MURDER BEFORE THE WEDDING

MURDER BEFORE THE WEDDING

Lorna Snowden

Copyright © 2022 Lorna Snowden

1st Edition – January 2022

All rights reserved

This is a work of fiction. Unless otherwise indicated, all the names, characters, events and incidents in this book are either the product of the author's imagination or used in a fictitious manner. Any resemblance to actual persons, living or dead, or actual events is purely coincidental.

Other titles in this series:
Murder After The Matinee
Winner of a Chill With A Book Readers' Award
(www.chillwithabook.com)
and
Longlisted on the 2021 Millenium Book Awards
(www.bookviralreviews.com)

Notes from the Author

I hope you enjoy the second book in my Ashdale series and if so, the third book *Murder Concealed By Snow,* will be published in 2022 and available on Amazon.

List of Main Characters

Will Appleton: Detective Chief Inspector Will Appleton is with the North Yorkshire Police and based in Harrogate. His wife Chloe is the sister of Greg and Tom Craven.

Brian & Elsa Armitage: Brian is a pleasant, easy-going man who tends to agree with his wife for a quiet life. Elsa has a tendency to chatter non-stop and could be described by some as nosey, but her heart is in the right place.

Eric Bentham: Eric is a photographer for the Harrogate Herald.

Zoe Birch: Zoe is the owner of the hair and beauty salon, *WOW!* and and although she has a tendency to be a bit feisty, she is kind-hearted.

Lydia Buckley: Lydia is an eyelash technician who works at both *WOW!* in Ashdale and *Lush Lashes* in Harrogate. She lives above the estate agency and is still dating Greg Craven.

Vinnie & Vivienne Buckley: Vinnie is Lydia's ex-husband and lives in Oxfordshire, he is a marketing executive for Major Marketing. His new wife, ex-pole dancer Vivienne, is some ten years younger than him.

Maggie Clark: is the hair salon manager and senior stylist at WOW! She is also wardrobe mistress for the Ashdale Players.

Greg Craven: Greg is Lydia's boyfriend and is an investigative journalist.

Tom & Amy Craven: Tom is Greg Craven's brother and has bought the estate agency from Charles Lewis and Hugo Marshall, he has renamed it *The Property Ladder*. Amy, his wife, works for the local council in Harrogate.

Mikey & Tasheka Dixon: Mikey is in partnership with Ben Simpson at Ashdale Autos where is specialises in classic cars and has both a taxi and two wedding cars. Tasheka is of Caribbean descent, large bosomed and loads of attitude. She now works at Lulabelle's boutique.

Fran & Michelle Garnett: Fran is Cliff Walker's sister, her husband Paul was in the army and tragically killed in a helicopter accident in Bosnia. Michelle is her daughter.

Derek & Sheila Houseman: Derek is a master baker and his cakes are renowned in the baking industry. His wife, Sheila, works in the bakery alongside him.

Lucy & Sarah Kirkwood: Lucy owns the flower shop, Flower Power, with her daughter, Sarah. They have recently arrived in Ashdale after having a floristry in Leeds.

Beatrice & Adam Lewis: Beatrice is a thin and mean-faced woman who was a stern local magistrate and seems to have little or no sense of humour. She is now widowed and a local councillor, having taken Hugo's seat. Adam, her son, has recently returned to Ashdale from London.

Saffron Lawson: Saffron is covering Bella's maternity leave at *WOW!*

Mr Lord: Mr Lord is an anonymous gangster type who is a loan shark, but also dabbles in prostitution and drugs.

Hugo & Celia Marshall: Hugo and Celia have moved to Mar Menor in Spain. Hugo works for *Spanish Sun* selling apartments and villas for various property developers. He and Celia enjoy their new life and play golf together.

Robbie Parker: Robbie is a journalist friend of Greg's who works for a sister newspaper in Leeds.

Sir Gerald Pemberton Bt: Sir Gerald is the owner of Claro Court and spends much of his time in London as a professional director on the boards of various companies.

Terry & Ray Sharp: Terry is a muscular thug who works for the mysterious Mr Lord. He has a striking resemblance to a tb soap star which he uses to his advantage. His not so bright brother, Ray, is very handy with a razor, hence his nickname Ray 'Razor' Sharp.

Penelope Sinclair-Sutton: Pen is Charlotte Worthington's best friend. She is now the owner of the Lulabelle's boutiques and has stores in Ashdale and Northallerton.

Cliff Walker: Cliff is ex-army, retired about ten years ago and about to start writing a social column for the newspaper.

Albert Wilks: Albert is the sole surviving partner of Babcock, Coombs & Wilks, local accountants in Ashdale.

Charlotte Worthington: lives at Ashdale Hall and is engaged to Sir Gerald, their wedding is imminent.

Alexandra (Lexie) Worthington: Lexie is Charlotte's younger sister and works for their father, Sir James at Ashdale Hall.

1

Lydia Buckley
The breeze, cool enough to raise goosebumps on her arms, ruffled her hair again and Lydia wished she had worn a cardigan over her black beautician's tunic. Today, she had a full list of appointments at Lush Lashes, an eyelash bar in Harrogate, but the first job of the day was a visit to Flower Power at the top of the east side of Ashdale's Market Place. The business had recently been bought by mother and daughter, Lucy and Sarah Kirkwood, following the retirement of the previous owner. The Kirkwoods had made significant changes to what had been a dark and dingy shop, turning it into a bright and welcoming space painted in a gorgeous eau de nil shade which made a lovely back drop for their flowers and plants. As Lydia pushed the door open, she breathed in the fragrance of fresh flowers, an armful of which Lucy was busily arranging in a large urn on one side of the shop, then she recognised the distinct voice of the current customer.

'So, you got that?' Tasheka Dixon was saying to Sarah, who merely nodded her head. 'I'll pick them up on Saturday evening jus' before closin'.' The dark-skinned woman turned her fulsome figure around at the sound of the door opening and smiled when she saw Lydia.

'Hi, how're you doin' Lydia?'

'I'm good thanks, Tasheka.'

'I'm jus' orderin' my flowers for my Mikey's stand at the weddin' fair next Sunday. I told him that he gotta have real flowers on his stand 'cos we don't have much to display, as his weddin' cars will be outside. Are you gettin' some flowers for Zoe's stand?'

Lydia shook her head. 'No, WOW! is Zoe's salon so I'll leave it up to her to decide what she wants on display, although I'll be with her at the wedding fair. I need some flowers to take to the Sturdy's this evening, there's a little get-together as today is Bella's birthday.'

Tasheka held up her right hand to claim attention.

'Y'see, although I didn't agree with her gettin' involved with Mr S-J and him cheatin' on Mrs S-J like he did…' Tasheka's very expressive right hand retracted all fingers leaving only an extended neon blue-tipped index finger which now wagged from side to side as she spoke. '…'cos by my reckonin' you don't mess with somebody else's man.' She looked at her audience one by one and Lydia silently chuckled as both Lucy and Sarah, wide-eyed in amazement nodded their heads.

'But…' Tasheka swept on, '…I also understand that young Bella thought he was gonna leave Mrs S-J when actually he had no intention of doin' so. All that bein' said…' all the fingers were extended as Tasheka's hand stopped in the 'hold on a minute' position, '…I would still like to send my best wishes to Bella and say that I hope everythin' goes well wit' the baby, 'cos, by my reckonin', I think she's due any day.' In one swift movement, the hand snatched the air and the fingers snapped closed.

'That's really sweet of you—' Lydia began.

'I mean, things have not been easy for any of us, an' let me tell you somethin' else…' the index finger appeared again, '…it gave me the heebie-jeebies. I said to my sister, I don't think I wanna have no more private clients.' With a dramatic flick of her wrist, the index finger retreated. 'So that's when I got myself a job at LulaBelle's boutique across the Market Place an' I know I have done the right thing 'cos I have an eye for fashion and a real good customer-service attitude, you know what I'm sayin'?' There was a pause whilst the three ladies cast their eyes over

Tasheka's current ensemble of a dress in the same shade of neon blue as her nails which clung seductively over the curve of large breasts and ample posterior, teamed with a pair of black ankle boots. However, before anyone could make a remark of any kind, the ringtone of a popular song burst forth and Tasheka rummaged in the depths of her copious handbag, which lay on the counter. The volume increased and Tasheka frowned.

'This is my sister, I gotta take this call,' she pressed the screen of the phone with her thumb to answer the call, 'Louella? Jus' hold on a minute,' Tasheka turned to Sarah, 'I gotta go, I'll see you on Saturday,' and then to Lydia, 'remember my good wishes to Bella.' She then picked up her large handbag, slung the strap over her plump shoulder and left the shop. There was a slight pause as all this information was digested, then Sarah spoke,

'What did Tasheka mean by "private clients"?' she asked hesitantly, not really sure if it was something she ought to be asking.

'Tasheka and her sister Louella have a business, *The Clean Team – Housekeeping and Domestic Assistance,*' said Lydia. 'Tasheka went to the Saxby-Jones house each Wednesday morning –, the '"S-Js"' as she refers to them –, but since the …er…incident, she's had the "heebie-jeebies", hence the latest job at LulaBelle's.'

'So, Annabelle had an affair with Mr Saxby-Jones?' Lucy murmured softly.

'She did, but it wasn't quite as you might imagine. Anyway, then she found out that she was expecting a baby.'

'Wow! How did Mrs Saxby-Jones take that?' asked Sarah.

'Not too well, actually,' replied Lydia wryly, 'Simon was a member of the *Ashdale Players*, which is how he and Bella met. He and his wife, Annabelle, lived in Harrogate so they were not known around here as a couple. Bella was the receptionist at Zoe's salon next door and to be fair to her, we all knew her and Simon as a couple – he had us all fooled.'

'What a rat!' snapped Sarah.

'Might it not be a bit awkward though, if he wants to see the baby or be a part of its life?' pondered Lucy.

'No, they're not … um, well … they're not around here anymore and Bella has the full support of her family. I'm not sure if you've come across the Sturdys yet, but they own the holiday park just outside the town –, Harefield Park.'

'Ahh, yes, I think Mrs Sturdy has been in?' Sarah turned to her mother for confirmation. Lucy nodded her head,

'That's right, she's opened an account with us – she seems a very nice lady, her name is Claire, I believe?'

'They're a lovely family. Anyway, it's Bella's birthday and Claire has invited a few friends to their home for a celebration and I thought I would take her some flowers as a thank you.'

'That's a lovely thought, Lydia. Shall I make a colourful bouquet for you?' Lucy asked.

'Yes please. How are you both settling in? It must be a couple of months now since you bought the shop,' Lydia asked as Lucy selected flowers from several large vases on one side of the shop.

'So far, we love it here, don't we, Mum?'

Lucy nodding in agreement,

'It's definitely much nicer than the centre of Leeds. How does this look?' Lucy showed a colourful selection to Lydia, who smiled in agreement,

'Lovely, thank you.'

'I'll just go and make them up,' Lucy took the flowers into the room at the back to prepare them.

'Have you taken a stand at the wedding fair?' Lydia asked.

'Oh yes, we were delighted when Lexie Worthington called to ask if we were interested. Does Ashdale Hall hold a wedding fair every year?'

'I believe this is their first. It's part of a new marketing strategy and I must say that to have a wedding at Ashdale Hall would be magnificent, it's a beautiful place,' Lydia told her.

'We're supplying flower arrangements for all of the Ashdale businesses who are attending the wedding fair, so we'll be able to showcase quite a lot of our designs.'

'That's one of the nice things about Ashdale, everyone supports each other.'

'Have you lived in Ashdale for a long time, Lydia?'

'Goodness no! I came here just before last Christmas, some ten months ago. My sister Kate, has the Forget-me-not Café on the other side of the Market Place and initially I lodged with her until I received my divorce settlement, then I bought my flat above the estate agents,' Lydia explained.

'Is it the one opposite here, The Property Ladder?'

'Yes, that's right.'

'We bought this place through them, Tom owns the business and he is ever such a nice chap. He knows a lot about this area even though he only bought the agency a few months ago.'

Lydia smiled, 'Yes, Tom is a lovely guy, absolutely trustworthy. He worked at the agency when it belonged to Charles Lewis and Hugo Marshall and when they retired he bought it from them. He and his wife Amy have lived in Ashdale for about twenty years, so he is very familiar with the surrounding area.'

'It was a pleasure doing business with them. On another note, you mentioned the *Ashdale Players* and um…I was wondering about joining them as I've enjoyed amateur acting before. Do you know who I should contact?' Sarah asked.

'Oh, that would be brilliant! I'm also a member and we have great fun. We will be having a read through for the next panto soon – I'll give you Desmond's email address so you can let him know you're interested.'

Just as Lydia had finished writing Desmond's email address for Sarah, Lucy reappeared with the flowers in a water balloon which was then encased in a gift bag with long handles.

'Here you are,' she said.

'They look fantastic, thank you.' As Lydia paid for her flowers, the shop door opened and a small bald-headed man entered, he had an expensive-looking camera around his neck and carried some small stepladders.

'Hello ladies,' he greeted them with a flourish of his camera, 'I'm Eric Bentham from the Harrogate Herald and I've come to take your photo.'

'Have you? What on earth for?' asked Lucy.

'There will be a double-page spread about the Ashdale Hall wedding fair in the paper next Thursday with a photo and little bit of blurb about each of the Ashdale businesses who have taken a stand. Now, will both of you ladies be on the stand for Flower Power?' He inclined his head at both Lucy and Sarah.

'Yes, we own the shop,' Lucy told him.

'Good. Good. Right. How about you stand in front of your display over there and then I'll have another shot of you behind the counter.'

Lucy ran her hands quickly through her pretty grey pixie cut, then they both obligingly did as Eric had asked. He set the stepladders a few feet in front of them and climbed up to the top broad step.

'Ok ladies, look happy…it's Friday, end of the week.'

He took a few photos and climbed down to reposition his step ladders.

'Excuse me,' interrupted Lydia, 'have you been next door to the salon yet?'

'No, that's my next stop. I'm working my way around the square.'

'In that case, I'll pop next door and check with Zoe the owner, she may be in the middle of a treatment and it might not be a good time for a photo shoot.' Lydia picked up her flowers, bade the Kirkwoods a hasty goodbye and hurried next door to the salon.

When she opened the door to the hair and beauty salon, Lydia revelled in the gorgeous mix of aromas from the botanical scents emanating from the beauty treatment rooms. The décor was predominantly cream and duck-egg blue with turquoise accents, and soft music added to the calming atmosphere. Lydia loved her occasional work here. The young receptionist covering Bella's maternity leave was studying her nails, her very long blonde hair was caught up in a high ponytail, yet it still hung to halfway down her back. Lydia had been briefly introduced to Saffron earlier in the week as she had worked alongside Bella, but today was her first day alone. The girl looked up as soon as she saw Lydia and smiled a welcome,

'Hello, Linda, I didn't realise you were like, coming in today?' her head immediately dipped to check the diary on the newly installed computer screen.

Lydia sighed. 'Lydia,' she corrected patiently.

'No, I'm like, called Saffron?' the girl replied slowly as she chewed her lip, her eyes never leaving the screen. She frowned as she clicked furiously with the mouse, 'I...err...like, can't see any clients booked in for you today, Linda?' Saffron glanced up, then her eyes widened in horror as she saw the black uniform Lydia was wearing. 'Oh! You're not wearing our uniform!'

'No, I'm not working here today,' Lydia explained, watching as Saffron mouthed the words 'Lush Lashes' which were embroidered in gold thread on Lydia's black tunic and then looked down at her own turquoise dress embroidered with the WOW! logo.

'Oh, right...' Saffron blinked as the penny appeared to drop.

'I just wondered – is Zoe available or is she in treatment?'

Saffron took a sharp intake of breath and looked a little shocked. 'I didn't know she was, like, *ill*,' she whispered and then glanced furtively around her as though she had stumbled on a secret, 'but I can be, like discreet, you know?'

'R–i–ght,' was all Lydia could find to say. Saffron resumed her professional smiling face and receptionist's voice at normal volume.

'Zoe is working today but she's like, with a client at the moment?'

Lydia wondered why young people included the word 'like' so many times in their speech and why all their sentences went up at the end as though they were asking a question. Not confident that leaving a message with Saffron about the photographer would be a good idea, she made a quick decision.

'That's fine, I'll just have a quick word with Maggie then.'

Saffron smiled, seemingly happy that she had been able to deal with the enquiry without having to ask for assistance. Lydia glanced in Maggie's direction and was relieved when the hair salon manager looked her way. Maggie Clark was a super-efficient and brilliant stylist who had worked with Zoe for years at a salon in Harrogate and then moved with her to Ashdale when Zoe had opened WOW! Lydia stepped around Saffron's desk and met Maggie as she approached,

'Is everything all right?' Maggie asked with a slight frown.

'Yes, fine. I just popped in to warn you about a photographer who will be calling in any time now to take a photo of you and Zoe for a spread about the wedding fair. He's currently next door with Sarah and Lucy, but he shouldn't take up too much of your time,' Lydia explained.

'Ok, thanks for the heads-up. Are you staying to be in it with us?'

'No, I've to get off to Harrogate...' Lydia glanced at her watch, 'in fact, I'm running a little late now so I'll dash off and see you later at Bella's.'

Maggie nodded as Lydia left the salon, hurried back to her car and set off for Harrogate.

As she drove, Lydia reflected on the past few months and how things had changed. Quite a few of the Ashdale residents seemed to believe that it was she who had solved the murder case, but in fact she had only put all the pieces of the jigsaw together to come to a conclusion. Although the police had been appreciative of her assistance, it had been made clear that it had been a one-off lucky break and she wouldn't be called upon to investigate any future criminal activities.

Lydia was happy and settled following her divorce from Vinnie. During their twenty-five year marriage she had turned a blind eye to a number of affairs, but the last one with Vivienne had been the final nail in the marital coffin. The divorce settlement had enabled her to buy a whole building containing her apartment and the estate agency office and she now received a decent rent from Tom at The Property Ladder. Her other income came from her two part-time jobs as an eyelash technician at Lush Lashes and WOW! along with royalties from the two published novels she had written. Lydia was seriously contemplating giving up her work in the salons to concentrate on her writing and had set herself a time limit of Christmas to make a decision. Her love life had also blossomed in the shape of Tom's older brother, Greg whom she had been dating since her move to Ashdale last year. Greg lived in a block of swish modern apartments not too far from the town centre, and they spent most weekends together either at his or her home. Yes, she was definitely happy with life!

Sheila Houseman
Over at the bakery, Sheila Houseman was busy loading a large tray with freshly baked bread and tea cakes, 'A double-page spread in the paper, that'll cost a pretty penny,' she commented to her husband, Derek.

'Aye it will, but it's the first time the hall has done anything like this, so I suppose they want to push the boat out. We're all relying on a big turnout for this wedding fair – it'll fair put Ashdale on the map if it goes well.' Derek opened the big oven door and slid his next batch of baking inside. Once the door was closed, he picked up a cloth and wiped his sweating face. He was a large man with sparse, blond hair and looked the epitome of a baker, rotund like a barrel with big meaty arms and a smiling, happy, plump face – always dressed in his chef's whites. Derek was at his happiest in his kitchen as he kneaded, mixed and iced to create the most amazing breads, buns and cakes.

The bakery was one of the oldest in the area with the original baking ovens and the date 1704 carved into the lintel over the door, of which the Housemans were very proud. On Thursdays, which was Market Day, Sheila usually dressed in a Victorian grey or navy dress with sleeves rolled up to her elbows under a spotless white pinafore apron complete with mob cap so visitors could be forgiven for thinking they had stepped back in time when they entered the shop. The Harrogate Tourist Information Office used this in their marketing and the town held a Dickensian market before Christmas in which all the businesses were involved. Busloads of tourists flocked to the town to enjoy the atmosphere and carol singing, and Santa often made a flying visit.

'If we win at the awards in a fortnight's time, it'll be the icing on the cake, so to speak.' Sheila was immensely proud of her husband and they were devoted to each other; they had worked together for all of their married life in their bakery and it seemed that at long last, Derek's talent was being recognised. She remembered opening the envelope from the British Bakers' Association Awards informing them that they had been nominated by their customers, and that a secret shopper had also been to their bakery and bought goods which had proved to be of a high standard. So they were now invited to a glittering awards dinner, which this year would be held, locally, in Harrogate.

Derek washed his hands, 'Winning a British Bakers' Association award will mean a lot to you, love, won't it?'

'Oh, Derek, it will be the culmination of our whole life's work. We've had this bakery for over thirty years and to be nominated and then supported by our customers is just so rewarding, but to win the award, to be proclaimed the best in the UK would be the most amazing accolade ever.' Her eyes shone with pride. 'But for me, the best part is that you'll be rewarded for your talent – and I'll be the proudest wife ever. You deserve this award, Derek.'

'Well, I'm not getting excited yet as we may not win but to get this far, I'll admit, has given me a bit of a boost.'

'Do you think I should splash out a bit and buy a new evening dress or just wear my faithful old green one?' Sheila pondered.

'I would be more than happy for you to buy a new one, love – it's not every day that we get to go to a posh do.'

'In that case, I might pop into Rathbones this afternoon when it quietens down a bit, is that ok with you? You'll have finished baking by four.'

Derek nodded and picked up an icing bag, 'That'll be fine, I can manage here. You know that Blenkhorn's bakery in Stonebridge are also in the running,' Derek began to pipe icing quickly and accurately onto a cake. 'It's hard to believe that in the whole of the UK, two bakeries within ten miles of each other are both in the final.'

'Pah! Blenkhorns aren't a patch on you, Derek love. You're way better than them!' Sheila smiled at her husband.

'As long as the judges think so. Blenkhorns also have a stand at the wedding fair, so maybe we can get someone to sneak us a tasting sample of their wedding cake – purely for comparison purposes, of course.'

'That's a good idea, it always helps to know what you're up against.'

Derek chuckled, 'Have you put the new cake-tasting samples out yet? I'm hoping that people like my almond Victoria sponge.'

'I have and I had a little taste myself, that cake is gorgeous. I'm sure our customers will like it, they always look forward to our little sample plates...' the bell over the shop door tinkled, 'Oh! Just a minute! I'll be right there!' Sheila called. She left the tray of teacakes and hurried into the shop, where she stopped suddenly as she saw who her customers were.

Councillor Beatrice Lewis was a thin, sour-faced woman with whom Sheila had had a bit of a disagreement some months previously, and Beatrice had said she would never step inside the bakery again. Standing behind his mother, Adam Lewis was a tall, good-looking man in his thirties. He had a chiselled jaw with high cheekbones, and wore his trench coat fashionably undone with the sleeves pushed up. He wouldn't have looked out of place as a model in a magazine. Adam looked down his nose at Sheila with an intimidating expression which suggested he knew something no one else did.

'Good morning, Councillor Lewis, Mr Lewis,' Sheila said tersely, 'How can I help you?' Sheila looked warily from mother to son as if expecting some kind of trouble.

'Good morning, Sheila,' began Beatrice, 'my son has a penchant for some toasted teacake and, as your baked goods are far superior to the supermarket variety, he has persuaded me to come here. Now, I know what I said about never coming here again, but I would like to think that we can set aside our differences and move on from that little episode earlier in the year when you were unwilling to support my campaign in the local by-election. We both said things that we perhaps now regret and I propose that we make a fresh start. I'm attending the forthcoming wedding fair on behalf of the mayor, who is unfortunately indisposed, and I'm sure you will agree that we want to avoid any unpleasantness on that day.'

Sheila was stunned at this little speech and studied Beatrice's thin face carefully before she shrugged, 'Ok,' she answered warily, 'I guess we can let bygones be bygones. So, teacakes you said. How many would you like?'

'Half a dozen, please,' replied Adam. He smiled warmly, his brown eyes soft and kind. 'I can freeze them, can't I?'

Sheila relaxed. 'Oh yes, they're fresh today. I was just about to put them out when I heard the bell, so I'll just go and get some for you.' Sheila returned to the kitchen and placed six teacakes into a paper bag.

'Can I get you anything else?' she asked, placing the bag of teacakes on the counter.

'I'd like a Viennese slice please and what about you, Mother? Something for elevenses? Mother? Mum! Bloody hell! What's the matter?' Adam stared at his mother in alarm.

Beatrice was struggling to breathe, turning first pink, then puce. She gasped for air, her eyes stared at Adam in horror, her hands clawing at her throat as she sank to her knees.

'Christ! Somebody *do* something! What the hell was in that cake?' Adam pointed to the plate of cake taster samples on the counter. 'You've poisoned her!' Adam shouted at Sheila who had not moved.

Derek appeared from the kitchen, took one look at Beatrice now writhing purple-faced on the floor and addressed Adam.

'Has she got a nut allergy?'

'Yes! For God's sake do something!'

Derek glanced out of the bakery window. 'Sheila, there's Dr Weston, go and get him!'

Sheila nodded and ran out of the bakery, shouting, 'Dr Weston! Dr Weston!'

Dr Tony Weston, who had been chatting to Brian and Elsa Armitage, turned as Sheila reached him and grabbed his arm. 'Come quickly, it's Beatrice Lewis – she's choking...turning purple...can't breathe.' Sheila gabbled as she towed Dr Weston back to the bakery.

As they entered the shop, Adam was cradling his mother as she lay on the floor, more or less unconscious.

'I think it's an allergic reaction to nuts, doctor,' Derek said urgently.

'Has she got an epi-pen? Where's her handbag? Somebody call an ambulance,' he ordered.

Adam passed the handbag over. The doctor opened it and tipped the contents onto the floor, and then finding what looked like a syringe, he pulled up Beatrice's skirt and stabbed it into her thigh. Brian and Elsa, who had followed Sheila and the doctor back to the bakery, stood open-mouthed. But Elsa now reached for her mobile phone, dialled the emergency services and asked for an ambulance. She then passed the phone to Dr Weston so he could talk medical speak to the operator.

As they waited for the paramedics, Elsa asked Adam what had happened.

'There are cake samples on the counter and my mother ate one. The next thing I know she couldn't breathe.'

'She's had an anaphylactic reaction, probably due to her nut allergy,' Dr Weston said before turning to Derek. 'Where are the nuts?'

Derek pointed to his cake-tasting samples and nodded miserably. 'It's a new recipe, the cake contains ground almonds.'

'What the hell are you doing putting a cake with nuts in it on the counter – without a warning?' Adam stormed.

'I did put a warning on the plate,' Sheila told him, firmly.

'I saw the plate and offered my mother a piece of cake, and there was no warning then, and there is no warning there now,' Adam asserted.

'What? Well, maybe it has fallen off in all the confusion.' Sheila looked fruitlessly around the counter and glanced on the floor but to no avail.

At that moment the ambulance arrived, and all attention was on Beatrice.

When the paramedics were happy that Beatrice was stable, she was transferred to the ambulance.

Everyone followed Adam outside, where an inquisitive crowd had gathered.

'If my mother dies, you'll both be charged with manslaughter,' Adam said savagely.

'There's no need for that kind of talk,' snapped Derek.

'You've not heard the last of this,' replied Adam before turning to the astonished crowd. 'My mother has been poisoned and may die because of this bakery, so avoid them at all costs,' he announced before climbing into the waiting ambulance. Everyone was silent as he and Beatrice were whisked away with blue lights flashing and sirens blaring.

As they disappeared, Sheila gasped in shock at Adam's words and Derek folded his arms across his ample chest frowning at anyone who caught his eye. The crowd began to mutter with much nudging of elbows and shaking of heads, before Brian took control. 'Right, let's go inside and put the kettle on, eh Elsa, love? I'll lock up. The bakery will be shut for the next hour or so,' he said firmly. 'Dr Weston, will you join us?'

Dr Weston shook his head. 'Thank you, but no, I've a surgery to attend to. Are you feeling all right, Mrs Houseman?'

Sheila simply nodded miserably.

Dr Weston glanced at Brian and Elsa. 'A nice cup of tea and a shoulder to lean on for the time being, ok?' he suggested.

'Leave her with us, Doctor,' Elsa replied determinedly as she led Sheila inside.

Ten minutes later, they were all settled in the bakery kitchen with hot mugs of tea. 'I didn't even see her take a piece of cake, she must have done it when I went back into the kitchen to get their teacakes. When I returned to the shop, he was just stood there and she was collapsing. I can't believe she might die, and it's our fault,' Sheila said miserably.

'That injection he gave her was doing its job when they took her away and she was still breathing then, so I think she'll live.' Brian patted Sheila's hand.

'What about the awful things that Adam said. We won't get arrested, Derek, will we?' Sheila looked beseechingly at her husband.

'No love, of course not, we haven't committed a crime,' he replied.

'I *know* I put that sign on the cake, I'm quite careful about things like that. It must have fallen off when they entered the shop – it's probably under the counter. Now everyone's talking about us and no one will come here again. Our chance of winning the bakery award is right out of the window now – the press will get to know about all this *and* we've a stand at the wedding fair. Oh God! Derek, what are we going to do? We shall have to cancel our stand...' Sheila was beside herself.

Derek scowled and clenched his fists, 'Adam had no right to yell to the crowd like that. When I next see him, I'll give him a piece of my mind,' he growled.

'I wouldn't do that if I were you,' warned Brian. 'I expect he'll calm down, it's all been a bit of a shock. Wait and see how Beatrice goes on before anyone does anything hasty.'

Derek huffed and folded his arms across his chest.

'Derek, us Ashdale folk have known you and Sheila for a long time, and we aren't going to just stop shopping here. And another thing, you didn't poison her – she had a reaction to them nuts,' Brian added.

'Well, I for one, will not hear a word said against either of you!' announced Elsa. 'The very idea that you would poison anyone! That Adam Lewis was too quick to point the finger. Now, Sheila, love, are you sure about that sign? Shall I have a quick look under the counter? I can see that you're fretting about it?'

'If it's under the counter, then you won't be able to see it and it's too heavy to shift. I can't think where else it can be,' Sheila pointed out.

'Well, I think it's a bit strange, to be honest, suddenly having a to-do like that.' Elsa sniffed before she got into her stride. 'I don't suppose you think she's faking it, do you? I mean what with her friends the Blenkhorns being in the same competition as you *and* having a stand at the wedding fair. Suppose she's trying to blacken your name or stop you from going? Nothing would surprise me about that woman...I mean she's only been a councillor for five minutes and already thinks she's the queen bee! Next thing, she'll be wanting to be mayor! The only reason she got to be councillor is because her brother-in-law had to stand down and retire...and that was due to some dodgy goings-on—'

'I don't think she was faking it, love,' Brian said quietly and patted his wife's hand. 'She's not *that* good an actress.'

Sheila was horrified. *Would Beatrice really stoop that low? Her coming into the bakery at all had been a bit strange.*

'Don't you worry Sheila, I'll make sure that everyone knows it was an accident and no one's fault.' Elsa tapped her forefinger on the stainless steel countertop to emphasise her point.

'That's very kind of you, Elsa, but once the press get hold of it—'

'I'll have a word with Lydia so she can tell her Greg. He'll make sure that nothing unpleasant is printed – he's quite well thought of at the newspaper offices, him being a journalist and all,' said Elsa.

'I think we should open up now. I've got bread and cake batter wanting attention and the sooner we face people the better. I don't see why we should hide away.' Derek stood up purposefully. Brian and Elsa took the cue to leave and said their goodbyes.

After they had gone, Derek returned to his kitchen and Sheila miserably took up her usual place behind the counter, her hands still shaking. She glanced out of the window and was somewhat relieved to see that life had appeared to have returned to normal and people were going about their business. She took a deep breath, and, as the shop door opened, she smiled to welcome her next customer.

2

Lydia Buckley
That evening, Lydia and her boyfriend Greg Craven were welcomed to Harefield Park by Jonathan Sturdy. He led them through the former farmhouse to a large lounge with French doors opening on to a patio where guests were already enjoying the warm evening.

Greg then followed Jonathan back to the bar area to get some drinks, Lydia looked around until she spotted Claire Sturdy a short distance away. Claire was an attractive woman in her late forties with honey-blonde hair. This evening she looked the picture of elegance in a striking berry-red soft, crepe trouser suit, with palazzo-style pants and a longline jacket. Lydia made her way over to where Claire stood listening to Elsa Armitage, although it appeared from her body language that she was trying to move away.

'Claire!' Lydia placed her hand on the woman's arm. 'I'm sorry to interrupt but I wanted to give you these flowers just to say thank you for inviting us this evening.'

Claire looked relieved as she turned around and smiled in response. 'Lydia! Thank you for the flowers – you didn't need to do that. My, aren't they beautiful? I'm so pleased you could come, Bella was only saying this morning how she was looking forward to seeing you. Please excuse me, Elsa, I'll have to put these in some water.' Claire walked away and Lydia turned to the older woman who looked a little put out that she had lost her audience.

'Elsa, I'm so sorry to interrupt your conversation with Claire, how are you keeping?'

Elsa, looking a little mollified that Lydia seemed happy to stay and talk, put her hand conspiratorially on the younger woman's arm. 'Well, actually I'm fine, but I can't say the same for Beatrice Lewis. She had a bit of a turn today.' Elsa nodded her head in emphasis and clasped her hands firmly together under her bosom.

Lydia frowned. 'How do you mean, "A bit of a turn"?'

'Well...' began Elsa, settling in for a gossip, but before she got into her stride, Lydia heard her name called from behind.

'Lydia! I'm so pleased to see you!' Lydia turned around to see a heavily pregnant Bella Sturdy waddling towards her. Her long blonde hair, usually styled in a bun for work, had been curled softly in a half updo, Lydia thought that Bella had simply blossomed. The two women hugged a greeting as best they could and then Lydia remembered that Elsa had something to say. 'Elsa was just going to tell me something about Beatrice Lewis having a funny turn,' she explained to Bella.

'Oh please, go on Elsa, I love a bit of gossip.' Bella nudged Elsa who sniffed and began again.

'Well, only this morning me and Brian were talking to Dr Weston on the Market Place – we were on our way to Rathbone's as I've seen a lovely new winter coat in there and I thought Brian might buy it for me, seeing as how my birthday is coming up. Anyway...' Elsa paused and drew breath before regaling them with the incident in the bakery. Lydia and Bella listened, their eyes growing wide as Elsa talked.

'Oh, it was a right to-do,' Elsa continued, relishing the rapt attention of her audience. 'Beatrice was gasping for breath and almost purple...as I said to Doreen Rider later when me and Brian had lunch at the Coach...it was just as well that Dr Weston was handy and knew what to do as Beatrice couldn't speak. I must admit I thought she was a gonner, and so did Sheila Houseman – white as a sheet *she* was.'

'Is Beatrice ok then?' asked Bella.

'Well, she went off in the ambulance with that son of hers. He's a handsome lad, I'll give him that – looks like an actor or singer or someone off the telly...but do you know, he shouted at Derek and Sheila just before they left... something about getting them arrested for poisoning his mother and we should all avoid the bakery from now on. There was quite a crowd, and that

Shatesha…err…Turkesha, or whatever her name is, came out from the frock shop next door wanting to know what was going on and I told her we had an emergency.' Elsa nodded her head for emphasis. 'But do you know what she said?'

Lydia and Bella both shook their heads.

'"Well, I can see that for myself! But I want to know what kind of emergency." that's what she said. I told her the kind that needs an ambulance and then she gave me a really funny look and said, "You don't say!" Now I'm not sure if she was just being flippant, or that she hadn't twigged—'

Lydia pressed her lips together to contain a giggle knowing that Tasheka and Elsa had 'misunderstood' each other in the past.

Bella cut in. 'Why on earth would Beatrice eat a piece of cake with ground almonds in it if she has a nut allergy?'

'Well, that's just the thing – there was no allergy sign, although Sheila said she had put one there earlier. Anyway, I've heard that Beatrice will be fine by tomorrow.' Elsa paused,'…I wondered whether Beatrice was just pulling a fast one, you know causing a scene on purpose, but my Brian said that she couldn't have pretended to go purple. Sheila was ever so upset about everything, what with the wedding fair coming up, not to mention those bakery awards.'

'But why would Beatrice eat almonds on purpose?' persisted Bella.

'Because she's friends with the Blenkhorns. They have a bakery in Stonebridge and they're also going to be at the wedding fair *and* they're in with a chance at the bakery awards. I guessed that she wanted to damage the Housemans' reputation.'

'It's a bit extreme though,' Lydia pointed out, 'people can die from reactions to nut allergies.'

'That's what my Brian said. Not only that, but apparently…' Elsa paused for effect, '… Beatrice had been quite nice to Sheila, wanting to put their differences aside, for the sake of the wedding fair, or so she said.'

'Differences?' queried Lydia.

'Oh yes,' continued Elsa, 'they had a bit of a falling out a few months back.'

'They did?' asked Bella.

It was after Beatrice had been elected as local councillor. She had a celebratory drinks party do and asked Sheila Houseman if they would *donate* one of Derek's gorgeous cakes. Well, I can't repeat Sheila's exact reply, but the short answer was a 'no' and Beatrice was fair put out 'cos she thinks she's the queen bee now.'

'To be honest, I'm not sure I know what Beatrice Lewis looks like, I don't think I've ever seen her, let alone met her,' Lydia said pensively.

'Me and Sheila have known Beatrice Lewis for years. I remember the Lewis's moving here and opening the estate agents along with the Marshalls – must be about thirty years ago now. They each bought one of them posh houses. And don't you remember? Celia Marshall was Charles Lewis's sister?'

Lydia nodded.

'I don't remember seeing Charles Lewis around much, actually,' Bella said thoughtfully.

'Well for the last ten years or so, Charles left most of the work to Hugo. He was busy with golf, horse racing and vintage cars, so Edna said—'

'Edna? I don't think I've heard anyone mention an Edna before,' Lydia interrupted and frowned.

'Oh, you won't have, love – you've only been here five minutes and Edna has gone now. Edna Brownlow used to do a bit of cleaning for a few folk and, well…what *she* didn't know wasn't worth talking about. One frosty New Year's Eve, Edna had a few too many gin and oranges in the Coach and on the way home, she slipped on some ice—'

'Oh no! Was she badly injured?' asked Bella with concern.

'Not so much injured…but she knocked herself out and was found the next morning by the milkman – frozen to death! I'll tell you what though – we had a great send-off for her and it was a good turnout – she would have been so chuffed.' Elsa smiled fondly at the memory. Lydia glanced uncertainly at Bella, whose mouth had dropped open in surprise.

'Anyway, Charles and Beatrice had a son, but he was sent to boarding school and Beatrice became a magistrate...did herself no favours in that department, I can tell you... always gave out the maximum sentence. And then what with her airs and graces. The point is that Beatrice Lewis and Celia Marshall didn't mix with the likes of us, they kept in with the rest of the posh houses lot. Mind you, they did a lot for charity, I'll give them that – but it wasn't any local charities, it was always the big national ones. We never saw the son, Adam, as after school, university and so on, he got some big important job in London.'

'How do you know all this?' enquired Lydia.

'Because after Edna, Beatrice's home help was Janice Dawkins – Sid's daughter.'

'Was?'

'Yes, up to March – then her shoplifting case came up at court and Beatrice felt she couldn't trust her no more. I suppose you could call it a conflict of interest...then as soon as Flora Simms became available, Beatrice snapped her up.'

'*Flora* Simms? Is that Mrs Simms who used to work at The Manor?' asked Bella.

'It is, of course me and Sheila are the only ones who call her Flora, 'cos we was at school with her – she was Flora Higginbottom in those days. Anyway, what was I saying? Oh yes! That son of Beatrice's – Adam, has only been back home since Charles upped and died a few months back. Anyway, for all she's our local councillor now, you won't see Beatrice out and about much because she doesn't usually do her shopping in Ashdale, she always gets her groceries from one of them posh supermarkets in Harrogate.'

'Well, I don't know what to say, Elsa, other than between you, Sheila and Mrs Simms – there's not much you don't know about Ashdale,' Lydia mused.

'It's never a dull moment here, is it?' chuckled Bella.

'Well, I'll tell you one thing, I won't hear a word said against Derek and Sheila... they're good people and Sheila is really upset about all this. She's talking about not doing the wedding fair and she also thinks their chances of winning at the awards have now been scuppered. So if I hear anyone repeat what Adam Lewis said, I'll...um...well I'll put them straight!' announced Elsa.

'I'm sure that people will still go to the bakery. My sister Kate gets all her cakes for the café from the Housemans and I don't suppose she's thinking of changing that. We all need to show support for Derek and Sheila right now,' Lydia assured Elsa firmly.

'You might like to ask Kate to say that to them, it might help Sheila to feel better. Will you girls excuse me? I need a quick word with Desmond over there.'

Bella and Lydia both nodded as Elsa slipped away and, after a slight pause they both giggled.

'I do love Elsa,' chuckled Lydia warmly, 'but, before I forget, Tasheka has asked me to send her regards for your birthday and she hopes all goes well with the birth,' Lydia told her friend.

'That's really kind of her. How is she?'

'Initially she had the "heebie-jeebies", but she's working in LulaBelle's with her own special brand of customer-service and sales technique.'

'I didn't know her very well, but I can tell from the way you talk about her that you like her quite a lot.'

'I do,' agreed Lydia, 'she's a heart of gold and a lovely personality. Anyway, tell me, are you all ready for the baby?'

'Yes, everything's ready. Baby Sturdy has a well-equipped nursery courtesy of two doting grandfathers, and an impressive wardrobe thanks to my mother.'

'How is your mother coping?'

'Well, you know my mother.' Bella gave Lydia a meaningful look. 'She refers to my pregnancy as "a minor indiscretion" and talks about me "regaining my figure shortly" and "everything getting back to normal." In her mind, I'm the victim of a "dastardly man who took advantage", which in a way I was, but she makes it sound as though I was a Victorian virgin whose reputation is now ruined.'

Lydia laughed. 'Poor Claire, I expect it will also take some time for her to get used to being called Granny.'

'I wouldn't dare call her that!' retorted Bella fiercely. 'She hasn't decided on what she wants to be called yet, but no doubt it will be something ridiculous. Nick has been amazing, he has bought the stroller.' They both glanced towards the smiling young man chatting with Bella's brother, Joe.

'It's great that he and Joe get on so well, bearing in mind Nick is Simon's son. It could have been very awkward,' commented Lydia.

'It could have been awkward indeed, as this baby is Nick's half-sibling. He was as shocked as everyone else when the whole story came out, and of course, he hadn't known Simon long.'

'Happily, Nick is a thoroughly decent young man who seems to take after his grandfather, Edward.'

'Edward is a complete sweetie. Do you know, he came to see me after…er…well, Simon's dastardly behaviour?'

'That is so typically thoughtful of Edward. Is he here this evening?' Lydia looked around but couldn't see the man they were discussing.

'Yes, he's here somewhere, he came with Elsa.'

'Anyway, I haven't said Happy Birthday yet, so Greg and I would like to give you this and hope you have had a lovely day.' Lydia pulled a small but beautifully wrapped gift out of her bag and gave it to Bella.

'Oh Lydia, thank you. Would you mind if I opened it later? I've received so many presents today, I want to make a list and send an individual thank-you to everyone tomorrow.'

'That's fine, don't worry. By the way, who is that girl over there with the long black curly hair? I don't think I've seen her before.' Lydia gestured with her glass to a tall slender girl talking to Claire.

'Oh, that's Alexandra Worthington, or Lexie, as she prefers to be called. She's riding Spritzer for me until Baby is born.'

'*That's* Lexie Worthington? She's organising the wedding fair at Ashdale Hall, isn't she? Zoe mentioned that she's been round all the businesses, but I've always just missed her.'

'She's lovely, she's down-to-earth and very friendly, and I like her a lot. She's hoping that the wedding fair brings in a lot of bookings as it's her idea. Ashdale Hall is already a popular venue for many conferences and balls which Lexie now organises with her event manager, Karen Hunter, but Lexie wants to tap into the weddings market.'

'I'll try and have a chat with her this evening. Hasn't she got a sister?'

'Yes, her elder sister Charlotte is the most stuck-up madam I've ever known – full of airs and graces and thinks she's a cut above everyone else. she's engaged to Sir Gerald Pemberton and when they get married in a couple of weeks, she becomes Lady Charlotte and swans off to live at Claro Court.'

'Charlotte doesn't work at the Hall, then?'

'Good heavens, no. Charlotte doesn't work at all. There are also two brothers, Jeremy – he works alongside his father, Sir James, mainly in estate management and Piers – he is a lawyer.'

'But how are you, Bella? Have you chosen any names yet?' asked Lydia, changing the subject.

'Apart from feeling like the size of a house, I'm fine. I'm looking forward to the baby's arrival, but I'm also just a bit scared. As for names, my mother suggested Agatha or Humphrey, neither of which I like, although I haven't told her that.' Bella pulled a face and Lydia laughed.

'You don't know whether it's a boy or a girl, then?'

Bella shook her head. 'I decided I didn't need to know although I wish now that I had asked, it would make name-choosing so much easier.' Bella shifted her weight from one foot to the other. 'I'm sorry Lydia, I'm going to have to go to the bathroom and then sit down.'

'Of course, Bella, off you go, I'll catch you later.' Lydia watched her friend waddle away and fervently hoped that she would not have a traumatic time with the birth of her baby.

As she glanced around the room, she noticed Desmond waving at her to come and join him. Desmond Carmichael was the director and producer for the Ashdale Players, and he had recently bought a house with his partner, Archie Staniforth. A neat two-bedroomed semi on the Treesdale Estate. He was now talking to Zoe and Maggie from the salon, as Elsa had already wandered off in the direction of the drinks table. Both Zoe and Maggie were members of the Ashdale Players, Zoe for make-up and Maggie as Wardrobe Mistress.

When Lydia joined their little group, Desmond stepped forward. 'Lydia darling, how marvellous to see you.' He kissed both of her cheeks. 'I've the most wonderful part for you in the next production, but I just need another lady to join us, so I was trying to persuade Zoe to take the part, but she simply refuses.'

Lydia glanced at Zoe who simply shrugged. 'I can't see myself learning lines *and* performing on stage,' she explained.

Lydia looked questioningly at Maggie. 'Don't look at me, I know my limits,' replied Maggie with a grin.

'What production are we doing?' asked Lydia.

'Cinderella!' announced Desmond, 'and I've got you down as the wicked step-mother – you will be marvellous, darling.'

Lydia gasped. 'But that's a major role.'

'I've every confidence in you. Now, all I need is my fairy godmother, do you know of anybody who would be willing and able? I would rather not do it myself.' Desmond pouted girlishly and they all laughed.

'Well actually, I wanted to tell you that Sarah Kirkwood is interested in joining us. She and her mother have taken over the florists, Flower Power. Apparently Sarah's done amateur stuff before, so I've given her your email.'

Desmond's eyes lit up. 'I know who you mean! Well, if she's up to scratch, she would be perfect for the role. I'll pop in and see her tomorrow. Thank you, Lydia darling, you have made me very happy,' he gushed.

At that moment, Bella's father tapped his glass with a spoon and the guests fell silent. He gave a short but heartfelt speech to thank the guests for attending, that he and Claire were very much looking forward to the birth of their first grandchild and finally asked everyone to raise their glasses and wish Bella a very happy birthday.

There was a chorus of 'Happy Birthday Bella,' and Bella beamed delightedly at her father's side. There was a cheer and a round of applause,

Lydia turned to Zoe. 'It's so lovely to see everyone getting on so well, isn't it? Especially after the whole Simon Saxby-Jones business.'

'It is and let's hope that Bella doesn't have too tough a time with the birth,' replied Zoe.

'Is she planning on coming back to the salon in a few months, do you know?'

'She hasn't said and I haven't pushed her. I think she'll take a good few months off and settle in to becoming a mum in the meantime.'

'How has today been with Saffron? It was her first day on her own, wasn't it?' asked Lydia as she sipped her wine.

'I am sure she'll be fine when she's got to grips with the salon terminology,' Maggie said with a grin. 'This morning, a client phoned to book a hair appointment and Saffron asked her if she "like, wanted a blow job"—'

Lydia burst out laughing and Zoe's eyes widened in shock.

'I explained it was a blow *dry*,' Maggie clarified.

'I had a similar experience when I popped in this morning.' And as Lydia told Zoe about the mix up over names, Zoe shook her head in mock despair.

'I think she's done ok on the whole, although she's been acting a bit strange around me,' replied Zoe.

'How do you mean strange?' Lydia queried.

'Well, I caught her looking at me almost sorrowfully from time to time and then before she went home, she patted me on my arm and told me that I wasn't to worry and that she wouldn't let me down. I've no idea what she was talking about,' Zoe said, looking somewhat perplexed.

'Actually, she told me that she thought you were very brave,' Maggie added, and Zoe frowned.

'Um…well, I think that all might have something to do with what I said this morning, to be honest,' admitted Lydia. 'After the confusion over names, I asked her if you were still "in treatment" and she replied that she didn't know you were ill…'

Maggie burst out laughing whilst Zoe's mouth dropped open. '*Seriously*?' Zoe gasped eventually, and Lydia nodded.

'Where did she work before?' asked Lydia regaining her composure.

'The accountants, Babcock, Coombes & Wilks. She was there quite a few months and Albert was full of praise so presumably they managed very well with her.'

Lydia felt another fit of giggles coming on and looked at Zoe, Both women laughed this time.

'As long as she does a good job for you, that's the main thing,' said Lydia.

'I'm sure that once we get used to her lingo and she gets used to ours, she'll be fine.'

Later, as the guests mingled once more, Lydia found herself next to Lexie Worthington who stood alone as she sipped her wine and surveyed the room. Lydia decided to introduce herself. 'It is Lexie, isn't it?'

Lexie turned and smiled. 'Yes.'

'I'm Lydia Buckley, I'm an eyelash technician at WOW! among other things.'

'Oh hi! I have an appointment with you on Tuesday so it's lovely to meet you beforehand.'

'I'm very pleased to meet you, too. You do a marvellous job of putting on fabulous events, a group of us had a table at the

Valentine's Ball and thought it was a brilliant evening, I'm already looking forward to the next one.'

'There was a time earlier this summer when I thought there wouldn't be a next one.'

'Oh? Why is that?'

'I'm not sure if you realised, but the Valentine Balls have been sponsored for the last few years by Aztec Developments, but when Carlton Banks moved away to Devon or Cornwall or somewhere and sold the company to a national builder, we were informed that the sponsorship would not continue.'

'Goodness, I hadn't thought about that – are you still looking for a sponsor?'

'Thankfully, no – Gerald has stepped in to sponsor at least the next one.'

'Gerald?' queried Lydia.

'Sorry, Sir Gerald Pemberton, my sister's fiancé – he owns Claro Court.'

'Oh yes, I know who you mean. Hopefully once he's your brother-in-law and attends the event, he'll see how successful it is and continue the sponsorship for a few more years.'

'That's my plan – a quick toast to Gerald.' Lexie grinned.

Lydia laughed and the two girls clinked glasses. 'When is your sister's wedding?' Lydia asked after she had taken a sip of wine.

'Two weeks tomorrow – it's the first wedding at Ashdale Hall since we got the licence and I'm quite nervous about it, as not only am I the wedding organiser, I'm also the chief bridesmaid. Charlotte has had me running ragged over the last few months as she kept changing her mind about things until in the end, I had to put my foot down and insist she made decisions and stuck to them.'

'You're also organising the wedding fair, which I'm attending with Zoe and we're both looking forward to it.' Lydia smiled.

'Ah, the wedding fair. I just hope it all goes smoothly and doesn't turn into a standoff between Stonebridge and Ashdale. I had hoped that the businesses from both towns would complement each other, but I get the feeling it's more competitive than I thought.' Lexie considered. 'I'm concerned that the rivalry is in full flow and I've heard snippets of gossip of how the towns think they can outdo each other, which is fine as long as it brings out the best in each business.'

'I'm sure it'll be ok. After all, the only *actual* competition between the towns is the Boxing Day tug-of-war over the canal, surely?'

'You might think that, but over the last twenty years or so, there has been a bit more sniping. The ward boundaries were changed so that Stonebridge and Ashdale are now in the same ward and have the same councillor. Stonebridge has always regarded itself as being a bit more upmarket that Ashdale – it has designer shops and a *plaza* rather than a market place – and it's a younger town. On the other hand, Ashdale has the canal, a bit more history, it used to have the train station and of course, it has the Hall. The nearest country pile to Stonebridge is Claro Court, which is where my sister will be moving to when she marries Gerald.'

'Well let's hope we don't have a tug-of war or even a civil war at the wedding fair then, that's not the notoriety you would be looking for,' teased Lydia, and then, as Lexie looked worried, she added, 'I am sure everything will be fine.'

'I do hope so. If this goes well, I plan to organise one every year to bring more business to both towns.'

'I'm sure everyone is very appreciative. Bella tells me you're riding her horse whilst she's pregnant.'

The ladies chattered and Lydia learned that Lexie had initially bumped into Bella in the Market Place and struck up a conversation. When Bella had told her about the pregnancy and her concern for her horse, Lexie had offered to ride Spritzer and use the opportunity to get away from work and the Hall, not that she didn't enjoy her work – she did, but sometimes living on the job was debilitating. Lexie spoke of how she had joined her family firm after leaving university, knowing that she wanted to make Ashdale Hall one of the most sought-after venues in the north of England. She had begun working with her father's secretary and as the bookings grew, had taken over responsibility for conference and banqueting. After Karen Hunter had joined her staff, Lexie had persuaded her father and elder brother Jeremy to let her obtain a licence to hold weddings at the Hall. She had then given the licenced rooms a makeover, bought some décor items including a rather expensive star cloth and then organised the wedding fair.

'It's been a lovely evening, hasn't it?' Lydia chatted.

'Oh, I've thoroughly enjoyed myself and I really appreciate the invitation to this party.' Lexie's eyes sparkled as she told Lydia about her evening. 'I've been introduced to Desmond, he writes, directs and produces the annual panto and he has made me laugh so much, he is so witty and flamboyant. Then there is Elsa, just like a favourite grandma, cuddly and gossipy but without malice – someone you would enjoy a cup of tea with. Maggie, I love her choppy black hair and ruby red highlights, she's so friendly and Zoe, who owns the salon, she comes across as an intelligent businesswoman-type, yet I picked up a mischievous glint in her eye, so she clearly has a sense of fun – oh!' Lexie stopped suddenly and clasped her hand over her mouth. 'But these are your friends, I'm sorry – I didn't mean to rabbit on,' she gabbled.

'There's no need to apologise, you've described them all to a tee,'

'You know, I would like to be more supportive of the Ashdale Players group in some way, perhaps Ashdale Hall could sponsor one of the evening shows? Maybe I should have a word with Desmond?'

'That would be fantastic, Lexie – I'm sure Desmond would be delighted.'

'If you'll excuse me then, I'll have a quick word now before he leaves and I shall look forward to seeing you on Tuesday, Lydia.'

'Ok, bye for now.' Lydia watched as Lexie made her way over to Desmond and lightly tapped his elbow. *What a lovely person. Now where has Greg got to?*

On the way home, Lydia told Greg about the incident with Beatrice in the bakery.

'I can just see the headline: Local Councillor Poisoned by Ashdale Bakery.'

'For God's sake don't write that! The Housemans are finalists in a national industry award, something like that might have an adverse effect on their chances and Elsa specifically asked me to ask you not to write about it.'

'Well, I'm not sure how they can keep it quiet, it must be around the whole town by now, especially with the ambulance turning up.'

'Oh, everyone in Ashdale knows about it, honestly between Elsa, Sheila and Flora Simms—'

'*Flora* Simms? Is that Mrs Simms? From The Manor? I didn't think she looked the gossipy type.'

'She was at school with Elsa and Sheila so naturally they share any titbits of news. Anyway, they didn't *poison* Beatrice, she had an allergic reaction, so really it's not even newsworthy.'

'It's the most exciting thing that has happened in Ashdale since the murder back in February.'

'The next big thing is the wedding fair, which is a week on Sunday and that is a much more pleasant story.'

Greg shrugged. As an investigative journalist, wedding fairs were not his thing. 'I had a long talk with young Nick – he's a great guy. He is quite like his father in a lot of ways but without the cold and calculating ambitious drive.'

'He has a look of Simon, but you're right, he is intelligent but not driven to the point of trampling over everyone. I liked him from the moment I met him,' agreed Lydia.

'He mentioned that Simon's house in Harrogate is rented out and told me confidentially – this is just between us by the way – that he hoped there could be some sort of provision for Bella's baby which is after all, Simon's child, his half-sibling. He talked about the possibility of transferring the rental income from the house to Bella, if that is possible.' Greg pulled the car into his parking space beneath the apartment block and as they made their way up to his apartment, Greg told Lydia more:

'The properties from Simon's partnership with Hugo and Freddie Flanigan, have all sold, via Tom and of course, and he's very pleased with that. Tom said that when the last one had completed, Freddie rubbed his little Irish hands together and told Tom that he was "…looking forward to his little pot o' gold, so he was."' Greg effected a rather bad Irish accent and waggled his eyebrows.

Lydia laughed at him. 'I don't think I ever met Freddie, but he does sound quite a character.'

Greg unlocked the door and they both entered his minimalistic white, glass and chrome apartment. 'Oh, he's a character all right, scruffy with a dingy office on a trading estate and looks as dodgy as they come, but he is a brilliant accountant. Some of his acquaintances are a bit dubious, but Freddie is always careful to keep himself *just* on the right side of the law. Nightcap?' he asked, waving a glass at Lydia.

'Mmm, I think I'll have a liqueur over ice, that coffee-flavoured one you bought the other day is lovely,' she replied as she slipped off her shoes and sank into a squashy sofa. 'Does Tom still have much to do with Hugo?'

'He is in fairly regular contact with him as he refers clients who want to buy a property in Spain and then Hugo pays him a small commission. I gather that he and Celia are happier now than they've ever been. Apparently, she's relaxed and taken up golf – they play as a couple now.'

'Goodness! I would never have seen Celia on a golf course, too pearls-and-twinset I would have thought. Thanks.' Lydia took the glass from Greg as he sat next to her. 'It was a lovely evening and Bella is positively glowing.'

'It was a good party, I also had a chat with Jonathan and Joe – now that is one level-headed and clever young man, no wonder

Jonathan was keen to include him in the Harefield Park business.'

'Thank goodness you were able to talk rationally to Jonathan back in February after you and Robbie had done your research. Talking of Robbie, are we taking anything to his party tomorrow night?'

'Just a bottle, he's provided everything else.'

'Have you met this new reporter chap yet?'

Greg shook his head. 'No, he's just arrived from Manchester. Robbie is having this party to welcome him to Yorkshire – ex-military, apparently.'

'Ah well, two parties in one weekend, we're living the high life at the moment,' sighed Lydia. She drained her glass. 'Time for bed?' she added putting her arms around Greg.

Greg didn't need time to consider that proposal. 'After you,' he said with a cheeky grin.

3

Adam Lewis
Adam reread the text message and then pressed Send. He stretched his back before returning to his computer and the work in progress. Adam was an attractive man with neat, short dark hair and eyes of brown velvet. He was a brilliant graphic artist and web designer who, until recently, had held down a rather well-paid job in London with a top international retail brand. Unfortunately, this had come to an abrupt end when his overspending and extravagant lifestyle had finally caught up with him, resulting in a hasty departure from the capital to the safety of his mother's house in Ashdale. He had been rather economical with the truth to his mother about his decision to return home and cited the main reason as the recent death of his father and the need to take time out.

In some ways he regretted having to move from London; he'd enjoyed the fast pace and high living. He missed his upmarket apartment, designer clothes and the amazing nightlife of the bars, clubs and restaurants, but in his heart of hearts, he realised that if he hadn't made the move, he probably would not be alive today. He had recklessly borrowed money from a faceless loan shark, always believing that he could repay the amount, but unfortunately, he had not invested wisely on the stock market and had to continue to borrow until the repayments became too expensive. Mr Lord had, through a visit from two tough and intimidating employees, made it clear that he expected to be reimbursed, and quickly. Adam had made new promises and agreements, none of which he had adhered to, whilst continuing his extravagant lifestyle until two things happened, almost at the same time. Firstly, his father had died suddenly of a heart attack, and secondly, Mr Lord had upped the ante and given him a deadline for the total repayment of his large debt or else, and Adam had been left in no doubt as what 'or else' meant. The sensible thing, of course, would have been to use his inheritance to pay off most of his loan, but Adam had considered that for all of five seconds before deciding to abscond back to the Yorkshire Dales. He reasoned that Mr Lord and his thugs would not be able to find him in the small market town of Ashdale, and it was a risk he was prepared to take.

Following his move back to his mother's house, Adam had started his own graphic design business, Graphicality, which provided a reasonable income for the quieter lifestyle he now endured. From time to time, he accompanied his mother to social events and met the local movers and shakers whom he had wooed as new clients for his business. But then he had met Charlotte Worthington, the eldest daughter of a local aristocrat. Charlotte – now there was someone who brought a smile to his face. He remembered their first meeting when she had smiled at him beguilingly, and then, when he had an opportunity to speak to her, there had been an instant chemistry. Since that first meeting, there had been several occasions when they had enjoyed wild and passionate sex and Adam was surprised at his own feelings for the raven-haired beauty. He wasn't dreaming of marriage and children – nothing as drastic as that – but he could see that an exclusive relationship with Charlotte and her generous allowance could pave the way for a return to the fast and expensive lifestyle he craved. The problem was that they had to keep their relationship under wraps as Charlotte was engaged to be married to the rather pompous and staid Sir Gerald Pemberton. Adam wanted her to call off the engagement and cancel the forthcoming wedding, however Charlotte had told him that it was not as simple as that because Sir Gerald was a good friend of her father for one thing, and the wedding was only a few weeks away for another. In fact, Charlotte had said that the only way she would abandon Gerald was if she could move abroad to a new life and not have to suffer the embarrassment of a cancelled wedding.

Adam was in no doubt that Charlotte's money and a life in Spain would suit them both, particularly as he could still continue with his new graphics business, and it was even less likely that Mr Lord would be able to track him down. With that in mind, and to demonstrate to Charlotte that he was serious, he had gone to see Tom Craven at the estate agency to discuss buying property abroad. Adam's uncle, Hugo Marshall, had moved to the Mar Menor area of Spain where he was involved in a Spanish property company. With Tom's estate agency acting as an intermediary, it wasn't long before Adam had put more or less all of his inheritance down as a deposit on a rather splendid detached, three-bedroomed villa with a pool. Only this morning, he had received a notification that the balance was now due and as soon as he had made the transfer, he would be the proud owner of his Spanish home. This was the news he had been waiting for; at last he could show Charlotte proof of his commitment to her and they could make plans for their future. The only minor technical hitch was that Adam didn't have enough funds to pay the balance, but he wasn't unduly worried as he knew his mother had plenty of money and he was sure that he could persuade her to lend him the amount he needed.

Adam glanced at his phone, anxiously awaiting a response to his message. He wondered if he should ring the hospital to see how his mother was, but seeing that it was still only 9.30, decided that it might be too early. Didn't doctors do their rounds later in the morning? And anyway, he was expecting a call. As he turned back to his laptop, the phone burst into life, but it was not Charlotte, whom he hoped had read his text message. Instead, the word Mother was displayed on the screen. He had been quite shocked yesterday as, although he knew she had a nut allergy and that it could be fatal, he had never seen an actual reaction. It was a very frightening experience when she had so quickly struggled to breathe and turned purple, almost dying right in front of him. However, she carried an epi-pen and that had probably saved her life – nevertheless, the hospital had deemed it necessary for Beatrice to remain overnight.

'Hi, how are you this morning?' he asked gently.

'I'm perfectly all right now and I want you to come and pick me up right away. I do not need to stay here any longer and I've things to do,' came the blunt response.

'Have you been discharged?'

'I'm fine, just come now, please!' The call was ended. Adam sighed, had that been anybody else, he would have taken umbrage, but that was how his mother spoke sometimes. She could be very sharp and she didn't suffer fools gladly – her curt manner was probably a remnant from her years as a magistrate.

Adam saved his work and closed the laptop. He could do with a break anyhow and a drive might just clear his mind, get the creative juices flowing. However, he first needed to call into MegaMart, so he parked on the Market Place and strolled towards the supermarket. Later, as he left the shop clutching his purchases, he thought he heard his phone chirp with an incoming message and whilst he fumbled with it, he continued to walk head down, in concentration. He was brought to a sudden halt as he cannoned into someone and a mobile phone clattered onto the pavement.

'Oof! Gosh I'm sorry – oh hell! Is it broken?' Adam bent down, retrieved the phone and, as he handed it back to its owner, he found himself looking into a beautiful pair of doll-like blue eyes fringed with long black lashes. The blonde girl's eyes immediately dropped to the phone and there was an anxious few seconds as she checked for damage.

'No, it like, looks ok,' she replied and smiled at Adam.

The salon door suddenly opened and a woman with dark hair highlighted in red poked her head out and looked in their direction. 'Saffron! Thank goodness I caught you, can you also get some milk please?'

Saffron nodded and the woman disappeared back inside.

'Right, well, as long as you and your phone are all right…' Adam looked at her for confirmation.

Saffron fluttered her eyelashes demurely, 'Yes, thank you.' She looked away. 'I'd better get on…they're like, waiting for coffee.' She flashed him a dazzling smile once more before heading towards the supermarket. Adam watched her go. He could see that beneath all the make-up she was stunningly beautiful, and those eyes – they had quite taken his breath away. As she turned to go into the shop, she looked to where he was still standing, vaguely waved and was gone. Adam mentally shook himself and headed back to his car.

As he drove to Harrogate, Adam's thoughts returned to his mother and he reflected on how she had seemed pleased to have him back home; how she had always been very supportive of his career choice and proud of his success in London. Adam had become aware that latterly his parents' marriage had been one of convenience, but he hadn't realised to what extent. They had apparently been living quite separate lives for a good many years, with his mother carving out her own life with friends in Stonebridge. After Hugo Marshall had stood down as the local borough councillor, the newly widowed Beatrice had been fired up, secured the necessary nominations and successfully campaigned for election in his place. The thought of living back at home again with his mother had filled Adam with trepidation, and indeed, although Beatrice appeared to have taken on a new lease of life, and even though she was busy with her bridge club, committees and council meetings, and they only really saw each other for their evening meal, she still had a need to constantly suggest things he ought to or should do. She questioned his motives on anything and everything, expressing her opinion on anyone he showed an interest in – usually unfavourable – so he knew that if she found out about his affair with Charlotte, she would hit the roof.

As he pulled into the hospital car park, Adam decided that, over all, living with his mother was a small price to pay for his current comfortable lifestyle and on the whole, as he didn't see much of her, they rattled along well enough together. However, as he got out of the car and locked it, he was mindful that not only would he have to pick his moment carefully to ask for the extra money to finalise his villa purchase, but that he would have to have a damn good reason for buying it at all. His mother saw Charlotte's parents, Sir James and Lady Victoria not so much as friends, but certainly as acquaintances, so the embarrassment of a broken engagement and cancelled wedding, would not go down well, never mind an elopement to Spain. So it was imperative that the whole business was kept quiet at all costs.

Lydia Buckley

Lydia was also stretching her back after a morning spent working on her novel. It was more or less lunchtime and the sun was shining, so she wandered out onto the roof terrace and turned her face, basking in the warmth for a few minutes. Deciding that a walk around the Market Place and lunch at Kate's café was in order, she picked up her handbag and sunglasses and left the flat. As she walked around to the front of the building and into the Market Place a new display in the estate agent's window caught her eye. Extolling the virtues of wintering in a warmer climate the reader was encouraged to consider viewing properties for sale in Spain. *Spain!* A country with an abundance of warm sunny days and a generally more predicable climate rather than the hit and miss weather of Britain. Lydia idly wondered if she could afford an apartment on a Costa Something-or-other, a bolt hole for improved writing. With two novels published and a third as work in progress, her mind now conjured up a vision of sitting on a balcony in a summery dress with her laptop and an uninterrupted sea view. She wandered closer to the window to check out the details of the advertised properties and as she admired the internal décor and fabulous views, a male voice garnered her attention.

'Hi Lydia, not thinking selling up and eloping to Spain with Greg, are you?'

Lydia turned to the man who now stood behind her clutching two paper bags from Houseman's Bakery and immediately decided to pull his leg,

'Shush Tom! Keep your voice down, it's supposed to be a secret. How did you know?' she stage-whispered.

The smile disappeared from Tom Craven's face as his mouth dropped open in surprise, but he was interrupted before he could say anything,

'Good morning Tom, Lydia. Lovely day isn't it?'

'Hello Doreen,' Tom replied warmly and Lydia nodded in acknowledgement to the blonde landlady from the Coach & Horses.

'Morning Doreen, how are you? Goodness it's suddenly turned chilly!'

As if to confirm Lydia's words, a small cloud momentarily blocked out the sun's rays sending the temperature down a degree or two, and a cooling breeze ruffled Lydia's chocolatey, shoulder-length curls, whilst Doreen's cropped and waxed hair, styled to within an inch of its life, never moved. Doreen shivered slightly,

'This is exactly why I told Jeff that we should sell the Coach and move to Spain, open a bar there,' announced Doreen, her hooped earrings swung as she spoke.

'Sell the Coach?' Tom was shocked.

'Oh yes, we could open a traditional English pub and then buy one of them posh apartments,' her head nodded in the direction of the window display. 'Jeff's none too keen at the moment but as soon as we get into winter, he'll see sense. Anyway, must get on, bye for now.' Doreen strode soundlessly away in her sneakers. She was a down-to-earth Yorkshire woman and although it was Jeff's name over the door as the licensee, it was Doreen who steered the Coach on its successful way. Lydia was in no doubt that if Doreen decided she wanted to move to Spain, then that is exactly what they would do.

'I wonder if they're serious about moving to Spain.' Tom muttered out loud, and then he remembered what had been said before Doreen had interrupted. '*Are* you and Greg eloping?'

Lydia burst out laughing and Tom visibly relaxed and smiled.

'Very funny! You had me going for a moment then.'

'Well actually I was just thinking how lovely these apartments looked, especially that one,' Lydia pointed to a photograph.

'They do look good, I must admit.'

'I can see myself sitting on that balcony…' Lydia returned her gaze to the photographs, 'and if I hadn't spent all my divorce settlement on buying *this* building,' Lydia waved her hand vaguely at the property in front of them, 'I would probably consider a two-bedroomed apartment. But seeing as I've settled here in Ashdale, a Spanish property will have to remain a dream, certainly for now.'

'Well, I'm pleased to hear that you aren't considering selling up and eloping! I was worried in case I had upset my landlord *and* my brother.'

Lydia laughed, 'I haven't been your landlord long enough for any upset, I was just taken by the idea of winter sun and as for your brother, Greg hasn't a clue I'm even looking at Spanish properties. You know, when I was looking at buying a property back in February, I didn't even consider investing abroad, but these look amazing.'

'They do, don't they? I'm taking Amy over there for a long weekend to have a look for myself, then I can recommend them with confidence, not that I don't trust Hugo but…' Tom tailed off and looked meaningfully at Lydia.

'How is Hugo?' she asked.

'To be honest, he and Celia have settled very well in Spain – which has surprised me. When he and Charles Lewis dissolved their partnership and sold me this estate agency business, I thought one or both of them would still interfere and "offer advice".' Tom did air quotes with his fingers, 'But Hugo took himself and Celia off to Spain pretty quickly leaving me to sell their house and then, as you know, Charles had a heart attack and died quite suddenly.' Tom pushed his hands casually into his trouser pockets, 'It was when they came back for the funeral that Hugo asked me about being a UK agent for Spanish Sun.' Tom pulled a hand out from a pocket and waved it in the direction of the poster and photographs. 'Initially I was a bit sceptical given that he had left under a bit of a cloud following some dodgy dealings, but he appears to have made a fresh start and is doing very well. I just want to check things out for myself.'

Lydia nodded. 'I think that's a good idea, then you'll be able to tell people about the area as well – you know, the amenities, etcetera.'

'Exactly!' agreed Tom.

'Hmm, I wonder if I *could* afford a small apartment – I could rent it out in between my visits,' Lydia mused out loud.

'You could probably get a loan to buy one as I believe you're currently mortgage free? Also, Hugo offers a managed letting service and would take care of handovers and cleaning,' Tom added helpfully.

Lydia nodded thoughtfully.'You know what, Tom? I'll give this some serious thought and come and have a chat with you at some point, maybe next week?'

'Sure, no problem, whenever suits you,' Tom smiled warmly, 'Have a good day!' he disappeared back inside the agency and Lydia wandered around the Market Place deep in thought. *I wonder if I really could get an affordable loan.*

Charlotte Worthington
Charlotte noticed the incoming text from Adam and sighed. She was beginning to think that perhaps she could stop seeing Adam until after the wedding and then once she was back from her honeymoon and Gerald was busy with whatever Gerald did in London, she and Adam could pick up from where they had left off.

'Are you ignoring that text?' asked her best friend, Pen. They were in Charlotte's sitting room contemplating what to do about lunch.

'For now,' replied Charlotte.

Pen raised her eyebrows in surprise. 'Getting bored with him, then?'

'Definitely not! I just think I should cool things a bit at the moment. But once I become Lady Charlotte Pemberton then I can see as much of him as I want. Gerald's pile will be my domain, away from parental prying eyes.'

'Isn't that a bit risky? I mean you will have some staff, what if one of them tells Gerald something?'

'Adam and I will still be discreet, it's not as though we shall be swinging from the chandeliers or anything, but he is far too delicious to give up.' Charlotte smiled mischievously at Pen, who looked doubtful.

'So, is Adam ok with you getting married? I know you have this thing where you talk of eloping.'

'Oh God, yes! We joke about running away to Spain or somewhere, but obviously it's not going to happen.'

'There was a time when I wouldn't have minded running away to Spain with someone…' Pen said dreamily.

Charlotte gave her friend a sharp look. 'I wouldn't have thought Spain would be your choice,' she remarked.

'And why not?' retorted Pen rather abruptly.

'Your fair skin and red hair are not exactly compatible with hot sun.'

Pen distractedly fingered her frizzy ginger hair. 'There is such a thing as factor fifty you know, anyway it's all irrelevant now that I've got my shops.'

Oh God! Here we go again! Charlotte smiled weakly, but inwardly grimaced at the thought of yet another conversation about Pen's blasted boutiques.

'I don't know whether to open a third shop, maybe in Skipton…'

'Listen Pen, you mustn't mention me running away to Spain to anyone at all – not even in jest. It's just a private joke between me and Adam when we're…well, you know – in the throes of passion. As if I would seriously consider giving up the title and Gerald's lovely money, not to mention the mansion, in exchange for some tatty apartment in Costa del Whatnot,' she retorted, tossing her black hair over her shoulder.

'…or maybe Ilkley, that's a bit like Harrogate only smaller. Or should I consider somewhere similar to here, like Helmsley?' Pen wondered.

'Penelope Sinclair-Sutton! Are you listening to anything I'm saying?' snapped Charlotte.

Pen blinked and stared at Charlotte guiltily. 'Um…yes, you're thinking of running away to Spain?' she answered vaguely.

'No! That's the whole point, I'm *not* going to Spain and you must never mention it again.'

'Right! So is Adam going on his own then?' Pen asked with a little more confidence.

Charlotte sighed in exasperation. 'Neither of us is going to Spain, it's just something we joke about – you know, going off into the sunset, eloping without a care in the world. Stuff we just dream about. Honestly, I wish I'd never mentioned it now! We'll probably just carry on seeing each other when I'm at Claro Court.'

'But what about when Gerald wants babies? You *will* have to stop sleeping with Adam then.'

'Not necessarily, Gerald will be no wiser as to whether they are his or not, in fact neither will I, nor Adam.'

'Charlotte! That's awful! Well, I think you're playing a dangerous game and that you need to be careful.'

'Anyway, I'm not sure Gerald or I will want babies, he already has a son from his previous marriage, not that I've ever met him. Once I'm married, Gerald will turn a blind eye to my little distractions, even if he does find out about Adam, there is no way he'll want a divorce – I just have to be careful *before* the wedding, I can't risk him calling it off.'

'God! You can be a heartless bee at times, Charlotte. I feel sorry for both Gerald *and* Adam, you're playing them both like puppets,' observed Pen.

Charlotte simply shrugged. 'Life is what you make it. One man gives me money and status, the other gives me pleasure – so much pleasure,' she purred.

'Does anyone else know you're seeing Adam?'

'God no!' Charlotte snapped, 'Nobody must find out either and I'm relying on your discretion, Pen.'

Pen simply shrugged and then delved into her handbag for her phone which had begun to ring. Charlotte felt safe chatting to Pen – she was the type of friend who didn't gossip. Pen was a make-up free, domestic goddess and downright decent sort of a girl, bordering on a being bit boring and, if she was completely honest, would probably have made a better wife for Gerald than Charlotte herself. Charlotte didn't know much about Gerald's first wife, Phoebe, who had left Claro Court many years ago and run off with an American, taking their son, Tobias with her.

'Are you still up for coming to that restaurant opening on Wednesday night? It might be fun,' she asked when Pen had finished her call.

'Definitely! I could do with a night out, I've spent so much time with the shops. So, what do you think, Ilkley or Helmsley?'

'For what? Shopping?'

'No,' replied Pen patiently, 'for my third Lulabelle's.'

Good grief! Not again! Charlotte stood up. 'Don't know, whatever. Come on, I'm hungry. Do you fancy lunch in the restaurant and then a lazy afternoon in the spa?'

'Yes, that would be lovely,' grinned Pen.

Lydia Buckley

Lydia had agreed to drive to Leeds this evening so Greg could enjoy a couple of drinks. Robbie was Greg's associate after all. Lydia smiled as she watched the handsome and slightly older version of Tom walk towards her car. Meeting Greg had been so very fortunate and Lydia couldn't imagine her life without him. As he dropped into the passenger seat beside her, he put a hand on her arm.

'We need to talk,' he said seriously.

Lydia looked at him, suddenly worried. 'We do?'

Greg stared into his lap and sighed. 'I think you know what about,' he said quietly.

Lydia took a sharp intake of breath. 'I do?'

'About us.'

Us? Surely, he wasn't going to break up with her now. They were about to go to a party. She couldn't think of any reason why he would want to suddenly do that and... Lydia realised that Greg was waiting for her to say something.

'What about us?' she asked quietly and with trepidation.

'Apparently we're eloping to Spain.' Greg's eyes twinkled and a smile played about his lips.

'Are we?' gasped Lydia, not sure whether to be surprised or relieved.

Greg feigned an innocent expression. 'Well, we are according to Elsa who I bumped into at MegaMart.'

'Elsa? Where on earth did she get that idea from?'

'Sheila Houseman!'

'Sheila Houseman? But I've not been to the bakery or seen Sheila for a few days, so why would she say that?'

'Sheila heard it from Doreen Rider who *has* been in the bakery and you saw Doreen this morning and *she* heard it direct from you! You and I are eloping to Spain,' he explained.

Lydia was momentarily speechless.

'You might have told me about the apartment. I might've gone halves with you and we could have bought a larger one,' he added.

Lydia found her voice. 'But I haven't bought an apartment!'

'No, I know.' Greg grinned. 'I happened to talk to Tom this afternoon and he told me about your conversation. He also mentioned that Doreen Rider had passed the time of day.'

The penny dropped and Lydia laughed. 'Well, yes! I was pulling Tom's leg about us eloping – Doreen must have overheard and taken it literally. Well, if we're talking gossip, I can also tell you that *she* said that her and Jeff were thinking of selling the Coach and opening a bar in Spain – perhaps I should mention it to Elsa and see quickly *that* piece of news travels.'

'Like wildfire, I should imagine,' remarked Greg.

'Just goes to show how things can be misinterpreted.'

'There are no secrets in Ashdale,' Greg chuckled. 'But seriously, I think we should discuss the possibility of buying one of these apartments. We could do it jointly. Let's have a chat about it over a pub lunch tomorrow. For now though, we had better get going.'

'You had me worried for a moment then,' Lydia replied as she started the car, 'but I'm happy to talk the idea through, I like the thought of an apartment in Spain.'

Robbie welcomed Greg and Lydia into his penthouse apartment in Leeds. They had been before and Lydia was quite envious of the magnificent wrap-around terrace and the views over the city. Robbie was a colleague of Greg's, although he worked on a sister newspaper in West Yorkshire.

'I'm so glad you could come. I know you won't know many people, but there is someone I would like you to meet.' Robbie led Greg and Lydia through a crowd of people to the other side of the room and out onto a terrace which overlooked the river below. He stopped in front of a tall man with a full head of neatly cut grey, almost white, hair, who wore a navy blazer with a pair of neatly pressed grey trousers.

'Cliff, may I introduce a colleague of mine, Greg Craven and his partner, Lydia Buckley.' The man turned immediately, smiled and shook both of their hands,

'Hello, I'm Cliff Walker, very pleased to meet you.' The greeting was enthusiastic and warm, 'I'm about to start writing a column for Robbie's paper so I may come into contact with you, Greg.'

Robbie slipped away to get them some drinks as Cliff explained his background. 'I'm ex-army, retired about ten years ago actually, but I've always had a hankering to do some writing – not a novel, nothing quite so long as that, but short, topical stuff with a smidgen of humour, possibly bordering on gossip.' His blue-grey eyes twinkled mischievously. Lydia immediately warmed to Cliff as he talked more about his ideas for the column.

'So, where do you live?' she asked chattily as she sipped the cold tonic water Robbie had presented her with.

'Here in Leeds, but I would like to move to a more rural location, Robbie tells me that you both live in a market town not far away.'

'Yes, we live in Ashdale, near Harrogate. It's about a thirty minute drive from Leeds. It's quite rural but not remote, it has a regular bus service, a weekly market, a supermarket – most of the things you need.'

'Ashdale? Well, what a coincidence! I was planning on going there on Monday. I believe there is a garage called Ashdale Autos – they do classic cars, do you know them?'

'We most certainly do,' replied Lydia, 'it's owned by Ben Simpson and Mikey Dixon. Ben just happens to be my brother-in-law, but Mikey is the classic car man.'

'I fancy buying an MGB, I used to have one you know, many years ago – a lovely classic car. I'm also looking to move out of Leeds, I'm not really a big-city kind of man, maybe I'll take a look at Ashdale whilst I'm there.'

'Greg's brother, Tom has the estate agents so you may like to have a look on his website, it's The Property Ladder.'

'Thank you, I'll do that. Oh, hello, Fran,' Cliff turned to greet a woman who had come to join them. 'This is my sister, Fran Garnett. Fran, this lovely couple Greg and Lydia live in a delightful sounding town called Ashdale.'

As they shook hands with Fran, Lydia observed that Cliff and Fran's features were so similar that it was obvious that they were related. Fran's pale blonde hair was styled into a neat chin length bob, but her blue-grey eyes and the shape of her face with its dimples echoed those of Cliff's.

'Ashdale?' repeated Fran, 'I'm going to a wedding fair at Ashdale Hall soon with my daughter. Is it the same place?'

'Yes, it is, and some of the local businesses will have stands there, we're so excited to be able to showcase our individual talents in this way,' replied Lydia.

'Are you attending, Lydia?' asked Fran.

'Yes, I'm an eyelash technician and I do some work for Zoe Birch's salon, WOW! so I'm helping her at the fair.'

'We're particularly looking for a florist and someone to make Michelle's cake.'

'Oh well in that case, you should certainly visit the Houseman's stand. They have a bakery in Ashdale and their cakes are simply divine – they are also finalists for a national industry award,' added Lydia enthusiastically. 'Mikey Dixon will be there with Ashdale Wedding Cars, Rebecca Miller of Bridal Beauty, and our newest residents, Sarah Kirkwood and her mother, Lucy, have recently taken over the florist's, Flower Power—'

'Lucy Kirkwood?' interrupted Fran, 'I once knew a florist called Lucy Kirkwood. You remember Lucy, don't you Cliff?' She nudged her brother. 'She shared a flat with Trissie Foxton, I wonder if it's the same Lucy.' Fran frowned as she tried recall the details then shook her head and looked at her brother for confirmation, but Cliff was staring over her head into the distance as though recalling memories of his own. 'Cliff?' Fran said again with another nudge.

Cliff returned to the present. 'Sorry, I was just trying to remember, and yes, you're right – it was Trissie Foxton, I've some lovely memories of her.'

'Really? About Trissie?' Fran was genuinely surprised.

'It was back then when I had one of those crossroads moments, you know the ones, when you have a choice of whether to do this or that and you make a decision to do "this". Then every so often you wonder what life would have been like if you had done "that" instead. Well, Trissie was my "that". I stayed with my wife rather than leave her and go off with Trissie, and, as I'm now divorced, I do wonder about Trissie and whether I made the right decision,' Cliff told them candidly.

'You were having an *affair*? With *Trissie Foxton*?' exclaimed Fran, 'Well, you kept that quiet!'

'My dear Fran, of course I kept it quiet, it doesn't do to shout one's affairs from the roof tops!'

'And Sandra never knew?'

'No, my dear wife never knew,' Cliff replied, with a sarcastic emphasis on the word 'dear'. 'I don't believe anyone knew,' he added.

'Well, I'm shocked. I can't believe you had an affair with Trissie Foxton. Whatever did you see in her?' Fran asked.

'Hidden depths, she had hidden depths,' Cliff replied mysteriously, tapping the side of his nose with his forefinger. 'Anyway, it was all a long time ago, plenty of water under the bridge since then,' he added brightly. 'Tell me a little more about Ashdale, Greg.'

The two men began to talk about the market town and Lydia turned to Fran. 'Do you live in Leeds?'

'No, we live in Northallerton. Michelle manages a boutique there and I have a part-time job at the county council,' replied Fran.

'A boutique? There is a newly opened boutique in Ashdale called Lulabelle's.'

''Yes, that's Michelle's. They are owned by a Penelope Sinclair-Sutton. She's a very nice young woman and she mentioned to Michelle that she was opening her second shop in Ashdale.'

'I believe ours only opened about three months ago. It's managed by a colourful character called Tasheka, and, although she's a friend of mine, I can guarantee that there will be a world of difference between her sales technique and that of Michelle's,' Lydia said with fond humour.

'Really?'

'Really.'

'Tell me, when is Michelle getting married?'

'Next June. She's set on a civil ceremony in a country house so we shall be very interested to see Ashdale Hall. I'm widowed, so Cliff will be giving Michelle away. He's taking his role of *de facto* father of the bride quite seriously and will be with us at the wedding fair.'

'I do hope he won't be bored with all the wedding talk, not many men attend wedding fairs.'

'He insisted on coming with us. He and Sandra had no children and when my Paul died, he was so supportive. In fact, between you and me, he is paying for the venue and reception, so he wants a say in the choice.'

'That's very generous of him and I doubt you will find better than Ashdale Hall. If you like the wedding retailers you see there, you might be able to get all the things you need organised on the same day.'

'You know, I wonder if the florist you mentioned *is* the same Lucy Kirkwood, I hope it is. It would be lovely to see her again. She and Trissie shared a flat whilst Sandra and I had the flat opposite. The four of us were great friends and went out together at weekends, but then I married one of Cliff's army friends, Paul Garnett and Sandra married Cliff. And, just before we were posted to Germany, Lucy got engaged and Trissie got a live-in teaching post in a posh girls' boarding school somewhere further south, so we all just went our separate ways. We heard later that Lucy's fiancé had been killed in a car crash and that she had subsequently had a baby, I did often wonder how she coped with that.'

'How awful for Lucy. I can tell you that the Lucy at Flower Power has a daughter who may be the right age to fit your story. Why don't you ring Flower Power and find out before you see her at the wedding fair?' suggested Lydia.

'Do you know, I think I will,' replied Fran.

They talked more about weddings, then Lydia told Fran about her novels and her eyelash business, and by the end of the evening Lydia felt as though she had known her for years. On their way home, she told Greg how much she had enjoyed the evening and she hoped that the Flower Power Lucy was Fran's long lost friend.

'Are you still serous about looking at the Spanish apartments or were you just joking?' she asked as they pulled into Ashdale.

'I'm very serious, we both need to think about it and I'm very serious about lunch at the Coach tomorrow. Right now though, do you fancy a hot chocolate?'

'I'd love a hot chocolate and a cuddle, please.'

'As it happens, I'm particularly good at both, Ms Buckley.'

They laughed as Lydia unlocked the door and they went upstairs to her flat.

4

Cliff Walker

As Cliff pulled into the Market Place in Ashdale on Monday morning, he smiled. This was just the sort of place he had in mind. Most of the businesses appeared to be individual rather than owned by national chains and he liked that idea. He drove around the square noting the café, the Coach & Horses, the travel agent next door, and then a line of shops including the florists – Ah that would be where Lucy Kirkwood was. He hoped it was the same Lucy Kirkwood as it would be great to chew over old times. Fran was going to phone sometime today and find out. He noted a salon called WOW! Lydia had mentioned that, and the supermarket which looked a decent size, but not out of place. Finally, the south end of the Market Place included an Italian restaurant and a department store. He turned his car into Quarry Lane and drove a short distance before he came to Ashdale Motors and EasyPeasy DIY, the businesses both occupying a huge warehouse-type structure built in what had once been a quarry.

Cliff parked his car and wandered through open, concertina doors into a workshop. A young man, wiping his hands on a rag approached him.

'Can I help you?' he asked politely.

'I'm wondering if I could talk to someone about MGs?'

'That'll be Mr Dixon. I'll just see if he's about.' The lad walked away in the direction of some offices that Cliff could just see at the back of the workshop. Whilst he waited, Cliff watched the mechanics at work; some were head bent over the engines of modern cars, but a couple of chaps were carefully manoeuvring a windscreen into position on an MG. Cliff smiled as he remembered the joy of driving his MG back in the day. He heard footsteps approaching and turned to see the young lad returning with a man of around forty years old, stockily built with a full head of brown hair.

'Good morning I'm Mikey Dixon, how can I help you?' The man smiled and held out his hand.

'Cliff Walker, thank you for seeing me without an appointment.' He shook Mikey's hand firmly. 'I'm considering buying an MG – had one years ago actually, and you were highly recommended by the MG Enthusiasts Club.'

'Nice to meet you, Mr Walker. What model of MG did you have in mind?' asked Mikey.

'I used to own a tartan-red Roadster, early 60s type and I quite fancy one again – purely for pleasure, I'm not thinking of competitions and such like,' replied Cliff as he glanced around the workshop.

'Well, I've two available from the 60s – one in tartan red and another in teal blue. Follow me and I'll show you.'

Cliff followed Mikey to a sectioned-off part of the workshop where five MGs were parked and pointed out the cars he had mentioned. Cliff wandered around both cars and did a double-take,

'I don't believe it!' he gasped. 'That's my old car, oh my God!'

'Is it? Are you sure?' Mikey asked with some scepticism.

'Well, it looks like it and the registration is very similar, four something something CRW. I particularly remember that as I got the car in the April, fourth month you see, and CRW are my initials. Well, I'll be damned!' Cliff stroked the front wing and wandered around the front of the car to stare at the bonnet.

'Brings back memories does this,' he mused. 'I loved my MG, drove all over the place and around Germany. I wonder if it *is* the same car...'

Cliff reminisced for a few minutes and then Mikey cleared his throat. 'Are you interested in any of the others or is it this one in particular?' he asked politely.

'Definitely this one. I see it has been converted to wire wheels – looks smart.' Cliff nodded his head and peered inside the car. 'New leather seats, new stereo I see, but the knobs and dashboard are exactly as I remember them. I'm sure it's the same car. Do you think I could take it for a spin?'

'Of course, I'll just go and collect the keys.'

Mikey disappeared and Cliff wandered around the car again – he was almost certain it was his old car. He ran his hand across the nearside wing and up the windscreen post, of course there was no sign of the damage now. Mikey returned and suggested that he drove them out of Ashdale and then they could swap over. They chatted about the car as they drove and when at last Cliff was able to slide into the driver's seat, he at once felt at ease with the car and enjoyed the feel of driving a classic car once again. Upon their return to the garage, Cliff sported a broad grin, 'It drives beautifully,' he commented.

'We've just rebuilt the engine and gearbox,' Mikey told him as they both got out of the car. The men chatted about the ins and outs of the engine and MGs in general until eventually Cliff took another stroll around the car.

'Good, good...' he nodded and smiled at Mikey, 'So I guess it's around twenty thousand then?'

'All but fifty pounds, yes,' confirmed Mikey.

Cliff wandered around the car again. 'Yes, this is my choice, I'm sure it's my old car. Have you got any history of it?'

'Only the invoices for the work we've done recently, some older invoices from other garages and a few old MOTs. One of the lads found a crumpled piece of paper when we removed the seats, but I'm not sure that he kept it.'

'Has it got an MOT?'

'Well, it doesn't require one by law, but as soon as it's sold, we'll obtain a new one.'

'I am really tempted but let me sleep on it and I'll come back to you before the end of the week.' Cliff ran his hand lovingly over the glossy front wing.

'I'll look forward to hearing from you in that case,' said Mikey as they shook hands. Cliff so wanted to believe that this was his old car and decided that he would have a rummage through his old photos to see if he could find a picture of the MG.

Now Cliff was something of a nosey man, he liked gossip which is why, he reasoned, he had opted to become a social reporter (he preferred that title rather than Gossip Columnist). Bearing that in mind, he decided to pay a visit to the café in the Market Place to get a feel for the 'local vibe' and a cup of tea as a bonus.

He entered the café and was immediately taken by the wonderful aroma of fresh coffee, the bright, welcoming décor of light blue walls, lemon yellow soft furnishings and dark wood beams and furniture. He approached the counter and a woman with dark hair swept up into a messy bun welcomed him, her face seeming surprisingly familiar.

'Good morning, what can I get for you?'

Cliff ordered a pot of tea for one and a chocolate muffin which was quickly placed on his tray. As he stirred his tea, Cliff tuned in to a conversation between two mature ladies (he knew better than to say 'older').

'I see Maureen Brown is back at work, but she doesn't look well,' commented the lady in the blue jacket.

'When have you seen Maureen?' asked her companion, sporting a red scarf.

'Oh, I haven't, but Sid Dawkins did when he dropped his accounts off at Babcock's. Back too soon, he says.'

'And what would Sid Dawkins know about it? I heard that she had problems…'

Cliff didn't hear the rest of the sentence as the woman lowered her voice, but out of the corner of his eye, he saw her mouth the words *down below* before continuing at normal volume,

'… had to have it all taken away, a mysterectomy,' she explained.

'I think you mean a hysterectomy,' corrected her friend as Cliff tried to contain a snigger.

The woman continued, 'Sid said she looked like death warmed up, but apparently she was worried about her job!'

'No, *get away!* Maureen Brown has worked at Babcock's for the past twenty years or so. At one time I thought Albert Wilks might take a shine to her. Why would *she* be worried about her job?'

'While she was off, Albert Wilks took on Saffron Lawson temporarily and Maureen didn't like it.' The lady in the blue jacket tapped her index finger on the table to emphasise Maureen's displeasure.

'Saffron Lawson? Surely Maureen doesn't think Albert has a thing for Saffron, why he's old enough to be her father!'

'*That* doesn't make any difference, look at Charlotte Worthington.'

There was a pause whilst both ladies considered Charlotte Worthington and sipped their drinks. Cliff glanced across and caught the eye of the lady in the blue jacket, he smiled cordially at them and turned away so they wouldn't think he was eavesdropping. He took a bite out of his chocolate muffin, which was absolutely delicious, and hoped the ladies would continue.

The lady in the blue jacket obliged, 'Oh! I knew I had something else to tell you – Lydia Buckley and Greg Craven are eloping to Spain!'

Cliff nearly choked on his muffin! *Lydia and Greg – eloping?* The lady with the red scarf put her cup sharply down back in its saucer,

'Eloping? Whatever for?'

'They're buying one of them fancy apartments that Tom Craven has advertised in his window.'

'No, really?'

'Oh yes, Doreen Rider actually heard Lydia tell Tom that she and Greg were eloping.'

'Well, Elsa, I *am* surprised. I thought they were both settled here. Such a nice couple – and she helped solve that murder a few months back.'

Cliff's eyes opened wide. *Murder?* He'd better ask Lydia about that before she disappeared! The lady in the blue jacket, Elsa, suddenly noticed the time.

'Goodness! It's almost eleven, I shall have to get back or Brian'll wonder where I've got to,' she said as she pushed her cup away.

The ladies collected their belongings and made their way out of the café. Cliff quietly chuckled to himself – this was exactly the sort of thing he was looking for – a small town with plenty of gossip. Just then, his mobile rang and the caller ID told him that it was Fran.

'Guess what?' his sister began excitedly, 'Ashdale's Lucy Kirkwood is the same Lucy that we knew! Isn't that a marvellous coincidence? We've just had a lovely chat, but obviously she's busy in the shop so I'm going to ring her again tonight for a proper catch-up. I just thought I would let you know.'

'Funnily enough, I'm just in the café opposite Lucy's shop, I may well pop in and say hello. It would be rude not to.'

'Ok, well don't overstay, they are trying to run a business.'

Promising not to linger in the shop and be a nuisance, Cliff ended the call.

Sarah Kirkwood

Sarah was in the back room of the shop making up an arrangement for an order. She listened to her mother chatting happily to a customer and thought how uplifted she had been since receiving a phone call from her long-lost friend, Fran. There hadn't been time for a lengthy conversation, but her mother was clearly looking forward to the promised catch-up this evening. Sarah had heard many stories from Lucy about the fun the four girls had had whilst they were young women living in Leeds and how they had eventually gone their separate ways after Fran and Sandra married the army chaps. Her mother had fallen in love with Sam Grayson, they had got engaged and were planning their life together, which left Trissie, who apparently hadn't got a boyfriend.

Her mother had told her about the dreadful time when she had found out about Sam's death. It had been Good Friday and Trissie had packed her bags and left that morning to travel south to her new live-in teaching post, apparently to get settled in during the school holidays, albeit earlier than originally planned. Sam's heartbroken mother had phoned with the devastating news that Sam had been knocked down by a car and killed. Sarah couldn't imagine how her mother had felt and then how she had coped when she subsequently discovered that she was pregnant.

Sarah had always felt that more should have been done to find the hit-and-run driver who must have been very drunk in order to mount the pavement and hit a pedestrian; surely, they must have known they had hit something. The police said it looked as though Sam had been hit on his left-hand side before hitting the ground – he had died almost instantaneously. There had been an investigation and the car would have been damaged but, despite appeals from the police for anyone with information to come forward, there had been nothing and neither the car nor the driver had ever been found. Although her mother had grown to live with the pain of losing Sam, Sarah had always felt a burning hatred for the person who had denied her the opportunity of knowing her father.

Their decision to move from Leeds to the quieter town of Ashdale had come about after an attempted break-in at their previous shop. Sarah had seen how frightened her mother had been and began her search for new premises more or less immediately, finding the shop in Ashdale had been a blessing. Since moving in, the local residents had made them feel so welcome and, following her emails with Desmond Carmichael, Sarah was now looking forward to joining the Ashdale Players. She heard the customer leave the shop and her mother came through to join her in the back room.

'Sarah! That arrangement looks gorgeous, I love the colours.'

Sarah stood back and admired her handiwork. 'I have to admit, I'm quite pleased with it.' Both the women studied the artfully arranged mix of peach and lemon garden roses, cinnamon spice roses, dahlias, orchids and pepper tree berries. The shop door opened again and they both returned to greet the man who entered. He was tall with a full head of neatly cut grey, almost white, hair, his grey-blue eyes had a twinkle and as he smiled, Sarah could see that he had dimples.

He held both his arms out as he spoke. 'Lucy! You haven't changed a bit! I would have recognised you even if Fran hadn't told me that you were here.'

Sarah glanced at her mother whose face had lit up with delight. 'Cliff! I can't believe it, after all this time! First I get Fran on the phone and then you walk through the door.' Lucy walked into Cliff's arms and they hugged each other warmly. Sarah was delighted that her mother seemed so pleased to see her old friend.

'This must be your daughter, she looks very like you, but she has Sam's eyes,' he said softly. Then, looking directly at Lucy he continued, 'We were absolutely devastated to hear about Sam's death and so upset that we didn't hear in time to pay our respects. As soon as I got back to Germany with the MG, we were sent away on manoeuvres and of course in those days, there were no mobile phones, communications were more difficult, I'm so sorry.' There was a pause whilst everyone reflected.

Lucy broke the silence. 'Yes, this is Sarah – we're in partnership here in the shop. Sarah, as you have probably gathered, this is Cliff Walker – he is Fran's brother.'

Cliff strode forward and put out his hand, which Sarah took. He shook it firmly. 'I'm very pleased to meet you, Sarah.' Then turning to Lucy, he said, 'Fran and I are so happy to have found you again and we've so much to catch up on. I understand you will be at the wedding fair next Sunday so I'll see you there and we shall arrange a proper get-together.'

Lucy nodded enthusiastically as the shop door opened to admit a customer. 'Now, I promised Fran I wouldn't be a nuisance and get in your way, so I'll go and leave it up to you and Fran to organise something, I'll just say au revoir.' He waggled his fingers at Sarah and squeezed Lucy's hand before closing the door behind him.

Having ascertained that the customer wanted to browse and choose flowers herself Lucy turned to her daughter, and Sarah was amazed at how animated and happy her mother looked.

'I can't wait to sit down with a glass of wine tonight and have a good natter with Fran – we've so much to talk about. Isn't Cliff a lovely man? I was speechless when he married Sandra. Between you and me, I'm not surprised to learn that they got divorced, he was too good for her!'

Sarah hadn't heard her mother be quite so catty before and she raised her eyebrows. 'Mother, really!' she admonished and then giggled before turning her attention to the customer who had approached the counter with an armful of flowers.

Lydia Buckley

Lydia was pleasantly surprised – she had just discovered that she could afford a decent loan as her half towards a Spanish apartment. She and Greg had talked about it yesterday and they had decided that they preferred a three-bedroomed apartment as it would rent out easily for a good return which would more than cover their borrowings. Greg had gone to London for most of the coming week on a secondment with a London newspaper, something about undercover operations, so Lydia had offered to go and see Tom to talk over some further details. A quick glance at her phone told her that she was due at The Property Ladder in five minutes, so she picked up her pad and pen and left the flat.

Once they were seated in Tom's office, he opened a file and spread the papers across his desk so Lydia could see them clearly. 'This is a plan of the site. You mentioned that you were both interested in a three-bedroomed property, the detached villas are marked in purple, the semi-detached villas are in green and the apartments are in blue. I have the various floor plans here which I can photocopy for you to take away, and if I log on to the website, we can see a virtual tour of the show homes.'

Tom took Lydia carefully through all the options and explained the costs and charges. He then showed her how it could be managed by Hugo via Spanish Sun.

Half an hour later, Lydia leant back in her chair. 'You make it sound so simple, Tom.'

'It is simple, everything is done via the internet. Hugo can even help you furnish it if you like.'

'Choosing the décor and furnishings would be something I'd enjoy, and I'm not sure Hugo and I would have the same taste,' commented Lydia.

Tom laughed. 'I don't mean Hugo does it personally, he has an interior designer who would work with you, but it means you don't have to spend time in Spain unnecessarily. I already have one client who has bought this property – here.' Tom pointed to a red outline on the site plan. 'It's a rather lovely detached villa with a pool, one of the more expensive properties at four hundred thousand and it's in a good private location within the site. This chap has not been to the site at all – he's just left everything to Hugo and as soon as the balance is paid and the sale is completed, which will probably be later this week, he can fly out, pick up his keys from Hugo and move in. It will be turn-key ready.'

'Four hundred thousand! Wow! I bet it's beautiful, I don't suppose you have any pictures so I can see the interior designer's work?'

'As a matter of fact, I do. It has only just been finished and I have some photos which I've emailed to my client.' Tom tapped on his keyboard and turned the screen towards Lydia. 'There you are, how amazing does that look?'

Lydia sighed as she looked at the screen. 'Gorgeous!' she exclaimed, 'I would be very happy if that was my villa.'

'I believe my client is looking to rent it out, to discerning guests, but he can look forward to a decent income of at least one and a half thousand pounds a week, possibly a bit more in the high season.'

'One and a half thousand pounds a week?' squeaked Lydia.

'Yes, Adam is quite impressed. Oh God! Sorry, I shouldn't have mentioned his name. Please forget I said that.' Tom appeared horrified at his slip of the tongue.

'Don't worry, I don't think I know anyone called Adam anyway. I can't wait to show Greg all this info, I'm so excited at the thought of actually owning a property like this.'

'I'll give you this folder with the photocopies of the properties we've looked at and you also have the website details.'

'Where would we be without the internet?' Lydia commented, 'I have to say, I think the website for Spanish Sun looks good. It's easy to use and very informative. Some websites you look at are difficult and trying to find the information you want is a nightmare.'

'Well, this one for Spanish Sun was created by Adam Lewis and I've just had mine for The Property Ladder revamped by him. I'm really pleased with what he's done.'

'Adam Lewis – is that Beatrice Lewis's son?'

'It is. He's started a graphics business here in Ashdale.'

'Hmm, I could do with overhauling my website, I did it myself a couple of years ago, but it could do with a professional makeover.'

'I've got his card here. You can take it, and at least let him give you his opinion on your current website. I think you will be impressed and he's not overpriced.'

'Tom, I can't thank you enough for all your help.'

Lydia left the agency and returned to her flat. She immediately logged on to the Spanish Sun website to look at the properties at leisure and wondered why on earth she hadn't thought of this before.

Adam Lewis

As Adam returned home from seeing a client, he thought about how he would broach the subject of money to his mother. He privately thought that she could have given him a bit more than what his father had bequeathed, but of course it would all come to him one day in any case, so in reality he was only asking for an advance. The death of Charles Lewis from a heart attack had shocked Adam. His father had been a large bear of a man who enjoyed the finer things in life, such as golf club dinners, a box at the racecourse, vintage cars, good wines, and so on. Charles had expected Adam to join the estate agency business at some point, but Adam had declined and had instead chosen graphic artistry and web design as his main degree subjects. Charles had been quite dismissive and told everyone that Adam would come to his senses and join the estate agency and not pursue an "arty farty" career. In the years before his heart attack, Charles had done very little actual work for his fifty percent share of the profits, instead leaving the day-to-day running of the business to Hugo. Eventually Hugo had had enough and, with some initial animosity, they had dissolved the partnership and sold the business to their sales manager, Tom Craven. Unfortunately, not long afterward, Charles had died.

Adam was pleased that his mother had been more than adequately provided for, but was disappointed with his own inheritance – a measly three hundred thousand pounds – which he attributed to being a sort of punishment for not joining his father in the business. However, his decision to invest the funds in a Spanish property, Adam felt, was essential for his future wellbeing. He figured that not only would it provide an immediate home for himself and Charlotte, but if the relationship fizzled out, then he would still have his money safely invested. Once his mother had been persuaded to transfer the necessary funds to his bank account, he would complete the purchase of the villa and look to booking their flights. He had arranged to see Charlotte tomorrow and planned to tell her the news about the villa purchase. He looked forward to seeing the joy on her face as their plans became a reality and they could finalise their escape. No one would know where they had gone, apart from his mother and even she wouldn't know the actual address – maybe he could tell her the villa was in a different part of Spain entirely…now that idea really had some appeal.

He pulled up outside the house and found himself humming *Viva España* as he walked up the path to the front door.

'Mother?' he called.

'I'm in the kitchen,'

Adam followed the delicious aroma of roast lamb and found his mother uncorking a bottle of red wine.

'That smells fantastic!' Adam commented as he reached into a cupboard for a couple of wine glasses.

'Oh, I haven't prepared this, Mrs Simms has been in today so I asked her to do a roast for us. It will be ready in half an hour – shall we just eat in here?' Beatrice poured the wine and glanced at her son.

Adam nodded. 'How are you feeling now? Have you had a busy day?'

'Oh, I'm fine now. I spoke with Lexie Worthington this morning and tried to persuade her to book Kerry's as an alternative to Ashdale Autos. Kerry's vintage wedding cars will look so much more appropriate at Ashdale Hall than those common saloon cars of Mikey Dixon's.'

'I would imagine that Mikey's saloon cars are a bit better than "common", Mother.'

'Oh, you know what I mean. Anyway, I think she'll take both businesses now.'

Adam twirled the wine glass stem between his fingers. 'Have you given any thought to pursuing the bakery for compensation?' he asked casually.

'Yes, I did consider doing that, but I'm not going to,' Beatrice replied decisively, 'I shall wait until after the wedding fair and then contact the British Bakers' Association. My complaint should scupper their chances of winning an award.'

'Really?' replied Adam, a little taken aback at the venom in Beatrice's voice.

'Yes, that will teach them not to have their food properly labelled. I could have *died!*'

'But why are you waiting until after the wedding fair? Surely it will do more harm to have it in the newspapers beforehand.'

'Precisely! I don't want to ruin the Worthington's first wedding fair with scandal like that. I'm also attending the event in my official capacity as councillor, as well as representing the mayor's office – the poor man has been taken poorly with shingles.'

Adam shrugged, he guessed his mother knew what she was doing although he personally would have sued for compensation. Beatrice stirred some gravy and continued talking,

'I also suggested to Lexie that, in the light of recent events with the Housemans, they should be denied a stand at the fair.'

'And what did Lexie say?'

'She said that they were still welcome to attend. I recommended that she discuss the situation with her mother. After all, Lady Victoria is far more experienced in these matters.'

Adam nodded in agreement and smiled warmly at his mother. He took a breath. 'I have some excellent news to tell you…' he began, then waited whilst his mother slid the lamb joint out of the oven and carefully lifted the meat onto the carving dish. Beatrice popped a dish of vegetables into the microwave, set the timer and turned to her son.

'Right, tell me your news now,' she said and sat down at the table opposite him.

'I've just been to see a major client in Harrogate and they have asked me to take over their website, it will be an incredible boost to my business.'

'Darling, that's marvellous news. How did that come about?'

'Well, I met this chap at a do when I went as your guest and we got talking, I told him about Graphicality, mentioned my job in London and he was impressed. He has since been in touch and *voila!*'

'Adam, I'm so pleased. You know it could lead to more work once word gets around.'

'As long as there is time for an odd holiday, I don't mind working hard – a bit like you, I suppose.' Adam tossed the comment out casually, but it was bait and Beatrice bit.

'Holiday? I can never plan a holiday these days, I'm busy most of the year except for August and I wouldn't want to go in the school holidays.'

'What you need is spontaneity, the ability to just decide to get a short haul flight to somewhere warm – just on a whim, which brings me to my next bit of news.'

Beatrice's eyes narrowed, 'Have you booked a holiday?' she asked suspiciously. 'One that you can't take now you have work to do?'

Adam chuckled, 'No, Mother, but I've done something quite serious, significant and, I hope, sensible.'

'Oh Adam, what have you got involved with?' Beatrice wailed.

'Nothing bad, don't worry, I've invested my inheritance from Father in a fabulous Spanish villa!'

'What?'

'I thought that we could let it for most of the year to get a return on the investment and enjoy it ourselves the rest of the time. I did it for us – as a surprise for you.'

Beatrice stared at him, 'You've bought a Spanish villa? As a surprise for me?' she repeated incredulously. 'You have never done anything for me in the past except cause me sleepless nights.'

'Well, when I say *bought*, I've put a hefty deposit on it. I just need to pay the balance, which is where I need your help.'

'Ahh! I was wondering where the catch was. I might have guessed you would want some money,' Beatrice replied wearily.

'Please, hear me out,' Adam had taken hold of his mother's hands, but now he let them go, stood up and began to pace around the kitchen as he chose his words carefully.

'When Father died so suddenly, I realised how tenuous life really is and that we should try to enjoy as much of it as we can.' He paused and glanced at his mother who took a sip of wine watching him with eyes full of scepticism.

'You work so hard, especially now you're a local councillor and I know you give no thought to proper rest and relaxation. It wouldn't have occurred to you to buy a property in Spain, or anywhere else, and I decided that if I took the plunge, we could both benefit.' Adam paused in case Beatrice wanted to make a comment, but she merely nodded her head thoughtfully.

'The thing is,' he continued, 'I've sunk my entire inheritance into the deposit for this villa and I thought I could make enough money from my business to pay the rest, but things have been a little slower than I imagined and now I'm in a bit of a hole.'

'How much do you want to borrow?'

'I need one hundred and fifty thousand, that's all.'

'*That's all?*' Beatrice put her wine glass down sharply.

'Yes, that's all.' Adam returned to the table and sat down again. 'I've already paid double that myself. For four hundred thousand – it's a fabulous place, and the extra fifty thousand is for the furnishings I've already agreed, but you'll love it and we can earn on average one and a half thousand pounds a week in rental, possibly more during the high season. I mean, it's not as if you can earn any interest on the money sitting in a bank account is it? I'll pay you back as my business grows, in fact you can keep the rental income, initially. Look, we can go together or separately on holidays, whichever you prefer.' He looked expectantly at his mother, wondering if he had said enough.

Beatrice still looked a little uncertain. 'How will you market the villa to potential renters?'

'I could do it through Uncle Hugo,' Adam replied carefully, trying to gauge his mother's reaction, and when she raised an eyebrow, he added, 'or I could do it for us on an owners' website – there are a number to choose from. I can look at all the possibilities and go through them with you at some point.'

'When do you need this money?' she asked.

'Straight away. I've had confirmation that the villa is ready and I'm being asked for the balance. Please say you'll do it or I will lose everything.' Adam held his mother's gaze whilst she considered her answer. Eventually Beatrice looked away.

'I can't get you that amount of money until, I believe, Thursday at the earliest. I have to give notice on that account.'

Adam stood up and reached across the table to kiss his mother on both cheeks. 'I can't thank you enough, Mum.'

Beatrice jerked back at the sudden display of emotion. 'Yes, well that's that decided. I'll speak to Albert Wilks tomorrow and put the wheels in motion.'

'Albert Wilks! I don't know why you're still with that old-fashioned firm. Freddie Flanigan is much more on the ball – a little close to the wire, but still legal.'

'Your father had all his financial affairs with Albert Wilks and I see no reason to change. In my view, Freddie Flanigan is a little – unsavoury, not a bit like his brother who owns Kerry's Classic Cars. Patrick and Bridget Flanigan are good friends of mine, although Bridget is prone to a little gossip, and to be honest, I would rather not have my private finances available to her as a topic. The lamb will be ready now so let's eat.' She bustled across to the dish and began to carve the joint. Adam stayed where he was and grinned. *Result!*

Later that night as Adam lay in bed, he pondered about whether he should have asked for an extra fifty thousand. After all there were the flights for himself and Charlotte *and* he would need interim spending money before he could expect her to start to contribute. However, he thought he might be pushing his luck to ask for the extra money at the moment – there must be another way. And then he had a light bulb moment.

Lydia Buckley
Lydia could hardly contain her excitement as she told Greg about her meeting with Tom. 'The properties are lovely. I'll text

the website details so you can take a look when you have a spare moment.'

'Spare moment?' laughed Greg. 'You have got to be kidding! Actually, what we're doing is quite fascinating. There is a current investigation about an anonymous loan shark called Mr Lord, and my colleagues here are helping the police via their own informants. This Mr Lord is a big player; he has a number of heavies who collect the debts and they think he is also laundering money. Not only that, he also has a harem of working girls – it's such a different world to Ashdale where the most exciting topic is a wedding fair!'

'Heavies? Money laundering? Prostitutes? Give me the wedding fair any day. Please be careful Greg. Are you involved at all?'

'No, don't worry. I'm not involved as such – just watching from the sidelines, that's all, but it's interesting to see how they amass information and see how the reporters work with the police, accessing something to really get their teeth into.'

'By the way, just getting back to the Spanish properties, Tom is taking Amy to Spain at some point to have a look for himself, so maybe we could go too.'

'That's sounds a great idea. Ok love, I'll say goodnight now and have a quick look. Let's speak tomorrow.'

After Greg had disconnected, Lydia sighed contentedly, Greg was lovely and they had a great relationship – she certainly had no qualms about buying a property with him. If she went ahead with the loan, she may need to work more hours at the salon, not reduce them, which reminded her that tomorrow she should contact Adam Lewis and arrange to meet him to discuss her website. She needed to up her literary game.

5

Sheila Houseman

Tuesday was another mild day, the bakery was warm and smelled deliciously of baking bread. Sheila tucked a strand of her layered blonde bob behind her ear as she leant on the open doorway to the kitchen watching her husband put the final touches to the coffee and walnut cake he had just prepared.

'Phew! It may not be a summer's day, but it's so warm in here – I'm going to prop the door open for a while,' she told Derek as she fanned her face. As Sheila secured a wedge under the open door, a slightly built man with an old-fashioned short-back-and-sides haircut, a thin section left long and combed over a bald head, hovered until he could enter the bakery. He wore black round-rimmed glasses which looked like original NHS issue and had a small, neat moustache. The three-piece black pinstripe suit, immaculate white shirt and black tie was a familiar uniform and Sheila welcomed him warmly.

'Morning, Albert, how are you?'

Albert Wilks, sole remaining partner in the local and long-standing accountancy firm Babcock, Coombes & Wilks, pushed his glasses further up his nose and squinted through them. Sheila wondered, not for the first time, why he wore them at all if they made him squint. He always had them on, for both long and short distances, which did not make much sense as they weren't bifocals. *Probably wears them in bed as well*, Sheila thought.

'Very well this morning, Mrs Houseman, and yourself?'

'Derek and I are both fine, thank you. Now, what can I get you?' Sheila asked as she returned behind her counter.

'Actually, I wanted to peruse your noticeboard. I'm looking for a cleaner,' explained Albert.

'Well, I think there is a card for Tasheka's cleaning company, only if there is, could you just take the details and leave the card there please? If it's not there, you could just pop next door and ask her for one.'

Albert inhaled quickly. 'Oh, I don't think I could go into *that* shop, Mrs Houseman.' He looked quite affronted at the suggestion.

'Why ever not?'

'It's a *ladies* shop,' he practically whispered as though it was quite something unmentionable.

Sheila tried hard not to giggle. Albert was so old-fashioned – straight out of the 1940s.

'In that case, take the card if it's there and I'll replace it, or, you could have a word with Elsa Armitage, she tends to know who is available to do whatever?'

Albert vigorously shook his head. 'No, no – I wouldn't want to trouble her, I'll…um… just have a look.' And Albert stepped out of sight behind the door.

Sheila shrugged and turned back to the kitchen doorway and seeing the coffee and walnut cake, she pointed at it. 'Is that ready to go out?' she asked her husband, who nodded in response. But before she could reach out to pick it up, she heard footsteps behind her. Sheila turned and gasped as she saw who her customer was.

'Good morning, I just wanted a quick word,' Adam said pleasantly. Sheila took a step forward as she felt Derek come and stand behind her,

'How can we help?' Sheila asked with some trepidation.

'Following my mother's unfortunate experience in this shop last Friday, she's asked me to call in and let you know that she intends asking for compensation.'

'*Compensation?*' repeated Sheila.

'Yes, well she was hospitalised due to your negligence and not only missed an important meeting on Friday afternoon, but you damn well nearly killed her!' Any pleasantness had disappeared.

'Now just a minute—' Derek began and stepped out from behind Sheila to face Adam, who put up his hand.

'Please, let me finish. I feel that it's only fair to give you an opportunity to make an offer prior to involving solicitors.'

'*Solicitors!*' gasped Sheila.

'Make an offer?' spluttered Derek. 'Why the hell should we make an offer? Your mother helped herself to the cake. It's not our fault.' Derek drew himself up to his considerable height, his round face had gone pink and his eyes flashed with anger.

'Actually, I think you will find that because the cake had no warning that it contained nuts, and let's face it, a Victoria sponge doesn't usually have ground almonds in it, you're liable,' Adam said coldly.

'But I had put a warning sign on the sample plate,' Sheila explained.

Adam put his head on one side, 'You say that now, but it wasn't there on Friday morning, was it? Do you really think my mother would have eaten that cake if she had known it contained nuts?'

'No, of course not!' replied Sheila.

Adam exhaled and shook his head sadly, 'You had a duty of care to ensure that a warning was in place before the cake was offered. My mother could have died. Look, I don't want to discuss this here, but I just want to advise you that we're looking for fifty thousand pounds in compensation and if you were to agree to pay that before, say, next Monday, then Mother would have no need to contact the British Bakers' Association.'

'Fifty thousand...' Sheila stumbled over the words.

'You must be out of your mind,' Derek blustered, 'we don't have that kind of money lying around. And what has the Bakers' Association got to do with this?'

'Well, it's my understanding that you're finalists in some sort of prestigious industry award and, well, it certainly wouldn't enhance your chances if they knew that you had almost killed one of your customers...' Adam tailed off to allow his words to sink in.

'Goddammit! Are you trying to blackmail us?' Derek shouted as he took a menacing step towards Adam, 'because if you are—'

He broke off as Sheila grabbed his arm. 'Derek love, calm down,' she said softly.

Adam grinned sardonically. 'I do hope I don't have to add threatening behaviour to our claim,' he said. 'Why don't I leave you to think it over for a while – let you consider ways to raise some money, hmm? I'm sure you will agree that to sort this out between ourselves is preferable to involving lawyers. I'll pop in later this week to see how you're getting on.' And with that, Adam turned and left the shop.

Sheila turned to Derek. 'What are we going to do, Derek? We haven't got that sort of money. Will you speak to the bank and see if they can lend it to us? Oh, if only I could find that notice!' Sheila felt tears welling in her eyes.

Derek put his arm around her. 'It wouldn't make any difference now even if you did find the notice, love. This is all *my* fault,' he said fiercely – 'I should never have baked that cake. He's right, you don't normally put ground almonds in a Victoria sponge.'

'It's your cake, you can put what you like in it,' sniffed Sheila as a tear ran down her cheek. 'I know that sign was on the plate, I *know* it!'

'It still doesn't alter the fact that she'll ruin any chance we have at the awards dinner and we've worked so hard to get into the final. All our customers have supported and voted for us. I feel as though we've let them down as well,' Derek pointed out, then he stomped back into his kitchen. 'Damn Adam Lewis!' he exploded.

Sheila watched her husband slam spoons and containers around and chewed her lip anxiously. She heard a discreet cough, and turning her head, she saw Albert Wilks step out from behind the door.

'Oh dear! Mrs Houseman—' he began sympathetically and took a couple of steps towards the counter.

'Albert! Whatever shall we do? We can't afford to pay that enormous sum! You heard him!'

'Well, err…no.'

'I mean, it sounded to me like blackmail. Was it blackmail?'

'I wouldn't go as far as—'

'My Derek *can* put what he likes in his cakes, can't he?'

'Of course, but—'

'I can assure you, Albert that I did put a sign there, whatever Adam Lewis says.'

'I'm sure you did —'

'Should we borrow some money, do you think?'

'To be honest, I—'

'He's right though, it may mean we're disqualified from the awards now –. And after all we've achieved, it's just not fair!' Sheila banged the countertop in frustration.

Albert Wilks looked nervous at Sheila's outburst and clasped his hands in alarm. Sobbing widows in his office he could deal with by offering cups of tea and tissues, but he was out of his comfort zone here in the bakery. However, before he could respond, he was almost pushed aside as Elsa Armitage marched in.

'Was that Adam Lewis I just saw leaving?' she demanded, 'What did he want? Was he threatening you again?'

Sheila cleared her throat and replied, 'Um, no…well yes – yes, it was Adam, he just called to let Derek and I know how Beatrice was, isn't that right Albert?'

Albert went a shade of red and merely nodded guiltily and Elsa glared accusingly at him. He gulped. 'I have what I need now, Mrs Houseman and… err… perhaps you had better call me about that other matter.' Albert scurried out of the bakery. Elsa stared after him and then turned her gaze on Sheila, raising her eyebrow.

'Is everything all right, love? You look a little upset?'

Sheila plastered a smile on her face. 'I'm fine now, I was a bit emotional after speaking to Adam – relieved I suppose. Now what can I get you?'

Elsa huffed, clearly not convinced at Sheila's story, but she asked for a curd tart and a Viennese finger. 'I can have a word with Adam if you like, Sheila,' she said as Sheila bagged the bakery goods. 'I don't think he should be hassling you like that. I know you said he dropped by to let you know about Beatrice, but he looked a bit smug and well, cocky actually, as far as I could see –. And as for that Albert Wilks, well he's not much use as a witness... he's frightened of his own shadow, is that one. Remember when he caught your daughter-in-law getting all up close and personal with Billy Pickles, who she eventually ran off with?'

Sheila inwardly winced at the memory as Elsa swept on. 'He wouldn't admit anything one way or the other –. Just ummed and arred and "didn't like to say". No, if you want to tell me anything confidential, well you know I can keep a secret...and I might even be able to offer some advice— '

'No! It's fine, thank you, Elsa,' Sheila said firmly. 'There's nothing I need to say right now.'

Elsa handed over her money and took the paper bag. 'Just bear it in mind then, and remember, a problem shared is as problem halved. Barb tells me everything...you do know that Beatrice Lewis is good friends with them Blenkhorns, so just watch out for any funny goings-on.'

Sheila nodded and smiled weakly as Elsa, having given her advice, left the shop.

As the day wore on, Sheila operated on auto pilot, but in quiet moments she reflected on the earlier conversation and went over the incident again and again. If only she had been in the shop when they had come in, none of this would have happened – but it had happened and now they were on the brink of ruin and embarrassment. Sheila couldn't see a way to solve this, as even if they could find fifty thousand, who was to say that Beatrice wouldn't ask for more? They could end up being blackmailed for months. On the other hand, if they refused and called her bluff, there could be some real damage to their business via the press and so on. Sheila could just see the sensational headline: Bakery Poisons Local Councillor. How could they live with that?

Lydia Buckley

Across the road in the salon, Lexie was settled on the couch with eyepads in place. Lydia told her to take a deep breath, relax and enjoy the wonderful aromas of the oils which she wafted under her client's nose.

'Oh my, that is so good. I must make more of an effort to fit in an odd treatment now and again,' she sighed.

'You have a spa at the Hall, don't you?' asked Lydia.

'We do, yes, but it's more spa than beauty. We have mud treatments, ice rooms, saunas, and although we do massage as well, it's...more therapeutic than relaxing.'

Lydia chuckled. 'Have you made a start on the layout for all the exhibitor stands yet? I remember doing one a few years ago and I can't tell you how many times I changed it in the run up to the event,' Lydia chatted as she prepared Lexie's eyelashes.

'You've organised a wedding fair?'

'Yes, when I was in Oxford. It's not an easy job, some businesses are very precious and picky as to where they are placed. Some don't speak to others; there are those with a high opinion of themselves, and there were some who thought they could have run the whole event better themselves. Oh yes! I remember it well.'

Lexie was silent for a few seconds, 'I don't suppose I could ask your advice on something – it's a bit confidential,' she said hesitantly.

'Anything you say in the treatment room is confidential, it's a bit like a church confessional. Seriously though, if I can help with something, then ask away.'

'The first question is – I've managed to attract more than one of each wedding business, for example two cake suppliers, a couple of photographers, two bridal retailers, etcetera but should I have had only had one of each?'

'No. In my opinion, you're doing the right thing. When I organised my fairs, I had more than one of each business and I found the brides really appreciated the choice. After all that is what people do, they look around for ideas and prices before making their final selection.'

'That was my feeling exactly!' agreed Lexie with relief. 'The second question is – what are your personal thoughts on Houseman's Bakery? I know that is a cheeky question, but I would really appreciate your honesty, as someone who has come to live here fairly recently.'

Lydia was surprised at the question but gave an honest answer. 'Sheila and Derek are lovely, genuine people. Derek is a marvel – he provides celebration cakes for just about everyone in Ashdale. My sister has the Forget-me-not Café next-door-but-one to the bakery and the Housemans provide all her baked goods. She wouldn't go anywhere else.'

'Really?' exclaimed Lexie, 'Even after last Friday's incident?'

'Last Friday? Oh! You mean with Beatrice Lewis. But how would that have anything to do with Kate's café?'

'I have it on good authority that your sister is moving her orders to Blenkhorn's' replied Lexie carefully,

'Not that I'm aware of,' replied Lydia, 'and I'm sure she would have mentioned it.'

'Hmm,' murmured Lexie.

'I hope you won't allow last Friday's incident to have a bearing on the wedding fair. Nothing the Housemans did or didn't do would have been deliberate. I wasn't there so I didn't see exactly what happened, but I do know that Sheila is very upset by it.'

Lexie sighed. 'I've been asked to reconsider allowing the Housemans to exhibit at the wedding fair because of last Friday's business. However, I tend to agree with you in that it should not have any bearing on the fair, especially as the Housemans have not been charged or fined, or even investigated as yet. But I just wanted another opinion. I was led to believe that the Housemans may pull out of the fair anyway though – because of allegations of negligence and incompetency.'

Lydia jerked in surprise, 'Negligence and incompetency? Not words I would use for that business. I do hope they won't back out, especially on those grounds. I had heard that Adam Lewis was shouting about something similar as the ambulance took his mother away, but I put that down to shock and a knee-jerk reaction at the time. I didn't think "negligence" and "incompetency" are words that would be banded about.'

'Maybe I should call in and talk to the Housemans and see how they feel about the fair for myself,' Lexie mused.

'I think that's the best idea. Look, don't hesitate to contact me if you want to chat about anything else or you need a hand with setting up. I'll give you my number – I'm only too happy to help if I can,' Lydia told her.

'Thanks Lydia, I really appreciate that.'

'Now tell me, how are the wedding preparations coming along for Charlotte's wedding?'

'Thankfully everything is fine as long as she doesn't change her mind about anything. This will be our first wedding since we got the licence for the Hall and it has attracted the attention of a glossy magazine, which has pleased Charlotte – but I'm not so sure about Gerald,' Lexie smiled.

'What's he like?' asked Lydia.

'Gerald? Oh, he's not bad looking, full head of greying hair – going to be a bit of a silver fox I guess – about fiftyish. I don't know him that well. Charlotte says he spends all week in London and according to my father, he is a professional director – you know, on the boards of a number of companies, fingers in pies – that sort of thing.'

'Presumably he has staff to look after Claro Court whilst he's in London?'

'There is a housekeeper, but Claro Court is a much smaller residence than the Hall, it only has ten bedrooms. The land is mostly rented out to local farmers and horsey people, so that takes care of itself, whilst the barns, outbuildings and stables have been converted into holiday accommodation which is all managed by a very efficient PA and an estate manager. Gerald tends to have people to stay most weekends. My parents often receive invitations to dinner parties, cocktail parties and so on, and now of course, Charlotte helps him host them. I used to go as well until Gerald began trying to pair me off with one of his acquaintances, so I just don't go at all now.'

'So, do you think Charlotte will be lonely at Claro Court?'

'I'm sure she'll still spend a lot of time at Ashdale – we have the spa, you see,' Lexie said wryly.

Lydia giggled and then had an idea. 'She might do charitable work, being Lady Charlotte will give her some sort of status. Perhaps holding fundraising lunches with your mother including a celebrity guest speaker – they could call it *Ladies Who Lunch,*' she suggested.

'You know, that's a brilliant idea,' enthused Lexie. 'May I suggest it to my mother?'

'Of course. They could be held at Claro Court and you could ask the glossy magazine if they would like exclusive rights to cover them.'

'Hmm, Charlotte would like that.' Lexie fell silent, so Lydia quietly got on with the job in hand, leaving Lexie to mull over the idea.

When, a couple of hours later, Lydia had finished, she handed Lexie a mirror.

'Oh my God!' Lexie exclaimed. 'They are amazing! I love them! I can almost guarantee that when Charlotte sees these, she'll want them also.'

'I'm so pleased you like them. If Charlotte is interested, remember to say that she will need a patch test at least two days before the application. If she wants them before her wedding, she'll have to check with Zoe and maybe Lush Lashes in Harrogate for an appointment.

'Ok, yes I'll do that. Before I forget, let me give you my mobile number – I may want to take you up on your offer of help.'

Numbers thus exchanged, Lydia took her client through to reception where they found Saffron almost hidden behind a huge bouquet of flowers.

'Goodness! Is it someone's birthday?' asked Lydia.

Saffron looked a bit shocked as she shook her head. 'They're, like, for me, but I don't know who sent them or why,' she replied in her sing-song voice.

'Lucky girl,' Lexie said, 'they're really lovely.'

'Boyfriend, perhaps?' suggested Lydia.

Saffron shook her head. 'Nah, Connor wouldn't do this. His idea of romance is, like, treating me to a Bailey's.'

'Is there a card with them? Look, underneath those peonies – I can see an envelope.' Lydia pointed to a tiny gap where she could see the white corner of a small envelope. Saffron carefully extracted it and opened it nervously whilst Lexie and Lydia hovered curiously. As Saffron read the card, her face dropped in disappointment.

'Well?' prompted Lydia.

'It says *Just for you.* And then there's a capital letter 'A' – that's it, there's, like, no name.'

'A secret admirer whose name begins with 'A',' decided Lexie with a smile.

'I don't want a secret admirer,' protested Saffron. 'It's, like, not cool and besides, Connor will think, like, I'm cheating on him.'

'Well, go and put them in water for now and they can sit in the relaxation room until you go home.'

'Oh, I'm not taking them home, Connor will, like, go mad.' Saffron stared at the offending flowers.

'Ok, I'll deal with them. In the meantime, can you take Miss Worthington's payment please?' Lydia asked. She left Lexie with Saffron, taking the bouquet of flowers into the kitchen, placing them into the washing bowl filled with water before returning to her room to prepare for her next client. As she did this, her mind mulled over her conversation with Lexie and she decided that she liked her very much.

Charlotte Worthington

Charlotte closed the study door and felt very self-satisfied. The discussion with her father had gone exactly the way she wanted. Daddy was such a pussycat. She pulled out her phone and sent a text: *I've got some good news for you!* x

That should have Adam jumping straight into his car. Charlotte chuckled, men were so malleable. It hadn't been difficult to persuade Daddy that Adam should take over their website management – that he would bring a fresh pair of eyes and make it more current and appealing. Daddy had insisted that Adam should liaise with their marketing company, Major Marketing, and had straight away called them to arrange for their account manager to come up for a meeting. Adam would be so pleased by her initiative, it would be an injection of money for his business and give him some great kudos, not to mention a damn good excuse for him to be at the Hall.

Actually, maybe she could suggest to Gerald that marketing Claro Court as a wedding venue might be a good idea, then Adam would be able to visit her in her new home – *what a brilliant idea*! Charlotte gave herself a mental pat on the back for her ingenuity. Of course she would have to have staff to organise everything as she didn't envisage doing much work herself. Perhaps she could even persuade Karen to leave Ashdale Hall and come to Claro Court – be a real manager and not second fiddle to Lexie. A decent salary raise should tempt her. There was always that toffee-nosed PA as well. *I wonder how Karen would cope with her!*

Gerald might take some persuading though, but then again, he always complained about how hard it was running the estate – maybe that was because he spent most of his time in London. He might be grateful of the suggestion and if he was difficult, there were ways to get him to agree. Charlotte allowed her imagination to flourish and had visions of Claro Court being featured in glossy magazines such as *Tatler* and *Vogue*. Photographs of herself as Lady Charlotte Pemberton 'at home' at Claro Court, a new and exclusive wedding and event venue. Oh yes, this idea had mileage and style. Maybe she could even employ Adam as her business manager – how delightfully and unashamedly wicked.

A while later, she and Adam sat in the newly refurbished pavilion in the secret garden, a secluded place in the beautiful grounds of the Hall which had become their regular meeting place in order to avoid questions about Adam's frequent visits.

Charlotte explained her ideas. 'So, what do you think? Isn't it a marvellous idea? We could be together ever such a lot on the pretext of working,' Charlotte was fairly bursting with excitement.

Adam took hold of her hands and looked deep into her eyes. 'If it's "together" you want, I also have an idea,' he said in his sexy voice.

'You do?'

'I've bought a fabulous villa in Spain, just for us.'

Charlotte gasped, 'You have? Well... God! Adam, I don't know what to say.' Charlotte was genuinely speechless.

'You can call off your wedding now, pack your bags and elope with me. Our dreams can become reality. I can work from our new villa in Spain – it's in Mar Menor, you'll love it – all the celebs go there. We can mingle with the rich and famous.' Adam's eyes shone with happiness, but Charlotte was lost for words, thoughts rushing around in her head. *What the hell has he done that for? I can't possibly elope to Spain. When did this little joke become so serious?*

Adam's smile faded as Charlotte failed to enthuse about his news, and then noticing his consternation, she mentally shook herself and took a deep breath. 'Adam,' she began, 'I really don't know what to say, I've a lot of thinking to do now. Calling off a wedding so close to the date is going to upset a lot of people—'

'In that case, don't tell anyone,' he broke in. 'Just pack your suitcases as you would for your honeymoon and we can just disappear on the morning of the wedding. Come on, Charlotte, we've talked about this so many times, let's just do it.'

Charlotte thought for a heartbeat – she needed to buy some time to think about how she was going to handle this, so she smiled at him. 'You're right, we can do this – on the morning of the wedding. We shall have to book flights and so on, but oh, how exciting!' She became serious. 'Just remember though, that we must carry on as normal until then. We don't want to raise any suspicions.'

'Oh my darling! I can't believe you've agreed to this.' Adam pulled Charlotte into his chest and hugged her tightly before releasing her, and then he kissed her so passionately that one thing inevitably led to another and the rest of the morning was spent in devouring each other's bodies in satisfying and passionate lovemaking.

Much later, as Charlotte watched Adam drive away, she knew that Adam was more smitten with her than she had realised. They had laughed about running away together but never had Charlotte thought that it was a serious proposition. Of course, it now meant that she would have to break it off with him, just before the wedding or, simply not turn up to meet him on that morning – she couldn't do it much sooner in case he let it slip to someone and Gerald heard about it. Charlotte sighed, she liked the idea of turning Claro Court into a small and intimate event venue, but she would just need a different business manager.

Vivienne Buckley
That evening in Oxfordshire, Vivienne Buckley scrolled through her phone as she spoke.

'I was thinking that we might go to that new restaurant on Saturday night, Vinnie and maybe a club afterwards, hmm?'

They had finished their microwaved dinner for two and Vinnie was idly flicking through the TV channels.

'Actually, I won't be around this weekend – I have to go to Ashdale,' he replied nonchalantly.

'Ashdale! Are you going to see *her* again?' Vivienne exploded.

Vinnie sighed. 'If by "her" you mean Lydia, then no, I'm not going to Ashdale to see her specifically. I'm going to meet the new website designer chap at Ashdale Hall, and, as they are holding their first wedding fair, I'm staying on so that I can see for myself how best to market it for future events.'

'But she'll be there, won't she?'

'I've no idea. I assume so, but I haven't spoken to Lydia for some time, so I don't have any plans to see her.'

'You spoke to her only a couple of months ago. In fact, you saw her as well.'

'For goodness sake, Viv, it was our son's graduation, of course I spoke to her. When are you going to get over this? Lydia is my *ex*-wife, it shouldn't still be a problem.'

'It's not a problem, she's just always there in our lives, sitting on the edge like the cat that got the cream – and for the millionth time, it's Vivienne not Viv.' Once Vivienne had pried Vinnie away from his wife, she had believed that being married to a high earning executive would provide her with all the materials things she desired. Initially of course it had, but then the divorce settlement had changed all of that as Vinnie had shelled out a quarter of a million pounds to Lydia, *a quarter of a million*! Well, that had changed things – a lot. Vivienne knew she was high-maintenance, well a girl had to take care of herself and Vinnie appreciated the way she looked, but hair extensions, manicures, spray tans and Botox – not to mention the designer wardrobe – all came at a price. The meagre limit on the credit card Vinnie had given her did not entirely cover her expenses and she had been forced to find an alternative means of financial support.

Vivienne had contemplated returning to her previous job as a pole-dancer, but that involved working late at night and Vinnie was definitely not keen on that idea. However, whilst meeting up with one of her ex-colleagues, an opportunity for a daytime job had presented itself.

Janey had moved on from pole-dancing into the more lucrative market of escort work and, along with her friend Angie, had rented an apartment in Oxford, purely for business purposes. Angie had a day job in an office and only used the apartment in the evenings, so they were looking for a third girl to work during the day and help with the costs. This suited Vivienne perfectly as Vinnie would never know and she could quietly keep the cash for herself.

That had been four months ago and it was working very well. She paid for some of her treatments with cash to keep her credit card balance well below the limit and Vinnie thought she had just cut back on her spending. On the whole, Vivienne had her life in check and the only real issue she had now was Lydia. It was bad enough that there was a son, Matt, although now he had left university, he was an independent adult and that alone should have ensured that Lydia was no longer a part of their lives, but Vinnie still talked about her. Many conversations included 'Lydia and I did this…' or 'When Lydia and I went there…' and Vivienne felt that deep down inside, Vinnie still had feelings for his ex-wife.

The last time Vivienne had seen Lydia was back in February when Vinnie had gone to Ashdale for a business meeting and accidentally sent a text to Vivienne that was clearly meant for Lydia. Vivienne had hotfooted it straight up to Ashdale to sort that out, so there was absolutely no way that she was allowing Vinnie to go to Ashdale again without her.

'You know, if you're going to Ashdale Hall, I might come with you. Maybe we could upgrade to a really nice suite and make a weekend break of it,' she suggested with a mischievous grin.

'I'm not staying at Ashdale Hall – my expenses won't cover their fancy prices, I'm booked in at the local pub,' Vinnie replied.

The mischievous grin disappeared. 'That downtrodden place! I'm not sure I like that.'

'You don't have to come Vivienne, it is business after all, and I won't have much time for entertaining you.'

Vivienne narrowed her lash-extended eyes. 'I could shop in Harrogate or Leeds, or maybe I could go to the spa at the Hall. No, I'll definitely come with you, it'll make a change from this place.'

Vinnie shrugged. 'As you wish. I'm going on Friday morning as I've a meeting in the afternoon, but we can get lunch in Leeds or somewhere if you like.'

'Great! I'm looking forward to it.' Vivienne smiled broadly at her husband, but he failed to look in her direction and appeared to be absorbed by the TV. Vivienne's smile faded, the magic was definitely disappearing from their relationship. What had started out with so much chemistry and lust had become mediocre and unimaginative. In the beginning, the clandestine meetings in various hotels had been salacious and longed-for, but now they shared the same bed every night, the sex was still satisfying but it had lost some sparkle and spontaneity.

As Vinnie laughed out loud at the comedy programme he had chosen to watch, Vivienne wondered where their relationship was going. They had gone on a cruise at the beginning of the year and it had been painfully obvious that they were on different pages. Vinnie had been quite hurtful about the way she had dressed on occasions, at one point refusing to go with her to dinner. It was as if the very charms and assets that had attracted him in the first place had to be contained and hidden from view, as though for his eyes only. Well Vivienne didn't hold with that old-fashioned view – she was gorgeous and wasn't afraid to flaunt it. If, and it was only an 'if, things did not work out between them, she wondered how much she could get in a divorce settlement; not a quarter of a million that was certain.

For now, though, Vivienne was content with her official 'home' lifestyle that Vinnie paid for, and the secretive day job that fed her nest egg and provided her with little treats. It was just as well, thought Vivienne, that she had a new and financially rewarding job to look forward to on a couple of days or so per week. At least she got the opportunity for flirting and tantalising men who not only appreciated her efforts, but paid her as well.

Lydia Buckley
That evening Lydia listened as Greg told her that his colleagues in London had identified two of Mr Lord's heavies and were now tailing them. 'One of them is a dead ringer for that actor chappie, Cody King – you know the one I mean? He's not handsome but for some reason women find him irresistible, a bit of a Bruce Willis.'

'A bad boy with a twinkle in his eye – that's what women like.'

'Well, the other one definitely hasn't got a twinkle. He's huge, well over six feet in height, incredible muscles and downright ugly. His face is slightly lopsided, definitely someone you don't want to get on the wrong side of. The idea of tailing them is, of course, to see if they will lead to Mr Lord or at least get evidence of illegal activities. The boys there tell me that these two are brothers, though you would never guess it, and the big one is a bit handy with a razor as well.'

'You're not involved with this surveillance, are you?' Lydia was apprehensive.

'Not too much.'

'Oh Greg! Please be careful, it sounds just too dangerous.'

'Don't worry, they're not letting me anywhere near. I'm just involved in the office discussions and online tracking, but it's a bit thrilling.'

They chatted a bit more but after Greg had said goodnight, Lydia chewed her lip thoughtfully. When Greg said he was going on a secondment to London, she hadn't anticipated any danger and although he told her that he was not directly involved, she knew he would volunteer in a heartbeat. It was only Tuesday – he wouldn't be back until Friday and Lydia knew she would worry until he was home safely.

6

Lydia Buckley
Lydia sat opposite Mikey in his office at Ashdale Autos as he tapped keys on the computer, then with one last click with his mouse, the printer came to life and churned out her invoice. Lydia paid with her debit card, put the folded invoice in her handbag and took her keys from Mikey's outstretched hand.

'Thanks Mikey, at least that's one job done for another twelve months.'

'It's in good order,' through replied Mikey, 'went straight the MOT without a problem.'

The door opened behind Lydia and a familiar voice said, 'Hello again!'

Lydia turned to see Cliff Walker standing in the doorway. 'Hello Cliff, lovely to see you again.'

'I've been to see Tom Craven this morning, thought I would go with your recommendation. He's a knowledgeable young chap, I'll say that. I'd seen a little townhouse on his website, don't know if you know it – Larch Gardens? Anyway, he suggested that it might not be my cup of tea, not quite the right area he said.' Cliff shrugged and shook his head, then frowned as Lydia giggled. 'What?' he asked her.

'Was it number 22 by any chance?' she asked with a twinkle in her eyes.

'As a matter of fact it was. What's wrong with number 22?'

'The fact that it's next door to number 20.'

'And what's wrong with number 20?'

'If you have a penchant for the Hound of the Baskervilles, then you would be right at home. However, your visitors may take a different view of the pooch called Satan who lives in the front garden at number twenty.'

Cliff stared at Lydia. 'Satan?' he queried.

'Yep! I viewed that property earlier in the year and almost had a close encounter with his slavering chops.'

'Good Lord! I see. Then I guess Tom was probably right. Anyway, he's setting up another viewing as we speak, so as I have time so spare, I thought I would come and have another look at that MG, I've given the matter a great deal of thought and—' Cliff broke off as the telephone on Mikey's desk rang.

'Hello, Mikey Dixon speaking… Just a moment please.' He put his hand over the mouthpiece. 'I might be five or ten minutes with this call, Cliff. Why don't you take Lydia and show her the MG? I'll join you as soon as I can.'

Cliff nodded and Mikey returned to his call.

'Come and have a look. I'm so excited about this car because I've dug out an old photo of my MG and I believe this could actually be it.' Cliff chatted about his old car as Lydia followed him through the workshop to the area where the available MGs were parked. He walked over to an MG parked separately from the others.

'Ta dah!' he said magician-like.

Lydia looked at the shiny red car with its glistening chrome wire wheels. It looked pretty enough but, if she was very honest, she preferred modern cars with as much gadgetry as possible. Cliff rummaged in his pocket and pulled out a photograph – he glanced at it and then checked the MG in front of him. His eyes lit up.

'It is! It is! It's my old car!' he exclaimed excitedly. 'Look!' he pushed the photograph into Lydia's hands and gazed lovingly at the vehicle. Lydia stared at the photograph, it seemed the same car, or at least it had the same registration, but the car in the picture had extensive damage to the passenger side. The front wing and bonnet were dented as though something had fallen onto it and the windscreen was cracked.

'Good grief! What happened to it?' she asked.

Cliff glanced down at the photo,'Trissie looked after my car when we first went to Germany with the regiment, and when I came back to collect it, that's what it looked like,' he explained.

'What on earth did she do to cause that sort of damage?' asked Lydia as she handed back the photo.

'She didn't do anything. She had parked up and when she returned, it was like that. Looks like someone dropped something onto it.'

'Did you find out what or who had done it?'

'Nope, but I had to pay for it – actually Trissie gave me some money towards it, said she felt responsible. I had it repaired, but this is the only photo of the car that I've got, unfortunately. Still at least I know it's definitely my old MG. What do you think of it?'

'It's lovely, Cliff, and I can just see you driving it next summer, with the roof down.'

'Come and have a sit in it, Mikey won't mind.' Cliff opened the passenger door and when Lydia was seated, he shut the door with a *thunk* before getting in the driver's side. 'Oh yes, I really want this car – takes me back a bit does this.'

Whilst Cliff vroom-vroomed to himself, Lydia looked more carefully at the interior. It was so basic compared to her hatchback, and the glove compartment looked tiny. She opened the small dropdown door and found a piece of paper,

'Oh! There's a piece of paper in here,' she exclaimed.

'Mikey mentioned that one of the lads in the workshop found an old piece of paper wedged under the driver's seat – is that it?' Lydia passed it to him and wondered how she was going to politely excuse herself and leave Cliff to his reminiscing.

'Oh God! Oh no, please God, no!' Cliff sounded distraught.

'Whatever is the matter?' Lydia asked with concern.

Cliff stared at the piece of paper then passed it back to her. 'Does that mean what I think it means?'

Lydia saw that it was a handwritten note from a Glebe Clinic in Leeds dated Thursday 7 April, 1977: *Miss Foxton – self-discharge following termination.* Lydia looked up at Cliff's stricken face. 'Um, well termination in the medical sense usually means…' she tailed off, unable to say the word.

'Abortion!' Cliff fairly spat the word. 'Trissie aborted our baby, and she didn't even tell me she was pregnant! If she had, it would have changed everything.'

'Are you sure?'

'What? That it would have changed everything? Absolutely. I loved Trissie with all my heart, but it was not easy to abandon my wife who had just moved to Germany with me. So, I did what I thought was the right thing – but if I had known Trissie was pregnant, I would have moved heaven and earth to look after her.'

'No, I meant are you sure it's your Miss Foxton?' Lydia said gently.

'It can't be anyone else, the name and the date fit...' Cliff exhaled and put his head on his hands that still clutched the steering wheel, '...and it's my old car. I need to try and find Trissie!'

'Cliff! Is that wise? After all, it's over forty years ago.' Lydia put her hand on his arm. 'You may not find her and... well, even if you do find her, she may not want to be reminded.'

'I always wanted to have a loving wife and a family, neither of which I've had, and now to find this!' Cliff snatched the piece of paper from Lydia's grasp. 'I know, I'll go and see Lucy – find out if she knows where Trissie went.'

'Lucy?'

'Oh yes, it turns out that your florist here is the same Lucy Kirkwood that shared a flat with Trissie all those years ago. She and Fran have had a long chat and I popped in to see her on Monday when I was last in Ashdale. There is just a chance that she might know something about Trissie.'

'But Cliff—,' Lydia began, but before she could continue, Cliff jumped out of the car and almost ran into Mikey who was making his way towards them.

'Gotta go. Sorry Mikey, I'll phone you later.' And with that he was gone. Mikey turned to Lydia, looking for an explanation,

'Something cropped up, Mikey, I'm sure he will be back as he loves this car,' she told him.

Mikey nodded,

'He thinks it's his old car – still, if that's what makes him happy,' he uttered as he turned away. Lydia fumbled for her car keys in her bag. *I do hope he doesn't do anything rash.*

Sheila Houseman

'It'll be all right, love – Albert'll help us,' said Derek confidently as he marched across the Market Place. It was late afternoon and they had an appointment with the accountant.

'He will?' Sheila quickened her pace to keep up with her husband.

'He's known us for a long time, he'll be on our side.'

'I'm…not…sure,' panted Sheila.

'No doubt about it! He might be an old fuddy-duddy, but he knows where his loyalties lie.' Derek lengthened his stride.

Sheila pulled up short, 'Derek! Albert is not old, he's younger than us!'

Derek stopped and turned round. Sheila stood a few paces behind him breathing heavily.

'Well, he may be *technically* younger than us, but he's been an old fuddy-duddy since he qualified thirty years ago – it was difficult to tell him and his father apart! Anyway, he heard everything and…' he added smugly, '…Adam Lewis doesn't know that.' Derek smiled and turned back to continue walking.

'Derek, stop!'

'What's matter, love?' he asked with concern.

'For God's sake slow down, I can't walk that fast,' Sheila gasped. Derek smiled, walked back to his wife and took her hand. 'Sorry love, come on.'

A little while later, Sheila sat nervously in the office of Albert Wilks. Next to her, Derek glared at Albert, his arms folded defiantly across his chest.

'What do you mean "not unreasonable"? Are you suggesting that it's perfectly acceptable for Adam Lewis to march into my bakery and make threats?' he boomed.

'He didn't actually—' Albert began.

'He damn well did! He's trying to blackmail us, you heard him!'

'It wasn't actually—'

'Are you telling me that you didn't hear him demand fifty thousand pounds?'

'No...I mean...yes...well, not demand exactly—' Albert broke off and pushed his chair six inches backwards as Derek leapt to his feet.

'Now look here, Albert Wilks, we've been clients of yours for the past thirty years or so—'

'Derek, love, calm down.' Sheila stood up and placed her hand on her husband's arm. 'Sit down and let Albert talk.'

Derek looked at his wife, Sheila smiled reassuringly, and with a huff he plonked himself back in his chair. Sheila turned to Albert who was still some way back from his desk. 'You were going to say...' she said softly.

Albert cleared his throat and repositioned his chair. He steepled his hands before he spoke. 'Mr Houseman, Mrs Houseman, I know this has been an upsetting incident but if you will allow me to explain exactly what I overheard and how it may be interpreted – you might understand my position.' Albert inhaled deeply, leaned back in his chair and perused the ceiling as he prepared himself for his speech. 'I am aware of the nature of the incident that took place last Friday morning which resulted in hospitalisation for Cllr Lewis—'

'It was a mishap, that's all!' snapped Derek. Sheila gave her husband a warning look. He wasn't generally an angry man, but since Adam's visit yesterday, he had been simmering with outrage which had given Sheila cause for concern.

Albert avoided Derek's stare by continuing to gaze at the ceiling. 'If one was to be completely honest and impartial, then one might conclude that in fact, Mr Lewis was being reasonable in that he was visiting your establishment to advise you of Cllr Lewis's intentions and thereby giving you a "heads-up", so to speak.'

Derek opened his mouth to say something, but Sheila nudged him, so he just closed it and glared at Albert, who deliberately hadn't lowered his gaze.

'There may possibly be a case to answer, therefore one might have to consider how much, if any, compensation would be appropriate for one to pay,' Albert told his fluorescent lights.

'One should just take a running jump,' muttered Derek. Albert glanced at him in alarm, and Sheila put a warning hand on her husband's arm and nodded reassuringly at Albert to continue.

Albert collected his thoughts and closed his eyes as he spoke. 'I've taken the liberty of speaking with a lawyer client of mine and, without naming names, I was able to explain your situation and give a brief resumé of the conversation which I inadvertently overheard. Compensation is a pecuniary remedy that is awarded to an individual who has sustained an injury, in order to replace the loss caused by said injury – also referred to as "damages". With respect to compensatory damages, a defendant is liable to a plaintiff for all the natural and direct consequences of the defendant's wrongful act—'

'Wrongful act! We haven't done anything wrong – yet, but if I get my hands on that woman...'

Albert sat up and faced Derek. 'Mr Houseman, please – I was not suggesting that you *have* done anything wrong, I'm merely quoting what I've been told.'

'Derek love, let Albert speak, we've come here for advice – let him give it.'

Derek huffed again and sank back into his chair.

Albert cleared his throat and continued. 'The measure of compensatory damages must be real and tangible, although it can be difficult to fix the amount with certainty, especially in cases involving claims such as pain and suffering or emotional distress—'

'We're the ones with emotional distress,' muttered Derek.

Albert ignored the remark and spoke at great length about the assessment of compensatory damages, consideration of mental trauma and anguish and whether the act was wilful or malicious, or done with extreme carelessness or recklessness.

Sheila listened with a sinking heart. They were finished. They would have to sell the bakery to pay the money and then move away from Ashdale. She couldn't possible live with people pointing their fingers and whispering.

Derek had managed to keep quiet throughout Albert's monologue but finally, he slapped his knees with his hands. 'Well, that's that then. I shall go to see Tom Craven about selling up.'

'Oh no, I wouldn't do that – you're not at that stage yet.'

'But they are trying to blackmail us!'

'Blackmail? Oh no, I wouldn't put it like that…' Albert shook his head.

'Well how would you put it? You were there, you heard every word!'

'I was there, yes but—'

'You were a witness.'

'But I'm not sure that I could—'

'In court, you could confirm that there was a demand for fifty thousand pounds, *fifty thousand!*' Derek leaned forward in his chair and Albert slid a smidgen backwards again.

'I wouldn't call it a demand, more of a reasonable suggestion of a compensatory amount.'

'Reasonable?' thundered Derek, standing up. Albert shrank back and his chair retreated further away from his desk.

'I…I didn't say the amount was reasonable, Mr Houseman, fifty thousand pounds is a lot of money, I meant he spoke in a reasonable manner – he wasn't demanding or threatening.'

'He bloody well threatened to destroy my business, well let me tell you—'

'Derek! Please stop shouting, this isn't helping.' Sheila stood up and faced her irate husband. 'And it's not Albert's fault.'

They both turned to the accountant, who was almost cowering in the chair which was now at least a foot away from his desk.

Albert looked from one to the other, gulped and straightened an already perfectly straight tie. He cleared his throat and pulled his chair back to the desk. 'Yes, well...I can see that you're a little upset about this matter, however at the moment there is nothing you can, or should, do about it; the proverbial ball is not in your court.'

Derek took a deep breath, nodded at Sheila and they both sat down. There were a few moments whilst each collected their thoughts,

'Um...Beatrice Lewis is one of your clients, isn't she?' Sheila spoke tentatively. 'You know our financial situation, so couldn't you just tell her that we don't have fifty thousand? She might listen to you.'

Albert looked at Sheila as though she had suggested that they play a game of strip poker.

'I couldn't possibly discuss your finances with Cllr Lewis, it would be totally inappropriate,' he replied.

'I didn't mean for you to go into detail, but you could confirm that finding such a large sum would be the end of our business...um...something like that?'

Albert rested his chin on clasped hands as he looked at Sheila. 'I'm afraid not, it would break our client confidentiality code, and in any case, the amount of compensation payable would have to be determined legally, usually by a judge.'

'So, you're saying that we can do nothing at all then?' asked Derek.

'Absolutely, Mr Houseman,' Albert smiled as he spoke. 'You must wait for Cllr Lewis to initiate proceedings – if she chooses to do so, of course.' Albert clearly thought he had solved their dilemma, if not completely, certainly in the short term. However his intention to soothe the Housemans had completely the opposite effect on Derek.

'All I can say is that she had better think twice before taking us on, councillor or not, *and* we've you as a witness to her son's demands – she won't know about that, will she?' he smirked.

Albert looked uneasy once more. 'Mr Houseman, as your wife pointed out, Cllr Lewis is also a client of mine so I feel that I should remain impartial,' he explained.

'Impartial!' Derek spluttered, 'Let me tell you this – I expected a bit more loyalty from you, Albert Wilks. But, if this matter *does* go to court, I'm calling you as a witness whether you like it or not – got it? Come on, Sheila, we're done here.'

Derek stood up and marched to the door. Sheila followed him unhappily. They were no further forward and Derek was still angry whilst Albert just looked terrified.

Albert visibly paled but didn't move. 'I'll add my charge for this consultation onto the annual bill, no need to worry about payment at the moment,' he ventured.

Derek turned back and opened his mouth to reply, but Sheila intervened,

'Don't say another word, Derek, just go!' She opened the door and Derek huffed before marching out. Before they reached the reception, Sheila caught his arm. 'Please, Derek, calm down. Stop with the anger. I'm worried about you, you'll give yourself a heart attack at this rate. Albert said there is nothing we can do so just leave it, let's get on with our lives including the wedding fair and the awards dinner. We'll deal with any consequences as they appear, there is no point in fretting until then.'

Derek exhaled a long breath. 'Ok love, I guess you're right. I'm just so frustrated when I think about Adam's smarmy face.'

'Then don't think about it,' was all Sheila replied.

As they walked through the reception of Babcock, Coombes & Wilks, Sheila nodded an acknowledgement at Maureen Brown as the receptionist picked up the phone, which had just buzzed.

'A weak tea, Mr Wilks? Right away.'

Derek held the door open for his wife. 'I don't know about a weak tea, but I could murder a drink. Fancy a quick one at the Coach?'

Sheila smiled. This was more like the Derek she knew. She nodded her head enthusiastically and, arm in arm, they headed towards the pub.

Charlotte Worthington

It was a cold and wet Wednesday evening when Charlotte and Pen arrived at the new restaurant for the opening night party. Charlotte immediately scanned the room, looking for familiar faces.

'Are you looking for anyone specifically?' asked Pen.

'Sophie Kingsley, she's dating that gorgeous hunk from the TV soap, Wes Garrett. She told me that the soap was supporting this do because the husband of one of the actresses owns this place.'

'Really?' Pen took a good look at the new restaurant, with its dark wood and tropical themed décor in a riot of colour which, as it was named Caribe, was very appropriate. A steel band had set up in one corner, a DJ currently mixed reggae sounds in another whilst palm trees swayed gently thanks to the air-conditioning. The professional barmen juggled bottles as they mixed rum cocktails and waitresses wove in and out of the crowd offering Caribbean finger food.

The guests were by invitation only and included the local media, influential business types, residents in selected postcodes and quite a number of the cast of the locally filmed TV soap.

Charlotte suddenly grabbed her friend's arm. 'Look! There's Fiona Whatshername, she's in that soap. I can't see Sophie and Wes though.'

'I think you mean Fiona Cavendish. Why are you so bothered about finding Sophie Kingsley? I didn't think you particularly liked her,' asked Pen curiously.

'I don't like her, she once made a play for Gerald because she fancied herself as Lady Pemberton.'

'Did she? When was that?'

'About two years ago, he had taken her out on a couple of occasions and she was already planning the wedding. Of course, as soon as I batted my eyelashes at him, he left her and came running after me.'

Pen frowned. 'So you took him off her?'

'I wouldn't put it quite like that, Pen. Gerald obviously wasn't that enamoured with her in the first place or he wouldn't have pursued me.' As she spoke, Charlotte's eyes darted about, seeking out the elusive Sophie and Wes.

'So why are you looking for her now?'

'Because she's with Wes Garrett and he is just so…Well, I'd like to meet him, that's all.'

Pen's eyes narrowed with suspicion. 'Why?'

'Because…' Charlotte hesitated as she picked up on the suspicion in her friend's voice and instantly changed her mind about what she was going to say. 'Because I thought he might be good for you,' she said and smiled indulgently.

'Why on earth would you think that? You've never met him!'

'For God's sake, Pen – lighten up, you could do with a good romp. When was the last time you saw any bedroom activity?'

Pen blushed. 'Well, none since Philip and I broke up, but—'

'Good grief! That was last year. Are you seriously telling me that you have not had sex for a year?'

'I've been too busy with the shops.'

'Your father bought you that shop in Northallerton to take your mind off your broken engagement. I didn't expect you to open a second shop and become the next businesswoman of the year. You have hardly been a barrel of laughs recently.'

'To be honest, Charlotte, I didn't expect to enjoy it – but I do. I've a purpose now, a reason to get out of bed. I love the marketing and buying, and well, just generally running the business. Lulabelle's in Northallerton is doing so well with Michelle in charge – she has an amazing sales technique and great customer-service skills. When the premises in Ashdale came available, I just grabbed the chance to open a second store.'

Charlotte huffed. 'Well, you're just not as much fun. We hardly ever go out and party.'

'That's not a bad thing Charlotte, because once you're married to Gerald, you won't be going out partying then, so consider yourself in training for your future married life.'

Charlotte took two glasses off the tray of a passing waitress and gave one to Pen. 'In that case, I've just over a week to party hard and enjoy myself, starting right now because I've just spotted Wes Garrett. Come on.' Charlotte set off, squeezing between people, determinedly on a mission to get to the other side of the restaurant.

As she approached the couple standing by the bar, she noticed Sophie do a double-take as their eyes met. Charlotte smiled sardonically and then, as Wes turned to see who Sophie had noticed, she slid her gaze in his direction and treated him to her best sexy come-hither expression. To Charlotte's delight, Wes responded immediately with a smouldering smile, and she caught her breath as his vivid green eyes met hers, the feeling was so intense that she was sure that actual electric sparks passed between them. Wes Garrett was of mixed race origin, around six feet tall and had an oval shaped face framed by a dark buzz-cut on top and minimal designer stubble on the lower half. Charlotte tore her eyes away from Wes to speak to Sophie, who made no attempt to conceal her contempt at Charlotte's appearance.

'Sophie darling! Long time no see, how are you?'

'I *was* doing fine thank you,' came the curt reply.

'Aren't you going to introduce me, Soph?'

'Sure' replied Sophie. 'Wes, this is Charlotte Worthington and Penelope Sinclair-Sutton. Charlotte is getting married in a few days, that's right, isn't it, Charlotte?' Sophie smiled sweetly as she made the introductions.

'Worthington?' repeated Wes as he took Charlotte's hand politely, 'Worthington as in Ashdale Hall?' Wes had a deep velvety voice and Charlotte inwardly shivered with delight – she had felt Wes staring at her as she had talked to Sophie.

'The very same,' replied Charlotte noticing that he kept hold of her hand.

'It's a beautiful place, and of course you know that we film some scenes in your garden and woodland.'

'Yes, I've often watched you all at work, although we've a new pavilion now, the last one fell down not long after you filmed that sizzling sex scene with Linda Thingummy,' Charlotte said boldly, her left eyebrow raised ever so slightly.

'Is that right?' Wes almost growled, his voice thick with implied lust.

'Yes, well of course once you're married Charlotte, you probably won't be able to watch them filming,' Sophie almost snapped. 'Charlotte is marrying Sir Gerald Pemberton and will move to Claro Court.'

Wes reluctantly let go of Charlotte's hand. 'That's another example of beautiful architecture, again with fine parkland. You know, the production team were looking for another country pile for filming purposes, I wonder if they could look at Claro Court?' he said airily and with a subtle wink, unseen by Sophie.

'I'm sure Sir Gerald would be delighted by that idea,' replied Charlotte, her eyes twinkling, 'I'll have a word with him.'

'As long as he doesn't mind being inconvenienced by us.' Wes had a mischievous look in his eye.

'Oh, Gerald spends most of his time in London so it will only inconvenience me...and I wouldn't be opposed to that.' Charlotte looked with meaning straight into Wes's eyes.

'In that case, let me give you a number to call when you have given the matter some thought.' Wes raised one eyebrow and Charlotte smiled as she handed over her phone. Wes tapped a number into it. 'That's Bert's number, leave a message if he doesn't answer as we all have our mobiles on silent whilst filming.'

'Thank you, I'll do that,' Charlotte said seductively.

Sophie nudged Wes suddenly. 'Wes, Fiona Cavendish is waving at us, I think she wants us over there.' Sophie hooked her hand into the crook of Wes's elbow and began to pull him away from Charlotte and Pen.

'See you around, girls,' Wes managed to say before he was swallowed up in the mass of people.

'OMG, he is so hot!' Charlotte gasped.

'I though you said he would do for me,' Pen commented dryly. 'If that's your way of finding me a man, please note that I'll make my own arrangements in future. I don't want your sloppy seconds.'

'I bet there's nothing sloppy about *him*,' Charlotte replied lasciviously. 'At least I've got his number now.'

'I thought he had given you Bert's number.'

'He's put his own name to it. I think a little dalliance after my honeymoon would prevent me from being bored, don't you?' Charlotte sighed with delight at the prospect of an hour or two in the company of Wes Garrett.

Pen opened her mouth to speak but before she could utter a word, the steel band started on their set and further talk was impossible. Charlotte found herself being towed into the ladies' loos where Pen could speak without shouting.

'Charlotte Worthington! Are you seriously considering starting an affair with Wes Garrett?' Pen demanded fiercely.

Charlotte took a step backwards in surprise. 'I'm not sure about a full-blown affair, but a little fun won't hurt, surely,' she replied with a dismissive wave of her hand.

'What about Adam and Gerald? Sleeping with three men is a little risqué wouldn't you say?'

Charlotte glanced hurriedly about, mindful of Pen's indiscreet name-dropping. Fortunately, she couldn't see or hear anyone else around. 'It'll be over with Adam very soon, he's become too serious and has actually bought a villa in Spain for us to run away to.'

'He's *what*?'

'He thinks I'm going to elope with him on the morning of my wedding.'

'And are you?'

'Elope? Of course not!'

'Have you told him this?'

'Not exactly.'

'For God's sake, Charlotte, why not? You can't go on letting him think you are, or he'll make plans, buy plane tickets and things.'

'But if I break it off with him now, he will be so angry, he might tell Gerald and then I'll have no wedding either,' Charlotte reasoned. 'He'll get over it – maybe you could take him off my hands. Anyway, he can always rent the place out, so he won't lose financially. What?' Charlotte asked as her friend stared at her in disbelief.

'Adam thinks you're going to elope with him on your wedding day, start a new life in Spain and be happy ever after. Gerald thinks he is marrying a well-brought up young lady who will make an excellent and faithful society wife. But in reality, however, you're going to leave Adam high and dry, deceive Gerald and begin a torrid relationship with Wes Garrett who can't wait to get into your knickers!'

'Don't be so coarse, Pen. You make it all sound a bit seedy,' Charlotte pulled her lipstick out of her bag.

'It *is* seedy. You may as well make a career out of it and charge them all for the privilege.' Pen glared at Charlotte's reflection in the large mirrors over the basins.

'I thought you were my friend, Penelope Sinclair-Sutton, I thought I could confide in you.'

'You are my friend, which is why I'm concerned that you're going too far. You're getting married Charlotte, you have to stop sleeping around. You wouldn't like it if Gerald did the same.'

Charlotte snapped the lid back on her lipstick and dropped it back in her bag. 'I wouldn't care, it would keep him off me a bit more often.' Charlotte noticed the disapproving look on Pen's face and felt an explanation was needed. 'Look, Gerald is all right, I mean we get on ok and he'll look after me. I'll be a good wife socially and so on but, although he is not bad looking for his age, he is not hot or desirable and, quite frankly, he is not great between the sheets. He thinks he just has to clamber on and—'

'Enough!' interrupted Pen, 'I get the picture – he has no finesse in the bedroom. But if you're going to have a lover, then you will have to be more discreet and not blatantly flirt with other people's boyfriends. Sophie Kingsley was fair bursting to slap your face when she got that you were after her man – *again*!'

Charlotte smiled at her reflection in the mirror and ran her hand through the long black curls. 'I can't help it if men find me attractive,' she said smugly.

'No, but you should be more subtle about it, certainly for the next ten days.'

Charlotte sighed. 'I suppose so. Anyway, let's go and enjoy the evening, this place has a fab vibe.' Charlotte held the door as Pen walked through, but as she turned to follow, she could have sworn she heard someone clear their throat. She stood still and listened but there was only silence, so she shrugged and allowed the door to close behind her.

Adam Lewis

Adam switched off the television, stood up and yawned. It was eleven o'clock and he wondered how late his mother was going to be. She had gone to a new restaurant opening in Harrogate. *Ah! Speak of the devil.* He heard the front door open and close.

'Adam? I need to talk to you!'

'In the sitting room, Mother.' Adam sat down again, her sharp tone hinted at trouble.

Beatrice marched into the sitting room. 'Are you having an affair with Charlotte Worthington?'

This took Adam completely by surprise, but he collected himself quickly,

'No, of course not. Why would you think that?'

'Because I've just overheard a conversation which leads me to believe that you are, and that you intend to elope with her – to the villa *we're* buying.'

Adam's mouth dropped open. *Bloody hell, Charlotte what have you been saying? And to whom?*

His mother's eyes narrowed with suspicion and Adam forced a laugh. 'Oh that! That's just a private joke between us. She was having a wedding wobble and I said that if she couldn't go through with it, we would elope to my new villa. It's not serious, of course she'll get married.' Adam hoped he sounded unfazed, but his mother did not smile.

'And since when have you been that friendly with Charlotte Worthington?'

'I met her at a do…I forget when, it was just talk.'

'But this evening's conversation wasn't said as a joke or "wobble", Adam. Apparently, you're both planning to elope on the morning of the wedding, however Charlotte intends going through with the wedding without telling you. She worries that, if she breaks it off now, then following the rejection, you might then have a word with Sir Gerald.'

Adam laughed. 'I don't even know Sir Gerald. Of course she intends going through with the wedding, this whole thing is a joke.' Adam sighed. 'Although I must admit, it does sound as though it's getting out of hand. Do you know who she was talking to?'

'Someone called Pen?'

'Oh, that's her best friend – I'm sure she's just over-dramatising things. I might have a word with her and suggest that enough is enough. After all, we don't want Sir Gerald to get the wrong end of the stick, as you obviously have.' Adam smiled at his mother, confident that his explanation sounded plausible, although he just felt a teeny bit apprehensive. His mother's next words only added to his anxiety.

'You should also know that you're not the only joker in the pack. Once she's finished with you, she has a reserve in the form of Wes Garrett, whom I believe she intends seeing after her honeymoon.'

Adam was rendered speechless, but one glance at the slightly triumphant look on Beatrice's face was enough to make him rapidly collect his thoughts. 'I'm sure you're mistaken, Mother, getting involved with a well-known actor would be the last thing Charlotte would do. I guess she was just flattered by some attention from him. Anyway, it's nothing to do with us what Charlotte does, is it?'

Beatrice pursed her lips. 'As long as you're not involved with her, Adam. I really don't like that girl and I just feel so sorry for Sir James and Lady Victoria – the sooner she's married off, the better in my view.'

Adam nodded and stood up. 'By the way, when I met Charlotte at that event, I mentioned my new business which she in turn mentioned to her father. The upshot is that I'm having a meeting on Friday with the Ashdale Hall marketing man, he's driving up from the south.'

'That sounds very promising.' Beatrice smiled tightly.

'Charlotte even suggested that after her wedding, Sir Gerald may be interested in a website for Claro Court.'

'Hmm, although if I were you, I wouldn't get involved with her at all – married or not.' Beatrice looked at her son pointedly.

'Well, I'm off to bed now, I'll see you in the morning.' Adam hurried up to his room and pulled out his mobile. He pressed Charlotte's name and waited for the connection.

'Charlotte, what the hell have you been saying? Mother has just come home and told me that she overheard you telling someone about us... Well, you shouldn't tell Pen everything and what is this about calling it off but not telling me? Yes, I told Mother that, but we're going through with it aren't we? We are going to Spain a week on Saturday as per our plan? Good! Of course I can't see you being happy if you marry Gerald, but Charlotte, promise me that you are serious about eloping. Tell me the truth, now... And I love you too, my darling girl. When can I see you next? How about this weekend? I'm at the wedding fair with the marketing chappie but I'm sure we can find some time...Two, at the pavilion? Ok.'

Adam hoped that Charlotte wasn't changing her mind, he needed to get away from the UK and he needed money – the villa solved the first problem and Charlotte's wealth the other.

He heard a bedroom door close further along the hallway. Tomorrow his mother would make the transfer to his bank account; he could make the final payment and the villa would then be his. He also wondered how the Housemans were coming along with their compensation payment, he needed them to pay up before his mother made her complaint to the British Bakers' Association. Ideally, he wanted her to wait until after he had escaped to Spain, he would have to work on that.

7

Adam Lewis
Adam drummed his fingers on the desk. What the hell was he going to do now? He had been relying on that transfer and now…honestly, you would have thought that she would know that the account required two weeks' notice and not two days. He recalled this morning's conversation and the casual way Beatrice had told him that by the way, she couldn't make the transfer today as planned. *By the way!* Adam had almost choked on his croissant in shock. He had tried to explain that waiting for two weeks was not really an option and suggested that perhaps she could use funds in other accounts, but his mother had pursed her lips and looked at him with 'that' look, so what with the recent references to eloping with Charlotte, Adam hadn't wanted to push any further.

He picked up a pen and doodled, the doodle resembled the sun, *damn it!* He had to come up with a plan B or he would be humiliated and might lose everything, including Charlotte. He would have to talk to Hugo and see if there was a chance of borrowing the money to tide him over. Now there was a man who understood that not everything was black and white. Adam knew that Hugo had left Ashdale under a cloud – something about not quite kosher property purchases – so he may have a more sympathetic ear than his mother had had this morning. The problem was of course that he couldn't tell his mother the real reason that he needed to complete the purchase in the next few days. Hopefully, she had believed his story of jesting with Charlotte about eloping on the pretence of pre-wedding jitters.

He had to admit that he was slightly concerned about what his mother had said she had overheard. What if Charlotte *was* leading him on and intended on going ahead with the wedding? How would he feel about that? Bloody furious, actually! Dammit, he was risking everything for that girl. He supposed he could rent the villa out if Charlotte did let him down, or maybe he could take Saffron there. Actually, the image of Saffron's big blue eyes and winning smile kept popping into his mind, but then he reminded himself of Charlotte's money and their intended Spanish lifestyle, not to mention the hot sex, and he reluctantly pushed thoughts of Saffron further back – although there was no harm in having her in reserve. No, he would have to soften up old Hugo, and with that in mind, Adam reached for his phone.

'Adam! The very person, I was just about to email you. No doubt, you're looking forward to receiving the virtual keys to your villa later today,' Hugo chattered.

'Well, I would but there is a technical hitch, or rather a financial one,' Adam said with a little trepidation.

'Oh? What's the problem?'

'Mother was all set to pay the balance, but she now finds that she has to give more notice than she realised to transfer the funds. I don't suppose you could help out, could you? It's only for a couple of weeks.'

'I see. To be honest, Adam, I don't have access to that amount of money immediately either, but I can speak with the developers and advise them of a change of completion date. They may not be very happy, but I can explain the situation, and hopefully it will all work out.'

'Ok, but…well the thing is, I was hoping to come out to Spain a week on Saturday with a young lady and stay in the villa, but now it's all a bit difficult.'

'You could always book a hotel.'

'I could but…look, can I speak frankly?' Adam knew that Hugo would appreciate "man-to-man" type talk.

'Of course.'

'The young lady and I would prefer privacy for various reasons, which a hotel would not provide. This little trip to Spain is special, and strictly private. I have, perhaps a little prematurely, told her about the villa and—' Adam broke off as Hugo roared with laughter.

'I get it,' he chortled, 'she's married and you've promised her a few days of sunshine and frolics where she won't be seen. I bet Beatrice doesn't know about this.'

Adam frowned at the phone. His relationship with Charlotte wasn't about 'sunshine and frolics for a few days', well it might *include* some frolics, but it certainly wasn't only for a few days. However, details as far as Hugo was concerned, were irrelevant.

'Something like that, Hugo,' he replied vaguely. 'So you see, I have to own the villa by then. Is there anything you can do to help me?'

'Have you thought about getting a bridging loan from a bank?'

'A bank wouldn't lend me that amount of money without some collateral, and that brings me back to mother, she doesn't need to know that I've asked you.'

There was silence for a few seconds and Adam crossed his fingers.

'Leave it with me and I'll see what I can do – I'm not making any promises, but I'll make some enquiries,' Hugo said at last.

'Thank you, Hugo, this is very much appreciated.'

'How is your mother these days? Still enjoying being a councillor?'

Adam relaxed somewhat and told Hugo about the incident in the bakery.

'I am surprised. The Housemans were always diligent, and Derek Houseman is a damn good baker. Is it absolutely necessary for Beatrice to dob them in?'

'She very nearly died, Hugo – it wouldn't be right for them to win an award now.'

'No, I suppose not. Look I have to go, someone has just come in. As I said, leave things with me and I'll get back to you. Bye for now.'

Adam stood up and paced around his small office, time was short and he hoped Hugo could come up with a solution somehow. It was very frustrating because his mother had oodles of money in various accounts, stock, shares and God-knows-what! If only his father had left him a decent sum of money, enough to do something with and not left everything to his mother who generally kept a tight hold on the purse strings. In the meantime, he would just have to wait for Hugo to contact him again, so he returned to his desk and tried to concentrate on his work.

Lydia Buckley

Thursday was Market Day in Ashdale and after wandering around the stalls, Lydia pushed open the door to LulaBelle's boutique. She was immediately treated to the sight of Tasheka, eyes closed, as she bounced gently and rhythmically to a beat that even Lydia could hear emanating from the earbuds. Her fisted hands, moved back and forth to the music in front of her ample bosom and her hips twerked and rolled side to side, back and forth as only women of colour seemed to do naturally. The music came to an end and Tasheka opened her eyes and jumped as she saw Lydia standing there. 'Hey girl! What's up?' she called as she pulled out the earbuds. How long have you been standin' there?'

'Only about two minutes. I've just popped in for a quick browse.'

'Well I'm glad that you did 'cos I was wanting a word with you anyway.'

'Oh, what about?'

'Well, you know how I'm the manager here now an' I've real responsibilities what with merchandisin', cash handlin', customer services an' other things?'

Lydia nodded as she wandered over to a rail and began looking through the clothes.

'The thing is,' Tasheka began as she followed Lydia around the shop, 'I don't know if I'm cut out for just bein' in a shop. I'm not dissing bein' in a shop of course, there's nothin' wrong with managin' a shop, it's just that I have to wait for customers to come in an' sometimes, only sometimes mind, I jus' might get a little bit bored.'

'Bored? The shop has only recently opened, Tasheka. I'm sure it will get busier in time.'

'Well maybe not bored, but I think I might miss gettin' out 'n' about. I'm not sure stayin' in one place is quite my thing, you gettin' me?' As she spoke Tasheka gesticulated with her hands and Lydia noticed that today, the long nails were an acid green to match the loose-fitting top Tasheka wore over a black mini skirt.

'You miss travelling from client to client.'

'I sure do, so I've had an idea…'

'Tell me all.' Lydia settled in for a long chat with Tasheka. Fortunately she had an hour or so to kill and she liked Tasheka, so, whilst she browsed the very stylish yet affordable Italian clothing she listened to Tasheka's latest plan.

'Now I'm thinkin' that I might want to be a lifestyle vlogger and social influencer—'

'A what?' interrupted Lydia.

'A lifestyle vlogger and social influencer,' repeated Tasheka. 'Y'see I've got a friend, Orlena, she lives in Leeds an' I went to see her last weekend. She has a daughter, Sandrine, an' I was talkin' to her an' she showed me her videos an' stuff an' I was thinkin' – I could do that! Sandrine earns good money from vlogging 'cos she gets paid to promote different brands. So I thought I might start with beauty products for black women an' talk about my life here in Ashdale, what d'ya think?'

Lydia turned to Tasheka who looked animated and enthusiastic. 'You know, you may be on to something there Tasheka. You have a great personality and always look well-groomed, but it will take time to build up a following and have lots of subscribers. How do you plan on getting started?' Lydia turned back to the rails and picked out a beautiful scarlet red top with a floaty chiffon hem.

'I've got a camera on order an' I thought I might interview you 'cos you're a famous writer an' then I thought I might film the weddin' fair an' talk to everyone with a stand. I thought maybe Mrs Houseman next door might talk about that incident last Friday with Councillor Lewis'.

'I wouldn't describe myself as a famous writer, but I'll happily do an interview if you want to although…' Lydia paused as she held up an emerald green dress, 'I wouldn't mention the bakery incident as it may be a touchy subject, but Mrs Houseman would probably talk to you about the award ceremony they are attending, as they have been nominated.'

Tasheka smiled broadly. 'Hey, that sure is a great idea,' she said picking up a hanger holding a pair of black velvet slinky trousers. 'You might like these with that red top?'

Lydia nodded appreciatively and took the hanger. 'I'll just go and try this lot on,' she said as she headed to the changing room.

'The other thing is…' Tasheka followed her and paused as Lydia hung up the clothes, '…well, I was wonderin' if you thought I should include some gossip in my vlogs.'

Lydia closed the curtain and began to undress. 'It depends on what type of gossip, I guess.' Lydia's voice was muffled as she removed her clothes.

'My sister, Louella, still works in our cleanin' business, you know, an' she's got a contract with Ashdale Hall, an' when she was there on Tuesday, she came across a situation.'

'A situation? What sort of situation? Do you think this looks ok?' Lydia stepped out of the cubicle wearing the red top and black velvet trousers.

'That looks real boujee on you, I like that a lot.' Tasheka nodded her head, the black curls shaking vigorously. 'Well, they have this pavilion place in a secret garden an' Louella went to give it a clean, but before she opened the door, she heard voices inside, so she looked through the window 'cos nobody was supposed to be in there.'

Lydia had disappeared back into the cubicle and now she reappeared in the green dress. 'So, what did she do? I'm not sure about this, what do you think?'

Tasheka shook her black curls. 'Tha's not your best look, it don' give you no shape, you know what I'm sayin'?

Lydia nodded and vanished back into the cubicle. 'Carry on about Louella's situation.'

'So, she's lookin' through the window an' guess what she sees?'

'No idea,' Lydia replied.

'Lexie Worthington havin' hot sex!'

'*What?*' Lydia's head popped out between the cubicle curtains.

'Mmm-hmm, tha's right. There was no shame in her game let me tell you, she was ridin' him like she was in a rodeo, so my sister said.' Tasheka's index finger waved back and forth as she spoke.

'A rodeo?' Lydia gasped faintly.

'She sure was, an' then Louella heard her call him "Adam", so I'm thinking that it's maybe Adam Lewis!'

'Adam Lewis?'

'Well, I don't know of any other Adams around here...' Tasheka's voice trailed off and she looked meaningfully at Lydia.

Lydia swished back the curtains and stepped out clutching the clothes and hangers. 'I'll take the top and trousers please.'

Tasheka took the things and headed to the cash desk whilst Lydia followed her, unsure of what to say next.

'My sister said that he was yellin' "Yes! Yes! Yes!" Anyways, she didn't want to hang around to get caught watchin' – you get my meanin'?' Tasheka said with relish as she neatly folded Lydia's new clothes into a pink Lulabelle's branded carrier.

'Well, I'm quite shocked, to be honest,' Lydia said. She simply could not imagine Lexie being compromised in that way, but then again, Lexie was a young single woman and making love in a private place was no crime.

'Anyways, what I was gonna ask you was, if you thought I could mention that in my vlog, you know as gossip?'

'God no! Tasheka, you can't mention it to anyone let alone spread it on the internet – it's a private matter.' Lydia handed over her card to pay for the goods.

'Hey girl! It's not so private if people can see you through a window. I would've drawn the blinds if I wanted to be private.'

'Well, they were clearly not expecting anyone to be around.'

'An' my sister said that she had a tattoo of a rose right there on her bootie, now that's not something you would expect to see on a girl like Lexie Worthington,' Tasheka said as she returned Lydia's card.

'Lots of girls have flower tattoos. The thing is, Tasheka, if you were to write, blog or whatever about that incident, it could be denied and then it would be your word against Lexie's. If I were you, I would stick to events you've attended or things you've seen yourself – you don't want to get into trouble.'

Tasheka chewed her lip as she mulled this over. 'I see what you're sayin' an' you're right, I don't want no bother. I'll just keep my eyes open to see if I can catch them myself!'

This wasn't quite what Lydia had meant however she decided to leave it there and if an opportunity arose, she may warn Lexie that her relationship with Adam had been discovered.

'Could I just say somethin' like, a couple were seen havin' hot sex in the pavilion an' not mention no names?' Tasheka handed the pink carrier over the counter.

Lydia looked straight at Tasheka. 'No!' she replied firmly, 'I wouldn't say anything about it at all. In fact, I think you should just forget it.'

Tasheka shrugged her plump shoulders. 'Hmmph! – It's a real shame though 'cos it would've made a great topic for my vlog.'

Lydia took the carrier and turned to go. 'Please keep it to yourself, Tasheka – Lexie will be mortified if she thought someone had seen her.'

'Ok. I'll probably jus' see you on Sunday then.'

Lydia nodded, said goodbye and left the shop.

Lydia went straight back to her flat and hung up her new purchases. She had an appointment with Adam Lewis in fifteen minutes, and how she was going to look him in the eye now, having just learned about his sexual exploits with Lexie, she wasn't sure. She set off for the five minute drive across town to Beatrice's house situated on a rather exclusive development dubbed "the posh houses", where Adam currently worked from home.'

Lydia had never met Adam before and her breath was almost taken away by his handsome face and toned physique – he could easily have been a model for a top brand.

'Come in, Lydia,' Adam welcomed her. 'I'm sorry, but I must just say, you're not a bit like I imagined.'

'I'm not?'

Adam led her through to an office off the hall. 'No, I sort of thought you would be more…bookish?'

'Bookish?' Lydia frowned.

'Coffee? Yes, a stereotypical old maid librarian, sort of person.'

Lydia raised her eyebrows as Adam indicated for her to sit down. 'Old maid librarian?' she repeated icily.

'I don't know, I just guessed that as you write books, you might be…Oh, look! It doesn't matter. Can I just say that you look far more attractive than I imagined. Actually, I think you should have your photo on your website…unless of course you wish to remain anonymous, which I don't think you should…but it's your decision…and I do think…' Adam broke off suddenly and looked at Lydia sheepishly. 'Sorry, I'm waffling – trying to cover up my embarrassment.'

Lydia softened at the sight of his discomfort. 'Let's start again,' she suggested.

'Ok,' Adam said with some apparent relief, 'Your profile on the current website led me to believe that you were a more mature lady, whereas to meet you in person, I find an attractive woman, dare I say it – around the age of forty, obviously intelligent and with a sense of humour for good measure.' He looked at her with soulful eyes. 'Have I just dug a bigger hole?' he added softly, but with a hint of sensuality. Lydia blushed and shifted uneasily in her chair, the movement caused her handbag to topple over and spill some of its contents. She bent down to cover her embarrassment and stuff her things back inside. When she straightened up, she was mortified to see Adam's smug expression and his satisfaction at the reaction he had caused. There was a moment before either of them moved, and then Adam switched into professional mode and began to talk about Lydia's website, suggesting some changes.

As he typed on the keyboard, Lydia found herself admiring his long fingers and manicured nails. His shirt sleeves had been folded back a few times to expose strong forearms with a light covering of dark hair. Her mind wandered back to the conversation with Tasheka and she wondered how Adam might look without his shirt, and whether he was a good lover. *I bet he is, I bet those fingers can work magic...*

'So, how does that sound?'

Lydia pulled herself back to the present with a sight jerk and realised that she had no idea what Adam had just said.

'Sorry, um...I was miles away...' she stammered, blushing furiously.

Adam raised an eyebrow and simply smiled. 'Sorry, I can get carried away...' he said softly, '...when I'm being creative.'

His dark brown eyes drew her in and for a few seconds, they stared at each other, then Lydia quickly looked away. *This is ridiculous, I need to get a grip!*

'Let me top up your coffee and I'll go over it again in English rather than IT speak. I tend to forget that a lot of my clients are not as familiar with tech words.' Adam stood up to fetch the coffee pot. He refreshed their coffees and they spent around half an hour discussing various options while Adam asked about her novels. When decisions had been made, Adam leaned back in his chair. 'Have you been in Ashdale long, Lydia?'

'No, only about a year. I moved up here from Oxford.' Lydia was on safer territory here, as long as Adam didn't flirt with her.

'Similar to me then, from a city to a small market town. How do you find living here?'

'I like it. I know quite a few people now – I joined the local am dram group and I enjoy being close to countryside. How about you?'

'Couldn't be more different to London and the glitzy, fast-paced lifestyle I had there – I don't miss the stress though,' he grinned.

'There is definitely no stress here.'

'Unless you include that business with my mother and the bakery – it gave me a fright, I can tell you.'

'It must have been awful. How is Cllr Lewis now?'

'She's fine, thank God. It was very fortunate that the doctor happened to be outside and knew what to do. I felt absolutely helpless. I knew about her allergy of course, but being away from home for so long, I've not had to use the epi-pen – to be honest, I didn't know she had one. I've learned what to do in future from the hospital, but hopefully, I won't need to put it to any use.'

'Let's hope not.'

'As a matter of interest…' Adam put his elbow on the desk, rested his chin in his hand and looked at her intently, '…how did you come to find me?' he spoke softly. Lydia tore her eyes away from his gaze and stared at her coffee cup.

'Tom Craven from The Property Ladder. I was looking at the properties on the Spanish Sun website and I found it a very easy and engaging website, and simple to navigate. Tom told me that you had created it.'

'Spanish Sun? So, you quite fancy Spain – not running away or eloping with someone are you?' Adam's eyes twinkled. Lydia raised her eyes and looked at him in amazement, this was the second time someone had mentioned eloping.

'I'm *not* eloping – have you been talking to Doreen Rider at the Coach?' she said, a trifle sharper than she intended.

Adam frowned in surprise. 'No, I was joking, why? What has Doreen Rider got to do with anything?'

'Doreen overheard Tom say something to me and then suddenly the word around Ashdale was that Greg and I were eloping, which is ridiculous as we've no need to elope.'

'Greg?' enquired Adam.

'My significant other.'

'Ahh! Well, if you're already living together, then I understand.'

'Oh! We don't live together,' Lydia answered, then immediately regretted it as Adam raised an eyebrow in interest.

'We're in a…committed relationship,' explained Lydia, wondering exactly why she felt she had to discuss her private life. '*And*, we don't need to elope, in fact I'm not sure anyone needs to elope these days.'

'There may be a variety of reasons, perhaps family members don't approve or maybe one or both parties are either engaged or married,' suggested Adam as he lifted his head off his hand, picked up a pencil and began to doodle.

'Surely people are not usually so bothered about family approval these days, and engagements can be broken, marriages can be ended. I think it's the idea of elopement – it has a romantic feel about it, you know running off into the sunset, that type of thing.'

Adam thought for a few moments and then shook his head sadly. 'There are circumstances when running away is the only way forward, perhaps calling off the engagement or wedding would cause too much heartache and embarrassment.'

Lydia said nothing and glanced at his doodle of the sun. Adam looked as though he was reminiscing, perhaps he knew a couple who had had no choice but to elope. The silence continued for a few seconds, before Adam snapped out of his reverie. 'Is there anything else I can help you with?' he said softly, looking straight into Lydia's eyes with an intensity that gave her goosebumps. She looked away, busily fussing with her handbag.

'No, it's fine. I really like your suggestions…err…ideas,' she blustered, feeling stupidly embarrassed.

Adam smiled winningly.

He knows. He knows exactly what he's doing and he's revelling in it!

'Right! I'll make a start on your new website using the images that you sent. I'll email a link once I have something for you to look at and we can take it from there, perhaps another meeting next week?' Adam was suddenly business-like.

Lydia stood up and picked up her bag and jacket. 'I'll have a look at what you send through and…um…get back to you. Thank you, bye for now.'

Adam saw her out and Lydia drove back to her flat. She was mortified about the effect Adam had had on her. She felt ridiculous and disloyal to Greg – talk about a mid-life crisis! On the other hand, it was so unprofessional for him to blatantly flirt with her and take pleasure in her obvious discomfort. Adam clearly had a very high opinion of himself. Lydia glanced at her phone – lunchtime, *thank God! A glass of wine with a sandwich would help and then she had to do some work on her novel.*

Later that evening, Lydia swung her legs onto her coffee table and leaned back into the sofa, it had not been a great afternoon. The glass of wine had been a mistake as it had totally wiped out any chance of concentration on her novel. She had gone over the conversation with Adam and decided that it wasn't so much what he had said but the way he had said things – how he had looked at her and had been slightly amused at her discomfort. She decided that if and when she had another meeting with him, she would be strictly professional and if he tried to flirt with her, she would get cross. There was absolutely no way she was putting herself in that situation again. Not only that, but he was involved with Lexie! She settled herself down for a long chat with Greg.

'… So, not only is Cliff likely to buy an MG, it turns out that it's the actual one he used to own,' she ended her story a little while later.

'I bet he was chuffed about that. I can't say I'd feel the same if my old Fiesta turned up though,' chuckled Greg.

'The thing is, I found something.' Lydia told him about the discharge note.

'So, Cliff has decided to track Trissie down?'

'He has, I warned him that, even if he finds her, she may not be happy about it and I don't know what he really hopes to achieve.'

'Perhaps Lucy doesn't know where Trissie went. To be honest, I haven't a clue where some of my past colleagues are.'

'The lovely thing is that Lucy Kirkwood is the same Lucy that Fran and Cliff used to know. They'll have loads to catch up on. Now, on a completely different note, I met with Adam Lewis today, and he's going to build me a new website.' Lydia explained to Greg what Adam had suggested. 'He had some very innovative ideas and I'm looking forward to seeing the result.'

'I must admit, I found the Spanish Sun website easy to navigate and very informative,' commented Greg. 'I've also seen an apartment I really like, when you next log on have a look at A405, it's situated next door to a large villa.'

'Ok, A405. By the way, I forgot to mention that Tom let slip about a sale of one of the villas, he said the owner was called Adam – I reckon it's Adam Lewis.'

'So, what with Doreen and Jeff from the Coach and now Adam Lewis buying property, it will be home from home in Spain,' laughed Greg.

'Maybe Tom and Amy will buy something as well.'

'We could talk to Ben and Kate about it.'

They joked about who else from Ashdale might buy a property from Spanish Sun and chatted some more about their plans for financing the apartment.

'It's so exciting, I can't believe we're actually seriously considering doing this.'

'We can talk some more about it tomorrow night over dinner and I'm also quietly excited.'

'Are you? It's quite a step for us, buying somewhere together – I know it's only a rental property but still, quite a...' Lydia struggled to find the right word.

'A commitment?' suggested Greg. 'I want you to know that I'm more than happy about doing this with you. Let's have a serious conversation about everything this weekend.'

'Ok. Now, how are things in London with your mysterious Mr Lord?'

'The boys here reckon that the two heavies they are tailing are responsible for a couple of murders – it's the Sharp brothers and they are well-known thugs. They've also had some reliable information from one of Mr Lord's prostitutes so hopefully they'll get closer to what's going on. Rick – that's the guy I'm working closely with – took me for a pint earlier this evening and we went to one of the pubs frequented by the Sharp brothers, and we actually saw them. I wouldn't like to get on their wrong side, the ugly one is bloody huge and the other really could be mistaken for Cody King, it's quite an incredible likeness.'

Lydia sucked in her breath. 'I really don't like the sound of this Greg, I'm glad you're coming home tomorrow.'

'In some ways it's quite exciting and I shall miss being involved, although Rick has promised to keep me informed of progress.'

'Hmm, I'm glad we live in the Yorkshire Dales where the worst thing to happen is a reaction to nuts!'

'We did have a murder earlier in the year,' Greg reminded Lydia.

'Oh yes, but that was a one-off, and we don't have criminal gangs, money laundering and suchlike on a regular basis.'

'No,' remarked Greg with a touch of wistfulness. 'Anyway I'll say goodnight for now and see you tomorrow.'

'Ok, sleep well and drive safely tomorrow.'

'Love you.'

'What?' but the connection was gone. *Did Greg just say what I think he said – he did!* Lydia stared at her phone is shock. That was the first time Greg had uttered the L-word, and her heart soared with joy. All that ridiculous business with Adam was pushed out of her mind as she realised that she also loved Greg. How did she feel about that? Absolutely delighted! As she got ready for bed, Lydia wondered what changes, if any, this new revelation would make to their relationship.

Terry Sharp

Somewhere in a pub in the east end of London, Terry put his mobile back in his pocket and turned to his younger brother who sat waiting patiently.

'Well bruv, we've a job on tonight 'cos they've found that bird that's been grassing us up, then tomorrow we're going up north for the weekend,' he said in his broad cockney accent.

'Cor, where're we going, Tel?' Ray's eyes shone with delight at the thought of a trip.

'Into the country and we're staying in a pub. What d'ya make of that, eh?'

'I've never stayed in a boozer before Tel, have I?'

Terry smiled indulgently at his brother who, to put it bluntly was a couple of cards short of a full deck,

'No Ray, you haven't. We've got a job to do mind, it's not a holiday, but there's no reason we can't enjoy a bit of country air.'

'Who we after then?'

'Remember that geezer who did a runner owing Mr Lord a right wodge of cash? Well, he's been tracked down and we've to get Mr Lord's money back, or else…'

'Or you'll let me persuade 'im,' guffawed Ray, miming cutting his throat.

'That's about it, bruv. Anyway, first things first and tonight, you can practise persuading on Sallie Fisher 'cos she 'as been a bit naughty chattin' to the old bill and Mr Lord's not happy about that.'

Ray pulled a sad face. 'Aww, I like Sallie Fisher, she's real pretty,' he pouted.

'Well maybe you can cuddle her first, yeah? Then do some persuading.'

'Oh yeah, I'd like that, Tel.'

'Come on then, let's get on wiv the business.' Terry stood up and put his hand on his brother's shoulder.

'Just need to go to the lav first.'

Terry sat down again to wait for Ray and cast his eyes around the pub. Terry fancied himself as a bit of a ladies' man, and he knew he was a dead ringer for a fancy actor off the telly called Cody King. He was shaven headed, very muscular with blue eyes and, on several occasions, Terry had been mistaken for this Cody chap which had some benefits. Some bird had once told her friends that she was dating Cody King – they had all turned up one night in the *Dog & Duck* and it had got a bit out of hand. Terry wasn't keen on being the centre of attention in his local area, he preferred keeping in the background, as his job demanded it, so he had given her a slap and she became his ex-girlfriend. His brother, Ray on the other hand, had a buzz-cut and a slightly lopsided face – he frightened women rather than attracted them. Unfortunately, he had also been born with learning difficulties, apparently as a result of their mother's drug habit, and Terry had looked out for his brother all through their childhood, protecting him from the bullies at the children's home and young offenders' units. However, once Ray had reached puberty, he had grown and continued to grow until now he stood at six feet six inches and had developed a powerful physique.

Terry and Ray had become Mr Lord's number one henchmen and were well rewarded financially, for the privilege. Terry's wit got them into places they needed to be, his looks and charm ensured that he didn't struggle to find a bed mate when he wanted one so life was as sweet as could be expected. Ray, on the other hand, well he just lived up to his nickname of Ray 'Razor' Sharp and having no seduction skills to speak of, he got his kicks from forcing himself onto some of Mr Lord's working girls, giving them 'a cuddle' as he put it. Any complaints fell onto deaf ears and if the girls got out of hand, then they required 'persuasion' to keep them quiet – permanently. However, this new job up north was a chance to get out of London as Terry had begun to feel uneasy recently, he was sure that they were being followed or monitored in some way and he didn't like feelings of that sort.

8

Vivienne Buckley
Vinnie pulled off the bypass onto the main road into Ashdale.
'Do we really have to stay in this grotty old pub?' Vivienne asked petulantly, 'I would much rather go to Harrogate.'
'In the first place, it's not a "grotty old pub", the rooms are spacious and are en suite, and in the second place, my business is at Ashdale Hall, not in Harrogate,' replied Vinnie.
'Well can't we stay at the Hall then?'
'No, my expenses won't cover that kind of luxury.'
'Pay for it yourself then, I'm sure we can afford a little treat, you have been so miserly recently.'
'I'm not being miserly, I'm being careful – and you know the reason why, the mortgage on the house is quite hefty now.'
'That's because *she* took you to the cleaners and I'm having to suffer for it.'
Vinnie sighed impatiently. 'Not this again! Look Viv—,' Vinnie caught the sharp glance out of the corner of his eye 'sorry – Vivienne. Lydia did not take me to the cleaners. The amount I paid was agreed in court and it's all finalised and done, so we are where we are.'
'But you never spend anything on me. This could have been an opportunity for a little pampering – please Vinnie, let's have a romantic weekend.' Vivienne put her hand on Vinnie's knee and slowly slid it further up his leg, but Vinnie removed her hand abruptly. 'Not whilst I'm driving, Vivienne, and I'm not changing my mind, The Coach & Horses it is. You insisted on coming with me, so you'll just have to fit in with my business plans.'
Vivienne folded her arms crossly, turned her head away from her husband and stared out of the window.
Half an hour later, as Vivienne unpacked their bags, Vinnie glanced at his watch.
'Right, I've got to go and meet Adam Lewis, I'll be back around five thirty in time to get ready and take you into

Harrogate to that new restaurant I mentioned. It has had great reviews with food to die for. It's Caribbean, apparently.'

Vivienne visibly brightened. 'Oh, that sounds lovely. I'll probably just have a browse around Ashdale then.' She smiled and Vinnie kissed her briefly on the lips before he headed off.

On leaving the pub, Vivienne turned left and wandered past the travel agents browsing the various holiday offers. She crossed over a road called Eastgate to walk down Market Place East and the first shop she came to was a bridal boutique. The dress in the window caught her eye and she sighed wistfully. Vinnie was her first husband and they had married quickly and quietly in a register office, and as she looked at the beautiful gown, she felt a pang of regret at missing out on the whole wedding razzmatazz. That's when the seed of an idea sprouted roots; of course, why not have a vow renewal and make a proper occasion out of it? She could wear a wedding dress and they could have a fancy reception. Vivienne looked beyond the white dress in the window and saw more beautiful gowns hanging on rails. *In fact, I could try on wedding gowns now – just to get an idea.* She pushed open the door and entered the shop.

The consultant introduced herself as Rebecca and asked if Vivienne would like to try on some wedding gowns.

'My husband and I only had a small and simple ceremony and we would like to have a vow renewal with a much bigger do,' Vivienne told Rebecca confidently. 'I think I would like something very fitted to show my figure.' Vivienne admired herself in a full length mirror as she spoke. Rebecca smiled pleasantly and steered Vivienne in the direction of a selection of fishtail dresses.

For the next hour, Vivienne was in her element as she tried on dress after dress. She told Rebecca that her ceremony was to be in spring of the following year and they had yet to decide on a venue. When she finally left the shop, Vivienne had fallen in love with *the* most beautiful wedding gown in the world which was priced only at £5,000 – an absolute bargain, given it was by a top designer. She was convinced that she could persuade

Vinnie to agree to the whole vow renewal event and, with that in mind, she would go with him to Ashdale Hall, and while he was busy with his client, she could browse all the stands at the wedding fair. Rebecca had said there would be a fashion show of her gowns and those of another bridal boutique from Harrogate along with several wedding service providers. Vivienne had a leaflet with all the details safely tucked away in her handbag.

Vivienne walked past Flower Power and looked at the treatments available at WOW!, both of whom were apparently attending the wedding fair, and then, spotting the independent department store, she decided to have a browse around Rathbones. She found a handbag that would go with a recently purchased pair of shoes and leaving Rathbones, holding a distinctive red branded carrier, she perused the properties in the windows of an estate agency. Spanish Sun! Now there was a good idea, a smart apartment in Mar Menor – all the celebs went there so it must be nice, she thought. Perhaps she and Vinnie could go there after their vow renewal on a sort of honeymoon – they could check out properties at the same time. Buying a property in Spain would be a great investment. It could be rented out when they weren't there – *in fact, I could go there by myself or with my friends, maybe even do a little business with the golfing chaps ... now that's a brilliant idea.* Feeling happy and positive about her latest idea, Vivienne walked past a few more shops and came to a stop in front of LulaBelle's. The clothing looked very much on trend in an Italian designer style, so Vivienne decided a closer look was necessary.

The buxom woman of colour behind the counter had her eyes closed and gently bouncing to music with a beat that Vivienne could just hear, even though it was playing through ear buds. The woman softly clicked her fluorescent pink-nailed fingers and her black curls bobbed as she moved her head. Vivienne huffed disparagingly and headed to the nearest clothes rail.

'Are you jus' lookin' or would you like some assistance?'

Vivienne jumped as the sales assistant, leaning on plump crossed arms behind the counter, spoke to her.

'I'm just browsing actually, although I do like the outfit in the window,' replied Vivienne.

'I did that display,' said the woman proudly, 'I jus' knew that the corset would look real hoochie wit' those jeans, you know wha' I'm sayin'?'

'Hoochie?'

'Yeah, hoochie. You know, those times when you go out wit' your husband an' you wanna look all hot an' sexy, you want your man to be real proud of you?'

'I know exactly what you mean,' agreed Vivienne, 'a woman needs to keep her man interested.'

The woman walked from behind the counter and beckoned Vivienne further towards the back of the shop. 'We have the corset in blue an' red as well as the black in the window an' I'm thinking that you would look real good in the red. I mean tha's not somethin' I myself could wear cos I would struggle to get my girls in it, as I am very generous in that department, you know what I'm sayin'?'

Vivienne glanced at the woman's ample bosom and simply nodded. 'Y'see honey,' the assistant continued, 'you gotta make the most of what your mama gave you, an' I'm not bein' rude when I say you have some real nice curves an' you would definitely look hoochie in this.' The pink fingernails indicated a beautiful scarlet and crystal embellished corset which laced down the back but had hook and eyes fastenings on the front.

Vivienne gasped, the corset was stunning and paired with some skinny black jeans and her high-heeled boots, Vinnie was bound to be appreciative. It might put him in such a good mood that she could mention the vow renewal.

'I have to try that on,' she breathed.

Five minutes later, Vivienne and the sales assistant stared at her reflection in the mirror. The black skinny jeans were an amazing fit and the red corset just looked incredible.

'Now *that's* hoochie! You're all set for a night on the town, girl.'

'We're going out into Harrogate tonight to a fancy new restaurant, so this will be perfect and when we get back...' Vivienne's eyes sparkled with delight.

'He's sure gonna be a lucky man, mmm-hmm!'

'I'll take both items,' Vivienne decided and disappeared back into the cubicle.

'I don' recall seein' you around here before,' the assistant chatted as she waited for Vivienne to reappear.

'I've been to Ashdale once before. I was almost involved in a murder!'

'Oh yes! I remember that – it gave me the heebie-jeebies an' that's when I decided to change jobs, so now I manage this shop.'

'Anyway, we're in Ashdale again because my husband has some business here, but there is something I need to persuade him to agree to and I think this little outfit might help.'

'Let me tell you something girl, if he don' want to park his car in your garage tonight, then my name's not Tasheka Dixon.'

Vivienne laughed at the expression as she passed the garments through the curtain.

'I love the way you say what you mean without actually saying it,' she chuckled.

'I got a real way wit' people so I'm startin' my own channel on the internet, my first gig is on Sunday at the weddin' fair.'

'I'm planning on going to that so I may well see you there,' Vivienne said as she handed over her credit card.

'I thought you said you was married?'

'Oh! I am, but we're planning a vow renewal and I want a big event.'

'Hey! That sounds a great idea, I wonder if my Mikey would like that...'

Terry Sharp

Terry had booked two double rooms at the Coach & Horses as Ray, being a large man, would have struggled with a smaller bed, and as for himself, well...you never knew what opportunities would present themselves. He had explained to Ray that they were pretending to be debt collection agents – which in a way they were, but not the sort that were sent by the court – so he wasn't to question anything and to just go along with whatever was said. They had taken up their overnight bags and now sat in the bar area with cups of coffee, which Ray had wanted to question, but a look from Terry had changed his mind.

'We need to pace ourselves, Ray,' Terry explained, 'we're going to be here all evening and I want to listen to the locals talk, see if we can pick up a trail on our man.'

'Can't we just ask someone, Tel?'

'We don't want to arouse suspicion. I need to have a cosy chat with the landlady first.'

''Er name's Mrs Rider innit, Tel? She looks really nice and friendly.'

'That's right Ray, but you leave the chatting to me, ok?'

Ray nodded and picking up his mug of coffee he turned his attention to the car magazine that Terry had bought for him. Terry felt a bit uneasy if he was honest – the brothers had never ventured out of London and here they were up north. It might not be as easy to deal with their target as Terry first thought, for one thing, the town was quite small and any incident would be noticed immediately and for another, there was nowhere to run and hide. It was clear that he would have to come up with a plan to try and ambush their man or somebody close to him, and that would require information. Terry glanced at the landlady, it was obvious that Mrs Rider knew all her customers as she kept up a constant flow of questions and answers, each pertinent to the individual. As Terry's brain pondered about what to do and how to do it, he heard his brother give a low whistle,

'Cor, she's pretty in't she, Tel?'

Terry looked up and saw a stunning blonde enter the pub, she had an even tan and the open jacket displayed luscious-looking breasts. As Terry stared, he noticed the heavy black eyelashes, plump cheeks and manicured nails – designer totty...interesting.

The blonde glanced around the pub and her eyes stopped when they reached Terry, her eyebrows raised and there was a hint of a cheeky smile – *Bingo!* The woman walked to the bar and rested her shopping bags on a bar stool whilst she waited to attract Mrs Rider's attention.

'Hello love, looks like you've been doing a bit of shopping, do you want your key?'

Terry had overheard. *Key? So, the doll is staying here.*

'Yes please and I'll have a gin and tonic.'

'I'll get that.' Terry was at the blonde's side in a flash. 'From one guest to another,'. He treated her to one of his best seductive smiles and was rewarded by a flirtatious grin in return. Terry knew in an instant that this woman was not a class act, he had seen girls like this before, and no doubt her husband was a something-or-other and she was his arm candy. Terry knew how to play this game so instead of coming on strong, he backed off. 'Sorry doll,' he growled sexily, 'I don't mean to be pushy or offensive.' He turned away having put a ten pound note on the bar for Mrs Rider, who was keeping her gaze averted, but Terry knew that her ears were flapping.

The blonde put her hand on his arm. 'No really, it's quite all right I'm not offended and as one guest to another, please accept my thanks.' She looked him straight in the eye and he felt a familiar stirring. 'You must get asked this all the time, but are you Cody King?'

Terry saw an opportunity and immediately switched into his alter ego, he glanced around the bar to make sure no one had overheard,

'Actually, yes,' he whispered, 'but I'm trying to keep it quiet.' He tapped his finger on the side of his nose, conspiratorially.

The woman's eyes flew open in surprise. 'Oh! Right! Gosh I'm sorry,' she apologised.

The landlady returned with their drinks and Terry gave her a winning smile. Doreen Rider smiled at him and retreated to serve another customer.

'How's about we go and sit down over there?'

'That would be lovely, yes.'

Terry picked up the gin and tonic and gestured for the woman to walk in front of him. As they approached, Ray looked up and Terry nodded his head in the direction of the door.

'I'm just off out for a walk round,' Ray grunted. He hauled himself to his feet, tucked his magazine under his arm and ambled off.

'That's my minder, Ray. So, what's a pretty girl like you doing here on her own?'

'Oh, I'm not on my own,' replied Vivienne, 'I'm here with my husband. He's here on business this weekend.'

'On business over the weekend? That's a bit rough – what business is he in?'

'He is a marketing executive and the Worthingtons at Ashdale Hall are his clients,' Vivienne told him importantly.

'Ok. Do you go with him on business often, then?'

'Definitely not! But the last time he came to Ashdale, I caught him texting his ex-wife – she lives here, so I had to come up real sharpish. Then I got involved in a murder…' Vivienne began the story of her previous visit to Ashdale, which Terry actually found very interesting.

'…this time however, he's going to the wedding fair at Ashdale Hall and he won't take me – says I'll be bored. But as I said, what woman doesn't like a wedding fair? Between me and you, I think he is going to see *her* – the ex-wife. Honestly, I feel a bit pushed out. I *so* wanted to go because I've had a brilliant idea…'

Terry tuned out of Vivienne's chattering and considered whether she was worth pursuing for a bit of bedroom activity or if he should just leave well alone.

'… so just because they have taken on a new website designer, Vinnie wants to make sure he is of the expected standard. I still don't see why I can't go to the wedding fair, I won't get involved in whatever he and Adam are talking about. I'll be quite happy collecting ideas for the vow renewal.'

Terry's ears pricked up at the sound of Adam's name and he probed a little further. 'Is he any good then – this website designer?'

Vivienne shrugged. 'Dunno, he's just moved up here from London, so Vinnie says. Apparently he had some hotshot job down there.'

'You know, I could do with a good website designer – my current site is a bit tired. Do you know this guy's name...or business name...?' Terry asked casually.

'All I know is that his name is Adam Lewis.'

Bingo!

'I could ask Vinnie about his details for you if you like, or tell him that you're interested?' Vivienne volunteered helpfully.

'No, don't do that. I wouldn't want to get you into trouble with your husband. He might not like you discussing his clients and their business – data protection and all that,'

'Oh, right...' Vivienne muttered dejectedly.

'I'll probably just call in at this wedding...er...thing.' Terry waved a hand casually.

Vivienne laughed. 'Wedding fair! That'll look a bit odd, the actor Cody King going to a wedding fair with his minder. People might get the wrong idea.'

Terry had forgotten for a minute that he was supposed to be a famous actor from a well-known soap opera, an actor who was already married, but then, an idea began to form in his mind.

'Look, I'll tell you what, I'm doing some research for a new role I'm thinking about doing and it's set up here in the north. I could do with going to this wedding fair, just to watch and listen, maybe bump into this Adam chap, but you're right, it will look a bit odd so...' Terry gave her his best cheeky chappie smile. '...if you pretend to be my wife, you can say we're looking at this vow renewal thing if you like, then we can both get in – legit like.'

Vivienne's eyes shone with delight. Not only could she attend the wedding fair, but she would get to be a celebrity wife for a few hours,

137

'Are you serious?' she gabbled. 'I can tell people who ask that I'm your wife? We'll get treated like stars – well, of course you already are, but wow!'

Terry smiled indulgently. 'Are you sure you'll be able to handle it? Ray will be with us, but he's cool.'

'I won't let you down.'

'Once we're in, mind, you go off and do whatever you want, and we'll meet up later when we're ready to leave.'

'You're on. Look, I'd best get off as me and Vinnie are going out tonight and I've got to get ready. I've bought something special to wear,' Vivienne whispered seductively. She picked up her bags and gave him a sly smile. Terry watched as she tottered her way upstairs and wondered if he could fit in a bit of rumpy pumpy on Sunday morning before they went to the wedding fair. He decided to see how things went.

Cliff Walker

When Cliff rushed away from Ashdale Autos on Wednesday, he had gone straight to Flower Power. Unfortunately, Lucy had no idea where Trissie had gone, and, although she remembered the name of the school, Cliff discovered that it no longer existed. He had been completely thrown by the revelation of Trissie's termination and had gone over the situation in his mind many times. Why had she not told him? Surely she could have confided something of that magnitude, after all he had been equally responsible – hadn't he? With a jolt, the sudden thought occurred to him that perhaps the reason Trissie had not told him about her pregnancy was because he was not the father. Then he shook his head. No, Trissie wasn't that kind of girl. It would have been his. His child! How could she have done that? Taken that decision by herself? If he was honest, he knew why; it was because he was married and Trissie *had* given him the choice of either her or Sandra and he had made the easy choice – Sandra. It was easy to look back in hindsight and realise that he had made the wrong choice. Sandra had never been right for him, but he had been a coward, not wanting to go through a divorce and create waves for himself whilst in the army. It had been a huge relief when Sandra had left him for somebody else – *Good luck with that mate!* He had thought about Trissie often, wondering how she was…but if he had known about the baby…

Finding that discharge note in the MG made him realise that she must have just returned from the hospital after having the termination. He remembered that night when he had last seen Trissie, her tear stained face as she showed him the damage to his beloved MG. God knows what had happened, but the front wing and passenger door were badly dented and the windscreen was cracked. Trissie had been very upset as she explained that, having parked the MG neatly at the side of the road, she had found it in this state when she returned. No one was around and there was nothing to indicate what might have happened, and mortified, she had just driven straight home. She had written out a cheque there and then, insisting that she should contribute to the cost of the repairs, but he had never banked it. Then, with tears running down her face, she had run back to the flat and he had not seen her since. There had been no fond farewell where he had taken her in his arms and kissed her, and, at the time, Cliff had been quite cross about the car. However, while he might have followed her back to the flat to console her and talk it through, he had a ferry to catch and so he had just driven away.

Looking back, he realised that Trissie must have been emotional following the termination, or maybe she was upset that he was leaving, but he would never know now. He had spoken to Fran on Wednesday evening and told her that he wanted to find Trissie again, to tell her that she should have told him about the pregnancy, that he would have left Sandra to be with her. Fran had been sympathetic and understood how upset he was, but she had been quite firm in her belief that he should now leave well alone. *You can't change the past! What's done is done.* He knew she was right of course, but it would take a little while for him to digest and come to terms with the knowledge of what Trissie had done. It had shaken him to his core and, upon reflection, he was not sure how he would feel even if he did come face-to-face with her. That being said, he now had to consider the MG sitting at Ashdale Autos. He had told Mikey that he would let him know by the end of the week and it was now Friday afternoon. Cliff took a deep breath – Fran was right, he had to move on, and the MG would always be a reminder of the fact that Trissie had taken the life of their child without considering his feelings at all, and he wasn't sure if he could just put it to the back of his mind.

Lydia Buckley

Lydia prodded the roasting chicken, then, determining that it was cooked, she hoisted it out of the oven. The intercom squawked and she lifted the receiver to hear Greg's familiar voice, and pressing the door release button, she carried the cutlery over to the table to set their places.

'Hi, something smells good,' Greg called as he entered the flat.

Lydia smiled at the tall, broad-shouldered man. She was so relieved to see him back safely from his London adventure.

'Roast chicken – I hope you're hungry!'

'Starving!' Greg strolled over to the table and kissed Lydia deeply, 'I've missed you,' he said.

'So, you're glad to be home then?'

'Definitely. London is big, busy and fast paced. I have to say, I'm glad I don't have their kind of pressure – trying to get across the capital quickly is a nightmare. Can I do anything?'

'Actually, can you pour the wine first whilst the chicken relaxes?'

'*I'm* looking forward to relaxing this weekend,' said Greg wearily. 'I've left a bit of a hornet's nest down there. You know I told you that Rick had an informant? One of the prostitutes – well she was found murdered this morning. She had been raped and then her throat cut, it was very nasty.'

Lydia put down the carving knife she was holding and shuddered. 'Oh God! Poor girl – was it the Sharp brothers do you think?'

Greg nodded. 'They think so, it was their typical MO, and it means they were getting close though. Unfortunately, it also means that none of the other girls will talk now, they'll be too frightened.'

'What will happen?'

'The Sharps are still being watched – there's a tracking device on their car. Rick is hoping that the brothers will lead them to Mr Lord at some point and they can get some photographic evidence.'

'It sounds absolutely frightful,' Lydia took a sip of wine as she digested what Greg had said.

'How has life been here?' Greg said after a few moments. 'Any more juicy details about the Housemans?'

'I had Lexie Worthington as a client on Tuesday and she asked me what I thought of the Housemans, as she had heard on good authority that Kate was moving her order away from Houseman's to Blenkhorn's – the bakery in Stonebridge.'

'Where on earth did she hear that? And *is* Kate moving her bakery order?' Greg leaned against the fridge freezer and took a drink from his glass of white wine.

Lydia repeated her conversation with Lexie as she stirred the gravy '… she didn't say where she had heard about Kate leaving the Housemans, but I checked with Kate and she has no plans to move anywhere.'

Greg shook his head. 'It must be upsetting for the Housemans, they need all the support they can get at the moment.'

'As far as I know, they haven't been charged with anything or put under investigation, so Lexie is being impartial. Right, everything is ready.'

Greg picked up the carving set and began to deal with the chicken. 'Well, I guess Beatrice Lewis might be able to sue for negligence…'

'It comes down to whether there was a sign about the nuts or not. Derek might have to move his counter to check underneath because...' Lydia suddenly stopped dishing up roast potatoes and put the spoon down. '...I've just had an idea! Have you got the number of the photographer you use at the paper – Eric something-or-other?'

'I have, why?' Greg placed slices of roast chicken onto their plates.

Lydia continued serving. 'Because when he took photos in the flower shop, and he took loads – all from different angles, he had already been to the bakery, so if he did the same there, maybe one of the photos will show whether there was a sign or not.' Lydia looked at Greg triumphantly.

'That's a real possibility, I'll send him a text whilst we eat. By the way, Cliff is covering the wedding fair as his first stint as the social reporter, and Beatrice Lewis is also attending in an official capacity on behalf of the mayor, who has shingles. I would say there is a distinct chance of something kicking off as Beatrice does her rounds, wouldn't you?' Greg grinned.

'I do hope not!' exclaimed Lydia, 'Lexie has put so much effort and energy into this, it's her venture and we don't need any additional excitement. I've already managed to scupper a sensational disclosure that would have knocked the wedding fair into a cocked hat!'

'What's the "sensational disclosure" thing you've scuppered? Is it something Cliff can use?'

Lydia put their plates on the table. 'Absolutely not! I'm not even sure I can tell *you*.'

'Cross my heart and hope to die...' Greg said without any conviction.

'This was told to me in confidence, well...actually it wasn't, but I'm hoping that it stays a secret because it's embarrassing for the person and—'

Greg put down his knife and touched Lydia's hand. 'If you don't want me to, I shan't breathe a word,' he said seriously.

'Cliff may have some competition in the gossip stakes,' Lydia began.

'What on earth do you mean?'

'Well, you know that Tasheka is working at LulaBelle's?'

Greg nodded as he ate.

'I popped in there today,' Lydia continued 'and she told me that she was considering a career change to become a lifestyle vlogger and social influencer.'

Greg choked on his food, Lydia slapped him on his back and got a glass of water, it was some minutes before he could speak again. 'A *what*?' he gasped eventually.

'You heard right the first time – a lifestyle vlogger and social influencer.'

Greg guffawed whilst Lydia sat stony-faced.

'Why is that so funny? She's a great personality and loads of people do it now. She's going to create her own channel and she's buying a camera. Her first major piece will be the wedding fair – maybe Cliff could mention her channel in his piece.'

Greg chuckled again. 'I don't think the newspaper will allow him to do that.'

'I don't see why not, it's local news.'

'Are you going to tell me about the scandal?'

'I'm getting to that.' Lydia repeated what Tasheka had told her about Lexie and Adam.

When she had finished, Greg whistled. 'I'm glad you advised her not to include it in a vlog, Lexie would not have been impressed. Seriously though, I hope she's careful about what she *does* include and that it doesn't detract from what Cliff writes. Talking about Cliff, do you know if he has managed to track down...what was her name? Tressy?'

'Trissie, and no, I haven't heard any more since Cliff left Mikey's on Wednesday.'

As they ate, Greg sent a text to Eric, and their talk turned to Spain.

'Are we really going to do it?' asked Lydia, her eyes shining with anticipation.

'I would like to.'

'What shall we do next, then? By the way, I had a look at the apartment you suggested, A405 – and I love it. Tom also said that Hugo uses an interior designer for the finishing touches. I saw some photos of Adam's villa and it was breathtaking.'

'I think we should arrange a trip to Spain to see the site for ourselves, check out the amenities and have a chat with Hugo. We can discuss the ins and outs, the nitty-gritty, cross the T's and dot the I's.'

'Are there any more clichés you want to use?' teased Lydia, however Greg remained serious.

'I'm really happy about buying an apartment with you, but I want you to be completely honest about how you feel. We've only known each other for just over a year and this is a financial obligation.'

'I'm fine, I really am,' replied Lydia, but the look on Greg's face told her that there was more he wanted to say.

He took a deep breath before speaking. 'I've come to realise that I do love you, but I'm also aware that you have just been through a divorce and whilst on the surface you look fine, I expect that it was quite an emotional ride.'

Lydia opened her mouth to say something, but Greg carried on talking. 'I don't want to push you into a full-on relationship whilst you're still a bit raw. What we've got now is good, it works and quite honestly, I don't want to change that at the moment. I just want you to know, that I do love you and I don't want to be without you, but I'm not expecting any changes to our current circumstances.' Greg raised his eyes and looked at Lydia with some trepidation, Lydia smiled at him reassuringly.

'I love you too, Greg Craven,' she told him, 'and you have just said the right thing. When you ended our call last night with the words "Love you," although I was immediately elated, I then began to worry about what would happen. I'm so happy the way things are now, and yes, I would hope that given time we might want to take the next step, but until we're both ready for that there is no need to change anything.'

Greg said nothing but simply took Lydia in his arms and kissed her deeply. As he released her, his mobile rang and he was surprised to see the caller ID was that of his brother-in-law, DCI Will Appleton.

'Hi, Will, what can I do for you?'

Lydia watched with dismay as the smile on Greg's face disappeared as he listened to whatever Will was saying. He answered a couple of questions, and then, after he had disconnected, he took Lydia's hands. 'You remember I told you that Rick and his team had put a tracking device on the Sharp brothers' car?' Lydia nodded and Greg continued. 'Well, they have been tracked here, to Ashdale.'

Lydia took a sharp intake of breath. 'What for? Oh God! They're not after you, are they?'

Greg shook his head. 'That's what London thought initially, especially as Rick and I had been in the same pub as the brothers. However, by the time I arrived in Ashdale, the Sharps were already here, so they haven't followed *me*. The thing is no one knows exactly why they are here, they haven't been known to leave London before.'

'So, what's going to happen?'

'A couple of detectives from London have driven up and are liaising with Will and his chaps, but they wanted to warn me in case I saw them about here in town. I'm only telling you all this because I described them to you and you may recognise them. If you do, you ring me and Will immediately and take yourself away to somewhere out of sight. The London guys will be on their tail, but just in case they lose them…'

Lydia nodded her head. Just when she thought everything was ok and Greg was safe, she was scared.

'Where are they now?' she asked in a small voice.

'They checked into the Coach and are in the bar. So far, they have shown no signs of suspicious behaviour so there's no reason to apprehend them at the moment. They may be just on a weekend jaunt for all we know, but I would have thought Leeds would have been preferable.'

'I can't see that Ashdale has anything that would be of interest to two London heavies,' Lydia commented.

'Neither can I, and there's no need to tell or warn anyone else. Just do whatever you were going to do, but be alert.'

Lydia sighed and shook her head. 'Well at least we should all be safe at the wedding fair on Sunday, I hardly think they'll go there,' she said with a wry grin.

Greg smiled in response as his phone chirped. 'It's reply from Eric. He's attached the photos he took at the bakery, I'll forward them on to you.'

Two minutes later, Lydia was looking at a photograph which clearly showed a nut allergy warning next to the plate with the taster cake.

'I'll pop into the bakery tomorrow morning and show it to them, it might help to ease some tension.'

'I'm not so sure,' Greg replied doubtfully, 'because the next question is…where did it go?'

9

Lydia Buckley
It was just after nine o'clock when Lydia left the flat. Greg had grumbled when she had determinedly got out of bed at eight o'clock, muttering about not having to get up early on a Saturday. However, Lydia wanted to call in at the bakery before they got too busy and let Derek and Sheila have the photo that she had printed out. She also needed to buy some bits and pieces from MegaMart and drop a parcel off at the post office – all that before her first client of the day at Lush Lashes. Lydia decided to go round to the back of the bakery rather than through the shop, and as she passed the window she could see Derek hard at work making pastry. She tapped gently on the back door and Derek looked up, obviously surprised to see her there. He shouted something and Sheila appeared, waved and unlocked the door.

'Hello Lydia, is something the matter?' she said with some concern.

'Not at all, I'm hoping to set your mind at ease, actually.'

'You haven't come up with a dastardly plan to get rid of Beatrice and Adam Lewis by any chance, have you?' joked Derek.

'No-o,' replied Lydia uncertainly, 'but regarding last Friday's incident...' the smile disappeared from Derek's face and he scowled as Lydia rummaged in her handbag,

'Elsa told me that you couldn't find the allergy notice, but that you were certain you had put one there, Sheila.'

'I did...I was so sure, but as we can't prove it...'

'Look at this,' Lydia handed the printed photograph to Sheila. 'It might help if there were any repercussions.'

'Derek!' gasped Sheila, 'It's a picture of the notice – it *was* there!'

Derek practically snatched the paper from Sheila. 'Where did you get this?'

'Eric Bentham, the photographer from the newspaper. I was in Flower Power when he called in there and I remembered that he took lots of photos from different angles, so I asked him for a set of your photos.'

'Lydia, I don't know what to say, this may make all the difference.' Derek looked almost emotional.

'Thank you, Lydia,' Sheila said with conviction, 'it sets my mind at rest. Whatever else happens, we can prove that we were neither negligent nor incompetent.'

'I'm sure you were neither,' Lydia said reassuringly.

'According to some people, we are,' muttered Sheila.

'No! We just assumed people would think that, Sheila!' Derek replied quickly.

Lydia, feeling a bit awkward and feeling that there was something *not* being said, decided she needed to get on with her day,

'Right, well I'll leave you to it. See you both tomorrow.'

As she closed the door behind her, Lydia's carrier bag slipped out of her grasp. As she bent down to retrieve it, she overheard Sheila and Derek talking:

'Derek, does this mean that we can prevent Beatrice Lewis from phoning the Bakers' Association?'

'Don't worry, Sheila love, after I've had a quiet word with Beatrice Lewis tomorrow at the wedding fair, she won't be making any phone calls.'

Lydia slipped away, hoping that Derek would have his quiet word at the end of the afternoon, Lexie wouldn't want any fireworks during the fair.

Adam Lewis

Adam was restless, his mother was pottering about the house and he hadn't yet heard from Hugo. On the one hand, that was good because he didn't want to have a conversation with Hugo while she was faffing around, but on the other hand, he was desperate to know what was going on and whether Hugo had sorted out the problem.

The office door opened and his mother's head appeared – he really wished she would knock first!

'I'm going into Stonebridge, I've a hair appointment, then I'm having lunch with Nigel and Denise Clarkson, so I probably won't be back until late afternoon.'

Adam nodded and smiled. 'Ok, what about dinner tonight?' he asked.

'I'm eating out at a charity do with the mayor's office, so you can do whatever you like,' she replied before her head disappeared and the door closed.

Adam shrugged and listened as the front door opened and closed, her car started and pulled away. He sighed, if only Charlotte had kept her mouth shut he wouldn't feel so edgy. His mother had not mentioned Charlotte since Wednesday night and had been distinctly snippy with him. He and Charlotte had not communicated in order to keep a low profile, although they had plans to see each other tomorrow. He thought about cultivating a friendship with Saffron – if nothing else, it might go some way in showing his mother that his love interest was not a Worthington daughter. He quite liked that idea and if Charlotte did renege on their plans, well Saffron would fill the gap in the short term.

His eyes caught sight of the notes he had taken about Lydia Buckley's website. Lydia…he could be very interested in her. She was a bit older than Adam, some ten years older he guessed, but he had found her very attractive and she had fancied him – he was absolutely sure about that and she was single. All right she had mentioned a partner, but obviously not a serious one as they didn't live together. She had money, he knew that because she had been looking at Spanish properties, and Adam also knew that very often these older women liked to splash their cash on a younger man in exchange for sexual favours, it made them feel desirable. The more he thought about it, the more he warmed to the idea of having Saffron as an official girlfriend with Lydia on the side. So, that was Plan B sorted! He chuckled to himself, pleased with his ingenuity.

His mobile rang, it was Hugo. 'Adam, my boy!' shouted Hugo, 'I've got good news, it's all sorted. Your mother has emailed her confirmation that she'll transfer the necessary funds in a fortnight and Mr Baron, that's the developer chappie who I deal with, has agreed to let you have the keys beforehand. You can make your arrangements for your little liaison, how about that, hey?' Hugo sniggered.

Adam grimaced at the smutty reference but replied with gratitude. 'That's fantastic! Thank you, Hugo, I really am most appreciative.'

'Turns out that this Baron chap was very understanding, been in that situation himself apparently, anyway he had a word with the top man who gave the ok,' chuckled Hugo. 'You know what they say – it's not what you know, it's who you know.'

'What did you tell mother?'

'Oh, just that they wanted an emailed reassurance because of the delay, nothing too detailed. All she had to do was attach a scan of her driving licence and a copy of a financial statement to prove who she was, confirm that funds were available, and so on. I also took the liberty of mentioning that I wanted you to come out here as I needed your signature and first-hand approval of the villa for one thing, and to look at the website again for another. Thought it would give you an excuse to get on the plane. Hope I did the right thing.'

'Yes, yes, that's great. I hadn't actually given the reason for going to Spain much thought,' Adam replied carefully.

'Do you want me to organise car hire or taxi or anything?'

'No, thank you. I can do all of that.' Adam decided that Hugo had had quite enough to do with organising his trip; it was supposed to be a secret, after all. 'Just keep it to yourself though, ok?'

'Mum's the word!' Hugo quipped.

After making arrangements to collect the keys, Adam said goodbye to Hugo, and checked out flight details. He made some notes and decided that he should pop into town towards the end of the day and see how the Housemans were getting on with raising the fifty thousand pounds. For now though, he had to focus on the website for Ashdale Hall as he had another meeting with Vinnie tomorrow and needed to have something substantial to show him.

Lydia Buckley
Lydia hadn't driven far from Harrogate on her way home when her mobile rang. She was surprised to see the caller was Lexie.
'Hi Lexie, how are you?'
'Oh Lydia! I'm so sorry to bother you on a Saturday afternoon, well it's almost evening, but I wonder if you can help me?' Lexie sounded desperate.
'Well, I'll try, what's the matter?'
'Karen, my event manager has just been taken into hospital with acute appendicitis and I'm setting up the wedding fair. I hate to ask – but I could use your help. I don't suppose you could spare me an hour?'
'Of course I can. Do you want me to come now? I'm on my way back from Harrogate early as my last client cancelled her appointment.'
'Oh, I would be so grateful. Mummy is out so I'm on my own and I just want it all to be right.'
'I'm happy to help. I'll be with you in ten minutes or so.'
Lydia disconnected and drove straight to Ashdale Hall where Lexie was waiting in the entrance hall looking effortlessly stylish in cropped jeans, ballet pumps, and a half tucked-in shirt.
'Thank you so much for coming! Honestly Lydia, I can't tell you how—' Lexie began.
'It's no problem, I think I shall quite enjoy dipping back into wedding fair organisation.'
'The first problem is that Karen was going to help backstage during the fashion show, so I need a replacement for her.' Lexie clutched her clipboard nervously.
'Right, well I can ask Maggie – you remember Maggie? She's the hairdresser at WOW! I think you will have met her at Bella's

birthday party. She's also wardrobe mistress for the Ashdale Players, and I'm sure she'll step in. What time is the show scheduled for?'

'Oh, would she? I hate to ask the exhibitors. The show is at two fifteen.'

'We're usually quiet during the fashion show, and anyway Zoe and I will be on the stand. Let me send her a text.' Lydia sent her text and smiled positively at Lexie. 'Ok, what next?'

'Karen was also doing the meet, greet and registration. I need someone who is confident, smiley and won't mind sitting at a table for most of the day.'

'I know the very person. Someone who is dying to attend the wedding fair but has not got a valid reason for doing so, other than to be nosey,' laughed Lydia.

'Who on earth would that be?'

'Elsa Armitage! She's very chatty and you met *her* at Bella's, too.'

'I remember, lovely lady…talked to everyone…even me!'

'That's Elsa. I'll text her.'

Lexie let out a long breath and visibly relaxed, 'Right, let me show you where we've got to in here,' she said positively as she turned towards the ballroom. Lexie's long black hair was caught up in a high ponytail which swung as she walked and Lydia quietly admired its glossiness.

'Patrick Flanigan and Mikey Dixon are each bringing two cars which will be parked on the terrace,' explained Lexie.

'Well, that's simple, they can have their table on either side of the French doors so they can pop out when someone wants to have a look at the cars,' suggested Lydia. 'Now, I suggest you put the Housemans next to Mikey on his left-hand side and Blenkhorns over there next to Kerry's. Both the bridal shops will want to be next to the stage and Zoe's stand should go there next to Bridal Beauty. The menswear can go over there between Blushing Brides and the Housemans. Then, if you put Flower Power next to us and Blooming Lovely across there next to Blenkhorns…'

When all the exhibitors were placed and Lydia had received confirmatory texts from both Maggie and Elsa, Lexie looked a lot happier.

'Thank you so much, Lydia – can I offer you a coffee? And I'd love to show you the bridal suite. I'm hoping that Sid Dawkins has been able to put up the new curtain rail around the four-poster in there – the curtains randomly fell down yesterday. I don't think the screws were strong enough.'

'A coffee would be welcome, and I would love to see the bridal suite.'

Lexie led the way upstairs chattering about tomorrow's weather, which was forecast to be dull but dry in the morning but the sun was predicted to come out around lunchtime. They reached the top of the grand staircase and were able to look out of a window to the terrace and across the lawn towards the dense copse beyond.

'In that small wood is our secret garden where we've just had a new fountain installed, and we've rebuilt the pavilion. It's used quite a lot by the television people now.'

'No wonder it's called a secret garden, you would never guess there was anything there other than trees. I might try to have a wander down there tomorrow.'

'You're more than welcome to pop down. We've asked Beatrice, as the mayor's representative, to have some official photos taken down there so we can use them in our marketing campaigns, but we're not promoting it specifically tomorrow as we would rather the brides stay in the Hall. I'm going to close it up for the winter unless the production company need it, and then we'll have a proper launch in spring.'

'How delightful, cocktails in the copse – a more modern take on a garden party,' Lydia mused thoughtfully.

'I like that idea – have you ever thought about becoming an events' organiser?' asked Lexie. 'By the way, Mum loved your last idea about the ladies' lunches.'

'I used to organise a few events for a charity and I really enjoyed doing it, although it was only voluntary in my spare time.'

'Hmm, if I tell Mum that, she'll have you on her charity committee in no time. She was only saying the other day that she could do with some fresh ideas.'

'As much as I would like to help out, I don't really have the time anymore, what with lashes and writing, then there's the panto during the winter. I'm happy to suggest a few ideas though.'

'In that case, I shall recruit you as my secret ideas-woman. Now I want your opinion on this special room.' Lexie opened a door, 'Ta dah! Behold – the bridal suite!'

The room was decorated in shades of cream and coffee, gold paint picked out the ornate plasterwork and there was an occasional pop of scarlet from the scatter cushions, vases and so on, but the massive four-poster bed dominated the room. It was hung with thick tapestry-like curtains which were held at each corner with matching tie-backs.

'Looks like Sid has been and gone,' commented Lexie, straightening the curtains. 'He told me that he wasn't sure he would have time to put them up and I told him he didn't have a choice.'

Lydia smiled. 'It's really beautiful…and so grand,' she said, gazing around in amazement. 'I love it!'

'Come on, we'll have coffee in my sitting room. Fortunately, we're lucky enough to have our own little apartments so I don't have to spend too much time with my sister – as much as I love her, she can be…well…trying, I guess.'

When they were settled with their coffees, Lydia asked if Charlotte had taken any interest in the wedding fair, bearing in mind she was planning her own nuptials.

'Not a jot!' replied Lexie, 'she's no idea about any of it…who's exhibiting, the fashion show – nothing!'

'I expect she's busy with her wedding preparations. I was watching a programme about brides choosing their wedding dresses and the price that these girls will pay – eyewatering!'

'I went with Charlotte to help her choose her dress, it was an exercise in damage limitation on Daddy's behalf.'

Lydia laughed. 'On the programme I saw, there was a girl who chose a beautiful dress with a price tag of £6,000, she looked absolutely stunning but what spoilt the whole image was her tattooed arms. It wasn't even a cute tattoo, it was a black and purple mess!'

'Charlotte has a tattoo, it's a rose – on her bottom. I think Daddy would have a fit if he knew.'

'A tattoo? Charlotte?' Lydia managed to say.

'Yes, it was a few years ago when she was in her rebellious stage – not that I've seen any real change since.'

'She's quite a feisty girl then?'

'You could say that! Oh! I mentioned about the lashes and I think she may have popped into WOW! today for a patch test and to make an appointment.'

'Ok, but I think I'm quite busy next week. Look, if she hasn't been able to book at either WOW! or Lush Lashes in Harrogate, then as a special favour and, if it's ok with you, I can come here and do them one evening…maybe use one of your treatment rooms? It's not something I would normally suggest but as it's her wedding in a week's time…'

'That's really generous of you, Lydia. I'll find out and let you know. Talking of lashes, I was going to ask if you could recommend a lash technician or knew of anyone who did training. I'm thinking that it may be something we could do here at the Hall, but I want to make it clear that I've no intention of poaching Zoe's clients – it would only be for our weekend spa guests and hen parties, that sort of thing.'

Lydia thought for a moment and then smiled as an idea began to form in her mind. 'If you're not in any rush to start that, then I may be able to help – you've just given me an idea. Leave it with me and I'll come back to you on that.'

'There's no rush, it's just a thought, but I'd be happy to discuss it further in due course.'

Lydia nodded. She liked Lexie, but there was something she needed to confirm, so she casually changed the subject. 'So, with Charlotte getting married and Sir Gerald's unwanted attempts to pair you up with one of his friends, have you got anyone special in your life?' she asked lightly.

Lexie shook her head. 'No!' she replied emphatically, 'there's no one around here that even remotely takes my fancy.'

'What about Beatrice's son, Adam? He looks an attractive man.'

'Definitely not! He's too smarmy and thinks he's God's gift to women, absolutely not my type. Charlotte's somehow managed to persuade Daddy to let him create a new website for the Hall, although why she did that, I've no idea. As for me, I'm happy as I am for now. I guess I'll meet somebody eventually, but I'm not desperate for marriage and babies.'

Lydia smiled at Lexie, but inwardly she was worried now that the knowledge about Charlotte's rose tattoo had confirmed which Worthington girl was involved with Adam. She fervently hoped Tasheka or her sister didn't tell anyone else about what they thought they knew.

Her phone beeped with an incoming message: *Are you coming home tonight? x*

Goodness, it was after six o'clock. The phone beeped again: *Are you ok? x*

'I have to go, Greg is concerned that I've not arrived home. Thank you for the coffee and I shall see you tomorrow. Everything is fine and there is nothing else you can do tonight, so don't worry.' Lydia sent Greg a brief text in reply then stood up and put on her jacket.

Lexie gave her a quick hug. 'Thank you for all your help and support, I really do appreciate it. One last favour – although we don't open the wedding fair until eleven tomorrow, could you come early, say nine thirty, in time to help me with the exhibitors arriving? I know it's a big ask, but we seem to work together so well and—'

'Of course I will. When this wedding fair is over, the next few that you organise will be a piece of cake!' laughed Lydia. 'Now don't bother seeing me out, I can manage.'

Lydia walked along the corridor, her footsteps making no sound on the thick carpet. As she neared the end, she became aware of a female voice and, from the occasional gaps in conversation, Lydia surmised that it was a phone call. The voice didn't fade away and Lydia realised that the person was ahead of her and that she was now in the awkward situation of either remaining where she was and eavesdropping, or boldly walking around the corner so the caller would know she was being overheard. Lydia hesitated and couldn't help but hear what was said:

'Look Pen, my dalliance with Adam has got to remain a secret and I'm relying on you to back me up if Adam's mother says anything... Of course I'll deny it, it was just unfortunate that she overheard us talking... Oh for goodness sake! It's not really lying, it's just not telling the truth... Well, I don't care if you think it's the same thing, stop splitting hairs. Honestly, you're supposed to be my best friend and confidante. Look, if it makes you feel any better, just say you don't know anything about Adam, then you don't have to actually lie... Oh, damn it! Where are my keys? Pen, this is serious, I'll do whatever it takes to marry Gerald and no one is going to stop me... Aha! There they are.'

There was the sound of keys, one was pushed into a lock, a door opened and closed and the voice was muffled and then silent. Lydia hurried back to her car and drove home, her mind full of thoughts and ideas.

When she opened the door, Greg was visibly relieved. 'I was a bit worried, sorry if I came across as possessive, but the Sharps have gone awol,' he explained.

'Awol? I thought they were being tracked?'

'Their car is, but that is still outside the Coach, and unfortunately it looks as though, the brothers got on a bus.'

'A *bus*? Where to?'

'The bus from Ashdale goes into Leeds eventually, but it stops numerous times before then, so they could be anywhere.'

'On the positive side, they're not in Ashdale, so *we* can relax until they come back.'

'I'm not sure that's how the police see it.'

'Perhaps not, but there's nothing we can do about it. In the meantime, I've had an idea which I would really like to run past you, it's about my work…'

Sheila Houseman

It was five thirty, Derek and Sheila were in the kitchen going over the items they were taking to the wedding fair as Derek nodded at the clock to remind Sheila to close up.

'We're more or less ready. Did you find those business cards and leaflets?'

Sheila nodded. 'Yes, I put them somewhere safe.' She chuckled as the shop door opened.

Derek groaned. 'Who the heck is this now?'

Sheila walked into the shop and pulled up short. 'I'm just about to close up. What do you want?' she spoke pithily, and Derek stuck his head around the door to see who the customer was.

'Oh! It's you. Well, now that you're here I've something to tell you,' he said derisively.

Sheila stood determinedly next to Derek as they both glared at Adam, who simply grinned maliciously,

'Well, I hope it's good news…for your sakes,' he sneered.

'Oh, it is good news for *us*,' began Derek confidently. 'Can't say as *you'll* be too chuffed though.'

Adam frowned. 'I do hope you're not going to make things difficult for yourselves. I thought I had explained the situation and made the consequences perfectly clear.'

'You did. However, we now have evidence to show that there was a nut allergy sign in place that morning—' Derek broke off as Adam roared with laughter.

'You mean to say that you have made another sign and that you're going to pass it off as the original one?' he chortled.

'Actually, no,' replied Derek calmly. 'We have a photograph of the original one in place, along with the time.'

'Don't be ridiculous, why would you have that? Who the hell would take a photograph of a nut allergy sign before it went missing? How would you *know* it would go missing?' Adam shook his head in disbelief.

'We didn't know it would go missing. But that morning, before you came in, the press photographer was in the shop taking pictures for the wedding fair article – turns out he took a photo that happens to show the allergy sign.'

Sheila smiled in delight as the grin disappeared from Adam's face and a look of fury took its place. '*What?*' he exploded.

'So, I just want to say that we'll not be paying you or your mother any sum of money. Now, if you don't mind, I'll ask you to leave so we can close the shop.'

Adam's mouth opened to say something, but he appeared to be lost for words, so he closed it again. Adam turned and pulled open the door, but before he left, he stopped and turned back to face them. 'You'll regret this, your business will be finished when my mother hears about this conversation.' He marched out, leaving the door open.

Sheila ran forward, closed it, and dropped the latch. Turning round, she leaned against and looked at Derek. 'Oh Derek!' she gasped. 'Have we done the right thing?'

Derek stood, arms defiantly crossed over his chest. 'We certainly have,' he said firmly.

'But what if we've made things worse?'

'We haven't, we've just made things…well, different. As I said earlier, I'll have a word with Beatrice tomorrow – somewhere quiet, just me and her. I want to make it clear that we'll not succumb to bully-boy tactics and she'll not get a penny from us. If she wants to take matters further, then she can do so via the proper channels and we'll deal with the consequences, *if any*, at that time. Until then, however, this is a private matter and if she makes any phone calls or causes any trouble, then I'll make sure that everyone knows that her son tried to blackmail us – and don't forget, we have a witness to that.'

Sheila was taken aback at this little speech, as Derek sounded so rational and in control. She smiled, 'My hero,' she beamed at him. 'Derek, I'm so proud of you.'

Derek uncrossed his arms and smiled softly at his wife. 'I'm putting my foot down about this, I'll not be messed about. Right love, let's get sammed up and ready for tomorrow.'

Sheila felt relieved that everything was going to be all right. Derek would talk to Beatrice, who would probably see sense and not ring the Bakers' Association.

Sarah Kirkwood

As the waiter poured their wine, Sarah watched as her mother happily chatted to Fran. This get-together at Fratelli's had been a good idea, giving the two old friends time to catch up at leisure rather than tomorrow at the wedding fair. They had all taken the opportunity to glam up a bit. Fran looked charming in a jade green devore dress and Sarah had been surprised how much Fran resembled her brother. Lucy had also taken time to put on make-up, which she rarely did, and she looked lovely in a sparkly top worn with a pair of black trousers. Fran's daughter, Michelle, was very pretty and looked elegant, her long blonde hair in a casual updo.

'So, I hear you work at the Northallerton LulaBelle's Boutique, do you enjoy it?' asked Sarah.

'Yes, I do and Pen is a lovely boss. She really takes an interest in her shops and her staff, and she always asks how we are.'

'I guess she appreciates good staff. How are your wedding plans coming along? Have you chosen your dress yet?'

The girls talked about Michelle's ideas for her wedding and Michelle told her that Cliff was standing in for her late father. Sarah knew that Michelle's father, Paul, had passed away a number of years ago which made them both fatherless. She spoke quietly. 'I – I just wanted to ask about your father. I guess you have some lovely memories of him?'

Michelle smiled nostalgically. 'I do, yes. Mum and I were devastated when he was killed, he died in a helicopter crash in Bosnia in 1996. I was only fourteen.'

'I'm so sorry to hear that, it must have been dreadful to have him taken from you so suddenly.'

'It was, but at least I had some time with him, whereas you never knew your father and I really feel for you.'

'In some ways, I find it hard to be sad – does that sound heartless? But I can't really grieve for someone I didn't know. My sympathies lie with Mum, she must have been devastated to lose her fiancé and then finding out she was expecting me. It's not been easy for either of our mums, but they coped – look at us and how well we've turned out,' said Sarah running her fingers through her glossy, brown wedge bob.

Michelle laughed and the mood lightened. 'They both did a good job with us,' she agreed.

'It is so lovely to see them together, look – they've gone all girly,' Sarah chuckled.

Fran and Lucy were indeed giggling as they chatted so easily and naturally. Sarah could imagine how they had been as young women enjoying nights out in Leeds.

'It's as though they have never been apart,' Michelle said softly.

'Perhaps you and I could track Sandra and Trissie down and have a proper reunion?' enthused Sarah.

Michelle's face darkened. 'Finding Sandra would definitely *not* be a positive thing,' she replied. 'She and Uncle Cliff didn't have a good marriage and apparently he has been much happier since she left. I think Mum has always felt a bit responsible for them getting married, she feels that Uncle Cliff kind of felt...well, obliged, I suppose, to marry Sandra because she was Mum's friend and Mum had married my dad, who was *his* best friend. I told her that was nonsense, but she said things were different in those days, and that in the end, Uncle Cliff hadn't got the heart to call the wedding off.'

'It kind of explains his affair with Trissie though,' remarked Sarah.

'Cliff came to the shop earlier this week and asked me about Trissie, but I don't know where she is now.' Lucy said, overhearing Sarah's remark.

'I'm hoping that I've talked him out of trying to trace her. It's too late now – what's done is done, but I have to say that I was completely taken aback when he mentioned his affair with her,' said Fran.

'Well, I shared a flat with her and I had no idea, although looking back I can remember wondering if she was seeing someone – she was very secretive. There were times when she could be quite snippy if I asked too many questions.'

'Uncle Cliff was quite upset about the termination though, wasn't he, Mum?'

'Aah, we weren't sure if he'd mentioned it to you,' said Lucy, recalling Cliff's distress following his visit to look at the MG.

'He told us about the discharge note which Lydia found in the car and then he told us how distraught Trissie had been on that night, the last time he had seen her. He is full of self-recrimination about what he should have done, could have done, but he has to let it go – it's over forty years ago,' explained Fran.

'I'm sure he will, he's just a bit shocked at the moment,' said Lucy, soothingly.

'He was so cross with her that night because of the damage to his beloved MG *and* he had a ferry to catch, so he just drove off. If she *had* told him about the termination, I'm not convinced he would have been any more sympathetic – probably even more furious,' Fran said.

'I think finding out about the termination has really shaken him. He kept saying that he couldn't believe she would do such a thing, ending a child's life and so on. One minute he was upset and the next he was angry,' said Lucy sadly.

'Thankfully, we didn't have any customers in the shop when he marched in. He slammed both a photo and the discharge note on the counter, then pushed them towards us telling us to "Look at that!" He wanted to know if Mum knew where Trissie had gone,' Sarah told them.

'I could remember the name of the school where she went after she left Leeds, but I've no idea how long she was there or what has happened since,' said Lucy.

'The MG was a bit of a mess, what on earth happened to it?' Sarah wanted to know.

'Apparently she didn't know. Cliff said she told him it was fine when she parked it and like that when she returned. Whatever it was must have been heavy to cause so much damage, it looked as though something had been dropped on it,' replied Michelle.

'Just a thought, but do you think Trissie could have hit something and didn't dare tell Cliff the truth? After all, didn't they have anaesthetics for abortions in those days? Perhaps she shouldn't have been driving at all if she had just left the clinic,' remarked Sarah.

'Well, whatever happened, we can't put the clock back, it was just a frightful night,' said Fran.

Lucy sighed. 'Well, it's one that I shan't forget – it was the night that Sam died,' she almost whispered.

'Oh God! I'm so sorry.' Fran was mortified, 'I didn't realise it was the same night. We shouldn't be raking up bad memories.'

'That night is the only bad memory and I remember it very clearly,' Lucy said. 'Thursday 7 April, 1977, the day before Good Friday. Cliff, Sandra, you and Paul had already gone to Germany. Cliff was coming back to collect his MG which he'd had to leave behind and he'd let Trissie use it for the week. Anyway, he came to our flat to get the car and drive it back to Germany. Trissie hadn't returned home so Cliff and I chatted – mainly about how you all had settled in. Trissie arrived all of a dither because she was late, Cliff said goodbye and that he would all see us at my wedding at the end of May. Trissie went back out with Cliff, I think she had left something in the car, and when she returned, she said Cliff had gone and she went straight to her room, I guessed she was just upset.'

'Was Sam killed instantly?' asked Michelle gently.

'He had two major head injuries, one from the car and one from hitting the pavement, along with internal injuries. Apparently he had been hit sideways on and he died more or less straight away. It was some sort of comfort knowing that he hadn't suffered.'

'It must have been dreadful when you found out. I can't imagine how you coped, especially then finding out you were expecting,' said Fran with genuine sympathy.

Lucy put her hand on her daughter's arm. 'I have my lovely Sarah – she keeps the good memories of Sam alive.'

Sarah blinked back some tears, it had been so hard not knowing her father as she grew up, with only her mother's memories and the odd old photograph of him. However, as she had listened to them talking about the MG's damage, she wondered if it could have been caused by hitting a pedestrian. A pedestrian hit on his left-hand side would cause damage to a car's passenger side. Cliff had driven off to the ferry and taken the car abroad that night – that in itself could explain why the car and driver had not been traced. Had Trissie been responsible? She had left the flat pretty sharpish the following morning according to her mother. The more Sarah thought about it, the more the idea seemed to come together, but she was brought back to the present as the waiter appeared with their meal. *Let's hope for your sake, Trissie Foxton, that Cliff doesn't track you down, because if he does...*

10

Lydia Buckley
Lydia arrived at the Hall on the dot of nine thirty to find Lexie smiling and looking elegant in a simple black shift dress.

'Thank you for helping me last night, I slept better than I would have done otherwise.'

'Well, I'm glad you're satisfied with the layout,' replied Lydia.

There was a scrunch on the gravel outside, and both women turned round to see a van with Bridal Beauty written on the side.

'Here comes your first exhibitor. Let's have them go around the side onto the terrace and unload straight into the ballroom, they can repark their vehicles when they've finished,' suggested Lydia.

Lexie nodded. 'Good idea.'

'Morning, Rebecca, could you take your van around the side to unload please? Then just repark out here?'

Rebecca nodded and returned to her van. Elsa was the next to arrive and Lexie spent some time getting her settled and explaining what was going on and what she was to do. Then leaving her in charge of redirecting the exhibitors, Lexie and Lydia went to the ballroom. It became a hive of activity and reminded Lydia of the dressing room before the panto curtain up. The curtains across the stage were open and an arch of flowers had been artfully installed. Each florist had been allocated a side of the arch and it was obvious that they had discussed colours as, although the arch was not symmetrical, each side was complimentary to the other. The runway from the stage was in position with chairs around it with a DJ positioned at the end. The tables for the exhibitors were set up around the edges of the room. By a quarter past ten, everyone had unpacked and reparked their vehicles, giving Mikey Dixon and Patrick Flannigan an opportunity to position the wedding cars to their best advantage.

Lydia was pleased to see that all the exhibitors were chatting to each other. The atmosphere was friendly with a touch of excitement, although she detected disparaging looks directed at the Housemans from the Blenkhorn's table. Lydia thought this was a bit off, but once the public arrived, it was less likely that the two bakeries would be able to see each other.

By ten forty-five, the exhibitors were wandering around looking at each other's tables and displays, and it occurred to Lydia that most of them had never met before. She strolled over to the French doors which were open on to the terrace and smiled when she saw that Mikey Dixon and Patrick Flannigan were deep in conversation, hands nonchalantly in pockets and rocking to and fro on their heels as they chatted about their cars. Occasionally one of them would point something out and the other would nod wisely in agreement. Mikey looked handsome in his light-grey suit and chauffeur's cap, whereas Patrick Flannigan had completely embraced the vintage theme by wearing a pair of black riding breeches and a mandarin-collared, double breasted jacket sporting two rows of shining brass buttons. It was a uniform straight out of Downton Abbey. Turning back into the room, Lydia walked over to the Housemans' stand, where Derek, resplendent in pristine chef's whites and Sheila, looking bonny in a long black dress over which she had fastened a snowy white apron, stood proudly behind their display. Lydia gasped. 'Derek! That cake looks amazing, how on earth do you do such intricate sugarwork? Not only that, but once you've done it, how do you dare move it?'

Derek beamed with pleasure. 'I've been doing this for years, Lydia love, it's an art form really, but I have to say, I'm pleased how this has turned out.'

At that moment, Lexie appeared at Lydia's elbow. 'We're ready to open,' she said excitedly, 'the only thing is, Mummy will not be putting in an appearance. As soon as she heard that Beatrice Lewis was coming in lieu of the mayor, she suddenly found something she had to do,' Lexie gave a knowing look.

'So, what are you going to do with Beatrice?' Lydia asked.

'I've explained to Elsa that she's to be super-nice and polite when Beatrice arrives and just say that she's welcome to wander around at her leisure, but to make sure that she goes to the pavilion at one forty-five for a photograph.'

'What time is she arriving?'

'She is due at one o'clock. Right, well, it's eleven exactly so the wedding fair is officially open.'

Lydia joined Zoe and Maggie at their table, all of them dressed in the turquoise uniform of the WOW! salon. Sarah and Lucy looked very smart in matching black trousers and white tops. *Ashdale has scrubbed up well*, thought Lydia, as she looked around the room at all the exhibitors eagerly anticipating the day ahead. The brides and their entourages came in good numbers and as the morning wore on, the exhibitors were kept busy and it became apparent that the event was heading for success. About an hour later, there was a slight lull in the numbers as some people made their way across the entrance hall to *The Sandringham Suite*, next door to *The Balmoral Bar*, where sandwiches, salads and drinks were available. Lydia exhaled, stretched her back and looked up from the table, her eyes making contact with Tasheka on the opposite side of the ballroom. Tasheka wiggled her fingers in acknowledgement. Today she looked vibrant in a fluorescent-orange oversized shirt worn with a lightweight black jacket-and-trousers combo, the jacket was fastened over her generous bosom with what looked like a huge brooch.

A voice at her elbow made Lydia jump and she was surprised to find Cliff standing beside her. 'I want a word with you, young lady,' he said mock-seriously.

'Do you? Why?'

'Well, in the first place you didn't mention that you and Greg were eloping, and in the second place, you didn't say there had been a murder in Ashdale a few months ago.'

Lydia rolled her eyes. 'For goodness sake, not you as well. In the first place, Greg and I are not eloping – somebody overheard something that was said in jest and has been repeating it seriously since, and secondly, the murder was well documented by the local press and is not really hot-off-the-press gossip,' she told him, not unkindly.

'Oh! I thought I might have had something there.' Cliff looked crestfallen. 'Never mind, how's it going today?' he added brightly.

'Very well, I think. I haven't seen much of Lexie since we opened, so I'm hoping that's because she's busy with appointments for her bridal tours.'

'Well, I'm going to have a wander round in here and have a chat to everyone before the mayor arrives.'

'The mayor's not coming as he has shingles – you'll have Cllr Lewis instead, she's due around one o'clock,' Lydia told him.

Cliff shrugged. 'All the same to me, still a bloomin' councillor,' he said somewhat irreverently.

Lydia giggled as Cliff wandered off. She watched him as he worked the room, introducing himself and seemingly taking a great interest in each exhibitor. He had a small voice recorder which he asked permission to use at each table, so everyone gave a little interview. Lydia was interested to see how Tasheka would handle an interview, but as Cliff approached her table, half a dozen girls gathered around Zoe's stand and it was impossible to watch. By the time the girls had moved on, Cliff was two tables further on.

A little while later, Cliff returned to Lydia. 'I don't suppose you could meet Cllr Lewis with me and introduce us, could you? I don't know her and she doesn't know me – wouldn't want to get the wrong lady,' he pleaded.

'Actually, I don't know her either, but Elsa is on registration duty and she'll help.'

'I don't know Elsa either,' Cliff pointed out.

Lydia told Zoe that she was stepping away for a while and Zoe nodded,

'That's fine, it's quietened down a bit now,' she said.

Cliff and Lydia walked into the entrance hall where Elsa sat importantly at a desk. She wore a floral wrap-over dress and her grey hair had been blow dried in a soft style around her face. She looked bonny today, Lydia thought,

'Hi Elsa, how are you coping?'

'I'm doing great. Thank you for thinking of me for this job, I'm really enjoying it. I can chat to them as they sign in. The sun has come out now which will be good for Mikey and that Flanigan man, people will wander outside and take a look at their cars.'

Lydia smiled at Elsa's happy face. 'Let me introduce you to Cliff Walker. Cliff is the social reporter with the *Yorkshire Press* and is covering the wedding fair today – he enjoys gossip,' Lydia added wickedly.

'What are you implying with that remark?' teased Elsa.

'Cliff, this is Elsa Armitage. I'm not being rude when I say that if you want to know anything about anybody, this is the lady to ask.'

Cliff smiled as he recognised the lady in the blue jacket from his visit to the café earlier in the week,

'I believe I've seen you before, Mrs Armitage, although you may not remember. I was taking a break in the café last Monday and I think you were at the table next door with a friend?'

'I knew I recognised you from somewhere!' Elsa said with a snap of her fingers, 'How do you like Ashdale? Do you live here?'

'I am planning to move here, but I'm not sure where would suit me, perhaps you could suggest an area?'

Lydia tuned out as Elsa extolled the virtues of living in a park home on the Canalside Residential Park. She checked her phone which, like everyone else's was on silent. There was a message from Greg to ask how the fair was going and to tell her that the Sharps had returned to the Coach late last night on the bus. *I hope they don't find a body somewhere,* she thought grimly. She sent a brief text back to say that the event was going well with a large number of people attending. Then, hearing footsteps behind her, she turned to see a po-faced, thin woman approaching them. She wore a navy blue suit and a cream blouse.

Lydia put on her best welcome smiley face which disappeared as Cliff gasped, 'Trissie? Bloody hell! Trissie!' Cliff raced forward and grabbed the woman's arms. Beatrice visibly paled and pulled back from Cliff's grasp.

'Trissie! It's me, Cliff Walker. I've been trying to find you.'

Lydia glanced at Elsa, whose mouth had dropped open in shock, and then, pointing a finger at the woman, Elsa mouthed: *That's Beatrice Lewis.*

'Cliff? I…I …' stammered Beatrice, retreating away from him.

'I need to talk to you. You should have told me. Oh Trissie, if only I had known. The clinic! I know you went to the clinic and—'

Cliff broke off as Beatrice's normal poker face turned from initial shock into an unpleasant grimace, one which an enraged Maleficent would have been proud of.

'Get your hands off me! I don't know what you're talking about!' she snarled.

'Trissie, I just want to talk to you.' Cliff was aghast at her reaction.

'I've nothing to say!' Beatrice snapped.

Lydia realised she had to do something to rectify the situation, so she put her hand on Cliff's arm,

'Perhaps it's not something to be discussed here,' she said firmly.

Beatrice pursed her lips, stalked past Cliff and glared at Lydia, who felt she had to smooth the obviously ruffled feathers,

'Good morning, Cllr Lewis, thank you for taking the time to attend the inaugural wedding fair at Ashdale Hall. I'm afraid that both Lady Victoria and Miss Worthington are engaged with potential clients and they have asked me to say that you're welcome to have a look around at your leisure. Perhaps you might like to have a chat with all the exhibitors, and a photo opportunity has been arranged for you at the pavilion in the secret garden at one forty-five.' Lydia smiled brightly at Beatrice, whose face softened somewhat.

'Thank you, it's Lydia Buckley, isn't it?' Beatrice asked. 'I've read your novels and enjoyed them.'

'Thank you,' replied Lydia, pleased to hear the softer tone in Beatrice's voice. 'Perhaps you would like to make your way into *The Buckingham Ballroom*?' Lydia gestured gracefully towards the open ballroom doors. Beatrice nodded and with a backward, hostile glance at Cliff, she walked away.

Lydia turned to Cliff who stood looking distraught, his arms hanging limply at his sides.

'I—we—she doesn't want to talk to me,' he stuttered.

'Come on, Cliff, let's go grab a coffee and take a breath, hmm?' Lydia stared hard at Cliff and when he looked at her, she slid her eyes to Elsa, open-mouthed and clearly enthralled in the little drama that had played out right in front of her. Cliff nodded disconsolately and followed Lydia to *The Sandringham Suite*.

When they were sitting with a coffee each, Lydia put her hand over Cliff's. 'Drink your coffee and take a deep breath,' she advised him quietly.

Cliff did as he was told.

'You perhaps shouldn't have mentioned the clinic straight away, it was a shock to her meeting you like that, let alone bringing up such a painful memory,' Lydia said gently.

Cliff nodded miserably. 'I know. It just all came out in a rush. Ever since we found that discharge note, I keep looking at it and thinking if only—'

'Cliff! I understand you want to talk to her about it, but you need to take it slowly. I imagine that day is indelibly imprinted in her mind, albeit pushed far to the back, and you just brought it to the fore, releasing emotions that she had buried deep.'

'But she said she didn't know what I was talking about.'

'Defence mechanism!' Lydia replied sharply. 'Beatrice Lewis sees herself as a pillar of the community; holier than thou; above reproach – that sort of thing. You have just reminded her that once, long ago, she had an illicit affair which ended in abortion.

So, of course she's going to deny it. She needs time to come to terms with the fact that you're here, which she will, because not only are *you* here, but so is Lucy and very soon, Fran.'

Cliff sighed resignedly. 'You're right, of course. So, shall I go and have a quiet word with her?'

'I would leave it for now, Beatrice is here on official business and will need to regain her composure. She'll meet Lucy when she reaches their table and that will be another surprise. If you don't find a quiet moment today, there are other days to talk to her, now you know where to contact her.'

'I don't know whether I'm happy or upset to see her again, or just plain bloody furious, actually.'

'Probably all three?' Lydia smiled at him and was relieved to see Cliff's smile back. 'Drink your coffee and keep out of her way for a while, let the dust settle.'

Cliff heaved a sigh. 'Ok, and thank you for the sensible advice. I'll stay here and listen to my interview recordings, make sure I don't need to redo anything.'

'I'm going back to our table, I want to make sure there are no dramas at the Flower Power stand either.'

Satisfied that Cliff had regained his equilibrium, Lydia returned to the ballroom and saw that Beatrice was chatting happily to the Blenkhorns. She glanced apprehensively at the Flower Power table and saw that both Lucy and Sarah had a number of brides with them, with no sign that they had noticed Beatrice. Lydia hoped for an opportunity to speak to Lucy about what had happened, but a young woman approached the table and she launched into her lash extension patter.

Vivienne Buckley

Vivienne was very excited about going to the wedding fair with Cody King, and she knew he had booked in at the Coach under the name of Terry Sharp, but she understood that celebrities did that sometimes. She and Vinnie had had an energetic start to the day, after all isn't that what Sunday mornings were all about?

She had done all the things he loved and been extra playful because when she had suggested the wedding vow renewal on Friday night, although he hadn't agreed or shown any enthusiasm for the idea, he hadn't actually said 'no' either – but then what man was excited about weddings? They had enjoyed a leisurely breakfast and Vinnie had gone off to his meeting with the Adam chappie. Cody had agreed to go in time for her to watch the fashion show, so they had settled on leaving at one thirty, although Cody had made it clear that he didn't intend to stay too long after that. Vivienne decided to keep away from the watchful eye of Mrs Rider as she didn't want her to arouse any suspicion, so after Vinnie had left, she took a scented bath and spent a long time over her hair and make-up. She perused her clothes for quite some time as the wife of a famous actor had to look good and, in the end, settled for a scarlet mini-dress and a cropped black jacket with scarlet piping teamed with black ankle boots and an oversized handbag. A glance out of the window told her that the sun kept popping out from behind clouds, so she dropped a pair of large sunglasses into the bag as well as her usual accessories. At last she was satisfied with her look and hoped that Cody would notice the effort she had put in. They had decided to meet in the car park behind MegaMart, so Vivienne left the Coach, strolled down Eastgate and around to the back of the shops. Cody had a Mercedes and, although it was a luxury car, Vivienne was a little disappointed that it wasn't a bit more flashy, like a Lamborghini. Not only that, but he failed to make any comment on her appearance, which Vinnie would have done, so his star status lost a little bit of its sparkle.

Cody drove the few miles to the Hall and at last they pulled up outside; the beautiful Georgian façade was impressive and he whistled in appreciation as they got out of the car.

'Ok, darlin', now remember, you're Mrs Cody King and we're looking at vow renewal stuff, and while you watch the dress show I'll just have a gander round and maybe bump into this Adam geezer. If he's with your husband, I'll keep schtum though, got it?'

Vivienne nodded enthusiastically and was thrilled when Cody held her hand as they entered the Hall. They approached the registration desk and the woman behind it smiled as she recognised Cody.

'Oh! I know you, you're off the telly,' she gushed. 'You're Cody King – wait till I tell my Brian that I've met Cody King.'

Cody smiled and leant forward conspiratorially. 'Just wait until after we leave before you tell anyone – please? We just want to have a look around quietly.'

Elsa nodded her head rapidly in agreement. 'You can rely on me to be discreet,' she told him glancing uncertainly at Ray.

'Don't worry about him, he's just my minder,' Cody winked at her and she blushed.

Cody signed the register with an illegible scrawl and they wandered through into the ballroom.

Vivienne was in her element. More than ever, now, she wanted a vow renewal. They stopped at each table, albeit not for long enough, and she was aware that as they moved on, there were nudges and pointed fingers as Cody was recognised. When they reached the French windows, Vivienne felt she didn't need to look at the cars, so Cody suggested that he and Ray go outside and that they would catch up later. The next table she came to was attended by someone she recognised, it was the woman from LulaBelle's – Tasha? Sasha? Something like that.

'Hey, girl, how ya doin?' You was in my shop on Friday. Did he like that fancy corset you bought? You should've said you was with that actor, I would've asked for an autograph or somethin'.'

Vivienne was taken aback for a moment, no one had ever wanted her autograph. 'I didn't like to brag,' she replied coyly.

'So, are you doin' this vow renewal? I spoke to my Mikey 'bout doin' ours, but he ain't so keen, you know? He says we don't *need* to do that, but I'm thinkin' that I might want to.'

'Yes, he agreed to it which is why we're here – he's outside talking about cars.'

'He'll be with my Mikey. Now, here's the thing,' Tasha gesticulated with her index finger, 'I'm settin' myself up as a social influencer and vlogger, I'm thinkin' of callin' my channel *Talking with Tasheka* 'cos my name's Tasheka, an' I was wonderin' if I could do an interview wit' you, just a girly chat about weddings and stuff? It would help me get some followers for my channel, you know?'

Vivienne hesitated, she wasn't at all sure if Cody would like her doing that. 'I'm not sure...we're keeping it secret for now,' she replied eventually.

'Well, how's about I record you and me havin' a chat about weddin's in general, so's you don' get no flim-flam from him?'

'Oh! That would be all right because I wouldn't have to pretend,' Vivienne blurted out, '... err...reveal any secrets, I mean,' she added quickly as Tasheka gave her an odd look. Then she gave her brightest smile. 'Ok, when shall we do it?'

'Well, we could do it now 'cos my Mikey can sit here and have his sandwich. We could go to the bridal suite on account of it will be quiet there. It won't take long an' you'll be back for the fashion show.'

Vivienne was thrilled at the prospect of being interviewed, quite forgetting for the moment that she wasn't actually married to Cody King. She waited whilst Tasheka told her Mikey that she was leaving the table and then happily followed Tasheka out of the ballroom and up the stairs. When they reached the top, they both looked out of the window across the terrace lawn toward a clump of trees and saw a female figure with long black hair disappearing into the foliage.

Tasheka pointed an orange-tipped finger. 'See her there, goin' into them trees? Well tha's Lexie Worthington – she's the daughter of Sir James and Lady Victoria who own this place. Now, I happen to know that she's goin' to meet someone for a bit of jiggy-jiggy.'

'How do you know that?' gasped Vivienne.

'Because my sister caught her in the act last time an' let me tell you, she wasn't holdin' back.'

'I see…' mumbled Vivienne, quite taken aback at the news.

'Now this is the bridal suite an' it will make a real nice settin' for our chat.' Tasheka flung a door open and Vivienne stepped inside.

It was perfect, a beautiful and romantic room with a real four-poster bed, and a lounge area with sofas upholstered to match the soft furnishings. Tasheka marched across to one of the sofas in the bay window, rearranged some scarlet cushions and plonked herself down. She then retrieved her phone from the bottom of a voluminous shoulder bag and set it on the coffee table between the sofas.

'Now if you sit opposite me, we can just chat real informal, so's you don't get all nervous and antsy.'

Vivienne suddenly felt very nervous, what on earth was she going to say?

But Tasheka made it all very simple, as she began by asking why they decided on a vow renewal. Well, of course that was easy *because they had a small and simple ceremony the first time and now, they wanted a big celebration.* As Tasheka asked questions, Vivienne's answers were real. She repeated her own reasons she had given Vinnie on Friday night, when trying to persuade him to agree.

They were a few minutes into the interview when Vivienne realised that Tasheka had forgotten to switch on the voice recorder on her phone, *Oh dear, still it's probably just as well this conversation is not recorded.* They talked about dresses, possible venues – abroad or a fairytale castle, themed or traditional, number of bridesmaids – if any – and when Tasheka asked if any other celebrities would be invited, Vivienne waved her hand vaguely and said that they hadn't decided on who exactly, but they were thinking 'star-studded'. Knowing that the conversation was not being recorded allowed Vivienne to relax and she name-dropped relentlessly about their imaginary, famous, dinner party guests, well-known godchildren and really anything she could think of that would impress Tasheka.

'It all sounds real exciting an' I might try again with my Mikey, but right now, we ought to get back downstairs for the fashion show,' Tasheka said a little while later.

As she stood up, Vivienne pointed to the phone laying with a blank screen on the coffee table. 'I hate to say this, but I don't remember you setting it to record and we haven't time to redo the interview.'

Tasheka heaved herself to her feet and dropped the phone back into her bag. 'Oh, that wasn't there to record us, that was so I could see if Mikey sent me a text 'cos we all have our phones on silent,' she explained.

'But, I thought…'

'Don't worry, it's all recorded 'cos I've a body cam…here! Tasheka indicated the large brooch holding her jacket together. 'I got this so people wouldn't get nervous when I interviewed them an' I think it worked, don't you?'

Vivienne looked closely at the brooch in horror and realised that it was indeed a small camera around which Tasheka had artfully arranged some beads.

She forced a weak smile and gulped. 'I would never have guessed it was a camera,' she mumbled, wondering how on earth she was going to persuade Tasheka to not upload the interview. Tasheka pulled the door open and Vivienne stepped out into the hall to herself face-to-face with Cody.

Charlotte Worthington

Charlotte spent Sunday morning pampering herself and when she was showered, moisturised and scented, she opened a white bag from Lovely Lingerie in Leeds and pulled out an exquisite, flimsy lace teddy which she had bought only yesterday. She hadn't seen Adam since Wednesday and they had not been in touch. Charlotte felt some relief about that, but she was also very anxious to know what he was thinking. She wanted confirmation that Beatrice had believed Adam when he had told her that they were not having an affair, and she also needed Adam to confirm that they actually *were*, so she could be sure he wouldn't speak to Gerald.

Charlotte sighed. Things had got so complicated since he bought that damned villa – she'd only wanted a bit of fun, and they could have continued enjoying each other after her wedding, but now, he had ruined her plans. She slipped on the new teddy on and decided she would have to be super-nice to him today and talk a lot about their assumed future together in Spain. Maybe she should ask him how he planned to finance their daily life; perhaps she had misjudged him and he actually did have a lot of money stashed away – the villa couldn't have been cheap. He might have been left a fortune in his father's will, and it was no secret that Charles Lewis had lived exceedingly well. Charlotte shook her head. But whatever money Adam had, it would not compare to a title and Claro Court. No, there was absolutely no doubt in her mind that she *would* marry Gerald, but today, she would have to charm Adam and convince him that she would elope with him. She stepped into a black short-sleeved dress, zipped it up and teamed it with a pair of sandals before setting off for the pavilion.

Charlotte was annoyed to see that the door was already open when she reached their love nest, as she wanted to be ready, and wearing only the teddy when he arrived. But then she had an idea. 'Adam? Close your eyes. I've got a surprise for you.' she sang as her hand reached around to her back and pulled the zipper halfway down. However, there was no response and it suddenly occurred to her that taking off her dress outside the pavilion might not be a good idea if he wasn't there.

She stepped inside. 'Adam?' she called again as she glanced around the room. The pavilion had been rebuilt as a larger building than the previous one, and instead of just one large room, it was now comprised of a decent sized kitchen, two toilets and a further room at the back which was currently used as storage for garden furniture. The main room at the front, referred to as 'the salon', was furnished with sofas and easy chairs with coffee tables interspersed between them. Charlotte's gaze went straight to a particular large and squashy sofa – their favourite place for lovemaking – and was horrified to see Beatrice sitting there.

Charlotte, stunned and shocked, was quite incapable of doing anything, whilst Beatrice looked her up and down with disdain. Then, as if things couldn't have got any worse, her partly unzipped dress slid from one shoulder revealing a barely-there strap and the lacy edge of her suggestively erotic underwear.

For a while neither woman spoke and then Beatrice's look of dislike turned into a sneer.

'Well, well, well…' she snarled, 'is this what you call pre-wedding jitters?'

'I…I …'

'What's the matter? Lost for words? Or are you desperately trying to think of a rational explanation for why you have turned up here half-undressed, expecting to see my son? You're a thorough disgrace to your family. You have beguiled Adam with promises of a life together in Spain – so much so, that he has used his entire inheritance to buy a villa for you.'

'No, I didn't ask him to buy the villa,' protested Charlotte.

'Not outright, no! But I'll bet that you used every trick in the book to suggest it. Well, let me tell you something else – he can't afford it unless I put up some money. He told me he was buying it for us, him and me – and I believed him. I would have made the transfer last Thursday but, as you know, I overheard you laughing about him with your friend, and mocking him. So, I decided to delay the transfer of funds until after you were safely married.' Beatrice's eyes narrowed as she continued to speak. 'I had to lie to him, *lie* to my son, about the account needing notice; I assumed you wouldn't elope if you had nowhere to go to.'

'It was entirely his idea, I didn't know he was even thinking about buying a villa.' Charlotte tried to explain and then took a step back as Beatrice stood up and, right at that moment, she was reminded of the Wicked Witch of the West.

'He still believes you're eloping with him but— hah! You have absolutely no intention of doing so, he's just your bit on the side, a plaything. How shall I put it? When Gerald's away, Charlotte will play,' Beatrice taunted her.

Charlotte felt a teeny bit scared, the woman was getting out of control, almost threatening, so she took another step back as Beatrice moved forward.

'I didn't realise he'd taken our little joke that seriously—' Charlotte began.

'Joke!' thundered Beatrice, 'Adam is just a *joke* to you?'

'I didn't mean Adam, I meant—'

'I know what you meant, but he *is* a joke to you, he is disposable – and as you said, if I remember rightly: "He'll get over it." After all, following your wedding, aren't you going to replace him with someone else – an actor?'

Charlotte inhaled sharply. What the hell was she going to do? She had to stand her ground and fight fire with fire! Let Beatrice know she was no pushover. She clenched her fists, steeled herself and lifted her chin in defiance. 'Apart from your financial stake in the villa, all this has nothing to do with you! My relationship with Adam is private – it's between him and me, so why don't you mind your own business!' she yelled at Beatrice, who looked surprised at the outburst.

Having said her piece, Charlotte turned and stomped outside, where she got as far as the fountain before her arm was roughly pulled back and she spun around.

'You're nothing more than a cheap little harlot!' Beatrice told her steadily, their faces inches apart. 'When I tell your parents *and* Sir Gerald about your goings-on, we'll see if it remains private. Let's put your friend's loyalty to the test. Will she lie for you, or tell the truth?'

Charlotte stared into Beatrice's eyes and knew she meant every word.

Adam Lewis

After spending the morning working with Vinnie, Adam had eventually stretched and suggested that they had a break.

'I don't know about you, Vinnie, but I could do with some fresh air.'

'Good idea, I'm going to take a mooch around, so I'll just see you back here later.'

Adam had hurried off to his rendezvous with Charlotte, although if he was honest, he wasn't that excited about it. He was still annoyed with her for blabbing to her friend, Pen, given the trouble it had caused with his mother. As he reached the top of the main staircase, he pulled up short as the two men that he had hoped he would never see again walked past the bottom of the stairs – two of Mr Lord's nasty debt collectors. What in God's name were they doing here? How the hell had they found him? His heart thumped as he watched them walk away around the back of the stairs. Adam certainly wasn't in the mood for sex now, he had to keep out of their way.

It was about ten past two when Charlotte sent Adam a text: *I'm in my apartment, we need to talk.*

Adam replied that he was on his way.

The minute he walked in, Charlotte threw herself at him and burst into tears.

'Oh God, Adam! Everything is ruined…she knows…she's going to tell everyone,' she sobbed. Adam led her to a sofa and, between hiccups and sobs, Charlotte told him about her encounter with Beatrice.

'What are we going to do?' she wailed.

'Right now, nothing at all,' Adam said sternly. 'My mother is here on official council business and she'll not want to ruin her day in the limelight. I'll speak to her tonight and see if we can sort it out and come to some arrangement.'

'As if she'll be that reasonable!' retorted Charlotte.

Adam ignored the remark. 'What do you think Gerald will say if you confess to a minor indiscretion before the wedding?' he asked gently.

'I'm not doing that!' Charlotte snapped. 'If she won't listen to you, then I shall deny everything and tell everyone that she's telling lies. It'll be her word against mine!'

'I don't think it will be that simple, Charlotte. Have you forgotten that Pen and I are also involved? Adam pointed out.

'Of course I haven't forgotten, but you will deny it, obviously, and Pen will say she knows nothing.'

'I don't understand why you want to deny our affair at all, it's the perfect excuse to call off the wedding, and there is something else…' Adam paused and Charlotte frowned.

'What?' she asked hesitantly.

'We can't wait until Saturday, we've got to go to Spain as soon as possible.'

'Why?'

'When I was in London, I…err…well, something happened and now there are two men after me.'

'What happened?'

'That doesn't really matter, the point is they are here now, at the Hall, I saw them downstairs, so we've got to get to Spain, and quickly.'

'But…I can't just pack up and leave tomorrow or the next day,' Charlotte protested.

'Why not? It won't matter whether we elope on Monday, Tuesday or Saturday, will it?'

Charlotte squirmed uncomfortably. 'I – I don't know, it's all a bit sudden, and anyway, you don't own the villa yet. Remember what I told you about your mother lying to you, she *could* have transferred the money, but decided to delay it until after I was "safely married."' Charlotte did air quotes with her fingers.

'I've made other arrangements and the keys are waiting for us. Charlotte, you *are* coming with me, aren't you? You don't sound at all excited, have you changed your mind?'

Charlotte swallowed nervously and stared at Adam with wide open eyes. 'Um…' she muttered.

'You have, haven't you? You've changed your mind. Mother was right!' Adam narrowed his eyes with suspicion.

'No!' Charlotte shouted. 'No! I haven't changed my mind, but I'm scared, Adam, not only is it a big decision, but now you tell me there are people after you – will they hurt us if they find us?'

'They won't find us, they won't have a clue that we've gone to Spain. Now, I need to book flights, I need your passport.'

'I haven't got it.'

'What?'

'I mean I have a passport, but it's in the safe. I don't know the code so I'll have to ask my father, obviously he would have given it to me by Saturday, so I'll just have to tell him that I'm getting organised early.'

Adam sighed. 'Ok, well text me when you have it and we'll arrange to meet up, but for God's sake do it tomorrow. I should get back to work, but in the meantime, say absolutely nothing about going to the pavilion. Let's just say that we had arranged to meet here to discuss business because you wanted to talk about a website for Claro Court, ok?'

Charlotte nodded fervently and gave a weak smile. Adam was not reassured, and now had serious misgivings about Charlotte. There was something she wasn't telling him, and it was since she had seen his mother.

11

Terry Sharp
Terry was getting fed up with all the wedding malarkey – he just wanted to find and deal with Adam Lewis and then get the hell out of this place, go back to London where he felt at home. Having got rid of Vivienne earlier, he and Ray had gone walkabout in the hope of finding the offices, and in the end, he'd had to ask a passing waitress where to go. The young girl had taken one look at Ray and nervously pointed up the big staircase. As they went up, they had passed a bloke coming down and Terry had smiled affably, but confidently carried on upwards. They had found a door marked Private, opened it and found the offices, all of which were empty. By now Terry was seriously considering plan B, which was to find Adam's mother and deal with her – Adam would get the message.

They retraced their steps along the carpeted corridor when suddenly a door on Terry's left opened, and Vivienne appeared.

'Hey doll, enjoying yourself?' Terry managed to smile at Vivienne and nodded an acknowledgement to the big dark-skinned woman behind her.

'Oh sweetheart!' Vivienne gushed. 'Just come and look at the bridal suite.' She grabbed his arm and pulled him back through the door as the other woman took a hasty step sideways. Terry allowed himself to be pulled into the room and tried to look interested. Vivienne chattered about how romantic the room was and playfully talked about enjoying the four-poster, when Ray's deep voice broke into the conversation.

'Can I give 'er a cuddle, Tel?' Ray pointed at the dark woman, his eyes glued to her large bosom.

The woman frowned at him. 'Hey!' she called and put her hands on her ample hips, 'Why're you askin' him?'

''Cos if 'e says I can, then I will,' was the short reply.

'I don' think so. If you wan' a cuddle from me, then you gotta ask *me*,' the woman said defiantly. Ray looked unsure as to what to do or say next, so he looked at Terry for guidance.

'Who's this?' Terry asked Vivienne gruffly.

'This is Tasheka, she very kindly brought me up to show me the bridal suite, isn't that right?' Vivienne replied a little too brightly and nodded at the woman, but Terry frowned, he wasn't wholly convinced.

'So, can I give 'er a cuddle?'

'Let me stop you right there.' Tasheka held up her hand, palm forward. 'Number one, you don' go askin' anyone else about cuddlin' me, and number two, the answer's No!' and with a quick flick of her wrist, the hand returned to her hip.

Ray wasn't used to women saying 'No', so he ignored it. He took a step forward and went to grab Tasheka. Unfortunately, he wasn't very quick and his eyes were still focused on her large breasts as they rose and fell with each breath. He never saw the handbag as it swung through the air, so that when the blow came, he was knocked off balance. He grabbed wildly and his hands found the fitted drapes on the four-poster bed. As Sid Dawkins said later, he *had* used super-strong screws for the heavy metal curtain pole, but even they had limits. The newly attached pole was wrenched from the bed frame and, as Ray fell forwards onto the bed, there was a sickening thud as it made contact with his head.

There was a stunned silence. 'I don't think you should've done that,' Vivienne said nervously as they stared at the huge man sprawled on the side of the bed, his hand slowly rubbing his head.

'He's jus' lucky that I didn't have my extra-large bag or he wouldn't be movin' at all,' replied Tasheka crossly.

Ray growled and then roared as he hauled himself to his feet. He stood, legs apart, his huge hands clenching and unclenching, his face an ugly grimace not dissimilar to the Incredible Hulk. Then his eyes vaguely focused on Tasheka.

Terry immediately realised they were in trouble, he rarely saw Ray out of control with rage, but he recognised the signs and knew the girls were in danger. The problem was that Ray stood between them and the door. 'Get in the bathroom!' he ordered. 'Now!'

Vivienne and Tasheka didn't need telling twice, and they ran inside the en suite, slammed the door shut and locked it. Ray charged after them like an angry bull and threw himself at the door. It splintered and cracked, but stayed in place.

'Ray!' thundered Terry, '*Stop!*'

Ray turned around, breathing heavily, his eyes glazed with rage.

'Come on, away from the door,' Terry commanded. 'We have other work to do – cuddles come later.'

Ray gave a backward glance to the damaged door and then walked begrudgingly toward his brother. 'Sorry Tel, I just thought she would be nice,' he grumbled, his rage visibly melting away.

'Come on, let's get out of here.' Terry put his hand on his brother's shoulder and gently pushed him towards the bedroom door.

They didn't speak as they walked down the stairs and through the entrance hall. Terry heard music coming from the ballroom and he saw that the woman who had signed them in earlier was in the doorway watching something going on. *Probably the damned fashion show*, he thought. She turned round as they walked past and Terry smiled pleasantly as he gently guided his brother outside into the fresh air.

'What now, Tel?' asked Ray in a slightly subdued voice.

'We get on with what we came to do. If we can't find him – we do the next best thing.'

Sarah Kirkwood

Sarah had been enjoying the wedding fair until *that woman* had turned up. Half an hour or so ago, Fran and Michelle had arrived and they all agreed that they had enjoyed their dinner together the previous night. Sarah had done a lot of thinking about the possibility that Trissie *might* have caused the damage to Cliff's car and that she *might* also be responsible for killing her father. In fact, the more she thought about it, the more feasible the idea became. When she had looked at that photograph and saw the damage to the car, she had been shocked and then surprised to learn that Cliff had accepted that something had fallen onto it. Well it didn't look like that to her.

Her mother and Fran were engrossed in a floristry magazine whilst she and Michelle were chatting about weddings in general, and then *she* had turned up. Of course, when Cllr Lewis had first approached the table, Sarah hadn't known who she was, but when Mum and Fran looked up and had gasped in surprise, it then became apparent that Cllr Beatrice Lewis was indeed Trissie Foxton. Initially, the woman had smiled and asked if Mum and Fran had kept in touch all these years. They told her that they had only met again recently and they were looking forward to a proper catch-up and why didn't Trissie join them. Lucy mentioned that Cliff would be so pleased to see her as he had been trying to track her down, and Sarah had quickly added that Cliff had found his original, beloved MG here in Ashdale and was considering buying it back. At this news, the woman had gone as white as a sheet. And then Sarah had known that *that woman* had killed her father. She had guilt written all over her face.

Lucy introduced Sarah as Sam's daughter, and 'Trissie' changed from being politely pleasant to downright rude. She told them bluntly that she had no wish to meet Cliff again, and that she must get on as she had a photo shoot at a quarter to two at the pavilion, before striding away.

They had all been rather stunned. Cliff had joined them and told them what had happened earlier. He was embarrassed about how he had first greeted Beatrice and admitted he could have been more subtle. However, Sarah knew exactly why Cllr Lewis had behaved in that way, she was scared her nasty little secret would be discovered.

Fran and Michelle eventually took their seats in readiness for the fashion show and Cliff wandered over to where Lydia stood at the next table. Sarah ordered her thoughts: Number one, Trissie Foxton had just had a termination. Sarah had researched online and knew that in the seventies, women generally had a general anaesthetic for abortions, so really she should not have been driving. Number two, because she had prematurely discharged herself, she may have been drowsy, and it was perfectly possible that she could have veered off the road, her car mounting the pavement. Number three, the damage to Cliff's car was on the passenger side which fitted with the injuries to her father's left side. Number four, she said she'd no idea what caused the damage. But she would say that if she knew exactly what she'd done and was scared to admit it. Number five, the road where her father died was the road Trissie would have been on after leaving the clinic, and finally, number six, the car was never traced because Cliff had unwittingly taken it abroad. Sarah wondered whether she should talk to her mother about her thoughts, but Lucy was one of those people who said things like, 'What's done is done.' and 'You can't put the clock back.' Well, that attitude was all fine and dandy, but somebody killed her father and got away with it and, right at this moment, all the evidence pointed to Cllr Beatrice Lewis, formerly Trissie Foxton, and she looked as guilty as hell to Sarah.

'Mum, do you think it's feasible that Trissie knocked Dad down?' Sarah asked quietly, and before Lucy could respond, she continued, 'Hang on! Let me explain.' Sarah calmly and quietly told her mother of her suspicions.

'Sarah, that's a serious allegation to make. I can see how you might have come to that conclusion but...well, you've no proof, it's just speculation and I can't believe that Trissie would do such a thing – she was my flatmate after all.'

'Between you and Cliff, you have the full story, why don't we go to the police and let them look into it?'

'Because it's just a...an idea. If we're wrong, it will cause no end of trouble.'

'... and if we're right, she'll be convicted and Dad will be avenged.'

'It won't bring him back, Sarah,' whispered Lucy, aware that their voices had risen a little. 'We can't discuss it here, wait until we get home. We can talk freely there.'

'We can do that, but in the meantime, I want to talk to her. You were delighted when you met up with Cliff and Fran again, and you assumed she would be pleased to see you all as well, but she wasn't and I want to know why. You saw her face when I told her Cliff was buying his old MG, she was shocked – and not in a good way. You introduced me to her and she was horrified, it's not the usual response I get from people at a first meeting. I think she's worried that Cliff will somehow find out what really happened to his MG, so she decided to just ignore everyone. Well, she damn well can't!' Sarah had got angrier as she spoke.

'Sarah, please...' Lucy began.

'I haven't seen her come back from the pavilion, so I'm going to take a walk down there and see what she has to say.' Sarah didn't wait for her mother to reply as she edged her way around the table and out through the French doors.

It was quite pleasant to get some fresh air and the sun had come out, but Sarah was in no mood to enjoy it. *Just you try and pull the wool over my eyes, Trissie Foxton – that was my father you knocked down and left to die.*

Sheila Houseman

Sheila had had a lovely day so far – they had been very busy and had taken deposits for several wedding cakes, with appointments made for further detailed discussions. Saffron, who was modelling in the fashion show, had even gone undercover to the Blenkhorn's stand and brought back a sample of their wedding cake for Sheila and Derek to taste. In Sheila's honest and unbiased opinion, she was delighted to be able to say it was not as good as her Derek's. The only tiny niggle was when Beatrice Lewis had come to their stand during her majestic tour of the wedding fair. There had been a smugness about her as though she knew something they didn't. When Derek told Sheila that he didn't think Adam had told Beatrice about the photo of the allergy sign, Sheila had to agree.

'Either that, or she's already put in her complaint to the Bakers' Association and knows that we're doomed,' he added.

'Surely not,' replied Sheila. 'But why do you think Adam hasn't told her?'

'He only found out himself yesterday evening, perhaps he hasn't had time to tell her. The thing is, I'm thinking of speaking to her myself and finding out what's going on.'

'Oh Derek, I'm not sure that's wise, it might make things worse.'

'Look love, we've got to sort this out. Either she's taking matters further or she isn't. I don't like dealing with her son, it's not something I think she would do – she's the type of person who would confront situations herself. I believe that a face-to-face chat would be better.'

Sheila looked at Derek doubtfully, a face-to-face sounded a good idea in theory but in practice…?'

'So, what are you planning?' she asked, somehow dreading the answer.

'She went off to have her photo taken and she hasn't come back yet. The fashion show has just started so it'll be quiet on the stand for a while. I'll have a walk in the direction of the pavilion and perhaps meet her on her way back. We can just have a little word in private.'

'Derek, please don't lose your temper and start an argument. Try to remain calm,' Sheila pleaded.

'Well, I'll show her the photo and see how she reacts to that. But I'm going to be firm with her, I can say that for definite. See you later.' Derek tucked the printed photo into his trouser pocket, squared his shoulders, and walked determinedly through the open French windows. Sheila chewed her lip uncertainly, she had a bad feeling about this.

Cliff Walker

Cliff had stayed in *The Sandringham Suite* drinking his coffee and listening to his interview recordings. He mulled over Lydia's well-meaning words and, yes, he could see that he had startled Trissie, and, with hindsight, he could have been a little more subtle – however that did not excuse her hostility. He had received a warmer welcome from Lucy last Wednesday and he hadn't had a relationship with her, although if Sam hadn't asked Lucy out all those years ago, then maybe he would have done. Sweet, kind Lucy, if he hadn't married Sandra, perhaps he would not have got involved with Trissie then he and Lucy could have…anyway, he *had* married Sandra. It was so tragic what had happened to Sam, he had been a great guy and they had never found the driver that had knocked him down and left him to die. Then Lucy had found out that she was pregnant. *I bet* she *didn't consider having an abortion,* thought Cliff sourly. It was so damned unfair. Lucy had brought up her daughter, alone, and made a very good job of it from what Cliff could see. Trissie, on the other hand, had got rid of their baby without a second thought. He would have loved that child and been a good father, if only she had told him. What had happened to the girl he once loved? Maybe he should find out a bit more about Trissie and her life. She had obviously married – what was Mr Lewis like? Thinking about Lydia's words, he decided he would go and talk to Elsa, ask her about Cllr Beatrice Lewis – more info for his column, that sort of thing. Having made his decision, he stood up and walked into the entrance hall where he waited until Elsa had finished registering a young, loved-up couple before he spoke.

'Elsa, I wonder if I might prevail upon you—'

'You'll never guess who I've signed in this morning – Mr and Mrs Cody King!' Elsa gasped, she was flushed with excitement.

'Have you?' exclaimed Cliff, glancing towards the ballroom.

'Yes, she was all dolled up and he smiled at me, he is much nicer in person,' Elsa chattered.

'Oh well, I'd best go and find them in a bit,' Cliff said, 'but look, I wondered if you could tell me a little about Cllr Lewis, for my column.'

'Seems to me that you already know her,' replied Elsa.

'I do, but that was about forty years ago. I meant a little more recent stuff about her background, you know, how she came to be a councillor, what she does, that sort of thing.'

'Well...' Elsa began, and Cliff switched on his voice recorder.

A little while later, he ventured into the ballroom and headed straight to the Flower Power table where he then learned from Lucy and Fran, that Trissie had not been pleased to see them either.

'Didn't surprise me,' Sarah muttered grumpily. 'You would think that she would be pleased to see her friends from the past, but she had a poker face and looked at me as though I was something she'd just walked in,' Sarah told him.

'She said she had to go and left,' added Fran.

Cliff noticed Michelle's glum face. 'Anyway, enough of that, we'll talk about her later, we're here on much happier business,' he said brightly. 'How are we getting on with your wedding preparations, Michelle?'

Michelle immediately smiled. 'We've definitely decided on Houseman's Bakery for the cake, it's absolutely gorgeous, you should try a piece. Clearly the flowers will be by Flower Power and I've an appointment with Lexie Worthington at three o'clock for a personal tour of Ashdale Hall and to see what they can offer. If you're available then, will you come with us?'

'Yes, of course, I can't see that I'll have much to do by then.'

'I think we should get some seats for the fashion show before the best ones are taken,' suggested Fran.

'Ok, I'll catch up with you ladies later, I'm just going for a quick chat with Lydia to see how the day has been for them.'

Cliff walked the few steps to the stand next door and found Zoe and Lydia chatting.

'Hello ladies, how has the day been for you?'

'Fantastic,' replied Zoe, 'we've made loads of appointments and not just from the brides, their mothers and bridesmaids have made bookings for treatments, and so on. I think the day has been a resounding success. I hope Lexie has done well for the Hall.'

'I'm seeing her later as Michelle has an appointment, I think she's considering the Hall for her own wedding,' Cliff said chattily. They talked for a few more minutes and then the lights were turned off and music began. It was around ten minutes later when Cliff felt his phone vibrating in his pocket so he left the ballroom, smiling at Elsa who now stood in the doorway and made his way to the bar.

'Cliff Walker,' he said crisply as he answered.

'Cliff, it's Lexie. Look, I've just had a call from Eric – the photographer. He's got stuck in traffic behind an accident and can't get here. I asked Cllr Lewis to go to the pavilion for a photo opportunity about thirty minutes ago and I'm not sure if she's still there or has returned.'

'I've just left the ballroom and I didn't see her in there, so I don't think she's come back,' replied Cliff.

'I'm with a potential client, would you be an angel and go find her, please? If she's still there, can you take a photo on your phone? If not, then I'll have to find her and apologise.'

'Well, I suppose—' Cliff began reluctantly.

'Thank you so much,' Lexie cut in, and ended the call.

Cliff sighed, the last thing he wanted to do was to go and find Trissie, but then again, he knew he had to talk to her at some point and at least the pavilion would be private. He slipped quietly back through the ballroom and out of the French windows, across the terrace and through the gates. As he walked, he thought about Michelle planning her wedding; he was so happy to be able to help finance it and he was looking forward to walking her down the aisle. If only he could have been a father. The thought that Trissie's child might not have been his reared its head again, and Cliff sighed. Maybe fate had given him an opportunity now, to seek some answers. He would try and be rational, but dammit he was entitled to an explanation and an explanation he would bloody well demand! He strode through the copse and the pavilion came into view.

Lydia Buckley

When Cliff left to take his call, it reminded Lydia to check her phone – there were two messages. The first from Greg was worrying: *Sharps at the Hall. Keep calm police there too. On my way. Keep in touch x*

Lydia glanced around the room, but as it was in semi-darkness, she couldn't really make out individual people. The second text was from Tasheka and she had to read it twice because the first time it made no sense: *Stuck in bridal suite bathroom. Can you come asap?* Really? What the heck was Tasheka doing in the bridal suite in the first place, never mind stuck in the en suite? Lydia silently made her way to the door of the ballroom and stopped in her tracks as she came face-to-face with Vinnie!

Vinnie grinned at her and followed her into the entrance hall.

'What are *you* doing here?' she asked incredulously.

'I came downstairs and heard our song playing, so I came to have a look and sort of just stayed watching the fashion show.'

'*Our* song?'

'Barry White, *Just the Way You Are*. We had our first dance to that at our wedding.'

'You still remember that? It was twenty-five years ago, more or less.'

'It was a perfect song and…well…it just brought back memories.'

Lydia felt that Vinnie was getting maudlin, so she changed the subject. 'Actually, I meant what are you doing here, in Ashdale?'

'Working with the new website guy, we're just up for the weekend.'

'We?'

'Yes, Vivienne won't let me come to Ashdale on my own in case I meet you,' he told her candidly.

Lydia looked back into the ballroom, 'Where is she?'

'Oh, she hasn't come here. I think she was going into Harrogate. Have you got time for a coffee or a drink?'

'Actually, I'm going to release someone from the bridal suite, apparently they're stuck in the bathroom. I don't suppose you would come with me in case I need some extra strength?'

Vinnie laughed. 'Well, that's the best excuse I've ever heard for refusing a drink,' he chuckled.

Lydia pulled a face at him. 'Are you going to help me or not?'

'Come on, it beats watching a parade of wedding dresses.'

They set off up the stairs. 'So, how are things with you? Still with Greg?' Vinnie asked casually.

'Yes, still with Greg. How are things with you and Vivienne?'

'Just the same,' Vinnie replied lightly, 'She wants a vow renewal now, though God knows why.'

'And you don't?'

Vinnie shook his head. 'I do not!' he replied fervently. 'If we could have a vow Undo-All, now that would be interesting.'

'What on earth has happened here?' gasped Lydia as they entered the bridal suite. The bed drapes lay in a tangled heap on the floor and a solid looking curtain pole was balanced half on and half off the bed. There were muffled noises coming from the en suite and when Vinnie and Lydia looked properly, they could see that the door was at a strange angle and the door handle was askew.

'Blimey, it looks as though it has been hit with a battering ram.' Vinnie tried to straighten the door by pulling at the door handle, but it came away in his hand, so he put it on the bed with the curtain pole. 'We'll have to break the door down to open it,' he said. 'Maybe if we push and she pulls?'

'Ok, let's give it a go,' agreed Lydia, and she banged on the door. 'Tasheka! You pull and we'll push, ok? Here we go, in three – one, two, three!'

As Vinnie put his weight behind the door and pushed hard, the door began to splinter around the latch and eventually, with an almighty crack, it just gave way. Vinnie shot forward straight into Tasheka's chest and they both ended up on the floor.

'You all right, doll?' a voice said from behind Lydia. She spun round and caught her breath as a Cody King lookalike with a hugely muscled companion stood in the doorway.

Oh God! The Sharps! Lydia instantly recognised them from Greg's description and guessed that the man who had spoken was Terry. But he was looking beyond Lydia into the en suite and when she turned back to see who he was talking to, she was surprised to see Vivienne smiling hesitantly at the newcomers. Terry Sharp stepped over the pile of bed drapes and held his hand out to Vivienne, who looked unsure as to what to do.

'Come on, doll – we have to leave now.' Terry spoke again his hand outstretched.

Vivienne came out of the bathroom slowly as Vinnie rolled off Tasheka. He blinked as he noticed Vivienne,

'What are *you* doing here and where are you going?' he demanded.

'Oi! That's my wife you're talking to and what's it got to do wiv you where she goes?' Terry said gruffly.

'*Your* wife?' exclaimed Vinnie. 'I think you'll find she's *my* wife,' he added as he stood up and squared his shoulders. In the meantime, Tasheka had pulled herself upright and was now glaring at Terry's hulk of a brother who stood just inside the entrance to the bridal suite, effectively blocking off the way out. The big man grinned salaciously, his eyes glued once again to Tasheka's breasts and he took a step forward. Tasheka grasped her large shoulder bag and looked ready to swipe him with it. Lydia felt suddenly very worried as it seemed that neither Vivienne nor Tasheka had any idea who the men really were.

'Can someone explain what is going on?' Lydia said loudly.

'That great oaf wants to cuddle me an' I told him that ain't gonna happen. So, when he asks Mr King here for permission, I said that no one is gonna cuddle me unless *I* say so.'

'Who wants to cuddle my wife?' Mikey demanded as he entered the room.

'He does!' replied Tasheka pointing at Ray. Now, in his youth, Mikey had always been able to take care of himself not that he was a fighter, but he could stand his ground. However, as he looked up at the man mountain stood next to him, he realised he was at a distinct disadvantage. Ray, clearly unsure of what was expected, looked at Terry for the next instruction, and everyone else followed his example.

'Right!' said Terry after a few moments' pause. 'This is how it is. I decided to come here as I'm planning a surprise for my wife. This lady here—' Terry jerked a thumb in Vivienne's direction, '—offered to stand in as my wife 'cos it looked a bit weird me coming here with my minder, see?'

Tasheka rounded on Vivienne. 'Now wait a minute – you're not his real wife? You're *not* Mrs Cody King?'

'Well, like he says, I'm just doing him a favour. He asked me to pretend to be his wife,' Vivienne replied snippily.

'Why did you agree to an interview then?' stormed Tasheka.

'You did an *interview*?' asked Terry.

'Well, she asked so…'

'What the hell for?' Terry yelled, 'we were supposed to keep a low profile.'

'Don't you shout at my wife, like that!' retorted Vinnie, stepping up to Terry.

'I've jus' wasted my time wit' you, I should've known when you was name-dropping like you did, that you was jus' making it all up.' Tasheka gesticulated with an orange-tipped finger.

'I gave you what you wanted, didn't I? An exclusive story!' Vivienne had her hands on her hips and sneered at Tasheka.

'An exclusive story? About *what*?' demanded Vinnie.

'Our vow renewal that we're planning,' replied Vivienne.

'What vow renewal?'

'We discussed it on Friday night.'

'I didn't agree to it though.'

'You didn't say "No" either!'

'So, is that why you wanted to come here?'

'That, and because you're always sneaking around with your ex-wife!'

'I am *not* sneaking around with my ex-wife!'

'Well, you're with her now!'

All eyes turned to Lydia.

'*She's* his ex-wife?' Terry asked.

'She is!' confirmed Vivienne, triumphantly.

'But we're not *together*!' protested Vinnie.

'Well, you were when we came in,' Terry pointed out, and Vivienne gasped in horror.

'We came into the room at the same time but we...' Vinnie tried to explain.

'So, you *did* meet up with her here!' Vivienne rounded on Vinnie furiously.

'It wasn't pre-planned, we only met just now and I came up here to help with the bathroom door,' Vinnie explained. 'Anyway, that's not the point! How the hell did you come to be locked in the bathroom in the first place? And why is this bedroom wrecked?'

'I wanna give her a cuddle!' roared Ray.

'You jus' take one more step towards me an' I'll whack you again!'

'Again? You hit him before?' asked Mikey, eyeing the big man carefully.

'I sure did an' he fell over, grabbed those curtains an' then the pole fell off an' hit him on the head.' Vinnie, Mikey and Lydia winced. 'I thought tha' might teach him a lesson, but I guess not.'

'I think it's time we left here,' Terry said, moving towards the door.

Out of the corner of her eye, Lydia saw Ray shift unsteadily, and she turned her head as he swayed and shook his head.

'I don't think he'll be going anywhere,' she told Terry, who turned and looked at her in surprise,

'And why not, darlin'?' he smirked.

'Because I think your minder is about to pass out.'

No sooner had the words left Lydia's mouth then there was a loud, dull thud as Ray crashed to the floor.

'Now what?' ventured Mikey after a slight pause.

As all eyes turned to Ray, Lydia knew she had to get Greg and the police here fast, but without causing alarm. Her brain worked furiously, then she came up with an idea. 'We need some first aid and assistance, I think he has concussion. I'll ring Gary in maintenance,' bluffed Lydia as she got out her phone and pressed Greg's number on her contact list.

'Hi Gary, it's Lydia,' she said when Greg answered.

'Lydia?'

'We have a bit of a problem in the bridal suite and I'm here with two VIP guests, Mr Cody King and his wife. Unfortunately, Mr King's minder has had a nasty bang on the head and has collapsed, I think he may have concussion, so we'll need some first aid.'

'Lydia, are you with the Sharp brothers?'

'Yes, that's right. The door to the en suite is damaged as well, so you might need to bring some help.'

'Are you ok?'

'Yes. Now, Mr King would like to leave as soon as possible and I'm concerned about his minder, so you might like to hurry.'

'Got it! We're on our way.'

Lydia hadn't dared look in Terry's direction throughout her conversation with Greg, but once she ended the call, she put a smile on her face and said, 'He'll be right up. Does anyone know if we should do anything with him in the meantime?' Lydia nodded her head in Ray's direction, but nobody suggested anything.

Terry looked at Lydia with suspicion. 'Who've you just called?' he asked as his eyes narrowed.

'Gary in maintenance. You heard what I said.'

'So, you work here, do you?'

'No, she doesn't!' Vivienne answered with a smug grin and crossed her arms.

'Then how come you know "Gary in maintenance"?' Terry persisted.

Lydia thought quickly. 'Because I came here yesterday to help Lexie Worthington set up and Gary was here as well. He told me that he would be working today and I should call him if I needed anything,' she lied. *Well, it was only half a lie.* Ray groaned. *For God's sake, hurry up Greg!*

The bridal suite door opened and Greg appeared. He looked surprised to see so many people in the bedroom. 'It's ok!' he called and suddenly there were police officers everywhere including DCI Will Appleton and DS Helen Oakley. Terry was grabbed, handcuffed and arrested on suspicion of the murder of Sallie Fisher and, as DS Oakley read him his rights, Terry stared at the floor defiantly, not meeting anyone's eye. After he was led away, Will spoke to the silent group.

'I am going to need statements from all of you about what happened here and who was where, including timings – No, separately please,' he added holding his hand up as Tasheka opened her mouth to speak. 'I am also sorry to have to tell you that Beatrice Lewis was found dead a few minutes ago.' There was a collective gasp. 'Please don't say any more until you have spoken to my officers.'

Everyone watched in stunned silence as Ray was strapped to a gurney and wheeled away.

Later that evening in Lydia's flat, Greg told her that Beatrice had been found with her head in the fountain. There was also an injury on the back of her head which suggested that she had been struck with a heavy object prior to being drowned, but that they were not going to release that bit of information yet. He added that Cliff had found her.

He told Lydia how the Sharp brothers had been followed to the Hall, but that the two male detectives following them had felt it would blow their cover if they went into a wedding fair and had called for assistance from the local police. By the time that had been organised and they had arrived at the Hall, they had been unable to find the Sharps, and Greg had volunteered to go in posing as a reporter. That was when he had sent the text to Lydia. The London police had enough evidence to arrest the Sharps for Sallie Fisher's murder, but they had no reason to suspect them of Beatrice's – yet.

'What the heck were you all doing in the bridal suite and why was it wrecked?' Greg asked. Lydia told him about the text from Tasheka and that the damage had something to do with the fact that she had whacked Ray Sharp with her handbag.

'She hit Ray Sharp with her handbag? What the hell does she carry in it?' Greg shook his head in amazement.

'I've no idea why Tasheka, Vivienne and the Sharps were in the bridal suite in the first place, but I'll be paying Tasheka a visit to find out. I don't suppose you've heard that Beatrice Lewis turned out to be Trissie Foxton – Cliff's ex-girlfriend?'

'Bloody hell!' exclaimed Greg. 'Really? Talk about a proper friends' reunion. How did the meeting between Cliff and Beatrice go? How dreadful that as soon as he finds her, she's murdered.'

'Actually, it didn't go well at all.'

Lydia told Greg about Beatrice's arrival at the Hall and how, apparently, she had not been overjoyed to see Fran and Lucy either.

Greg shook his head in disbelief. 'I wonder why? Cliff and Fran were chuffed to bits to see Lucy again.'

'I don't know and perhaps now we shall never know. Do the police think that the Sharp brothers had anything to do with Beatrice's murder?'

'I don't know just yet. Will says he can give me more information tomorrow when he has interviewed everyone.'

'It might have something to do with Adam Lewis – he has recently returned from London, perhaps they were after him. Then again, how would they know that Beatrice was his mother and that she would be at the pavilion at that particular time? Lexie only told me about the photo opportunity this morning. In fact, how did they even know where the pavilion was?'

'Well, Miss Marple, put your gossip ears on tomorrow and start listening,' Greg teased her.

'Ok, but if you find out more information from Will, we'll compare notes tomorrow night. I'm just glad the Sharp brothers are behind bars now, Ray Sharp is seriously scary.'

12

Adam Lewis
Adam took a mouthful of coffee and leaned back in the chair, the events of yesterday still going round and round in his mind. Adam hadn't known what to say when the DCI had told him that his mother's body had been found at the pavilion. *My mother's body – not my mother, but 'her body'*. He'd hated that word – 'body', it made his mother sound like a thing and she was…had been, definitely not a thing. She may have been standoffish and seriously lacking in any sense of humour, but she was his mother and she had been supportive of him. When he had turned up from London, unannounced, claiming distress over his father's death, she had pursed her lips, given him her magistrate's look, but had not asked probing questions. She had carried on with her life and allowed him time to settle and calm down which, after his encounter with the Sharp brothers in London, he had seriously needed to do. She had never shown him much love and affection, even as a child, but he realised now that she had always been supportive, and well…*there* for him.

This morning, the house was too quiet – silent even, and as his numbness wore off, Adam realised that he would never see or speak to Beatrice again. She was gone, passed away. When the police told him that two known criminals from London with a connection to a Mr Lord had been followed up to Ashdale, Adam had decided not to mention his dealings with the loan shark. The men had already been arrested on suspicion of the death of a prostitute and they were trying to establish if they also had a connection to Beatrice. Adam figured that the Sharps wouldn't talk to the police at all, let alone give any indication as to why they were in Ashdale, but *he* knew why they were here. How had they found him? Then an idea suddenly occurred to him – had the Sharps fitted a tracking device to his car? Now there was a possibility! He would sell his car as soon as possible and use his mother's until he left the country.

Leaving the UK – he would be able to start again, but, as Adam contemplated his coffee mug, he thought back over the last few years and his decadent lifestyle in London. He had really enjoyed his job working with the huge retail company which owned a number of high street brands. He had commanded an impressive salary and lived in a swish docklands apartment. His evenings began at expensive restaurants and ended at swanky nightclubs where he'd mixed with celebrities and minor royals. His film-star looks ensured he was never short of female company, but he was careful never to get too emotionally involved or father unwanted children. He went to the Cannes Film Festival, partied on yachts in St Tropez and Puerto Banus, and holidayed in the Caribbean, but this all came at a price, and one day he'd realised that he needed to borrow money – immediately, or suffer the embarrassment of being taken to court or face eviction.

That is when he became embroiled in Mr Lord's web of never ending debt and it didn't take long for him grasp that he would never be free. When his father died, he had left Adam 'a paltry sum'. But even so, he knew now that he should have used it to repay his debt with Mr Lord. But, at the time he had felt that, hell, life was too short, deciding instead to take the holiday he had already booked. He would work out what to do when he got back. Upon his return from Barbados, he had a visit from the Sharp brothers with their final threat that unless he paid a substantial sum of money to Mr Lord, then Ray would have to use his 'powers of persuasion' and that it would be the last thing he remembered.

Adam couldn't bear the thought that his extravagance was probably the catalyst that had set all the events in motion that had ultimately brought about his mother's demise. But then he thought about Charlotte. Everything might have been fine if Charlotte had only kept her mouth shut. His mother would have been none the wiser and probably have made the transfer of money, and he would have been looking forward to Saturday.

Suddenly, without warning, Adam felt tears welling up. He broke down and sobbed, as the tears ran down his cheeks. He hoped she hadn't suffered too much. Eventually, Adam calmed down and got his emotions under control. There was only one person who he could turn to – Hugo. Hugo had been of great assistance to his mother when his father had died, and Adam quite liked the old boy. He reached for his phone and called his uncle – he would support Adam now that his mother was dead.

Charlotte Worthington
Charlotte had taken a couple of sleeping pills last night and now she felt groggy. It was the first time she had ever been asked to provide a statement and she hoped it would be the last. She considered herself to be a confident young woman and very much in control of her life, but the events of yesterday had shaken her to the core. She had been caught completely off guard when she saw Beatrice sitting on their sofa in the pavilion, and the embarrassing fact that her dress had been seductively sliding off her shoulder had made her feel cheap. As Beatrice had sneered at her, threatening to ruin her life by telling tales to Gerald and her parents, Charlotte had envisioned herself as the laughing stock of her contemporaries, her story splashed across the tabloids for the masses to chortle about – and it was just unbearable.

She had led a charmed life so far, enjoying boarding school where she hadn't worked too hard, family holidays in Spanish villas, ponies and gymkhanas, and now her days were filled with lunches, parties and shopping trips to London with a west-end show thrown in. Her father had offered her a job working at the Hall, but Charlotte had no interest in that. Her mother had asked if she had wanted to join her charity committee and Charlotte, to her credit, had given it a go, but the rest of the committee had been boring do-gooders and they only wanted to organise the same events time and time again. They had turned down her one and only idea of staging a music festival in the grounds of the

Hall without even giving it proper consideration, so Charlotte had resigned from the committee. But, seeing how the committee ladies had deferred to her mother had given her a taste for the same status, and Sir Gerald provided that opportunity.

Sir Gerald Pemberton was the Worthingtons' nearest neighbour and Charlotte, her parents and Lexie, were frequent guests at his cocktail parties and dinners, although Lexie hadn't been at all this year. Charlotte liked the house, although it was smaller than the Hall, and Sir Gerald had been honest about looking for a society wife to host his social life in Yorkshire; someone who would not want to have any involvement in his business dealings in London – and of course, he came with a title. Whilst Sir Gerald had not actually said that she could 'enjoy' herself whilst he was away during the week, Charlotte had assumed that as long as she was discreet, he would probably turn a blind eye. After all, she would not enquire about his activities in London. However, Adam had threatened all of that with his ridiculous idea of eloping to Spain, it had been only a joke for God's sake! And then Beatrice had complicated everything even more. Charlotte was under no illusion that if Beatrice had carried out her threat to tell all and sundry, Gerald would have called off the wedding and she would have had to keep a very low profile for quite some time.

This whole mess was Adam's fault. If he had only been content with a simple affair with no strings or promises, then she wouldn't be in this predicament. Charlotte felt Adam had let her down. Where on earth had he been yesterday? Why hadn't he been at the pavilion as arranged? Why was Beatrice there? Had Adam sent her? If he had turned up, he could have confronted his mother and calmed her down instead of leaving her to deal with it!

Charlotte poured her second cup of coffee. All she had to do was keep calm and allow Adam to believe that they were still eloping – that way he would stick to their story about not going anywhere near the pavilion. However, *if* Adam told the police that she had met his mother at the pavilion, then she would say that it had been arranged and was non-confrontational – a story that was plausible. An idea formed in her mind and she smiled; she would confess to the meeting and say that her chat with Beatrice was about Adam and her concerns that he was delusional about being in love with her. Perhaps she could infer that she was a bit scared of Adam because he had threatened to tell Gerald about a non-existent affair, and that is why she'd agreed to elope with him, just to keep him amenable. *All I have to do is deny that I argued with Beatrice and suggest that Adam is lying.* The more Charlotte thought about her plan, the more she liked it. It was only a few more days until her wedding, and after that there was nothing he could do.

As Charlotte considered her idea, her phone rang and the ID told her that it was Gerald. She sighed and rolled her eyes. 'Gerald! Oh Gerald, something dreadful has happened...' Charlotte began in her best tearful voice. '...Cllr Beatrice Lewis, I think you may remember her? Well, she's been murdered... Yes, murdered...yesterday, here at the Hall... Yes, I'm fine, just really shaken up. The police were here and they interviewed me. Oh Gerald! It's just so awful... They've arrested two known criminals from London. I don't know why they were here or why they murdered Beatrice... No, I don't think we shall have to postpone the wedding. When are you coming back?... Well, will you let me know? Don't forget that we've a rehearsal and family dinner on Friday.' They chatted some more and when Charlotte finally disconnected, she exhaled a long breath. Adam was her only problem, now that Beatrice was dead.

Terry Sharp

Terry's interview at the police station was simple and repetitive, he just answered 'No comment.' to every question apart from the one to confirm his name. He had been told that Ray was spending the night under observation at the hospital but was expected to make a full recovery. He requested a solicitor and when the man turned up, Terry had explained that he and his brother had decided on a weekend away, having picked Ashdale at random and booked in at the pub. The idea of pretending to be Cody King had been a bit of a joke and it had given Vivienne a thrill and got her in to the wedding fair, but he had no idea who the dead woman was. He shrugged and remained expressionless when the solicitor had told him her name – Cllr Beatrice Lewis. When asked what he and his brother had done after leaving the women in the bathroom of the bridal suite, Terry explained that he had taken Ray outside to calm him down and they had walked around a bit. He didn't mention that they had noticed a cop car parked down by the gates at the entrance to the Hall and that Terry had therefore decided it was time to go. They needed to get Vivienne, so they could leave as the couple who had arrived and they had returned to the bridal suite.

This morning, Terry had eaten a surprisingly good breakfast, but was concerned about Ray and how he was coping without his brother. When Ray had lost it yesterday, Terry had been bloody scared at the big man's fury – he hadn't seen Ray lose control over a woman before, but he hadn't seen a woman stand up to him, never mind bash him with her handbag, Terry chuckled at the memory. She'd been one hell of a woman, fierce, strong, brave and bloody sexy as… His thoughts were interrupted as he heard the door being unlocked.

'Your solicitor's here again,' said the copper. Terry stood up and followed him without a word, bracing himself for the day ahead. He realised that they would be charged with Sallie Fisher's murder, after all it was what it was – but what about this other business, now that this Beatrice Lewis was dead?

Sheila Houseman
Sheila watched Derek as, humming, he kneaded the dough. *Humming?* Derek only hummed when he was content, but how could he be so relaxed when they were involved in a murder investigation? This was the first time Sheila had felt fearful about Derek, yes fearful. She had been so supportive of him all

through the years as he honed his bakery skills, bursting with pride as he collected awards for his magnificent cakes. Their bakery was featured in the tourist office leaflets and website and in the local bakery world, the Houseman name was recognised and respected. It was no surprised to Sheila that Derek had eventually been nominated for the British Bakery Awards in the category of Best Independent Baker – winning that would put him into the final with a chance to win British Champion Baker, elevating them to dizzy heights in the bakery industry.

The nut allergy incident had almost scuppered this opportunity, especially after the visit from Adam Lewis and his suggestion of paying compensation. Sheila had been quietly shocked at the strength of feeling Derek had shown during their meeting with Albert Wilks. She had never seen her husband so angry and although they had gone for a drink afterwards and talked it through, Sheila could see that underneath, Derek still seethed.

When Lydia had turned up with the photograph clearly showing the nut allergy sign in place, Sheila had breathed a sigh of relief and thought that it would be the end of the matter, but Derek had gone on and on about talking directly to Beatrice. She had tried to persuade him to leave it and not ruffle any feathers before the awards, but Derek had still insisted, wanting to clear the matter up completely and he had left their table during the fashion show.

Of course Sheila didn't really think Derek had murdered Beatrice, she knew him too well to think that, but then there were cases where people had surprised those who knew them best, doing something completely out of character.

The problem was that Derek hadn't liked Beatrice ever since she became a local councillor and seemed to think that she now had unfair privileges. Derek had donated cakes in the past for charity events and to the old folks' home at Christmas, and he was chairman of the Christmas Committee – he did his bit for the community. However, when Beatrice had wanted a large cake for free for her post-election party, he'd refused and there had been ill feelings ever since. There was no denying the fact that, now Beatrice had passed, Adam had no reason to pursue them for the fifty thousand pounds and he would also be unlikely to contact the British Bakers' Association to make a complaint, especially as they now had the photograph. Derek had perked up since he'd had this evidence to wave at Adam and Beatrice and didn't appear to be concerned that he was possibly a murder suspect, '...*because I didn't murder her.*' was what he'd told Sheila, and of course she believed him – he was her husband, but he *had* gone walkabout at the time of the murder.

They opened up as usual at nine o'clock to find Elsa waiting at the door. She was slightly breathless as she bustled in.

'Are you all right, Elsa?' asked Sheila with concern.

'Oh Sheila, what a to-do yesterday.' Elsa's eyes were bright with excitement. 'They've arrested those two men – the Cody King lookalike and his accomplice.'

'Have they? How do you know?'

Derek appeared at the kitchen door wiping his floury hands on a towel. 'Now Elsa,' he warned, 'this is no time for gossip.'

'This is no gossip,' announced Elsa, 'this is fact. I'm a star witness for the prosecution. I saw the police taking the Cody King man away in handcuffs...and his minder was wheeled away on a stretcher.'

'A stretcher? Why?' Sheila wanted to know.

'Well, I haven't found that out yet...but at least they have the murderers in custody. I was with the police ever such a long time because of what I witnessed – you see I was the one who signed in that chap who claimed he was Cody King. Did you see him?'

Sheila nodded her head and Elsa told them, in great detail, about Cody King, his minder and *that* woman who claimed to be his wife.

'It turns out that it wasn't Cody King at all...apparently *he* was in Manchester. The real Cody King was, getting himself arrested for being under the influence from the night before...so this chappie was a fake...and you'll never guess who the woman was!' Elsa looked fit to burst. 'She was Lydia's ex-husband's new wife!' she announced triumphantly with a smart nod of her head.

'Lydia's —?'

'—ex-husband's new wife!' Elsa finished the sentence.

'Are you one hundred per cent sure these chaps were arrested, Elsa?' Derek asked.

'I saw it with my own eyes. Anyway, I thought I would come and tell you because I knew you'd be worried, seeing as how you had a bit of an incident with Beatrice last week. I thought you might see yourself as the prime suspect...and I know you had a run-in with that Adam Lewis, for all you denied it.'

Sheila looked at Derek who just frowned, then she remembered something. 'Oh Elsa, that reminds me – Lydia came by on Saturday morning and gave us a copy of a photograph which showed that we *had* put a nut allergy sign on the taster cake. She remembered that we had a press photographer in earlier that morning and she thought that he may have a photograph which just happened to show the sign – and he did!'

'Well at least you can prove there was a sign, but it doesn't explain where it got to.'

'Under the counter! It's the only logical answer, but hopefully we won't need to retrieve it as I don't think Adam will pursue us for compensation now that Beatrice is dead.'

Too late, Sheila realised that Elsa hadn't known the reason for Adam's visit to the bakery.

Elsa narrowed her eyes. 'Compensation? Is that what he was doing here? No wonder you were upset. How much did he want? And what did Albert Wilks have to say about it?'

'Oh, it was nothing.' Sheila flapped her hands dismissively. 'Albert told us to ignore him until they went through the proper channels.'

Derek cleared his throat and cut in as Elsa opened her mouth to say something,

'Elsa, thank you for telling us. You're right, we have been worried. I...we, have not been caught up in a murder investigation before. Anyway, I must get on, I've got a cake in the oven. Sheila love, could you give me a hand in the kitchen?' he asked smiling at Elsa. Elsa took the hint, and with a sniff she left the bakery.

Sheila turned to her husband. 'Does that mean you're in the clear now?'

'It certainly looks that way, love. Let's hope it's the end of the matter.'

Derek returned to the kitchen and Sheila stared out of the shop window chewing her lip thoughtfully. She thought about last night and how Derek had told her that he believed all their troubles would be over, now that Beatrice was dead.

Sarah Kirkwood

When everyone had been told that an incident had occurred, the wedding fair had come to an abrupt end. Sarah had given her statement and told the police that the last time she had seen Beatrice was around one forty-five, immediately before she went to the pavilion for a photograph. She could honestly say that she hadn't met Cllr Lewis before the wedding fair, as she and her mother had only recently moved to Ashdale. This morning, Sarah stayed in the back room of the shop concentrating on various admin tasks and going over the notes she had made from conversations with the brides from yesterday. Her mother stayed out front dealing with their customers until Sarah became aware that Lucy was leaning against the door frame watching her,

'Mum?' Sarah looked up from her laptop. 'Whatever is the matter?'

'You know perfectly well what the matter is – I'm worried about you!'

'Oh, not this again!'

'Do you blame me for being concerned? You left our table in an angry mood to go and find Trissie at around the time the murder took place!'

'Are you telling me that you think *I* did it?' Sarah snapped. 'You're supposed to be on *my* side.'

'I wasn't aware I had to take sides at all. Sarah, please let's not argue, I'm just concerned that the police may think that you did it.'

The shop door opened and Lucy turned to welcome the customer. Sarah sighed and stood up to put the kettle on. She recalled the surprise on Beatrice Lewis's face when she'd first seen her mother and Fran, and the expression hadn't been one of delight – not like her mother's face when she first saw Cliff or Fran – no Beatrice's horrified expression had swiftly been replaced by her formal-occasion fand. However, a frown had appeared at the mention of Cliff's name and then Sarah's deliberate comment about his MG had turned Beatrice's face to a rather sickly pallor. That's when she had known for sure.

Each year on the seventh of April, Sarah went to the spot where her father had died and laid flowers. There was a straight bit of road immediately before a right-hand bend which the driver, drunk or drowsy, had been unable to negotiate. It wasn't a particularly bad bend, but a driver with slow reactions would have mounted the pavement before turning the steering wheel.

Today of course, the road had CCTV cameras, but back then there was no such thing and the police had no evidence to help them find out who had been driving. When she thought back, Sarah had realised that the route from the clinic to the girls' flat passed the exact place she went every year with her flowers. The more Sarah thought about her six reasons for believing that Trissie Foxton aka Beatrice Lewis was the driver who killed her father, the more she instinctively knew she was right.

Her mother appeared at the door again.

'I'm making a drink, do you want one of your fruit teas?' Saah asked her.

Lucy nodded. 'Yes please. This murder is all anyone can talk about, it's just awful.'

'Quite frankly, Mum, I didn't take to Trissie at all. I thought she was unfriendly and rude. Was she like that back then?'

'Sometimes, although I don't think it was intentional. It wasn't so much as *what* she said as in the *way* she said it. She wasn't a bad person, but her manner could be a bit standoffish, you know? She didn't have many friends—'.

'I'm not surprised,' interrupted Sarah.

'However, I was completely taken aback when we found out about her affair with Cliff.'

Sarah handed a steaming mug to her mother. 'I can't understand what Cliff saw in her. I like him, she doesn't seem right for him.'

'He was obviously unhappy with Sandra and she may have been a shoulder to cry on which turned into the affair. It's very sad that she was murdered, especially as we had all just found out that she was Trissie. And as for your theory about her being responsible for Sam's death, we'll never know now what really happened that night.'

'But we *do* know, Mum, really – don't we? And I for one, feel justice has been served now that Beatrice Lewis is dead.'

Cliff Walker

Yesterday, after Lexie's phone call about going to the pavilion to find Trissie, Cliff had wandered down towards the wood and carefully considered what he might say to her. It would be a difficult conversation, if she would speak to him at all, but he needed answers.

This morning, Cliff made himself a cup of tea and a slice of toast, then he sat to try and marshal the thoughts spinning around in his head. It had been a week of such mixed emotions: firstly, his joy at finding his old MG, then shock on discovering that Trissie had had a termination, happiness on finding Lucy, elation on seeing Trissie, the devastation of her dismissal of him, and finally, the distress of her death. Cliff knew he had handled their initial meeting badly, but it didn't excuse her hostility. However, none of that compared with the horror of finding her body. He was distraught that she had been taken from him as soon as he had found her.

Later, from the window of the bar, where everyone was being questioned, he'd seen a man in handcuffs being led away followed a few minutes later by another chap on a stretcher. As he drank his tea, Cliff wondered who the two men were. He could ask Greg – he seemed to be well in with the police. Somebody else he might chat to was Elsa – a woman after his own heart, who kept her eyes and ears open. He would go into Ashdale later this week to track her down. Cliff also wanted to talk to Tom Craven again and seek his advice on buying a park home, as Elsa had suggested. He might even have a little drive around the site.

However, his first priority this morning was to write his column. His recorded interviews would give the exhibitors' perspectives of the fair, and he also wanted to speak to Lexie and see if, before the incident, she'd had any positive feedback from the visiting brides. It was a shame that there were no photographs, although he could ask around. He and Lexie had assumed that Eric had been busy with his camera during the day, not realising that he hadn't been there at all.

Cliff began to write and the words flowed as he used his recordings to recapture the excitement in the voices of the exhibitors. An hour or so later, he sat back. The remains of his tea and toast had gone cold so he stood up, stretched and put the kettle on again.

Elsa had told him that Trissie was now widowed and the thought had crossed his mind that she may be amenable to an odd night out, possibly rekindling their romance, but he was still struggling to get past the abortion. If only she had told him about the baby. Cliff thumped the worktop in frustration. He would have…what? Would he really have left Sandra? How would he have done it? He'd had to return to Germany that night, otherwise he would have been in serious trouble with the army. But the next step would have been to tell Sandra. As things turned out, she left him two years later, so may be telling her about Trissie might not have been such a shock. He was almost as angry now as he had been yesterday as he walked towards the pavilion. Cliff had worked out what he was going to say to her and hoped she wouldn't simply push him away again. His army training had steeled him to deal with death, and he had seen his colleagues killed needlessly because of some despot's delusional viewpoint. But Trissie had murdered their child, seemingly because *she* had made her mind up that it was the best way forward for her. Cliff took deep breaths in an effort to come to terms with how he felt now that Beatrice was dead.

Lydia Buckley

Lydia had spent the day at Lush Lashes in Harrogate and Greg had been in the office. At last, they sat down after dinner and the conversation inevitably turned to the murder of Beatrice Lewis.

'How was Cliff when you spoke to him earlier?' Lydia asked.

'He's been working on his gossip column. Fortunately, he had gone round all the exhibitors and recorded a chat with them before the upset of the murder, so he has some material to work with.'

'Yes, I saw him doing that before Beatrice arrived, and then he asked me to introduce him to Elsa.'

'It's a shame that Eric didn't manage to attend as there are no official photos, so he is going to ask the exhibitors if they have any.'

'I could ask Vinnie, he may have taken some for marketing purposes, perhaps of the various rooms before people arrived.'

'Good idea. Cliff is a bit miffed that Eric didn't call earlier as he could easily have taken some.'

'Things may have been very different if Eric had turned up. Beatrice probably wouldn't have been killed and Cliff wouldn't have found her body.'

'But he's really concerned that the police think he might have killed Beatrice, given that he found her, and of course, their past history...'

'That would give him a possible motive for murder, albeit a weak one. Surely the police can't think that he murdered Beatrice because he was so upset about an abortion that took place forty odd years ago.'

'He's just not thinking straight, and maybe he still feels a little bit guilty about the affair or possible not leaving his wife for her, who knows?'

'Anyway, he doesn't need to worry, the Sharps have been arrested.'

'What on earth was *Vivienne* doing with the Sharp brothers?' asked Greg.

'God knows! I don't think Vinnie was impressed either and at one point, when we were in the bridal suite, I thought he was going to square up to Terry Sharp. Mikey was already frowning at Ray for staring at Tasheka's chest.'

'Flipping heck! I hope Mikey wasn't thinking of taking on Ray Sharp.'

'I wouldn't like to bet on Ray's chances if he had taken a swipe at Mikey, Tasheka would have floored him again.'

Greg laughed. 'I would have so loved to have seen that. I bet Ray has never been knocked down by a woman's handbag before – it would totally destroy his street cred if *that* ever got out.'

Just then, Greg's mobile rang. 'Hi bro...' Greg listened and smiled. 'Yes, that would be lovely. Hang on, I'll just check with Lydia, she's right here.' Greg held the phone away from his face. 'It's Tom and Amy's wedding anniversary on Thursday, so do you fancy a night out at Caribe in Harrogate? I know it's a school night, but we don't have to be late.' Lydia nodded in reply and Greg passed her assent onto Tom. They made the arrangements and then Greg ended the call.

'I'll get a card and we can pay for the dinner, is that ok?' Lydia suggested.

'Yep, no problem with that. I've been meaning to take you to that restaurant, it's had such good reviews.'

Greg's mobile rang again – it was DCI Will Appleton. 'Hi Will...' Greg frowned as he listened, and at the end of the conversation he turned to Lydia. 'They're not going to charge the Sharp brothers with Beatrice's murder, at least not yet.'

'Really? Why not?'

'Will has some doubts about whether they actually did it. There are questions he needs answers to, for example: Did they know who Beatrice was? How did they know she would be at the pavilion, and how did they know where the pavilion even was? All of which you pointed out last night.'

'Perhaps they weren't after Beatrice and it was a case of wrong place, wrong time.'

'Maybe, but from the time they were seen leaving via the entrance hall by Elsa at around two fifteen to the time you saw them return to the bridal suite at about two thirty, no one else saw them going to or from the wood.'

'That's probably because everyone was watching the fashion show.'

'Not everyone. Tasheka and Vivienne were in the en suite, you and Vinnie were heading to the bridal suite, and Cliff was in the bar and then went to the pavilion, so there may have been others who went walkabout. The point is, no one saw the Sharps anywhere. They are not being released, however, and you'll be pleased to know they've been charged with Sallie Fisher's murder and are being transferred back to London.'

'Do we know what the Sharps say in their statement?'

'Will wouldn't say just on the phone, although he did say that he would tell me what he could tomorrow.'

'If the police don't think that the Sharps murdered Beatrice, then that puts other people in the frame, possibly Cliff. I think I'll go and see Lucy and Sarah tomorrow. When I left the ballroom to go to the bridal suite, I noticed that Sarah wasn't at her table.'

'Let's hope she can prove where she went and what she did then,' said Greg with raised eyebrows. Lydia nodded in agreement.

13

Lydia Buckley
Greg left after breakfast saying he was going back to his flat to work from home and Lydia sat down to concentrate on her novel. But she kept thinking about Will's call last night and the fact that the Sharps were not being charged with Beatrice's murder, and after an hour of writing she realised that her mind was not on the job. She stood up and stretched, deciding to pay a visit to Flower Power and see how the ladies were. The day was overcast and not many people were around. Those who were in the Market Place were going about their business and there was no indication that a murder had taken place in their midst.

Lydia pushed open the door to the flower shop and breathed in the heavenly scent of fresh blooms.

'Oh Lydia!' Lucy said in an anguished tone. 'The police have taken Sarah to the station for further questioning, but Elsa popped in earlier and told us that the suspects had already been arrested. What's going on?'

'The Sharp brothers have been arrested and charged with a murder that took place in London, but apparently the police don't have enough evidence to charge them with Beatrice's murder, so they're keeping an open mind,' replied Lydia.

'That means that Sarah must be a suspect now. It's because she keeps insisting that Beatrice ran down her father in Cliff's MG.' Lucy told Lydia about Sarah's reasoning. 'She shouldn't have admitted that she had left our table, I would have backed her up,' Lucy finished.

'Lucy, you know that wouldn't have worked. I noticed that she wasn't with you and someone else may also have seen her go outside. Do you remember what time Sarah left your table to go and speak to Beatrice, and what time she came back?'

'She left a few minutes before the fashion show started and came back came back just before it finished. She told me that when she went out through the French doors onto the terrace, she was waylaid by a bride who wanted to talk about flowers for her wedding. She doesn't know who the bride was, only that her wedding was in four weeks' time and that she would come into the shop, in other words – she has no real alibi.' Lucy tapped a pen rapidly on the counter as she spoke, clearly anxious.

Just at that moment the shop door opened and the landlady of the Coach came in.

'Hello, it's Mrs Rider, isn't it?' welcomed Lucy. 'I'm Lucy, pleased to meet you.'

Doreen Rider was dressed in her trademark cropped jeans and sneakers, her hair waxed to attention in stiff little peaks.

'Hello Lucy, morning Lydia. I just want to order a bunch of flowers to be delivered to Jeff's mum, it's her seventieth birthday on Friday.'

'No problem.' Lucy brought out a brochure with pictures of various arrangements and Doreen quickly pointed to one. 'That'll do,' she said irreverently. 'Now, Lydia, have you made your plans to elope yet?' she added, turning her gaze in Lydia's direction. Lucy looked up in surprise.

'No, we're not going to elope—' Lydia began.

'Oh! You've not fallen out, have you?'

'No, we—'

'That would be a real shame. I was only just saying to Shirley Collins when I was in the post office the other day that I thought you and Greg make a lovely couple. There'll be wedding bells there, I said, you mark my words.'

Lydia blushed. 'I don't think wedding bells—'

'I mean, I don't know why you want to keep it quiet, we'd all love a good wedding, don't you agree Lucy?'

Lucy's mouth had dropped open in surprise as she struggled for an answer.

'Doreen – Greg and I have no plans to get married – or elope,' Lydia said firmly. 'What you overheard me say to Tom was just a joke, I was pulling his leg, that's all.'

'Oh! I see,' replied Doreen looking rather crestfallen. 'His mum's address is seventy-six Cliff Drive, Bridlington,' she told Lucy who scribbled it down on a pad.

'You must feel relieved now that the Sharp brothers have gone.' Lydia changed the subject.

'I knew they were up to no good from the moment they checked in. I said to Jeff, they looked dodgy and I wouldn't have trusted them as far as I could throw them – and I was right! Sweet-talked that Mrs Buckley they did. I felt right sorry for Mr Buckley...he's stayed with us before, you know...although I think *she's* a bit of a floozy – as my mother would say, all fur coat and no knickers. I had to give a statement to the police and everything. Well at least they are behind bars now, the Sharps obviously, not the Buckleys. Poor Cllr Lewis, *murdered*!'

Doreen handed over her credit card to Lucy. 'I don't know what Ashdale is coming to. Maybe me and Jeff should seriously consider selling up and moving to Spain.'

Lucy completed the transaction and hand the card back to Doreen. 'Well, I hope you and Greg can sort out your differences, because whatever anyone says, I still think you make a lovely couple. See you later.' Doreen stuffed her credit card back into her purse and was gone.

Lucy raised her eyebrows questioningly at Lydia. 'The short answer is, no we haven't broken up, no we're not getting married, and yes, we're considering buying an apartment in Spain.'

Lucy giggled at Lydia's answer and then rather hesitantly asked, 'The Buckleys that Doreen mentioned, are they any relation to you? You're Lydia Buckley...' Lucy blushed, 'I'm reading one of your novels,' she admitted.

Lydia sighed. 'Vinnie Buckley is my ex-husband and Vivienne is his wife. Vinnie has business at the Hall – he's a marketing executive and the Worthington are his clients.'

'Doreen didn't give a very flattering description of Mrs Buckley, did she?'

'No. No, she didn't,' Lydia replied quietly.

Lucy nodded, then glanced at her watch. 'Sarah's been gone ages, I hope she's not been arrested,' she said with a worried look.

'I don't think there's enough to arrest her at this stage, but they may well want to talk about her allegations about Sam's death, though. Please try not to worry, Lucy. If this girl does come into the shop and is able to corroborate Sarah's story, she'll be all right. Did anybody see them talking on the terrace do you think?'

'I don't know, Sarah did say that she saw Derek Houseman going towards the wood and the pavilion though.'

'Derek? Oh dear, he also had an issue with Beatrice, and of course, Cliff found the body and we know he was upset with her too. I expect, they will all be called back in for further questioning.'

'Elsa told me all about the other murder that you solved back in February, will you help with this one too?'

Lydia's mouth dropped open. 'I didn't really solve it, I just...well...came up with the answer, I suppose. I'm not an official investigator, but I'll help if I'm asked.'

'If you can, will you let me know whether Sarah will be ok. Please?' Lucy looked beseechingly at Lydia. 'She was so angry with Trissie...er...Beatrice, and she really believes it was her who killed Sam.'

'And you, Lucy? Do you think the same?'

'I don't know what to think,' Lucy whispered. 'All that Sarah says makes sense, but...'

'You don't want to incriminate her, do you?'

'No! No, I don't and I'm scared in case she...' Lucy broke off suddenly and caught her breath.

'Do you really think that Sarah *would* be capable of murder?'

'Normally, of course not! But this isn't normal. She's borne a grudge for years about this unknown driver who disappeared, always blaming the police for not investigating enough and for longer. Suddenly, she meets this woman who *may* have been that driver and she wanted answers – I'm worried that she might have got them.'

After reassuring Lucy that she would impress upon the police that they needed to try and find the girl who could provide Sarah's alibi, Lydia said goodbye and left the shop.

Crossing the Market Place, she saw Elsa coming out of the Forget-me-not Café with Mrs Simms. Elsa waved, said something to Mrs Simms and hurried in Lydia's direction.

'Lydia!' she called, 'I'm so glad I've caught you.'

Literally thought Lydia as Elsa grabbed her arm.

'I popped into the bakery this morning to tell Derek and Sheila the good news—'

'Good news?'

'Yes, about the killers being arrested…surely you know about that? Anyway, it's just as well I did as Sheila was in a bit of a state…and I was able to reassure her about them Sharps…she said that you had a photo of that nut allergy sign—'

'Yes, I—'

'It's as well you got that because last week, Adam Lewis was in the bakery demanding compensation…it fair upset Sheila, did that.'

'Compensation?'

'Oh yes, after their money he was. Albert Wilks was there at the time and heard what was said…not that he'll admit it to me or anyone else for that matter. Doesn't like to get involved doesn't Albert. Anyway, the thing is, all's well that ends well…apart from Adam Lewis. But I guess he'll be a wealthy young man now, what with inheriting all of his parents' money.'

'I suppose so.'

'Y'see, I think that Sheila was worried about Derek…in case the police thought he might have done it…what with the nut incident and Adam demanding money. It'd upset anyone, would that, wouldn't it? I mean, it might give Derek a motive. It's just as well he was behind his table and in full view of everyone. Well, not everyone because I couldn't see him when I watched the fashion show…but then I didn't really look over to their stand.'

Elsa paused to draw breath and Lydia didn't know what to say, her mind was whirling with all the information,

'Umm...no,' was all she managed. According to Lucy, Sarah saw Derek going towards the pavilion, so he *had* left his table.

'I've got to get back home and do some lunch for me and Brian. I've been out all morning, so as much as I'd like to stay and chat some more, I'll have to say goodbye and get on.'

Lydia hurried home, she needed to write down all the information she had gleaned from her conversations this morning. Once she had opened a document on her laptop, she started with Sarah and quickly typed the reasons why the young woman had come to the conclusion that it was Beatrice who had knocked down her father whilst driving Cliff's MG. Then she noted that Sarah had gone out of the ballroom around ten past two and not returned until around two thirty. Then she wrote some notes about Derek and what Elsa had said about the visit from Adam and the compensation, noting that Derek was also absent from the ballroom around the same time as Sarah. Then in capitals, she typed: *NEED TO FIND SARAH'S BRIDE.*

Adam Lewis

Fortunately, Hugo had recognised Adam, who would not have picked the Marshalls out of the throng of tourists who streamed through the doors. He remembered them as both being on the portly side, but now they seemed slimmer and fitter, not to mention tanned. Celia's usual bouffant hair-do had been replaced by a softer bob and there was no string of pearls – he recalled that she had always worn pearls around her neck. Hugo was still ebullient and shook Adam's hand vigorously, chortling about how good it was to see him again, and that he looked jolly well, considering. As Adam drove back from the airport – he was using his mother's car, *just because it's more roomy and comfortable,* he told himself – Celia Marshall chattered incessantly.

'I'm struggling to believe it...in Ashdale of all places. What is the world coming to? It wasn't like that when we were there, was it, Hugo? Well, apart from that business with Simon Saxby-Jones...but then again, the Saxby-Jones's lived in Harrogate, so it doesn't really count, does it? *Murdered!* Poor Beatrice and she was only doing the council a favour by standing in for the mayor...and you say he had shingles, Adam?'

'Yes.'

'And this happened at a wedding fair at Ashdale Hall?'

'Yes.'

'How simply dreadful for the Worthingtons. What on earth were those men doing there in the first place? You don't get men on their own at wedding fairs, unless they're well...umm...very modern, do you?'

'No.'

'... and you say they were from London?'

'Yes.'

'But why were they in Ashdale?'

'I don't know.'

'Why would they kill Beatrice?'

'I don't know.'

'Were the Blenkhorns at the wedding fair?'

'I don't know.'

'I bet they were, I'll go and see them. They'll tell me what happened. Oh! I haven't got a car. Hugo! We shall have to hire a car, I can't be stuck in Ashdale without a car.'

'You can borrow mine, I'll keep Mother's.'

Once Hugo and Celia were settled in the Lewis's guest room and Celia had been given the keys to Adam's car, she called the Blenkhorns and told them that she was on her way. Hugo had made an appointment to see Albert Wilks and suggested a cup of tea before they went. As they sat at the table in the kitchen, Hugo asked if Adam had given any thought to Beatrice's send-off and whether he had spoken to the mayor's office at the council. Adam shook his head.

'No, I can't seem to find the impetus to get started with all that, and, to be honest, I thought you might help. You were so good with Mother when my father died.'

Hugo clapped him on the shoulder. 'No problem, my boy! Now, as a serving councillor, Beatrice is entitled to a civic funeral – is that what you want for her?'

'Definitely, I think she would like the formality of that.'

'Leave it with me and I'll deal with it.'

'Thanks Hugo, I knew I could rely on you for help and advice.'

'I know you're only my nephew through marriage, Adam, but you're the closest I'll ever get to having a son and I'll do whatever I can to help you through this. Do you know when the police will release Beatrice's body?'

'No, they were going to do a post-mortem and then let me know,' replied Adam with a shrug.

Hugo winced as Adam mentioned the post-mortem,

'Ok, well I'll make some calls tomorrow, but for now, let's go and see what Albert can advise.'

Hugo marched into Albert's neat little office and extended his hand in greeting. 'Albert! How are you, old boy?'

Albert hesitantly extended his hand and tried not to grimace as Hugo pumped it up and down vigorously. Adam merely nodded an acknowledgement at Albert but kept his hands by his side.

'Mr Marshall, lovely to see you again. Are you and Mrs Marshall both well?'

'Oh, we're both tickety-boo, apart from this terrible business.'

Albert talked them through Beatrice's finances which were not complex, and when he had finished, Hugo frowned.

'So, where is the account which requires two weeks' notice to withdraw funds?'

'There isn't one.' Albert replied.

'Well, why did she say there was? Is this anything to do with that young woman you're involved with, Adam?'

Adam gave a curt nod, but remained tight-lipped, hoping his uncle would realise he didn't want to discuss it in front of Albert.

However, Hugo pressed on. 'Why would two weeks have made a difference to the purchase of the villa?'

'Because we were going to elope before her wedding and live there,' Adam eventually muttered, glancing at Albert who was studiously reading some papers and feigning disinterest.

'I see, well we still have a problem, as I assume that a transfer of funds that was due to take place next week cannot happen now. Albert?'

Albert's head jerked up. 'What? Oh, yes well unfortunately, until the entire estate has been valued and probate granted, I'm not in a position to release any money in the immediate future, especially an amount of one hundred and fifty thousand pounds. Perhaps you could explain the circumstances and ask the seller not to rescind the contract?'

'Hmm, I'll see what I can do. But in the meantime, thank you for seeing us at such short notice, Albert.'

Throughout most of the meeting, Adam had said very little. It was now abundantly clear that his mother *had* been deliberately deceitful in not making the transfer last Thursday as agreed.

As they left the accountant's offices, Hugo wanted to know what was going on. 'Adam, you had better explain more about this two weeks' notice business,' he said rather sternly.

'Mother found out about the affair, and the young lady in question is Charlotte Worthington,' Adam said simply.

'Good Lord! *She's* the one who's getting married?'

Adam sighed and explained that he and Charlotte were actually going to elope on the morning of her wedding and his mother had thought that if she delayed making the transfer, the sale would not be completed before Charlotte was safely married.'

'All a bit dramatic, isn't it? Eloping with a damsel in distress – why not just call off the wedding?'

'That's what I suggested, but Charlotte couldn't bring herself to do it, she was embarrassed I suppose. Mother was also horrified at the thought of all the scandal, honestly you'd have thought we were in the 1800s.'

'Women! I think you've had a lucky escape there, my boy,' chortled Hugo. 'But on a more serious note, I shall have to contact Top Drawer Properties again to advise them of the situation, and to be honest, I'm not sure what they will say. We shall keep this between ourselves for now though. Celia was an acquaintance of the Worthingtons, so it's probably best if she remains in the dark.'

Adam wholeheartedly agreed. There were enough people who already knew about the affair. The men returned home and Hugo phoned the police to begin enquiries as when they could start arranging a funeral.

Vivienne Buckley

Vivienne crossed her legs as she sat on the high barstool, her short skirt rode up and exposed a good deal of tanned thigh. She took a drink from her glass of fizz and began relating her version of events to her friend, Janey,

'I had this idea that me and Vinnie could have a vow renewal, you know that I only had a quick wedding with a white summer dress from Boohoo and, as lovely as it was, it wasn't a glamorous wedding gown. I found an absolutely gorgeous gown in a bridal boutique – top designer and only five grand and that's when the idea came to me.' Vivienne continued her story and Janey listened with rapt attention, her eyes growing wide as Vivienne told her about being locked in the en suite.

'He introduced himself as Cody King, he looked like Cody King – why would I not believe he *was* Cody King? Honestly, Vinnie is just being *so* unreasonable, because if he had agreed to the vow renewal and been ok with me going to the wedding fair – none of it would have happened, so it's all his fault really,' she complained as she finished her tale.

'Did you have some fun with this Cody King chap?' smirked Janey as she twiddled a tendril of blonde hair.

'No! *I* was absolutely as good as gold, unlike Vinnie. There really is nothing for him to be so tetchy about. Let me tell you, when Vinnie finally opened the bathroom door, guess who was stood in the bedroom with him? *Her*!' Vivienne took another mouthful of fizz.

'Listen, Viv, why don't you just leave him and work full-time with me? Come on, at least think about it. We could have such fun, we might even spend the summer in Marbella.'

'I don't know Janey, I live in a nice house—'

'A nice house! *A nice house*? Is that all he has to provide to keep you happy – a nice house? Bloody hell, Viv you've lowered your expectations, a nice house indeed!'

Vivienne giggled. 'It doesn't sound a lot, does it?'

'If you come and work with me, we can earn shedloads and we could afford a real swanky apartment, working holidays and non-working holidays, freedom to do as you please, and – let's face it, you didn't marry him just for a nice house.'

'I wouldn't mind working in Mar Menor – all the celebs go there. You know, it was quite nice being asked for an interview and people really thought I was his wife. I could get used to the celeb lifestyle.'

Janey drained her glass. 'I've got a client now, so I'll be about an hour. Are you staying here or moving on?'

'I don't know, things are looking promising with the guy sat behind you. Let's keep it flexible.' Vivienne smiled seductively over Janey's shoulder at the man sitting on his own at the bar.

'Ok, I'll text you when I'm done, but if I don't catch up with you later today, please think about what I've just said. Life is too short to spend daydreaming in a nice house.' Janey slipped off her stool and walked away.

Vivienne watched her go before turning her head back, and then, from under her eyelashes, she caught the eye of the man looking at her. She had already taken in the designer suit and expensive watch and wondered why he was on his own. She casually looked away and, knowing he was watching her every move, she uncrossed her legs and twisted her body slightly to top up her glass from the bottle sitting in an ice bucket beside her. The twisting action meant that her legs parted, and, as her skirt rode higher, the man was treated to a glimpse of a tiny scrap of sheer fabric – the treasure beneath, just out of sight.

Out of the corner of her eye, Vivienne was delighted to see that he'd shifted on his seat to try to get a better view. So, quite deliberately and very wickedly, she straightened her body and arched her back, letting her thighs open wider, then she fluffed her hair before lowering her eyes to look straight at him as he gazed between her legs. It was only a few seconds before he realised that she was watching him, watching her. As their eyes met, Vivienne gracefully crossed her legs again, picked up her glass and took a small sip, her eyes never moved from his face. The man smiled, a knowing smile. *Gotcha!* thought Vivienne and lowered her head as she pulled out her phone pretending to read a text message. *Now just come over here and we can get on with it, I might just have time for a lucrative quickie this afternoon.* Vivienne slid her phone back into her handbag as she became aware that the man had made his move towards her.

'Good afternoon,' he said quietly with a lilting Welsh accent.

Vivienne gave him her best seductive smile. 'Good afternoon to you. Let's hope it is.'

Lydia Buckley

Lydia had managed to do some writing during the afternoon but now she needed a break. She made herself a cup of coffee and whilst she waited for the kettle to boil, her mind wandered back to the wedding fair. She wondered if Lexie had managed to book any weddings before Beatrice's body had been discovered and decided that she would give Lexie a call and see how she was, if nothing else.

'Lexie, how are you?'

'Oh Lydia, I've been meaning to call you and thank you for all your help and support with the wedding fair.'

'Don't mention it, I enjoyed being involved. How are things at the Hall?'

'All the exhibitors have done well and, aside from the murder, it was a success.'

'How is business for the Hall though? I really hope that brides weren't put off by what happened.'

'Quite the opposite. Between you and me, I think the publicity has done us a power of good. I've taken so many enquiries about weddings because the press mentioned that it was our first wedding fair. It's quite macabre. If I didn't have an alibi, I think the police might have considered me as a suspect given the business we've gained,' Lexie laughed nervously.

'An alibi? Were you asked for one?'

'I was asked where I was, and fortunately I could tell them that I was showing a couple around from one until two and then I was with another lovely couple from two o'clock until three, and they have corroborated my story. I think they may book their wedding with us, they loved *The Kensington Suite* as the wedding room. The sun had come out and the terrace garden looked amazing for photographs.'

'I am so pleased for you Lexie. It was dreadful about Beatrice and it has likely cast a shadow over what would have been an out-and-out success, but if the press coverage helps your wedding business, so be it. Although, I completely understand how you have mixed feelings.'

'I am a bit concerned about Charlotte, she's like a cat on hot coals – so jumpy and haunted-looking.'

'Perhaps it's just pre-wedding jitters and shock. The wedding is this Saturday, isn't it? Presumably it can still go ahead?'

'Yes, it's still going ahead. Oh! By the way, I think Charlotte is booked in for her lashes with you on Thursday. However, she wondered if you could fit Pen in on Friday here at the Hall, if she pops into WOW! for her patch test tomorrow?'

'Yes, I can manage that, probably late afternoon – is that ok?'

'That would be lovely. We've got the rehearsal dinner on Friday and Pen is staying the night with us.'

'I haven't met Pen yet, is she very much like Charlotte?'

'God no! Totally the opposite. I don't know if you know, but she owns the Lulabelle's shops. Her father bought her the one in Northallerton to help her get over a broken engagement and she enjoyed it so much that she opened another in Ashdale.'

'I've been in the shop and I love the clothes. Pen has turned out to be quite the businesswoman. What a shame it hasn't rubbed off on Charlotte.'

'It is, but then again I don't know if I could ever work with my sister, we rarely agree on anything.'

Lydia laughed. 'It doesn't matter anyway as you do a great job without her. I'll see you on Friday then. Bye for now.'

After the call, Lydia thought about what Lexie had said and made a note on the laptop regarding her whereabouts at the wedding fair. She didn't suspect Lexie for a minute, but it just added to the overall picture of who was where.

Later that evening after she and Greg had finished eating and were relaxing on the sofa, Lydia showed Greg her notes and they consolidated what they knew.

'If we take the Sharp brothers first, we know that they arrived with Vivienne at one thirty or thereabouts and split from Vivienne around two o'clock. We don't know where they were after then, but Elsa saw them go past her on their way outside at the start of the fashion show at two fifteen. You said they turned up in the bridal suite at about half past two and then they were arrested,' summarised Greg.

'So, they could have gone to the pavilion between two and two fifteen,' suggested Lydia.

'Elsa said they were coming from the staircase and walking towards the door, so they were not returning from the pavilion. We still have the problem about them knowing where the pavilion was,' Greg pointed out. 'Let's assume for now that it wasn't the Sharps. Who else have we got?'

'Sarah. Lucy says Sarah left their table before the fashion show and returned more or less as it finished, say two thirty which was only a few minutes before the police arrived,' Lydia said, referring to her notes.

'So, Sarah is a possibility and, at the moment, does not have an alibi. But does she have a motive?'

Lydia repeated what Lucy had told her about Sarah's reasons for accusing Beatrice of knocking down Sam. 'Lucy asked me to help as she's heard about the last murder I was involved in,' she finished up.

'There's not much you can do though, is there?'

'I did wonder if I could contact all the brides that registered with Elsa to try and find the one who talked to Sarah on the terrace. What do you think?'

'I think it's a great idea, but perhaps you should suggest it to the police and leave it to them. So, Sarah stays as a suspect for now,' said Greg as he circled Sarah's name on the paper.

'There's Derek to consider as well.'

'Derek? Derek Houseman?' asked Greg in surprise.

Lydia nodded. 'Apparently, Sarah saw Derek going towards the pavilion whilst she was talking on the terrace, presumably in search of Beatrice as he knew she would be there. I know that because Lexie told me about the photo opportunity in front of the Housemans' table. The other thing to bear in mind is that after the nut allergy incident, which seems such a long time ago now, Adam demanded compensation from Derek and Sheila.'

'What? Are you sure Elsa has that right? There are proper channels to go through for compensation and I don't think "demanding it" is one of them.'

'Well apparently Albert Wilks was a witness…'

'Albert Wilks?' exclaimed Greg.

'So Elsa says.'

'You see, that won't help Derek at all because if Adam or Beatrice were talking about compensation, then it strengthens Derek's motive for murder.'

'He was really upset about that nut business and Sheila was mortified that it might impact on their chances in the awards – which are this Friday,' said Lydia.

'Surely when you gave them that photograph, they were a bit relieved?'

'They were, but I also overheard Derek say that he wanted a quiet word with Beatrice.'

'Hmm, by killing Beatrice, there would be no need for compensation. It's a bit drastic though,' Greg pointed out.

'The awards are very prestigious, who knows how furious or desperate Derek was? Especially if the Lewis's were also demanding money?'

'Ok, what about Cliff? You confirmed that Cliff took a phone call just after the fashion show started and left the ballroom.'

'That's right,' replied Lydia, 'because Cliff was with me when he got a phone call – he went out of the ballroom to take it. That's when I picked up your message about the Sharps and Tasheka's message about being stuck in the bathroom, which was at two twenty-one precisely. When I got Tasheka's message and left the ballroom, Lucy was behind her table, but Sarah wasn't there.'

'Cliff told me that as he walked towards the pavilion, he got another call, this time from Eric Bentham apologising for not being able to get to the Hall. Cliff said he heard someone walking about in the wood and saw a flash of white – could that have been Derek in his chef's whites? If so, then the problem now, is that Derek could have killed Beatrice and been on his way back to the ballroom or Cliff could have killed her before he called the police,' said Greg.

'So that's Sarah, Derek or Cliff as a possible murderer?'

'It looks like it.'

'But they are all nice people, I don't want it to be one of them,' Lydia moaned.

'Who else could it have been? Lexie? Where were Adam and Charlotte? I've got to admit that I was a bit stunned when you told me the other evening that it was Charlotte having the steamy affair, and not Lexie. Beatrice also knew, didn't she? I'll bet she would have been upset about that,' Greg pondered out loud.

'I don't know where Charlotte was on Sunday, I didn't see her at all. I expect she was keeping well out of Beatrice's way. She must have been very worried in case Beatrice mentioned the affair.'

'Well, from now on, Charlotte should keep her knickers well and truly up – as high as her armpits!' said Greg somewhat primly.

Lydia giggled at that and a very weird vision floated around in her head.

'Anyhow, Lexie was with prospective clients between two and three and that has been corroborated by the couples themselves,' she said when her giggles had subsided.

'Adam?'

'I think Vinnie said he and Adam had been working for most of the morning. But why would Adam kill his mother?'

'No idea really.' Greg sighed. 'So, just the three so far.'

'Have you had any more information from Will?' asked Lydia.

'Will knows I'm likely to speak to you about this as you tend to find things out that he doesn't – and he is grateful,' Greg added as Lydia opened her mouth. 'However, I'm not sure how much is public knowledge so perhaps keep it to yourself for now. Beatrice was knocked unconscious by a blow to the back of her head, probably with one of the rocks from around the fountain, she was then held under the water until she drowned.'

Lydia shuddered. 'So, it was quite deliberate, I did wonder if she had possibly just fainted, but knocked out and then held under the water…Do the police still think it's unlikely to be the Sharps?' she asked.

'He didn't say, although going by their previous murders, they would probably have just cut her throat.'

'Eww! Even so, is it possible that Beatrice was targeted because of Adam? After all he has just returned from London?'

'It's possible. I suppose that's something they will look into.'

'Will the London police be able to find Mr Lord now that they have the Sharps in custody?' asked Lydia.

'Terry Sharp reckons they don't know who Mr Lord is, that they only receive anonymous phone calls. Ray knows nothing at all – he just does as Terry tells him.'

'Can they use Terry's phone to track down Mr Lord?'

'The number used by Mr Lord or his contact, has been discontinued and the Sharps are now on their own, so it's a bit of a dead end.'

'Where does that leave the investigation up here then?' Lydia drained her coffee cup.

'Will said they are still keeping an open mind about it being someone else who murdered Beatrice.'

'Oh dear! It's not looking good, is it? How was Cliff when you spoke to him today? How is he coping?'

'I think he is over the shock of finding a body, being an ex-military man it's not the first body he has seen, but he was quite upset that it was Beatrice. He said that he had to tell the police about the night Sam died because Sarah admitted leaving the ballroom through the French windows and she told the police that she believes Beatrice killed her father. He just wishes he'd had the chance to speak to Beatrice about the termination and the allegation about Sam. He feels it's all – "unfinished business" was how he put it.'

'Oh! I don't know! We're just going around in circles.' Lydia pushed the laptop away. 'Anyway, the police will have worked out who was where by now, so why are we poking our noses in?' she asked him with raised eyebrows.

'Because people gossip to you and that usually includes things that they don't necessarily tell the police.'

'Are you calling me a gossip?' Lydia said indignantly and poked him in the ribs.

'Ow! No, it's just part of your job to gossip. Unfortunately, the only conclusion that we've come to is that Sarah, Cliff and Derek are all viable as suspects.'

'I simply cannot believe that one of them murdered Beatrice,' declared Lydia.

'Neither can I. But they all have a damned good motive, and that's the problem.'

14

Cliff Walker
Cliff pulled his car into the Canalside Residential Park and noted the park homes laid out in neat rows. The park homes were bungalows, and each had their own plot which the owners had either lawned, decked, or paved, depending on their personal preference. Cliff had offered to drive so Tom could leave his car at the office, and now Tom directed Cliff to number 85. As some of the homes had names and others had numbers, the sequence of which was not always logical, specific bungalows sometimes were hard to find.

Cliff parked outside and looked enthusiastically at what might be his next home.

'This is one of the larger models,' explained Tom, 'and as such, has quite a large garden at the rear. It came onto the market on Monday and you're the first person to view it.'

Tom opened the front door of the park home and they walked inside. It was quite large with three good-sized bedrooms all with fitted wardrobes, and an en suite in the master bedroom. The open-plan lounge/diner/kitchen was exactly what Cliff had in mind and it was all newly fitted out, as was the main bathroom. When Cliff stepped through the French windows onto a decked area which faced south, he knew this was where he wanted to be. To the side of the decking was a paved area. *That's for the bar and barbecue,* he decided. Further down was a rockery with a water feature and an area laid with exceptionally good quality artificial grass. *No need for a lawn mower.* The end of the garden had a tall fence to separate his plot from the park home on the other side, which he couldn't see. *Very private.* As Cliff stood on the decking, he listened, and the only sound was birdsong – a far cry from the noise of his Leeds flat. Tom had said very little, allowing Cliff time to take everything in.

But as Cliff smiled, Tom spoke. 'What are your thoughts on this?'

'I like it, very much. I just need to redecorate – it's a bit chintzy for my taste, but that's not a deal-breaker.'

As Tom locked the front door on their way out, Cliff heard his name being called. He looked up and saw Elsa waving from the park home opposite.

'Yoo-hoo!' she called and walked towards them. 'I was hoping you would come and view that. Janet had ever such a lot of work done and then she just upped and left…went to live with her daughter in Scarborough. It's nice, isn't it?'

Cliff smiled in recognition. 'Elsa! You see, I did take your advice. Now how are you after Sunday's episode? I've been meaning to come to Ashdale, and was hoping to bump into you, thought we might have a little chat.'

Elsa beamed. 'Well, come right in – I can soon put the kettle on. Me and Brian live here at number 84, so if you bought that, we would be neighbours. I have to say that I'm glad those two thugs are behind bars…tricking me into believing he was Cody King, indeed! And as for that woman with him, well…you do know that she's Lydia's ex-husband's current wife, don't you?'

'Lydia's…?'

'…ex-husband's current wife.'

'No! Really?' gasped Cliff.

'Oh yes…she was around when we had our last murder—'

'That was something else I wanted to talk to you about.'

'Well, at number 87 is Edward Jones…now he is a nice chap…moved in just before Christmas. But unfortunately, his son—'

Tom cleared his throat. 'Mrs Armitage,' he interrupted, 'as much as a cup of tea is a very kind offer, I'm afraid I must ask Mr Walker to take me back to the office. Perhaps you could arrange some other time for your chat?'

Cliff would have loved a cup of tea and a gossip about Lydia's ex-husband's current wife and Edward's involvement in the previous murder, but he understood that Tom had a business to run and that he needed to get back,

'Absolutely, Tom, quite understand. Well, dear lady,' he turned to Elsa, 'I would very much like to take a rain-check, if I may?'

Elsa's face had lost its sparkle when Tom turned down the offer of a cuppa, but now she lit up again. 'I'll look forward to that, Cliff.'

As Cliff drove back to the Market Place, Tom asked what, if anything, he wanted to do about the park home.

'I would like a second opinion and I'm planning to ask Lucy Kirkwood – you know Lucy from the florists? Anyhow, I would like to take her with me, on a second viewing.'

'Yes, I remember the Kirkwoods, I sold the shop to them.'

'Let me speak to Lucy and see when she would be free, then I'll contact you and make arrangements for a second visit.'

Cliff parked his car, and as he and Tom approached the office, they saw Lydia coming towards them.

'Cliff! Lovely to see you again. Have you been house-hunting?' she asked.

'I most certainly have. I took Elsa's advice and we've just been to view a park home, which I liked very much, so I could be a resident very soon.'

'I'm pleased to hear that, I'm sure you won't be disappointed.'

'We bumped into the lovely Elsa, she offered us a cup of tea, but we had to decline due to Tom's work commitments,' Cliff inclined his head at Tom, who smiled ruefully,

'As much as I would have loved a cup of tea, I don't have the time to spend all day with Elsa, in fact—'

'Tom, dear boy!' the door of the estate agency was wrenched open and a well-built man stepped outside to join them on the pavement. He wore a navy linen suit, fashionably crumpled, and a white cotton shirt.

'Hugo! I didn't know you were back in town,' said Tom in surprise.

'Came back rather urgently, helping Adam with arrangements and so forth,' Hugo explained. The mood became a little more sombre.

'Yes, sorry to hear about Beatrice,' replied Tom.

'Of course, she was your sister-in-law – please accept my condolences, Hugo,' said Lydia gently.

Cliff shuffled his feet awkwardly and Tom glanced at him, probably realising that Cliff wouldn't know Hugo.

'Hugo, this is Cliff Walker – he discovered Beatrice's…umm…found her,' Tom said awkwardly.

Hugo's hand shot out. 'Hugo Marshall. Must have been a bit of a shock, old boy?'

Cliff shook Hugo's hand and nodded. 'It certainly was; nasty business, murder.'

Hugo nodded in agreement. 'Adam is my nephew, has no one else now, just myself and my wife, Celia. He needs some guidance and advice about what to do next, so we've just popped over. We live in Spain now, involved in these properties here as a matter of fact.' Hugo's hand waved at the poster in the window, then he turned to Lydia. 'Talking of that, Tom tells me that you and Greg are interested, Lydia.'

'We are, but we would like to come over and visit first. We want to know a bit more about the area before we decide,' she replied.

'Oh! They are absolutely first class, you can't go wrong, well the company name says it all really – Top Drawer Properties, eh?' Hugo chuckled.

'It's an unusual name for a property company, don't you think?'

'That's because of the directors, Mr Baron and Mr Lord – top drawer, see?' Hugo laughed. 'Clever play on their aristocratic names.'

Cliff was puzzled to see Lydia's mouth drop open in surprise. He turned to Hugo. 'You know, I'd not considered buying in Spain, but I might look at that idea, too,' he said.

'Great investment! Good rental income too. If you're interested—'

'Hugo, did you need to see me or were you calling in socially?' Tom interrupted.

'Actually, I just need a word about Adam's villa.'

'Right! I'll get off and be in touch about that second viewing, Tom,' said Cliff. 'Lydia, have you got a few moments? I'd like a word,' he added.

'Yes, no problem.'

Tom and Hugo disappeared back inside the office and Lydia waited for Cliff to speak.

'When I met Elsa earlier, she mentioned that the woman who was with one of the London thugs turned out to be your ex-husband's current wife.'

'You mean Vivienne,' said Lydia warily.

'I don't want to pry, but I have written a piece for the paper and I hope that I've not compromised you in any way.'

'It's fine. Vinnie and I are fairly amicable, although I'm not Vivienne's best friend. I don't think anything you write will affect me,' Lydia told him. 'However, there is something I would like to ask you…'

'Is it about Sunday?'

Lydia nodded.

'Have you got time for a cuppa? Shall we go to the café?' asked Cliff.

As they approached the counter, Lydia greeted the woman behind it, 'Hi Kate. I'm not sure if you have met Ashdale's new social reporter, Cliff Walker? Cliff this is my sister Kate who owns this lovely café.'

'Hello Kate, pleased to meet you, I have popped in before.'

'Hello Cliff, welcome to Ashdale.' As Kate made their drinks, it dawned on Cliff why he had thought she looked familiar – the sisters were very much alike.

Lydia Buckley

Once they were settled with their drinks, Lydia asked Cliff what had happened on Sunday when he went to find Beatrice, and he gladly told her how he had gone to the secret garden, stood for a moment and taken a deep breath. He could see the new pavilion at the far side and noticed that the door was open, then his phone had vibrated and it was Eric Bentham. He said that Eric had prattled on, apologising for not being there and so on, and after the call, he'd heard a twig snap, the rustle of foliage and a startled bird had flapped through the tree canopy. He'd turned and caught a glimpse of something white through the woods and how he'd first thought that it might have been Trissie, sneaking away to avoid him.

Cliff paused to have a mouthful of coffee before he continued, 'I turned back to the pavilion and that's when I saw her – lying there. For a moment I just stood there staring at her, lying face down in the fountain, and then I ran over and reached for a pulse, but I already knew that I was unlikely to find one. People don't lie face down in water if they're breathing, do they? That's when I called the police.'

'I'm so sorry Cliff, it must have been a dreadful shock to you, having just found her again and not being able to have that talk that you so desperately wanted.'

'Then there's Sarah, you do know her feelings about Trissie…umm, Beatrice, don't you?'

Lydia nodded. 'I spoke at length to Lucy yesterday and she told me how Sarah had come to her conclusion. How do you feel about that?' she asked gently.

'I have to regretfully admit that she has a point and that all the pieces fit. Trissie was beside herself that night and I put it down to shock, which in essence it was, but there was fear in her eyes and she begged me to keep quiet…oh I don't know, it was so long ago and now Trissie is…has gone! We'll probably never know. Anyway, I'm going to see Lucy and ask her if she'll come with me on a second viewing of the park home, I would like her opinion.'

'I'm sure she would love to see it. I'm on my way to see Tasheka, I'm hoping to find out why she and Vivienne ended up in the bathroom of the bridal suite.'

'Now that is something I would also like to know! Perhaps I might interview her,' said Cliff hopefully.

'I'll mention it to her, you'll find it an interesting exercise.'

They stood up and left the café, Lydia watched as Cliff crossed the Market Place before turning and heading towards LulaBelle's.

When Lydia entered the boutique, she saw that Tasheka had two customers at the counter, both of whom clutched garments they wanted to buy, so she browsed through the rails of clothes. Once the ladies had left the boutique, Tasheka looked up and her smile showed that she was clearly pleased to see Lydia, but her manner was subdued.

'Hey girl, how's it goin'?' she said flatly.

'Everything's ok. You don't sound your usual bouncy self. What's the matter?'

'You know Lydia, I'm not sure as I'm cut out for this job an' I might want to do somethin' else, so I'm thinkin' of talkin' to Miss Sinclair-Sutton.' Her red tipped fingers absent-mindedly traced a circle on the counter top.

'But I thought you enjoyed working here.'

'I think I feel too confined, you know what I'm sayin? When I was at the wedding fair on Sunday, it was real nice to be busy until…well, you know.'

'But I'm sure the shop will get busier, it's only just opened. Or have you already thought about what you might like to do instead?'

'Now here's the thing. I might like to do what you do – eyelashes. 'Cos by my reckonin', I would have regular clients that I could chat to but still not be confined. I don't wanna be confined.' Tasheka's index finger wagged from side to side as she spoke. 'So, I thought maybe you could teach me how to do eyelashes an' maybe put in a word at Zoe's or that other place you go to in Harrogate. I mean I don' wanna take your clients, but you said that they want you to do more hours an' you don't have time, you know wha' I'm sayin'?'

'O-kay,' said Lydia thoughtfully. 'The thing is, I'm not a registered tutor and you would have to do an accredited course to get your qualification. I can give you details and costs of those and I've no problem in helping you with the technique.'

'Hey! That would real good, I could see myself doin' that. I could practice on my sister, my cousin, my friend Orleana – when can I start?' Tasheka's characteristic energy and enthusiasm had bounced back into life.

Lydia laughed. 'I'll look into it as soon as I get home and I'll text you when I've got some info for you.'

'I would really appreciate that, Lydia.' Tasheka smiled, her eyes lit up and she did two fist pumps with joy.

'Now, how do you feel after the incident on Sunday?'

'I keep wonderin' why I've gotten mixed up with murder again. I keep gettin' the heebie-jeebies.'

'It was a bit of a shock, wasn't it?'

'Can you believe I was wit' two murderers all that time? I said to my Mikey, I'm not sure I wanna do this all interviewin' 'n' stuff.' The index finger drew a snappy 'Z' shape as Tasheka made her point.

'You weren't to know that he *wasn't* Cody King. Other people were fooled as well.'

'And as for *her*, she was married to somebody else, wastin' my time like that, tellin' me all sorts of nonsense – what did she think she was doin'?' Tasheka pursed her lips and her black curls shook indignantly. 'An' if I remember correctly, that somebody else was your husband!'

'*Ex*-husband, Tasheka,' admitted Lydia. 'They got married last summer.'

'No prizes for guessin' how she enticed him away from you.'

'Who says she did?' asked Lydia, but Tasheka gave her a knowing look and raised her eyebrows. 'Anyway, what actually happened to that bathroom door in the bridal suite?'

Tasheka told Lydia how she had come to be in the bridal suite and eventually hit Ray with her handbag, which had resulted in the incident with the bed drapes.

'Anyways, when he got up he was like real angry, you know?'

Lydia nodded, trying very hard not to giggle as her imagination pictured the scene and the big man's shock at being floored by a handbag.

'Then the man who said he was Cody King told us to get in the bathroom. I took one look at the ugly one's face an' I didn't need tellin' twice, so we ran inside an' locked the door. The ugly one must have charged at the door like it wasn't even there 'cos we thought he was comin' through. The Cody King man shouted at him, then they just left an' I was stuck in the bathroom wit' *her*.'

'I see,' was all Lydia could manage.

'So that's when I texted you an' Mikey, although I knew tha' you would read it first 'cos Mikey's phone is never where it's supposed to be, you getting' me?'

'I get you.'

'Anyway, she got no class. She told me tha' she met that Cody King, who wasn't Cody King, at a pole dancin' club, you know what I'm sayin'? Now, tha's not somethin' a girl jus' admits to. An' another thing, my cousin Karenna is a professional escort an' she telled me tha' these pole dancers often try an' do her job as well, so it wouldn't surprise me if she was an escort tryin' it on. I should've known she wasn't who she said she was. I've looked at my recordin' and she just tells lies. It took me a while to get to it 'cos I recorded the whole day, you know?'

Lydia frowned. 'What do you mean, you "recorded the whole day"?'

'Well, you see I got myself this real small body cam thing an' it looked jus' like a brooch on my jacket, especially when I put those beads around it, an' I recorded everythin' from when I got set up to when it switched off automatic 'cos I forgot it was recordin'.'

'Have you still got the recording or did you give it to the police?'

'I still got it 'cos my Shanice hid it an' after I gave my statement, I got the heebie-jeebies an' I forgot about it. Then I found it this mornin' an' I was gonna speak to you an' ask what you thought I should do wit' it.'

'Do you think I could have it, or at least a copy of it?'

'Sure, I saved it onto a memory stick in case someone wanted it.'

Tasheka rummaged in a large handbag and pulled out a small pouch which she handed to Lydia.

'Are you ok with me watching this? If it has anything of use, may I give it to the police?'

Tasheka shrugged. 'Sure thing, Lydia – it ain't no use to me now.'

Lydia put the pouch in her own bag and then remembered Cliff. 'By the way, you know Cliff – the new reporter? Well, I've just seen him, and he wants to know if he could come and interview you for his column.'

Tasheka laughed. 'That'd be ok, I think I might learn somethin' from him.'

'I've got to go now, but I'll let Cliff know that he can contact you and I'll look into lash courses and text you, ok?'

Lydia left LulaBelle's, returned home and put the pouch containing the memory stick into her desk drawer. Then, collecting some notes, she drove to Adam's house for a pre-arranged meeting. As she drove, the sun disappeared behind the clouds which were no longer the fluffy white variety of earlier, but the grey, full-of-rain type. She parked outside the house and wondered if she was being wise coming here again after the awkwardness of her previous visit. However, she felt much more in control now, especially since she and Greg had clarified the status of their relationship. She was determined not to be taken in by Adam's good looks or seductive charms a second time.

Adam Lewis
Adam had decided not to flirt with Lydia, as it wouldn't do for Hugo to think he was after someone else who had a partner, and who might also be deemed inappropriate. He had come to the conclusion that Saffron would be a useful girlfriend until his mother's affairs were sorted out. So, bearing all that in mind, when he answered the door to Lydia, he was professional as he greeted her and kept his manner strictly business-like with no undertones of flirtatious behaviour.

Adam showed Lydia how he would make the changes to her website, including the addition of new pictures and links to social media, all of which she seemed delighted with.

'Adam, I really like what you have done, you're a talented web designer. I expect you have had a positive reaction from the Worthingtons, also?'

'Would you like to see their proposed new website?' Adam asked, 'Your opinion would be appreciated.'

'Of course, I would be delighted.'

Adam tapped on the keyboard and Ashdale Hall appeared on the screen. He chose the weddings tab and the screen displayed a beautiful picture of *The Kensington Suite* dressed as the wedding room. The French windows were open and the full length voile curtains had wafted inwards in a gentle breeze, and through the gap in the curtains was a small glimpse of a sun-drenched terrace garden. He clicked another photo of *The Sandringham Suite* laid out for a wedding reception, complete with white chair covers and sumptuous table centres – each comprising a tall lily vase filled with pale pink and white water beads topped with a beautiful display of pale pink garden roses, ostrich feathers, and strands of ivy, as a centrepiece.

'I took these photos early, before the wedding fair started,' he told Lydia.

'They are really impressive and capture the wow factor that brides are looking for. As for my website, I'm impressed – can we talk finances now?'

They discussed Adam's costs and Lydia agreed for him to continue with his work. As she was on her way out, Lydia came across Celia rummaging around in the coat rack. She wore a simple cotton blouse and tailored trousers with a pair of sensible low-heeled shoes.

'Hello Lydia, how are you?' She turned to greet Lydia.

'I'm very well and I've got to say, you look amazing, Celia, Spain clearly suits you.'

'Oh it does – we play so much golf now. Hugo tells me that you're considering buying one of the lovely apartments in Mar Menor. You would be neighbours with Adam. He's bought a villa, haven't you, dear?' Celia smiled at her nephew.

Adam smiled half-heartedly. *The whole bloody town will know now!*

'I've read your last two novels and I have to say that I enjoyed them,' chatted Celia.

'Thank you, Celia, I'm currently working on the third.'

'I'll look forward to reading that in due course, then. Have you seen the weather? It's throwing it down,' she exclaimed. 'Hugo has taken Beatrice's car and it has my raincoat in it. I don't feel comfortable wearing Beatrice's and it probably wouldn't fit.' She sighed in frustration.

'You could borrow my trench coat, if you like,' Adam suggested.

'What? I'll look ridiculous in a man's coat. What do think, Lydia?'

'Well try it and see – trench coats are pretty much unisex, aren't they?'

Celia pulled Adam's coat off the peg and slid her arms into it. The sleeves came down a little too long over her hands and when she buttoned it, it was clearly too big.

'Far too big, see?' announced Celia, pulling the front away from her body.

'Look, why don't you unbutton it, wrap it across and just tie the belt in front, then push the sleeves up? It will give you a very current look,' said Lydia. Adam leaned against the front door and watched as Lydia put down her bag and helped Celia to adjust the coat. Once the changes had been made, Celia stuck her hands in the large pockets and twirled in front of the hall mirror.

'Well goodness me!' she exclaimed. 'It looks a different coat altogether now. I quite like this idea.' She twisted from side to side and took two or three steps forward and back, admiring her reflection, nodding in satisfaction. 'Yes, this will do very nicely. Thank you, Lydia.'

Adam picked up a handbag and a small umbrella from the hall table. He held them out with one hand, whilst opening the front door with the other. When Celia took her hands out of the coat pockets to reach for her handbag and umbrella, a crumpled piece of paper came out of one of the pockets and fell onto the floor.

'Oh! What's that?' she asked. 'Is it something important?'

'It's ok, I've got it,' said Lydia as she bent down to retrieve the paper whilst picking up her own bag.

'I'm popping over to Stonebridge to see Bridget Flanigan, she's quite upset about this whole murder business. I mean, she and Beatrice were quite good friends.' Adam held out his car keys which Celia took. 'Bridget says she actually spoke to those dreadful men, you know – the murderers. Can you believe it?' Celia poked the umbrella through the doorway and opened it, and without waiting for anyone to reply, she swept out of the door and hurried down the path.

Adam closed the door and turned to Lydia, who, having read what was on the paper, was now looking at him with a raised eyebrow.

'What have you got there?' Adam asked tentatively, although he already knew the answer.

'It's the nut allergy sign from Houseman's Bakery.'

'I'd forgotten that it was still in my pocket.'

'Why was it in there at all?'

Adam lowered his gaze to the floor and exhaled. Then he chewed his lip as he thought rapidly, he didn't really want to admit what had actually happened. *Dammit! If only he'd thrown the blasted note away.*

He sighed resignedly before beginning his explanation, 'My mother saw the sign and said I should put it in my pocket, then she nibbled a tiny bit of the cake and, well…everyone knows what happened next.'

'Are you seriously suggesting that Beatrice ate the cake on purpose?' Lydia gasped.

Adam slowly nodded his head. 'I had no idea that the reaction would be so severe, and it scared me I can tell you that. My mother's idea was that she could inform the British Bakers' Association that the Housemans had almost killed one of their customers and then they would be disqualified, leaving the way clear for the Blenkhorns.'

Lydia stared at him and shook her head in disbelief. '*Really?* Your mother would go that far?' she said with some scepticism.

'She wasn't always the most forgiving person. She had crossed swords with the Housemans once before and she couldn't bear the thought of them winning an award over her friends. Look, I'm really sorry and of course now that she's…no longer with us, there will be no repercussions or compensation claims. Can we just forget about it?' Adam said beseechingly.

'The Housemans have been really upset about this, dreading a negative story in the press or an investigation that could have ruined their business. Did you know that someone suggested to Lexie that they shouldn't even be allowed to have a stand at the wedding fair? Was it Beatrice?' Lydia was quite cross now and Adam couldn't meet her gaze.

He stuffed his hands in his pockets and scuffed the floor with his shoes. 'I'm just so embarrassed. I don't know what I can say or do to put things right,' he muttered.

'I think the first step is to apologise to the Housemans and tell them what you have just told me. I would also suggest that you write a letter saying that the reaction that your mother suffered was due to a mistake on your mother's part and that Houseman's Bakery were not to blame. This letter should be signed by you and be something that they can display in their shop.' Lydia folded her arms and waited for an answer.

Adam chewed his lips for a few moments. 'I suppose I could do that,' he replied begrudgingly.

'It's the least you can do, and you should do it with humility and good grace.'

Adam felt like he was back at school. *Bloody hell, I'm glad I didn't pursue a relationship of any kind with her. I thought older women were supposed to be more compliant.*

He nodded sullenly. 'Ok,' he replied, 'but it wasn't my fault in the first place.'

'You should have refused to go along with the ridiculous idea – it was completely irresponsible. Your mother could have died and the Housemans may have been charged with accidental death. Seriously, Adam, I thought you would have had more sense!'

Adam had had enough. 'Right! Fine! I'll do it. Can we leave it now? I think you were on your way out!' he snapped and opened the front door. Lydia said no more and marched past him. Adam pushed the door closed a little harder than he intended and it slammed shut. He leaned against it, folded his arms and scowled. *Bloody hell! Bloody, bloody hell! The sooner I can get to Spain, the better.*

Lydia Buckley

'I've loads to tell you, so much has happened today,' Lydia began as she and Greg ate dinner that evening.

'Have you? Ok, fire away.'

Lydia began with the revelation about Mr Lord, Mr Baron and Top Drawer Properties.

'We have to tell Will about this, it could mean a major breakthrough in their search for Mr Lord, and I'm not sure the police were even aware of a Mr Baron,' Greg said.

'We might need to rethink our idea of buying one of the apartments now – if it's the same Mr Lord. Should we speak to Tom about this?'

'I'll ask Tom if he knows anything about the directors, in the first instance, and maybe give him a quiet heads-up – I know he can be discreet,' replied Greg.

'They'll call Hugo in for questioning now, won't they – maybe Tom as well?'

'I would think so. It's a bit complicated because there are two investigations, one about Mr Lord and one for Beatrice's murder.'

'And now we've a Mr Baron as well,' Lydia added.

'I hope there is not a Mr Earl lurking somewhere,' said Greg with a mischievous grin.

Lydia pulled a face. 'Be serious!' she told him. 'The thing is, that if it's the same Mr Lord that the Sharps work for, then there is a vague connection with Adam. Adam lived in London, he may well have come into contact with Mr Lord – maybe he borrowed money? And if they *were* looking for Adam, it might explain how they knew where Adam lives. It doesn't explain why the Sharps went to the Hall though, but it's a start.' Lydia pointed out.

'You could be right there and, I've just thought of something else. Vivienne was with the Sharps and she might have known that Vinnie was meeting Adam – maybe she mentioned it in passing and they used her as an excuse to get to him.'

'Of course! The Sharps were staying at the Coach, as were Vinnie and Vivienne. Doreen said that Terry was flirting with Vivienne, I bet she was bragging about how important her husband was and maybe mentioned Adam's name!'

'That would certainly explain why they were there, but it doesn't help with Beatrice's murder.' Greg stroked his chin thoughtfully.

'No, it doesn't,' said Lydia with a touch of disappointment, 'unless it was a revenge killing?'

'But they still wouldn't know that Beatrice would have been at the pavilion,' replied Greg.

'That means that we go back to our original list of suspects – Sarah, Derek, and Cliff.'

'There is something else which might help Will's investigation.' Lydia told Greg about her conversation with Tasheka and that she had the memory stick.

'Why on earth didn't Tasheka tell the police she had all that evidence?'

'Because after she got home, her daughter hid it, she had her heebie-jeebies and she forgot about it until today. It presumably just carried on recording until it was full or went flat.'

'Has she watched it?'

'Only her exclusive interview with the fake Mrs Cody King. So, I thought we would look at it first and see if there is anything that might be of help to Will.'

'Of course we should!' agreed Greg with a twinkle in his eye.

'Why are you looking at me like that?' asked Lydia suspiciously.

'Because we both know that we want to see it before we have to hand it over and it's nothing to do with checking the quality – it's because we're both nosey.'

'We're only trying to help,' Lydia said.

They settled down to watch the footage, which was quite clear but jerky as Tasheka moved about. Greg speeded it up until they saw Beatrice enter the ballroom. In between Tasheka talking to people who came up to her table, they could see that Beatrice chatted to the people at each table until, eventually, she reached Tasheka. Beatrice looked disdainfully at her table with its rather lovely display of flowers and various photographs of the wedding cars, and the conversation could clearly be heard:

'Are you a photographer?' Beatrice asked.

'No, I'm Tasheka Dixon and I'm with Ashdale Wedding Cars.'

'Oh yes, the *ordinary* cars – interesting,' Beatrice said in a dismissive voice before turning and walking away.

'Wha' d'you mean, "ordinary cars"?' Tasheka called after her, but Beatrice had gone.

Greg and Lydia watched as Beatrice made her way across the ballroom towards Flower Power and the ensuing interaction.

'Whoa! I can tell from the body language that that was no happy reunion,' commented Greg as they watched the brief vocal exchange before Beatrice walked away. Even the limited view from Tasheka's table across the ballroom clearly showed the shocked faces of Fran and Lucy. The view was then obscured as Tasheka's camera was blocked by a customer, but there was a glimpse of Beatrice as she walked out through the French windows next to Tasheka's table. The time on the recording was thirteen forty-six. As Tasheka's customer left, they were then able to see Vivienne and the Sharp brothers making their way from table to table.

'I have to admit, he does look very much like Cody King, especially on this video,' admitted Greg.

'I suppose you can forgive people for believing that he was Cody. Everyone was taken in. I might have been, had you not told me about him,' replied Lydia.

'Right, let's see if we can see where they go,' said Greg screwing his eyes up in concentration. 'Look, the Sharps have stepped out of the French windows and Vivienne has come to Tasheka's table.'

'The time is thirteen fifty-two,' said Lydia, reaching for a pen and her notes.

They listened to the conversation between Vivienne and Tasheka. 'This is where Tasheka suggests the interview and leaves the table with Vivienne, and it's now thirteen fifty-four.' Lydia wrote the time down.

The video wobbled as Tasheka climbed the stairs and then steadied as she stopped in front of the window overlooking the terrace garden. Then she could quite clearly be heard telling Vivienne that the woman they could see going into the woods was Lexie Worthington who was on her way for a bit of jiggy-jiggy.

'Oh my God!' gasped Lydia, 'That can't be Lexie, she would have been in the Hall either finishing a tour with one couple or greeting the next, so it must be…Charlotte!'

'So why is Charlotte going into the woods?' asked Greg as he paused the video.

'We know she's having an affair with Adam so she may have been going to meet him there. Don't forget she's been seen there before, in a compromising situation, with Adam. What time does it say? Thirteen fifty-seven.'

'But if Adam and Charlotte were in the pavilion, they must know what happened to Beatrice. Why haven't they said anything?' Greg scratched his head.

'Because they want to keep the affair quiet? Remember that Charlotte is getting married on Saturday,' replied Lydia.

'But his mother was *murdered* for God's sake! Surely he would say something. You don't think *they* killed her, do you?' Greg exclaimed.

Lydia looked at Greg for a minute, then shook her head. 'Maybe we're wrong then and she wasn't going to the pavilion to meet Adam. Maybe she was going to look at flowers in the secret garden – I don't know. When I saw Vinnie just after the start of the fashion show, he said he had been working with Adam all morning. I rather got the impression that they had only just gone their separate ways.'

'So, she might not have been there when the murderer was, but she would definitely have seen Beatrice, and I bet that wasn't a pleasant exchange given that Beatrice had found out about the affair,' said Greg.

'Hmm, but for now, it puts Charlotte at the scene, so we have to add her to the suspect list. I'm seeing her tomorrow for her lash extensions, I'll see what that reveals.'

'Now *that* is what I meant when I said people talk to you. I bet you find out more than the police have, because she won't realise you're questioning her.'

'I don't question people, they simply chat,' retorted Lydia.

'That's what I meant to say. In the meantime, Will defo needs to see this footage. I'll call in and give it to him first thing tomorrow.'

'There's something else. I need to tell you, about my meeting with Adam.'

Lydia told Greg about finding the allergy note and why Adam had taken it.

'That's ridiculous!' exclaimed Greg. 'It's a helluva risk to take for a friend. I bet the Blenkhorns would be horrified if they knew she had done that on their behalf, I know I would be.'

'I think you need to tell Will about this as well, because he knows about the bakery incident. The good thing is that there will be no repercussions as far as the Housemans are concerned,' said Lydia.

'Yes, Will needs to know about the note,' agreed Greg. 'I have to say that it would be dreadful if Derek killed Beatrice because of this nut allergy business – I mean it's dreadful anyway, but if Beatrice took that risk out of sheer spite, well, talk of getting your comeuppance.' Greg shook his head sadly.

'It was a very stupid thing to do and I'm surprised at her, to be honest,' said Lydia.

'Let's watch the rest of this recording, although I don't suppose we shall learn much as it's not far off the time when Tasheka was locked in the en suite.'

They listened to Tasheka's interview with Vivienne, amazed at how glibly Vivienne was able to spin a story, and then they saw the ladies bumping into the Sharps as they left the bridal suite.

'What were the Sharps doing upstairs?' asked Lydia.

'They were looking for someone and I bet it was Adam. They must have wandered upstairs after they left the ballroom. What time is it?'

'Fourteen eleven.'

'Well, that proves they didn't go to the pavilion before the fashion show because they would have been seen from the window by Tasheka and Vivienne, or by Charlotte at the pavilion. Equally, if they weren't seen by either Derek, Sarah or Cliff afterwards, then I don't see how they could have done it,' concluded Greg.

They watched the next few minutes and when Tasheka hit Ray soundly on the side of his head with her handbag, Greg winced.

'Ow! Good God! Remind me to never, ever get on the wrong side of Tasheka – especially if she has a handbag to hand.'

Lydia laughed and then inhaled sharply as the camera picked up the moment when the bathroom door took the full impact of Ray's body.

'That man is an animal!' she gasped.

'Didn't frighten Tasheka though,' commented Greg.

There was more bluffing and posturing from Vivienne as she tried to maintain her character of Mrs Cody King and Greg fast forwarded the video, until it stopped abruptly as Ray was wheeled out on a stretcher.

'That's all there is, but we know what happened after that.' Greg extracted the memory stick and put it carefully back in the pouch. 'Will and his team are going to find that very interesting, it might help to corroborate some of the statements they already have, but as for the bit including Charlotte…'

Lydia stretched after being hunched over the laptop. 'There's nothing there to help our three original suspects and we've now added Charlotte. Surely there must be someone else we've missed,' said Lydia a little despondently.

'What about this Mr Baron? What if he was at the wedding fair? That might not be his real name. I'm going to look into him tomorrow – he's a new lead. I'll also speak to Rick in London and find out what they know, if anything.'

'Good idea. Now do you fancy coffee or a nightcap?'

'Actually neither, thanks. I'm going to get off home and have an early start tomorrow.' Greg stood up. 'I do love you, you know,' he added tenderly.

'I know you do, and I love you too.'

After Greg had left, Lydia felt warm and fuzzy inside. She smiled happily as she prepared for bed.

15

Charlotte Worthington
Charlotte slid behind the wheel of her red Audi TT and set off for Ashdale. She was getting very edgy – the wedding was in two days' time and quite frankly, she couldn't wait until it was all over. It wasn't so much the wedding itself that was making her nervous, it was Adam and the total lack of any communication since Sunday. Charlotte had no idea what his plan was regarding the elopement scenario. The fact that they hadn't spoken led her to believe that he wasn't expecting her to go with him, which was fine, but she felt some clarification was needed. He clearly hadn't told the police about her argument with Beatrice, but Charlotte wondered if he was saving that up for a dramatic revelation at the wedding.

Maybe she should go to the police and confess. Obviously, she wouldn't confess the exact truth, but a story of Adam trying to sabotage her wedding because of his obsession with her and that she had tried to enlist Beatrice's help – hence their conversation, might be the way forward. On the other hand, the cliché 'let sleeping dogs lie' came to mind. She had told Pen that this would be her story if things got tricky with the police and Pen had got a bit po-faced and muttered about not lying to the police. However, as Charlotte had pointed out, Pen could only repeat what she had been told and if Charlotte said that Adam was pressuring her into going to Spain, which he technically was, then that is what Pen should say. Once she was married to Gerald and safely on honeymoon, then Adam could say what he damn well liked, it would be seen as jealousy and have no detrimental effect on her marriage.

Charlotte tutted as she realised it was Thursday and therefore Market Day, which meant she couldn't park on the Market Place, so she had to use the large car park behind MegaMart.

When she arrived at the salon, there seemed to be a bit of a flurry at the reception desk where the receptionist was staring at a large bouquet of red roses and gypsophila with fragrant eucalyptus and palm leaves. The arrangement was stunning, but the girl looked horrified.

Lydia smiled as she saw Charlotte. 'These have just arrived for Saffron, aren't they beautiful?' she said.

'But I don't want them,' said Saffron, pushing the flowers away.

'Don't you? Why not?' exclaimed Charlotte.

'Because I, like, have a boyfriend.'

Charlotte frowned, puzzled as to why the girl didn't want flowers from her boyfriend.

'This is the second time a beautiful bouquet has arrived for Saffron. The card says, *Thinking of you* and is signed with a capital 'A', just as it was last time. Saffron doesn't know who 'A' is, as her boyfriend is called Connor,' explained Lydia.

'How exciting – to have a secret admirer,' said Charlotte with a smile, remembering how she had felt at the beginning of her affair with Adam.

A woman with dark hair and red highlights also stood by reception. She had been quiet so far, but now she spoke. 'You know, I've been thinking and I believe I know who 'A' is,' she said.

'Who?' asked Lydia.

'Saffron, do you remember that day when you I saw you talking to Adam Lewis – you had gone for milk? Well, I reckon it's him,' the woman said.

'Adam Lewis! Why on earth would you think that, Maggie?' exclaimed Lydia.

Adam? Adam had sent this girl some flowers? Not once, but twice? Charlotte was stunned.

'When you came back from MegaMart with the milk, you said that you had been talking to a really nice man and you thought you had…a connection, was how you put it. Well, that man was Adam Lewis and I did think at the time, that he had a certain interested look in his eye,' said Maggie sagely.

All eyes turned to Saffron. 'Oh yes…I remember that,' she said slowly, 'but I'd only just like, bumped into him. Why would he like, send me flowers?'

'Years ago, I met a chap once and he sent me flowers prior to asking me out on a date,' replied Maggie.

'So, you think he's, like, going to ask me out? I don't want him to. Connor will go mad and accuse me of like, flirting with him.' Saffron looked worried.

Adam might be going to ask her out? Is that why he has ignored me this week? Charlotte's mind was in a whirl.

'When did you receive the first bouquet?' Charlotte asked casually.

'Umm…it was, like, last week. I had to leave the flowers here so Connor wouldn't see them. He's, like, not very happy if other men look at me,' replied Saffron.

'It was last Tuesday,' added Lydia, 'I remember because Lexie was here for her appointment.'

Last Tuesday! Charlotte thought back, but Adam had already told her about his villa purchase and his idea of eloping by then. Had he seen through her pretended enthusiasm or rather lack of it and cast his net in a different direction? Was Adam seriously considering finishing with her for this Barbie doll?

'If I were you, I'd give Connor the elbow and go out with Adam if he asks. Connor sounds altogether too possessive,' advised Maggie.

'But I love Connor,' protested Saffron.

Charlotte had heard enough and she cleared her throat.

Lydia turned to her client. 'Ok, Miss Worthington – please come with me, I'm sorry to have kept you waiting.'

Charlotte followed Lydia into a lovely aromatic treatment room and it wasn't long before she was relaxing on the couch with her eyes closed. They discussed what type and style of lashes would be best and Lydia began to apply them. Lydia asked Charlotte about her wedding, the theme and colours she had chosen, where they were going for honeymoon and if she was looking forward to moving to Claro Court. Towards the end of the appointment, Charlotte decided to probe a bit further as to what Lydia might know about the Adam/Saffron situation,

'That receptionist, Saffron, didn't seem too keen to go out with Adam Lewis, did she?' she began.

'She is quite smitten with her current boyfriend and she's a very loyal girl,' replied Lydia.

'So, you don't agree that she should drop him to go out with Adam?'

'I don't know Adam very well, but I understand you recommended him to design a new website for Ashdale Hall, so, actually you may know him better than I do.'

Charlotte thought about her answer and made a decision. 'I met him at a function, he was there with his mother and I thought that designing our website would be a great opportunity for his new business. I was also able to introduce him to some people who could open other doors for him.' Charlotte paused before adding, 'I'm embarrassed to say that I regret it now.'

'Regret it? How?'

'Well…' Charlotte replied carefully, '…look, what I'm about to say is quite confidential and I'm only telling you this so you can advise Saffron accordingly.'

'Whatever you say in the treatment room *is* confidential, unless you say otherwise of course,' Lydia told her pleasantly.

'I believe Adam to be…obsessed with me. I know that sounds ridiculous, but he is imagining that we're having an affair – of course we're not, but he has threatened to tell my fiancé that we are, unless I agree to elope with him to Spain.'

'Really? Adam said that?'

'Yes, and the problem is that Gerald is a little like Saffron's boyfriend in that he can be quite possessive…only because he loves me, obviously.'

'Obviously,' Lydia commented.

'So, if Adam were to tell Gerald that I was having an affair, it's likely that Gerald would believe Adam over me and he might call off the wedding, then everyone would assume I was...well, I would be tainted, do you see?'

'Yes, I can see how that would leave you in a very difficult situation.'

'So, I rashly agreed to this eloping idea, but he has taken it too far and bought a villa in Spain for us to live in!'

'A villa? He is very serious about this, then.'

'He is, the whole thing is very upsetting, but it gets worse...'

'Worse, how?'

'I was absolutely desperate, so I decided to speak to his mother – you know, woman to woman. So, I met with Beatrice and we had a really lovely talk, and she was so understanding. Did you know Beatrice?'

'No, I met her for the first time on Sunday at the wedding fair,' replied Lydia.

'Well, she told me not to worry, that she quite understood my anxiety and that she would try and persuade Adam to drop this whole affair idea. She even suggested that she would try and talk him into going to Spain with her sometime this week just to get him out of Ashdale before my wedding.'

'Wow, that's very considerate of her, but you said things got worse. This sounds as though things actually got better.'

'I saw Beatrice for this little chat at the pavilion on Sunday around two o'clock and I haven't dared tell the police in case I get arrested and the whole story comes out.' Charlotte held her breath. *There – she had said it. Now what would Lydia say?* The tweezers lifted away from Charlotte's eyes as Lydia digested this revelation.

'Does Adam know you saw Beatrice on Sunday?' Lydia asked as she completed her task and peeled away the eyelash pads covering Charlotte's lower lashes. 'Just keep your eyes closed for a few minutes, please.'

'Yes, I told him when we met up after my chat with Beatrice because he asked me where I had been. I didn't tell him exactly what Beatrice and I had talked about – I just said we had bumped into each other in the secret garden.'

'Why has he not told the police you had been with Beatrice?'

'I don't know, maybe he is planning to make an announcement at the wedding to ruin my big day. I'm just so stressed and I don't know what to do,' Charlotte said plaintively.

'My advice would be to be honest with the police. You can get into a lot of trouble if you withhold information. And I think you should also tell Gerald that Adam might be threatening to derail your wedding, it will be very awkward if Adam pipes up in the bit where everyone should forever hold their peace.'

Charlotte thought for a moment. 'Do you think the police will arrest me?'

'Not at this point as, presumably, you don't have a motive and there is no evidence to suggest that you killed Beatrice, otherwise you would already have been arrested; but if you don't tell them, you may be charged with making a false statement. You can open your eyes now and sit up when you're ready.'

Charlotte carefully opened her eyes and blinked before she sat up. 'I'm scared, Lydia,' she said in a small voice. 'I'm scared about telling the police, and there's something else – Adam told me that he saw two men at the Hall who were after him. Are they the ones who were eventually arrested?'

'They may have been. Why were they after Adam? Did they find him?' Lydia asked.

'He said that something happened when he was in London, that's why they were after him, but I don't think they saw him. He said they were downstairs when he saw them. I'm really worried that Gerald will cancel the wedding.'

Lydia sighed. 'If you don't say anything, you're taking a risk. You had no reason to kill Beatrice, did you? Adam could tell the police at any opportunity and then you will be in much worse position.'

Lydia passed a hand mirror to Charlotte. 'Oh! They look amazing, simply fabulous, I love them. You're doing Pen's aren't you? God knows, *her* eyelashes need perking up. She's got ginger hair and her lashes are so fair. She does try with mascara, but somehow she gets it everywhere and I want my pictures to look fabulous, without a panda involved.' Charlotte swung her legs over the edge of the couch and stood up.

'Yes, I'm seeing Ms Sinclair-Sutton tomorrow afternoon.'

'Please keep our conversation yourself, at least for now, and I'll think very hard about what you said.'

'Charlotte, you're going away on a two-week honeymoon – on Monday, I think you said? You must speak to the police before you go or I'll have no choice but to do so. I can't keep this a secret otherwise I'm also implicated in your deceit.' Lydia looked at Charlotte and Charlotte knew she meant what she said.

'Ok, I understand, but I may wait until Sunday, then at least I shall be married and it's one less thing to be worried about.' Charlotte saw Lydia shrug resignedly and she mentally crossed her fingers that she had now covered herself in case Adam either talked to the police or gatecrashed her wedding.

Lydia escorted Charlotte to reception and Saffron smiled at her. 'Those lashes look amazing. Lydia does, like, such a good job. My sister, Scarlett, gets married in four weeks' time and I've suggested that she gets hers done as well.'

Charlotte rummaged in her handbag for her purse as Saffron chatted on. 'Scarlett was at the wedding fair last Sunday, and, apart from what happened, she thought it was like, so brilliant. She's decided to book her flowers with the shop next door, Flower Power, because she thought their flowers were, like, so pretty and she talked for ages with the owner, Sarah, who she thought was, like, so amazing.'

Charlotte nodded benignly and handed over her credit card. 'You know, I may well come back after my honeymoon for infills, I really think these lashes suit me,' she said to Lydia. 'I'll certainly recommend you to my friends and I would think that having Lady Charlotte Pemberton as a client will certainly raise your profile.'

Lydia smiled gracefully and Saffron handed back her credit card. Charlotte tucked the card away and, confident that Lydia had been taken in by her version of events, she left the salon and headed back to her car.

Sarah Kirkwood

Sarah knew she was a prime suspect for Beatrice's murder. When taken in for questioning on Tuesday, she had been calm and honest when answering the police's questions. She reiterated her belief that Beatrice Lewis, formerly Trissie Foxton, had been the driver of the car that had killed her father, and that the only person she had seen walking towards the secret garden had been Derek. The bride who had stopped her on the terrace to talk about wedding flowers had not yet made contact, and, although this worried her mother, Sarah was confident that she would not ultimately be charged with killing Beatrice because of course she hadn't done it.

Around lunchtime, Lydia called in. 'Hi Sarah, how are you?'

'I'm fine…considering.'

'I've just popped in with some good news – I know who the young bride is – the one you were talking to on the terrace.'

'You do?' exclaimed Sarah.

'Saffron Lawson's sister, Scarlett. You know Saffron? She's the new receptionist at WOW!'

'How did you find that out?'

'Saffron just happened to mention it. Apparently, Scarlett works in Harrogate and intends to come here on Saturday to organise her flowers. I've asked Saffron if Scarlett can contact the police as soon as possible to offer a statement and confirm that she *did* spend some time talking to you on the terrace sometime after two o'clock.'

'Oh Lydia! That's fantastic news, Mum will be so relieved,' gushed Sarah.

'I hope you're relieved as well.'

'Oh, well, of course I am, but I knew I hadn't committed murder – I just couldn't prove it, but now I can – I've got my alibi.' Sarah felt almost giddy with delight and suddenly she realised that for all her bravado and calm exterior, underneath she really had been very anxious. As she felt the stress and strain of the week melting away, the shop door opened and her mother walked in.

'Mum! Lydia has found our missing bride! I've got my alibi!' she gabbled.

Lucy looked at Lydia, who smiled and nodded. 'Scarlett Lawson, Saffron's sister.'

Lucy put her handbag on the counter. 'I can't tell you how happy I'm to hear that, thank you, Lydia.'

'I didn't do anything. Saffron just happened to mention that Scarlett was getting married in four weeks' time, and bingo!'

'Well, it's a huge weight off our shoulders. Sarah says that she was told by the police that they are not charging the Sharp brothers with Beatrice's murder and are still continuing with the investigation, so the murderer is still at large,' said Lucy.

The door opened and Elsa bustled in. 'Lydia! I saw you come in here and I just wanted to catch you.' Elsa was slightly out of breath. 'I've just seen Dr Weston and I happened to ask him if Beatrice could possibly have faked that reaction she had to them nuts 'cos it's been bothering me – and do you know what he said?'

Lucy and Sarah stared in amazement at this sudden intrusion and Lydia shook her head in answer to Elsa's question.

'He said, "No." Then I asked if she would do such a thing deliberately, you know just to cause trouble and do you know what he said to that?'

Sarah felt certain that they all knew the answer, but they all shook their heads obligingly,

'He said that anyone with a nut allergy would not take the risk as they know it can be fatal,' announced Elsa, looking very pleased with herself.

'I don't think anyone thought she *had* done it on purpose,' said Lucy carefully.

'But that's just the point!' said Elsa, her eyes shining. 'It proves it was an accident.'

Sarah frowned. 'I don't understand why that's significant because, surely, it only makes Derek's motive stronger,' she said.

Elsa's smile faded. 'Well given that there is a photo of the nut allergy sign in place and Beatrice didn't eat the cake on purpose, I thought it proved that the sign blew under the counter,' she said hesitantly.

'Does it matter anyway, now that Beatrice is dead?' asked Sarah bluntly.

'I suppose not,' admitted Elsa, visibly deflated. 'Oh well, I just thought it might be an important piece of information.'

'It still might be, if there are any further developments about the incident,' said Lydia kindly.

Elsa sniffed. 'I must get back and do lunch for me and Brian, so bye for now.' And she left the shop.

Sarah giggled. 'Poor Elsa, she really thought she had stumbled onto something important, didn't she?'

'Bless her,' replied Lucy with feeling.

'How did you like the park home, Mum?' asked Sarah, changing the subject.

'I've just been with Cliff on his second viewing,' Lucy explained to Lydia. 'I'm really impressed, it's absolutely ideal for him and I told him so. I think he had already decided as he showed me where he intended putting his things as if he has already begun to pack.'

'That's good news, it will be lovely to have him as a local,' said Lydia.

'He has asked me to help with colour schemes as he wants to redecorate, it's a bit floral at the moment, and I shall look forward to that. Do you know, with park homes, the whole purchase process can be completed in about two weeks? It's much quicker than houses,' Lucy told them.

Lydia glanced at the nurses fob watch pinned to her uniform. 'Look, I shall have to go and get back to work, so I'll see you later at some point.' She wiggled her fingers as she left.

The phone rang just then and Sarah answered it, as Lucy took her handbag to their kitchen and put the kettle on.

Sheila Houseman

Later that afternoon as Sheila wiped the counter before closing up, the door opened and Lydia entered the bakery.

'Hello love.' She smiled warmly at Lydia. Sheila liked the budding author, and remembered how helpful and kind she had been to young Mrs Saxby-Jones earlier in the year, well until ...

'Sheila, I wanted to pop in and wish you and Derek the very best of luck for tomorrow night, my fingers and toes are all crossed.'

Sheila beamed with delight. 'That's very thoughtful of you, not many people have remembered about the awards, what with Beatrice's murder and so on.' Then her smile faded. 'But Derek is at the police station, being questioned again.' Sheila fought to hold back the tears and Lydia stepped behind the counter and put out a reassuring hand.

'Sheila, I'm sure it's just routine—'

'Oh Lydia!' Sheila grasped Lydia's hand, 'I don't know what to think, I'm so frightened in case he...he ...'

'Sheila?'

Sheila took a deep breath and told Lydia about giving her statement including the story of the nut incident, and Adam Lewis and his demand for fifty thousand pounds.

'Later, when me and Derek were at home, he told me that when he had left our table and gone down to the pavilion, as he walked along the path through the trees, he stopped short because he had heard a man's voice ahead of him. He realised that the man was on the phone as he could only hear one voice and the only words he heard clearly were: "You were supposed to be here and do this, it's what you get paid for." Derek then changed his mind about speaking with Beatrice and decided to return to the wedding fair. He had no idea who he had overheard, but I thought that it was likely to be the murderer!' she told

Lydia. 'I can't tell you how thankful I was that Derek had had the common sense to simply turn back.'

'But…why are you so worried that *Derek* may have killed Beatrice if he heard someone else there?' asked Lydia.

'Because, if those two men have been arrested, then why has Derek been taken in again? He said he only heard *one* man, so it doesn't fit, does it?'

'Maybe the other man just kept quiet whilst his mate was on the phone?' suggested Lydia.

'Maybe…' agreed Sheila, not sounding at all convinced.

At that moment, the door opened and Derek walked in, looking a little apprehensive.

'They've found the nut allergy sign although they wouldn't say where, and the man I heard on the phone in the wood was not either of those two chaps from London.'

Sheila's mouth dropped open. 'So where does that leave you?' she gasped.

'Still "a person of interest" is how they put it, so we won't be gadding off abroad any time soon. The best news is that the nut incident is well and truly behind us and we can look forward to tomorrow night now.' Derek smiled whilst Sheila still felt uncertain. 'Come on love, buck up, this time tomorrow, we shall be getting our glad rags on for a grand night out.'

Sheila glanced at Lydia who simply smiled and nodded positively. 'That's mostly good news, Derek. I'll leave you to talk and good luck for tomorrow,' she said as she turned and left the bakery.

'A person of interest?' repeated Sheila.

'That's what they said.'

'So, if the person you heard on the phone was not the London men, who was it?'

'Don't know love, but between you and me, I think it was the murderer!'

Lydia Buckley

Lydia was glad to get home after work. It had been a busy day at the salon and, although she was looking forward to going out tonight with Tom and Amy, she had a lot of information to add to her notes. She made herself a gin and tonic, sat at the table and picked up a pen. She wrote that Charlotte had admitted that she had gone to the pavilion and spoke with Beatrice, that Scarlett was Sarah's missing alibi, about the interesting but brief conversation with Elsa, and Sheila's information about Derek.

Lydia thought it was likely that Derek was the person that Cliff had noticed through the trees. Her next job was to gather the information for Tasheka regarding her request for eyelash technician training, and once that was done, she sent a text to Tasheka and suggested they meet in the Coach tomorrow evening after work at around six o'clock. An idea had been bubbling in her head ever since Lexie had mentioned about needing an eyelash technician for the Ashdale Hall spa, and now she had made a start on her plan. Greg had told her that her idea to become a tutor and create an academy and agency for eyelash technicians was a great idea, so Lydia had applied for the tutor training course. Her ultimate goal would be to train her technicians to a high standard, including customer-service skills, and then she would market her academy as *the* place for top notch technicians who would be available for both temporary and permanent positions.

Lydia knew that currently, if she took time off from work, it left her clients at both Lush Lashes and WOW! without appointments, whereas if she could rely on someone to cover whilst she was away, it would ensure continuity of the business. It followed therefore, that other salons may have the same problem and were possibly unable to find suitably efficient and qualified technicians to cover.

Satisfied that she hadn't forgotten anything, Lydia headed for the shower, pondering what she should wear for her evening out. Ten minutes later, as she looked through her wardrobe, her phone chirped with a message from Tasheka confirming their early doors meeting at the pub the next day.

Greg had booked a taxi to take them all into Harrogate and during the journey, Lydia told them that Lucy has been for a second viewing with Cliff and it sounded as though he was set to buy the park home.

'And I can confirm that Cliff's offer has been accepted only this afternoon,' added Tom.

'I'm really pleased about that, he did a great job with the wedding fair article. You know, I really like Cliff, he gets on easily with people,' said Greg.

'I bet Elsa can't wait to have him as a neighbour, she'll be forever at his door with gossip,' giggled Amy, her long brunette hair caught up in an elegant, but effortless bun.

Caribe was buzzing and vibrant with the Caribbean sound of reggae, and Lydia loved the atmosphere. They were shown to their table and ordered cocktails whilst they perused the menu.

When their food order had been taken and the drinks placed in front of them, Tom started the conversation. 'I'm glad you gave me a heads-up, Greg, as I had a phone call from Will this morning to say that he was sending his sergeant down to talk to me about Top Drawer Properties – you know, the developers of the Mar Menor site? Apparently, they are interested in the two directors Mr Lord and Mr Baron and what I knew about them, but unfortunately, I couldn't be of any real help as I don't get involved with Top Drawer, it's Hugo's thing really – I simply refer enquiries to him,' he told them.

'I expect the police will want to talk to Hugo, in that case,' said Greg. 'It's fortunate that he's over here at the moment.'

'He's helping Adam with Beatrice's affairs and the funeral and so on, although there has been a major hiccup with Adam's villa purchase,' replied Tom.

'Oh? I thought he had already bought it,' Lydia frowned.

'He had, more or less. The final balance of one hundred and fifty thousand pounds was due last Thursday, and Adam had asked Beatrice for money to make the final payment, but for some reason she had decided to deliberately delay this payment for two weeks. Following her death, Hugo and Adam have been to see Albert Wilks, who confirmed that, until the estate was settled and probate granted, no payments can be made.

'So, where does that leave Adam?' asked Lydia.

'Top Drawer have issued a Notice to Complete which requires Adam to make the final payment within ten working days. As Adam is not in a position to comply with the notice, Top Drawer will have the right to rescind the contract and keep the deposit. But unfortunately he has paid a lot more than the required ten percent deposit of forty thousand...he has actually paid two hundred and fifty thousand.'

Lydia gasped. 'Will Top Drawer have to pay back the two hundred and ten thousand pounds he overpaid?'.

'If they are a scrupulous company, then they will, although it may take some time. If, on the other hand, they are not, then Adam may have to take them to court. Either way, he will not be getting any money back any time soon.'

Greg whistled. 'Bloody hell, that's a lot of money *not* to have,' he said.

'So, it's not looking good for our Spanish property investment and a long weekend in Mar Menor then?' queried Amy. They all looked at her. 'What? We agreed we would go.'

'Amy, sweetheart, I think we all felt a little bit sorry for Adam for a minute there, rather than disappointment at a possibly thwarted weekend away.'

Amy opened her mouth to speak but was prevented from doing so by the arrival of their food. Lydia caught Greg's eye and raised her eyebrows knowingly, she knew that they would not disclose what they knew about Beatrice's murder as they both had an understanding with Will, that not all they were told or found out could be repeated. She hoped Greg intended coming back to her flat later so she could update him on the information she had found out earlier that day.

When the waiter left their table, Amy raised her finger. 'Talking about Mar Menor,' she began and Tom rolled his eyes, '...not about us, someone else,' she said to him.

'My sister Steph has a flatmate called Pam and Pam's friend Lindsay spent last weekend in her boyfriend's villa in Mar Menor. She says it's absolutely fabulous, she loved it – so exclusive and she saw loads of celebs,' Amy continued.

'Sounds expensive,' quipped Tom.

Amy ignored him. 'I say, boyfriend, but actually, Lindsay is having a relationship with an older man called Gerry and apparently he is rich, single and lives in his villa. He only comes to the UK at weekends. I think she's hoping for a permanent thing with him, but the problem is that he smokes cigars.'

'Lucky Lindsay, I don't mind an odd cigar. Now why couldn't I have met a Gerry instead of a Greg?' Lydia wondered with a smirk at Greg.

'Oh! You wouldn't like Gerry, he's much older than you, in fact he's a bit of a Cosmo Smallpiece,' deadpanned Greg as he topped up everyone's wine.

'Cosmo Smallpiece!' spluttered Tom, 'who the heck is Cosmo Smallpiece?'

'Google it!' said Greg. Tom obliged and roared with laughter as he showed his phone first to Amy who also laughed and then Lydia, who waved the phone away.

'I know who Cosmo Smallpiece is – a pervy character courtesy of Les Dawson,' she said and shook her head despairingly at Greg.

'I loved watching Les Dawson, and what were the names of the old ladies that he used to do with Roy...um, whatshisname?' Greg clicked his fingers as he searched his memory.

'Roy Barraclough,' Lydia said.

'That's it! Loved that. What were their names?' He tapped the table.

'Cissie and Ada,' replied Lydia.

Greg stopped tapping and looked at her,

'You'd be quite good in a pub quiz,' he said.

Everyone laughed and they began to chat about the comedians they liked.

At last, the taxi pulled up outside Lydia's flat. 'Will you come up? I've loads to tell you,' she asked.

'I'll come for a quick coffee, but I'm going to London tomorrow to meet Rick and the other chaps to try and make sense of some info they have on Adam Lewis. I'm getting the seven thirty train from Harrogate in the morning.'

As they sat with cups of coffee, Lydia told Greg about her day.

'I had Charlotte as a client this morning and she confided in me about Adam and her reasons for going to the pavilion on Sunday.' Lydia told Greg what Charlotte had said during the appointment. 'And I told her to speak to the police before she goes on honeymoon on Monday, or I would have to. The thing is, we know she's lying.'

'You did the right thing, although if I were you, I might mention something to Will beforehand, just in case she doesn't get round to speaking to him – to cover yourself as well.'

'Good point. You know, I bet that, if asked, Adam will say that his mother was not pleased about this affair and I wonder if that was why she delayed the final payment on the villa until after Charlotte's wedding,' said Lydia.

'Hmm, does that give Adam a motive for murder?' asked Greg.

'It might do.'

'But Adam is now worse off because he might lose the villa altogether whereas if Beatrice had *not* been killed, she would have paid the balance. The person with the most lose is probably Charlotte – she was worried in case Adam, or indeed Beatrice, might tell Sir Gerald about her affair. Beatrice's death seems to have solved her problem,' Greg remarked.

'Don't forget that Adam was with Vinnie during Sunday morning.'

'So, Adam can't really be in the frame.'

'I'm seeing Pen tomorrow to do her lashes, so it will be interesting to see what she says, if anything.'

Greg yawned. 'Ok, what else have you got?' he asked and took a drink of coffee.

'I think we can cross Sarah off our suspect list as I found out that Scarlett Lawson is the bride who can provide Sarah with her alibi,' Lydia said. 'Saffron works at Zoe's salon and she happened to mention that her sister had been talking to Sarah on Sunday and intends to book her flowers, but she just hasn't had time yet. I asked Saffron to tell Scarlett to contact the police.'

'That is good news, and depending on what Scarlett has to say, they may be able to eliminate Sarah. Next?'

Lydia was very much aware that Greg was tired and had a long day to look forward to tomorrow, so she quickly told him what Elsa had said about her conversation with Dr Weston.

'...which totally contradicts what Adam told me, so I give up on the nut allergy incident. It's all irrelevant anyway now that Beatrice has died.'

Greg nodded. 'Oh! I nearly forgot!' he said suddenly. 'When I gave Will the memory stick, I asked him if he could tell me where the Sharps went after leaving Vivienne and Tasheka in the bridal suite. He said that Terry took Ray outside and talked to him to calm him down, and that as they talked, Terry noticed the police presence at the main gate and decided to go back, get Vivienne and leave. He reckoned that they needed Vivienne so they could blend in with other couples leaving the Hall.'

'I think "blend in" is stretching it a bit,' laughed Lydia.

Greg nodded in agreement and chuckled. 'If you want my opinion, I think Charlotte is looking like a prime suspect – she had means, motive and opportunity. Hey! I've just thought of something; if Charlotte tells the police the same story she told you, and Adam says something very different – maybe they are in cahoots? He told her where Beatrice would be and she did it! Now they are just blaming each other.' Greg looked excited about his theory.

'You could be right there, but something is bothering me and I don't know what it is. I'm missing something or I've seen something that is significant or doesn't add up, but I can't think what.'

'Maybe Adam saw the Sharp brothers and thought it was an opportunity to bump off his mother and blame them, so he tells Charlotte to do the necessary.'

Lydia stopped rinsing cups and looked Greg straight in the eye. 'Are you serious?'

'I certainly am. What if Adam wants his mother's money *and* Charlotte – perhaps Charlotte really *does* want to escape marriage to Gerald. After all, Sir Gerald Pemberton is not a man you would typically put Charlotte with, is he?'

'No, but Adam wouldn't need to kill Beatrice to elope with Charlotte, I'm guessing she has a pretty hefty allowance from her father.' Lydia finished at the sink and wiped the counters.

'Yes, but calling off a wedding this close to the date would be tricky and embarrassing for the Worthingtons.'

'I suppose so, but this feels more of a crime of passion, not premeditated murder.'

'Hmm. See what you can get from Pen tomorrow – without questioning her!' Greg teased and Lydia swiped him with the tea towel.

'Right, I'm going home now. It's been a lovely evening and we'll catch up properly tomorrow.' Greg put his arms around Lydia.

'I'm meeting Tasheka in the pub at six, so if I'm not at home, that's where I'll be,' she told him.

Greg kissed her deeply and when he pulled away, he smiled. 'In that case, I'll go straight to the Coach when I get back.'

After Greg had left, Lydia locked up and headed to bed. *What was it that was bugging her?*

16

Lydia Buckley
Lydia left Lush Lashes at three o'clock and drove straight to the Hall for her appointment with Pen, scheduled for three thirty. As she walked through the entrance hall, she noticed activity in *The Kensington Suite* and the ballroom, and then she saw Lexie.

'Wow!' she exclaimed, gazing around in wonder. The large folding doors that separated the two rooms had been opened to create one huge room, all the French doors were open as the sun had been shining directly into the large space, the voile curtains wafted gently to and fro.

'This is the wedding room,' explained Lexie. 'I'm having to use both rooms as there are so many guests, and the reception is in a marquee that's already erected. Mummy's in charge of operations in there.'

'It'll be absolutely wonderful, I can't wait to see the photos.'

'It will be a fabulous showcase for the Hall as a wedding venue, so naturally we're pulling out all the stops. Call in here on your way out after doing Pen's lashes and you'll see the transformation.'

'I certainly will, see you later.' Lydia left Lexie to get on with her work and made her way to the spa.

The theme of the spa was Thai, the colours were grey and cream with accents of muted gold. Buddha statues sat on plinths in niches, and the ceiling was softly arched culminating to a point in the style of a typical Thai temple. It was an oasis of calm, and Lydia breathed in the botanical aromas and listened to soothing spa music, and with sounds of water lapping gently, she felt herself relax.

Having been shown to her designated room, Lydia set out the things she had brought for the appointment. Pen arrived on time and, after a brief chat about what she wanted, Pen laid back on the couch with eye pads in place. Lydia hadn't met Pen before and asked her where she and Charlotte had met. Pen told her that they were friends from school, that they were completely opposite in character and that she had no idea what drew them together. She talked about her broken engagement to Philip Montgomery, the son of a very wealthy judge and how her father had bought her a shop in Northallerton – her first LulaBelle's boutique.

As she chatted about her beloved LulaBelle's and her plans for expansion, it became clear to Lydia that Pen had found her *raison d'être* – she was so focused, and determined that her shops would be successful. She talked about her plans for a marketing campaign around Christmas time after she had opened her third shop, which would be in Skipton.

'In fact,' she said, 'I was wondering if it would be possible to sponsor the Christmas lights in Ashdale, Northallerton, and Skipton – do you know who I should contact?'

'I think each town has its own Christmas Committee, I know Ashdale does. Derek Houseman is the chairman so perhaps he should be your first port of call, his bakery is next door to your boutique.'

'Oh, in that case I'll call in and see him sometime next week,' Pen decided.

'These lashes are going to look lovely, I'm using mostly brown with some black so that your eyes don't look too heavy as your own lashes are quite fair,' Lydia explained.

'Charlotte loves hers. She'll look stunning tomorrow, I've seen her dress and it's breathtaking. Sir Gerald is very lucky.'

'Charlotte is very worried about Adam Lewis ruining her day, so she may look to you for support if he turns up,' Lydia said gently.

Pen chewed her lip. 'She spoke to you about that?'

'She did and she asked my advice about something, and whether she should tell the police.'

'I was questioned by the police only this morning. I was absolutely terrified that I would say the wrong thing.'

'If you tell the truth, you can't say the wrong thing, surely.'

'You can if you know Charlotte. I'm really worried about her, Lydia, I think she's getting herself into trouble.'

Lydia thought for a moment. *I wonder which version of events Pen thinks that Charlotte has told me?*

'This whole Adam situation is trouble,' Lydia said carefully.

Pen sighed. 'She should never have started the affair with Adam in the first place. She told me about their little joke of eloping if her wedding jitters got too much, but I don't think she ever considered that Adam would take it so seriously. She said that Adam's plan was for them to elope on the morning of the wedding, but of course she wasn't going to go along with that because she *wants* to marry Gerald.'

'So, when was Charlotte going to tell Adam?' asked Lydia.

'She wasn't, she was worried if she told him any time this last week, that he would spill the beans to Gerald and then he would be so cross, and that he would refuse to marry her.'

'She was going to jilt Adam?'

'Yes, by simply not turning up to their pre-arranged meeting.'

'He would have been furious.'

'Probably, but by the time it dawned on him that she wasn't going to turn up, she would have been married.'

'Oh dear! What an acrimonious end to an affair – still at least she could start her marriage with a clean slate, I suppose.'

'I'm afraid it wouldn't have stayed that way,' Pen muttered.

'Surely she wouldn't have started the affair with Adam again? I wouldn't have thought he would come back for more.'

'Not with Adam, Wes Garrett.'

'Wes Garrett? Oh Lordy!'

'Charlotte and I went to the opening of Caribe in Harrogate, and he was there with Sophie Kingsley, one of our friends. Charlotte was going to dump Adam and take up with Wes Garrett after she moved to Claro Court – Gerald is away such a lot.'

Lydia paused as she thought about what Pen had just said. 'Sophie won't be impressed,' she commented and then resumed her work.

'No, Sophie was furious to see Charlotte making eyes at Wes because she's quite smitten with him. What makes it worse is that Sophie was once dating Gerald, then Charlotte appeared on the scene and fluttered her eyelashes at him, and Gerald simply abandoned Sophie. I'm afraid Charlotte was rather dismissive about that, however, I spoke to Sophie later and she said that she had been having second thoughts about Gerald in any case because she hated his smelly cigars, but that's not the point.' Pen's voice had raised a little at her exasperation with Charlotte.

'But what if Sophie or someone else found out about Charlotte's intended affair with Wes?' asked Lydia.

'Unfortunately, someone did,' replied Pen. 'Charlotte told me all this in the ladies' loo that same evening, and unbeknownst to us, Beatrice was in there and she heard every word.'

Lydia inhaled sharply. *So that's how Beatrice knew about the affair!* 'And did Charlotte find out that Beatrice had heard all this?'

'Yes, because Beatrice tackled Adam when she got home that night and then Adam questioned Charlotte, then that's when things got complicated. Adam had to tell Beatrice that he *wasn't* planning to elope when in fact he *was* and Charlotte had to convince Adam that she *was* eloping with him, when in fact she *wasn't*.

'Good grief!' Lydia shook her head, and then decided to press on. 'The thing is, Pen, that's not what Charlotte told *me*.'

'I guess she told you that Adam was more or less stalking her and that she went to talk to Beatrice about it?'

'She did.'

'That's to cover herself in case Adam tells the police about their affair. But I'm really concerned that the police will find out that Charlotte is lying and become suspicious of her or charge her with something – I don't know, falsifying evidence? Perverting the course of justice? Wasting police time?'

'She could certainly find herself in trouble when the truth comes out.'

'This latest plan is what really worries me, because she asked me to confirm this stalking story to the police, however, I couldn't lie to them, so I told the truth.' Pen was clearly worried.

'You did the right thing.'

'As much as I'm Charlotte's friend, I couldn't go along with that,' Pen admitted miserably. 'She's going to hate me from now on. I've no idea how she'll feel about my being a bridesmaid tomorrow now that I've let her down.'

Lydia laid down her tweezers and gently removed the eye pads. 'Keep your eyes closed for a few minutes, Pen,' she said. 'Look, for what it's worth, in my opinion you have not let Charlotte down. This situation has come about through Charlotte's own behaviour, it was always going to end in tears whether the police were involved or not. If Beatrice had not been killed, she would probably have spoken to Sir Gerald and he might well have refused to go ahead with the wedding, anyway. Similarly, if Charlotte had simply not turned up to meet Adam as arranged, he might have gatecrashed the wedding – he may well still do, as I doubt he is still planning to go to Spain tomorrow. But none of this is because you have told the police the truth.'

'You're right, of course,' sighed Pen, 'I just feel a bit guilty for not supporting her, I suppose.'

'Charlotte cannot and should not expect you to lie to the police for her, it's not on.'

Pen chewed her lip thoughtfully. 'I suppose not,' she admitted.

'You can open your eyes now,' Lydia told her.

Pen slowly opened her eyes and blinked as Lydia passed her a hand mirror.

'Goodness! What a difference!' Pen exclaimed.

'Do you like them? I hope they're not too heavy for you.'

'Lydia, they are gorgeous. I don't like mascara, it never seems to stay on me and I end up with panda eyes, but now...' Pen fluttered her new eyelashes.

'My only other suggestion would be to add a little brown pencil or eyeshadow to your brows, it will balance the look,' Lydia advised as she packed away her products.

Pen nodded appreciatively. 'I think I can manage that.' She handed back the mirror. 'Thank you for listening to me, it has helped me put this situation into perspective and you're right, this is *Charlotte's* problem, not mine.'

'I hope tomorrow goes smoothly and you enjoy the day.'

'I'm sure it will, and hopefully, this business will be cleared up soon and Charlotte will settle down at Claro Court.'

Pen went to meet Charlotte in her sitting room, and Lydia returned to *The Kensington Suite* to see how Lexie was getting on. At one end of the room was a dais over which an art deco arch had been installed, a florist was decorating the arch with roses, carnations, freesias and greenery. Flower displays on plinths were positioned either side of each set of French windows and the chairs were placed in neat rows with a gap down the middle to form a central aisle. Lexie saw Lydia in the doorway and came over, smiling.

'It's taking shape nicely,' she said. 'There are flower posies to be attached to the end chairs of alternate rows and there is another flower arch to go down there where we'll all make our entrance.'

'It's looking beautiful already. It's a good thing the sun has moved round or it may have been too hot for the flowers, will they be ok for tomorrow?' asked Lydia.

'They should be fine, the wedding is at three o'clock and the forecast is fine and warm but not very sunny. It's usually around one o'clock when this room gets the sun and, since the wedding fair, it has crossed my mind to look into installing a retractable canopy over the terrace for future events,' replied Lexie.

'I hope you have a lovely day tomorrow, Lexie, and that all goes well,' said Lydia as they wandered towards the main entrance. They turned at the sound of car tyres scrunching on the gravel and watched as a silver Porsche Cayenne pulled up.

'Here's Gerald – he and Charlotte are giving a pre-wedding interview to Cliff for our local paper this evening, which is very generous of them. We also have our rehearsal dinner tonight, so I really need to finish in here.'

'I won't keep you, I've got to meet someone at six.'

'Thank you for everything, Lydia, I'll speak to you next week.' Lexie hurried back into *The Kensington Suite* to continue her preparations, and Lydia walked outside to her car which was parked next to Gerald's Porsche. He was getting out of his car as she approached. Gerald was a tall, broad-shouldered man with a full head of dark but greying hair and Lydia thought he was probably in his fifties. He wasn't good looking in the classic sense, but not abhorrent either. *He doesn't float my boat and if he didn't have a title, I guess he wouldn't float Charlotte's either,* Lydia thought. He was talking on his mobile and didn't even register her presence.

'Are you sure it's Adam Lewis she's been seeing? ... Well, I have to say I'm a bit put out... Yes, I realise that it changes everything, but to call it off the day before... What do you mean the police are looking into Top Drawer?... Now look here, Lord, we're both directors and are in this together... What?... But you can't do that... Hello? Goddammit!'

Lydia reached her car and quickly got inside without making eye contact with Sir Gerald who, having been cut off mid-conversation, marched into the Hall, clearly not in the best of moods. She thought about what she had just heard. *So, if Sir Gerald was talking to Mr Lord as a co-director and mentioning Top Drawer, does that make him Mr Baron? Of course! He is actually an aristocratic baronet. Does that mean that Mr Lord is actually an aristocratic lord?* Lydia thought about what else Gerald had said about knowing about the affair and possibly calling off the wedding. *I have to tell Will and Greg what I've overheard.*

Cliff Walker

Cliff arrived at Ashdale Hall and parked next to a silver Porsche Cayenne. *Nice car*, he thought as he stood and admired it for a few minutes. He walked in through the grand porticoed entrance and could see a lot of activity in the *Kensington Room* on his left.

'Good evening, Lexie,' he called. Lexie looked up and pushed a strand of loose hair away from her face as she smiled and walked towards him.

'Wow! You look fantastic but – aren't you a little overdressed for an interview?' she asked cheekily, indicating Cliff's black-tie outfit.

Cliff smiled at her. 'Nothing but the best for Sir Gerald and the future Lady Charlotte.'

Lexie gasped then Cliff laughed out loud. 'Just joking!' he chuckled, 'I'm going on from here to the British Bakery Awards in Harrogate. I thought I would just blend in with the guests dressed like this.'

'Cliff – you devil!' laughed Lexie. 'I thought I had embarrassed you for a moment there. Thank you for coming out on a Friday evening to do this interview, I thought our local paper should have an exclusive before the magazines do their thing.'

'Thank *you* for thinking about that. I'm looking forward to meeting the happy couple, it's quite reminiscent of royal weddings, isn't it?'

'It certainly feels like it from my angle, only the royals have far more aides than I've got. This room is practically finished now. Would you like to take photographs in here, then the marquee before you do the interview?'

'I think that's the best plan,' replied Cliff, still smiling. He looked around the room and was immediately impressed with how it had been arranged. It looked so different now that the adjoining doors to the ballroom had been opened. He took several pictures of the wedding ceremony layout and then Lexie took him across the hall and into *The Sandringham Suite* which was laid out for reception drinks. He took more photos there, and then he was shown through the French doors and out onto a lawn, where a huge white marquee had been erected. Inside, the sight was breathtaking. The far side of the marquee was fitted with full-size clear windows and looked across the beautiful lawn and beyond over the acres of the Ashdale parkland.

Flowers had been wrapped around all the poles supporting the draped roof, but over the black and white chequered dance floor the roof was clear, which would give a panoramic view of the night sky. Round tables were covered with snowy white cloths, the table centres were gold candelabra holding magnificent displays of white ostrich feathers, white spray stocks and draped crystals. Gold Chiavari chairs completed the look. Cliff was momentarily speechless at the sheer opulence of the décor.

'Charlotte went for an art deco theme and we shall have martini glasses for our cocktails and a jazz band for music during the drinks and canapés before the main reception dinner. I have to admit, I'm very pleased with how everything has turned out. By all means take some photos whilst I text Charlotte and let her know you're here.'

'You've done an amazing job, Lexie. I'll take some photos for you which you can use later in any PR if you wish,' replied Cliff.

Cliff took his photos and then Lexie led them both back through *The Sandringham Suite* and into the entrance hall.

She frowned. 'Charlotte hasn't replied to my text so I'll take you on up to her apartment,' she told Cliff, but before they took a step forward, Charlotte came running down the stairs. She was dressed for dinner in a red cocktail dress and sparkling jewellery, clutching a black jacket and handbag in one hand. Cliff thought she looked stunning, but she also looked furious.

'The wedding's cancelled!' she announced as she flounced past them and out of the open front door.

'Charlotte? Charlotte! Wait a minute,' called Lexie. She and Cliff took two steps towards the door and then stopped. Cliff heard footsteps behind them, he turned back to see a man in a silver grey expensive-looking suit approaching them.

'Gerald! What's going on?' Lexie asked him.

'I'm really sorry, Lexie my dear, but there will be no wedding,' he replied gravely.

'*What?*' exclaimed Lexie.

'I simply cannot go through with it now.'

'Are you serious, Gerald? But why?'

There was the sound of car tyres spinning on the gravel before it drove away.

'You should ask Charlotte,' was Gerald's curt reply.

'Where is she going?' asked Lexie, totally perplexed.

'I've absolutely no idea,' Gerald said haughtily.

'But—' Lexie was interrupted as two cars came to a stop outside.

Cliff remained silent. This little drama was far more interesting than a pre-wedding interview. Lexie gasped as DCI Will Appleton and DS Helen Oakley, along with two uniformed policemen appeared in the doorway.

'Good evening Ms Worthington, Mr Walker,' Will said gravely. 'I'm sorry to arrive unannounced, but I'm afraid I need a word with Sir Gerald.'

Lexie and Cliff turned to the baronet and were completely taken aback when DS Oakley stepped forward, handcuffs at the ready. 'Sir Gerald Reeves Pemberton, I am arresting you on suspicion of money laundering under The Proceeds of Crime Act 2002. You do not have to say anything, but it may harm your defence if you do not mention, when questioned, something which you later rely on in court.'

'What are you talking about?' blustered Sir Gerald. 'And there's no need for those!' He snatched his hands away from the detective sergeant.

'Sir Gerald,' DS Oakley said firmly, 'you don't want a charge of resisting arrest added to the list we already have, do you?'

'This is ridiculous! I want to call my lawyer! You'll regret this!' Sir Gerald shouted. Lexie and Cliff watched in stunned silence as the uniformed officers handcuffed the baronet and led him away.

'DCI Appleton, is…will…Sir Gerald is…' stuttered Lexie.

'Ms Worthington, I saw your sister leaving just as we arrived, but unfortunately I was unable to speak to her. I'm afraid that her wedding tomorrow to Sir Gerald Pemberton will not now be able to take place,' the Chief Inspector said apologetically.

'But...'

'I'm really sorry that you have to cancel the wedding at such short notice, but information regarding Sir Gerald has only just come to light. Now if you will excuse us?' DCI Appleton raised his eyebrows questioningly.

'Right...ok...I'll...umm, deal with it, thank you,' was all Lexie managed to say. The police left, and Cliff and Lexie looked at each other for a moment before Cliff spoke.

'Lexie, I'm so sorry. I guess I'll just get off. You'll have an enormous amount of work to do cancelling everything at this late stage. I'm not sure what help I can be, but if anything occurs to you, please give me a call,' he said kindly. Lexie nodded, still dumbfounded, and Cliff slipped away.

Vivienne Buckley

They were on their way to Ashdale again. *Honestly! Vinnie can't stay away from the place*, thought Vivienne grumpily. However, he wasn't in the best of moods, and he was decidedly off with her although she had no idea why. Vivienne thought she was looking particularly hot at the moment because since her little bonus afternoon on Tuesday, she had treated herself to a discreet lip enhancement. Vinnie had asked her about it and she had told a little white lie and said that she had a part-time job working a few hours in a friend's boutique. It was the first time that she had had her lips Botoxed and the result was fantastic – and even if Vinnie didn't appreciate it, Vivienne had a number of clients who would.

Vinnie had told her that he was liaising with one of the high-end glossy magazines re Charlotte Worthington's wedding and this time, he had agreed that she could go to the Hall with him provided she kept a low profile. Vivienne was happy to keep a low profile if that meant staying out of Vinnie's way, after all this was a society wedding and you never know just who you might meet.

They pulled onto the Market Place and parked, and Vinnie hauled their overnight cases out of the car. Vivienne had been unable to decide what she might want to wear tomorrow, so she had brought a generous selection of outfits. Sometimes, if she decided what to wear in advance, it felt wrong on the actual day, so this way she could choose in the morning and feel right.

'Mr and Mrs Buckley, lovely to see you again,' Doreen Rider greeted them warmly. 'Let's hope there isn't another murder – they do seem to happen when you're around, don't they?' she laughed at her own little joke and handed over their key.

As Vivienne unpacked and carefully hung up her various outfits for the next day, Vinnie was busy on his phone. Vivienne sighed and turned back to her shoes and handbags.

'Where are we going to eat tonight, Vinnie?' she asked eventually. Vinnie pushed his phone away and took off his jacket.

'Fratelli's, the Italian on the other side of the Market Place, we can have a drink downstairs first and then wander across. I'm just going to take a quick shower,' he replied as he undid his trousers letting them fall to the floor.

Vivienne smiled seductively. 'I know a better way to spend some time,' she purred.

'No thanks, Vivienne, not right now,' was Vinnie's rather curt reply as he headed into the en suite.

Vivienne was shocked, Vinnie rarely said no to sex, so she decided that there was definitely something on his mind. It was a pity really because she was feeling so sexy right now and she had bought some new lingerie, which would now have to wait for some appreciation. Vivienne stripped off and selected a cream silky oversized blouse and a pair of black super-skinny jeans to wear for their evening meal. After his shower, Vinnie dressed in his favourite Hugo Boss trousers and shirt, and once Vivienne had pushed her feet into her high-heeled ankle boots, they made their way downstairs.

As they walked, Vinnie's mobile rang and Vivienne stopped in her tracks. 'Can't you turn that damned thing off? It's Friday night, we're supposed to be relaxing,' she snapped.

Vinnie flapped his hand in response and then frowned at her. She shrugged, walked into the bar, and then she saw who was sitting there.

Adam Lewis

Adam wondered when the relationship with Charlotte had gone so wrong. She was very much like him in that she wanted the good life, no ties, no hassle and she enjoyed sex! It didn't bother Adam one jot that she was engaged. He had looked Sir Gerald Pemberton up on the internet and saw that, although he obviously had style and class, he didn't have the classic good looks associated with handsome men. Charlotte had told him that her fiancé was no competition in the bedroom stakes and spent most of his time in London as a full-time executive director on several company boards. He knew that she didn't love Sir Gerald, or anyone else for that matter, and that she just wanted to party and have a good time – a girl after his own heart. He'd figured that once the initial thrill of being Lady Charlotte had worn off, she would be bored, and when, after a particularly energetic lovemaking session on a warm summer's afternoon, Charlotte had poured them some bubbly and he had joked about how he would whisk her away to a new life in Spain, he'd been genuinely surprised at how her eyes had lit up and that she had asked him if he really would run away with her. And so the idea was born.

What was he going to do about Charlotte? There hadn't been an opportunity to speak to her again, and neither had made the effort to make any sort of communication with the other at all. In any event, he would be in line to inherit all the money from both his parents, and the house of course, which must be worth at least half a million – probably more. He would be able to pay off his debt to Mr Lord and enjoy his life in Spain. That being the case, he wouldn't need Charlotte's money now, so if she didn't want to go to Spain with him, so be it.

Adam had had a very uncomfortable afternoon at the police station where he had been questioned on his relationship with Charlotte. He had admitted that they'd been having an affair, but that it was over now, and yes, his mother had found out about it. What took Adam by surprise was the fact that Charlotte had been seen going to the pavilion on Sunday to meet his mother, apparently to discuss him! He was able to truthfully tell the police that he hadn't known about their meeting until Charlotte told him about it upon her return to her apartment. He showed them her text message along with his reply and related the ensuing conversation with Charlotte, explaining how upset she had been about his mother's apparent attitude towards her.

Adam had certainly not been prepared for the accusation that he had stalked her and fabricated an affair with the intent of ruining her marriage, because his intimate relations with Charlotte had been entirely acquiescent, and he was quite clear on that point. When he was asked if he believed his mother would carry out her threat to tell both Sir Gerald and the Worthingtons about the affair, he answered very firmly that, yes, he believed she would.

As the questions continued, Adam began to realise that the police suspected Charlotte of murdering his mother, and the more he thought about it, the stronger the possibility became.

At last he'd been allowed to ring Hugo and ask him to come and pick him up, and when Adam was finally in the car, Hugo suggested that they call in at the Coach for an early doors drink. Adam really wasn't in the mood, but Hugo admitted that he wanted some time away from Celia and that they really needed to talk about the villa, the funeral arrangements, finances, etcetera so Adam wearily agreed.

As Hugo drove from Harrogate to Ashdale, he broke the news that Top Drawer Properties had confirmed that they would rescind the contract regarding the purchase of the villa and keep the ten per cent deposit as was their entitlement.

'But I've paid them a damn sight more than ten percent, Hugo, as you know. Presumably they will refund the difference?'

'I did suggest that that was what you expected, but Mr Lord – he's the top man – wasn't very positive about that.'

'Lord? Did you say Mr Lord?' gasped Adam.

'Yes, why? It's unlikely that you know him, he's quite elusive and private, and leaves all the day-to-day running of the business to Mr Baron.'

Adam sank into his seat, knowing at once that he wouldn't get any money back. Out of all the property developments in Spain, he had to buy from the one owned by Mr Lord!

The pieces began to fall into place – when Hugo had arranged the delay, his mother had sent various documents as proof of identity and finances – that's how they had found out where he lived. Adam felt sick as Hugo swung the car onto the Market Place and parked.

'Come on then, Adam – the first drink is on me. What tickles your taste buds, eh?' he chortled as they got out of the car.

'A brandy!' Adam muttered half to himself.

'A brandy? Bit of a tough time this afternoon, was it?'

Adam smiled weakly and followed Hugo into the Coach.

17

Lydia Buckley
Lydia drove home, her mind whirling with information. The first thing she did when she reached her flat was to pull out her notes on the murder and add what she had just learned, and then she suddenly remembered the elusive something that had been bothering her – was it possible that…?

Lydia stared at her notes, she needed to make three phone calls to prove her theory. If she was right, then she knew who the murderer was. She pulled out her phone and rang Vinnie, Elsa, and Tom, asking them each a question, and having received the answers she needed, she circled a name on her notes and stuffed them into her handbag. As an afterthought, she phoned Amy and asked a few questions about the man called Gerry she had mentioned the previous night. Lydia thought that he sounded very much like Sir Gerald Pemberton. Her phone told her that she was due to meet Tasheka at the Coach, so she left a voicemail for Will outlining her theory, and her thoughts on "Gerry". She then sent a text to Greg.

When they were settled with their drinks, Lydia pulled out all the information she had collected for Tasheka. They talked about it in depth and Lydia explained the training process, how long it would take for Tasheka to become proficient, and what would be expected of her in the meantime.

'I spoke to my Mikey 'bout this an' he said I should go for it 'cos he knows how I like to communicate with people an' that I get on with everyone – mostly,' said Tasheka, casting a glance in Elsa's direction, who was having a quiet drink with Brian.

'The thing is, Tasheka, it's my intention to become a qualified tutor and have my own academy…' Lydia explained her idea to Tasheka and was pleased to see her eyes shine with delight.

'You mean I would be your number one technician?'

'Well…' Lydia began hesitantly, '… you would be my first, so I guess that would make you number one.'

'You know, I wouldn't let you down Lydia an' I think we will work real good together.' Tasheka then nudged Lydia and nodded her head in the direction of the door, where Adam and Hugo had just entered the pub. They walked to the bar to order their drinks.

'Look! there's that Adam Lewis. Y'know I was so shook that she went to meet him for some hanky-panky on Sunday on account of it was her wedding fair.'

Lydia wondered whether she should clear Lexie's name regarding Adam, but in doing so, she would implicate Charlotte. Just as she pondered what to do, a loud and shrill voice cut through the congenial ambience of the pub.

'You see? There she is again, I *knew* you would arrange to meet up with her!'

Lydia recognised Vivienne's voice before she turned her head. She sighed and looked at the furious blonde, glammed up in a silky blouse with skinny jeans and high-heeled ankle boots. Vinnie, trailing behind her, was on his phone and frowning. *What on earth are they doing back in Ashdale?*

'Vivienne, I haven't arranged to meet Vinnie,' Lydia explained calmly, very much aware that the pub had gone silent and they now had an audience. But Vivienne wasn't listening, she turned round to face Vinnie who finished his call and began to tap on the screen.

'It's every time we come here that we bump into *her*,' shrieked Vivienne.

'I *live* in Ashdale, Vivienne,' Lydia said reasonably.

Vivienne spun round angrily. 'You need to get over him, *I'm* married to him now. Wasn't taking him to the cleaners enough?' she spat.

'Now just a minute—' Lydia began.

'Vivienne...' Vinnie took hold of her arm, which she shook off as she turned back angrily to her husband.

'You always make me feel second best, that's why I wanted a vow renewal, but you couldn't agree to that could you? Oh no, we have to scrimp and save now because of *her*!' Vivienne yelled at Vinnie and at the same time, flung a pointed finger at Lydia, all eyes turned to follow.

Tasheka leaned forward and clapped her palms together as she spoke. 'Hey, Mr Buckley, I'm mighty surprised at you.' Tasheka's lilting Caribbean accent filled the silence as she commanded the attention of the drinkers. 'I've no idea why you would wanna swap this lovely lady here...' her left hand flipped towards Lydia, '...for a person like that!' Tasheka's right hand flipped towards Vivienne, who scowled.

'And what *exactly* do you mean by "a person like that"?' she snapped.

'I mean a person who has to wrap herself round a pole to find herself a man an' enhance her body cos she don't have no curves of her own. I mean a person who pretends to be somebody's wife an' tells lies when she had no business doin' so – that kinda person, you know what I'm sayin'?' Tasheka's right hand flicked to and fro as she spoke.

'What do you mean "tells lies"? I was not lying, I was pretending and that is not the same thing!'

'Vivienne!' Vinnie said loudly and firmly. 'I suppose you call this "pretending" do you?' he thrust his phone at Vivienne and she stared in horror at the screen. 'I wondered how you could afford all your beauty maintenance without maxing out your credit card, but if you had wanted a part-time job, perhaps you could have chosen something other than escort work,' he said.

There was a gasp from the crowd and Lydia could see the hurt on his face.

'I knew that! I said she was like an escort! Didn't I say I thought she was an escort?' Tasheka nudged Lydia's arm triumphantly.

Vivienne appeared to be lost for words as she just stared at Vinnie who glared at her as he slid his phone back into his pocket. The pub was silent, so when the door opened everyone turned to see who it was.

Lydia caught her breath as Charlotte marched in. She was dressed in an expensive-looking red dress with a black jacket, her sparkling earrings danced as they caught the lights, clearly ready for her rehearsal dinner. Charlotte looked furious, and she stood still as her eyes scanned the room, coming to a stop when she saw Adam. She strode across the short distance to the bar and soundly slapped him across the face. There was another audible collective intake of breath from the onlookers.

'You just couldn't keep your mouth shut, could you?' she hissed.

Adam looked genuinely shocked. 'What? What the hell are you talking about?' he spluttered.

'Don't pretend you don't know! You told Gerald and now he's called off the wedding. Well, if you think for one minute—'

'Hang on! I haven't told Gerald anything.'

'Do you really expect me to believe that?' snapped Charlotte. 'It's what you wanted, isn't it? You just couldn't leave things as they were, could you?'

Lydia quickly sent a text to both Will and Greg to let them know that things were kicking off in the Coach.

'I say, steady on…erm…you might want to take this little chat somewhere more private, eh?' said Hugo, placing a placating hand on Charlotte's arm, which she immediately shook off.

'Private? That's a joke, this whole town will know by tomorrow morning that my wedding has been cancelled by my fiancé.'

'Fiancé? *That's* the joke!' shouted Adam, clearly riled. 'You didn't really want to marry him—'

'I did!' shouted Charlotte back.

'Only because he had a title and money. My mother was right when she called you a cheap little harlot!' Adam flung his arm out and pointed at Vivienne. 'You should join forces with her and charge for it!'

There was another gasp from the drinkers as Vivienne marched over and stood in front of Adam. 'Who are you calling a cheap harlot?' she slung back. 'I'll have you know that I'm a respectable married woman.'

'Respectable? Hah! Then how come your husband has just accused you of being an escort?' Adam sneered. Then looking at Vinnie, he added, 'I'm sorry Vinnie, I couldn't help but overhear what you said.'

Vinnie shrugged despondently.

'You're putting *me* on same level as *her*?' exclaimed Charlotte. 'How dare you! All this is because you hounded me, making false insinuations about us having an affair, threatening to tell Gerald unless I went along with it.' Charlotte looked down her nose haughtily at Vivienne, who, not receiving any backup from Vinnie, resorted to giving Charlotte an evil stare.

Oh dear, thought Lydia, *this is going to get messy.*

'It was no insinuation, Charlotte, you were hot for it and even had someone else lined up for after your honeymoon, I believe.'

'So, it was her an' not Lexie?' Tasheka said, none too quietly to Lydia.

Unfortunately, Charlotte overhead and she turned to face Tasheka. 'What did you just say?' she demanded.

Tasheka looked Charlotte in the eye defiantly, and replied, 'I thought it was your sister who was in the pavilion…wit' him.' Tasheka nodded at Adam.

'My sister? Lexie wouldn't give *him* the time of day!'

'I know that now, girl. So, it must have been you who was seen partyin' with him real hard, you know what I'm sayin'?'

There was a snigger from some of the Coach's customers and Charlotte turned her back on Tasheka to address everyone. 'Don't listen to her, she's lying,' she announced.

Big mistake! Lydia thought to herself.

Tasheka stood up and clicked the fingers on her right hand. 'Hey girl! Don' you get all shady wit' me. My sister looked through the window of your pavilion an' she saw you an' him getting' all hot an' sweaty. You was yellin' his name an' that's how we knew it was him, you get me?' Now, in full attitude mode, Tasheka continued. 'At first, I thought it was your sister, on account of you being engaged an' all, but you just tol' everyone that your sister didn't even like him, which means it had to be you!' Tasheka's black curls bounced as her head snapped to and fro, her fingers clicked again and drew an imaginary 'Z'. Tasheka stared at Charlotte challenging her to call her out.

'Well, your sister was mistaken, it was probably some other floozy that he picked up,' retorted Charlotte without conviction.

'Well, Louella says she had long black hair an' a rose tattoo on her butt!'

Adam roared with laughter. 'Oh, it was Charlotte all right!' he confirmed.

Charlotte inhaled deeply and looked as though she was holding back tears. Lydia thought this was turning into a bit of a witch hunt and that perhaps it was time to bring it to a close, but before she could say anything, Charlotte spoke again.

'None of you understand,' she whined theatrically, 'he made me do it, he threatened to tell Gerald we were having an affair, so I went along with him just to keep him quiet – I thought it would be for the best.' Her voice wavered.

Everyone was so enthralled by the drama unfolding in front of them that Will and Greg were able to slip inside the pub unnoticed.

'Is she who we saw on Sunday? Going for some "jiggy-jiggy", I think you said,' piped up Vivienne with a smirk.

'That's her,' replied Tasheka firmly.

'I beg your pardon?' asked Charlotte haughtily.

'We saw you on Sunday at the wedding fair. We were looking out of a window and we watched you going to the woods,' explained Vivienne, clearly enjoying putting Charlotte on the spot. She pointed at Tasheka. '*She* said you were going to the pavilion to meet someone for some jiggy-jiggy.'

'How dare you say that I was going for…for…that!' Charlotte shouted at Tasheka, and then, waving her hand in Adam's direction, she continued, 'In fact, I went to meet his *mother* to talk to her about his behaviour.'

'That's not what you told me,' Adam said with a shake of his head. 'You told me that you had a blazing row with her because she threatened to tell both your parents and Gerald about our affair.'

Charlotte's eyes narrowed. 'Well, you would say that, wouldn't you?' she sneered.

'You *know* she would have done that because there you were, half-undressed and looking very much as she described you – what was it again? A cheap little harlot! Perhaps you thought there was only one way to keep her quiet.'

Charlotte stared at Adam, stunned for a moment, then her eyes opened wide as his words dawned on her. 'Are you trying to blame me for your mother's murder? Because let me assure you that she was very much alive when I left her,' she said.

'Well, maybe you just picked up a rock and hit the back of her head in a fit of temper – I'm not suggesting you planned it. However, horrified at what you had done, you had to finish the job so you held her under the water until she drowned – after all, you had the most to lose.' Having said his piece, Adam folded his arms and leaned back against the bar. He raised an eyebrow challenging Charlotte to answer that.

Lydia glanced at Will who was standing silently by the door. He caught her eye and nodded encouragingly, so she stood up and pulled her notes out of her handbag,

'The thing is Adam,' Lydia began and all eyes swivelled in her direction, 'you were there too, and you overheard their argument, because it was an argument, wasn't it Charlotte?'

Charlotte stared at Lydia for a moment and then turned to Adam. '*You were there?* You let her speak to me like that? Why didn't you say something?'

Adam shook his head. 'I wasn't there,' he said calmly, 'I was with Vinnie until after two o'clock, and then I met you in your apartment – *to discuss business.*'

Vinnie scratched his head, frowned and pulled out his phone again as Lydia continued. 'You left Vinnie in the office *before* two o'clock to go and meet Charlotte at the pavilion. However, when you got to the top of the main staircase, you saw the Sharp brothers walking across the hall. That must have been quite a shock.'

'It was after two when I left Vinnie—'

Vinnie interrupted him. 'No, it must have been before because I got a phone call from my son – at thirteen fifty-eight, according to my phone, and you had already left the office.'

'Well, what's a few minutes? When I saw the Sharps, I panicked and got confused about the time. I think I just walked up and down the corridor upstairs to steady my nerves,' explained Adam.

'No, you didn't do that, you went downstairs after the Sharps had walked past and went straight into *The Kensington Suite*, out of the French windows and down to the pavilion where you overheard the altercation between Beatrice and Charlotte.' Lydia spoke calmly and steadily.

'If I had gone downstairs, then *she* would have seen me,' said Adam pointing at Elsa, who clutched Brian's hand in alarm.

'No, because in the few minutes it took for the Sharps to walk past the stairs and for you to sneak down and into *The Kensington Suite*, Elsa was taking a comfort break.'

'I never went downstairs at all! I went for a comfort break myself'.

'Had you done that, you would have seen the Sharps at some point, because they went upstairs looking for you,' said Lydia.

Adam went very pale. 'Perhaps I just missed them. I think I went into the bridal suite, just to have a look,' he suggested.

'No, you didn't do that either because Tasheka and Vivienne were in there. In a nutshell Adam, the only time you could have seen the Sharps downstairs is when they walked across the bottom of the stairs whilst Elsa was on her break, and that was just after Tasheka and Vivienne went upstairs at…' Lydia consulted her notes, '…one fifty-seven.'

'How do you know when the Sharps went upstairs, you shouldn't believe what they say,' Adam said nervously.

'I saw them going up as I was coming down just after two o'clock,' Vinnie said helpfully.

'So, the only time you could have slipped downstairs unnoticed was when Elsa was absent from her desk between one fifty-seven and around five past two when Vinnie went downstairs,' Lydia said.

'But all that doesn't prove I actually went to the pavilion, does it?' Adam said with a smug grin.

'No, but you described Charlotte as being half-undressed and repeated exactly what Beatrice called her. How could you have known that if you were not there?' asked Lydia.

Everybody seemed to hold their breath as they waited for Adam's reply.

'Because Charlotte told me what she said,' replied Adam cockily.

'I did not say that!' snapped Charlotte, 'I never mentioned my dress at all!'

Adam shrugged. 'Your word against mine, darling,' he quipped.

'You also said that Beatrice was hit on the back of the head with a rock, how did you know that?' Lydia pointed out.

'Everyone knows that's what happened, it was in the paper.'

There was a general muttering and shaking of heads.

'Actually, the newspapers reported that Beatrice was drowned – there was no mention of a head injury,' Lydia told Adam, who was looking increasingly agitated.

'Anyway, this is all supposition. Charlotte told me about it because *she* killed my mother.'

'I did *not* kill your mother!' objected Charlotte.

'Well, you bloody well didn't have a cosy chat with her,' Adam retorted in reply.

'You did go downstairs and into *The Kensington Suite* because you took a photograph of it,' Lydia persisted.

'Of course I took a photograph of it! I showed it to you on the website, but I took it earlier in the morning before the wedding fair began. Is that your only proof?' Adam scoffed.

'You couldn't have taken it earlier in the day because the sun wasn't shining. Your photograph shows full sunshine streaming through the French windows, and the sun came out around lunchtime,' replied Lydia.

Adam's mouth opened and shut like a goldfish. He turned to Charlotte and shouted at her. 'If only you and my mother had kept to the plan and done what you said you were going to do. She agreed to transfer money so I could pay the balance on the villa and then, because of you, she changed her mind and decided to delay it! You agreed to go to Spain with me if I bought you a villa, so I did – and then you changed your mind and reneged on the idea! You both just trashed *my* plan with no thought or regards for the consequences. I put all my money into that villa and you just cast me aside!'

Adam was furious now and as no one seemed to want to comment on his rant, he continued. 'When I heard you both shouting, I thought it might be amusing to watch and that you would give as good as you got, but you just ran away in tears and left me to deal with her. She mocked me and gloated at being right all along about you, saying "I told you so" and "You should have listened to me." Well, I'm sick of listening and being manipulated, so I had no choice but to silence her.'

There was another gasp from the crowd, as Adam, breathing heavily, his eyes wild, turned to where Elsa and Brian sat transfixed. 'If you two hadn't been gossiping to that doctor, then she would have died that day in the bakery from her nut allergy and it would have been that baker's fault, but because you interfered, I had to think of something else.'

'Adam…' Charlotte whispered and put out her arm, but Adam swiped her arm away,

'All *you* had to do was keep your mouth shut and none of this would have happened. My mother would have paid the balance and we could have been going to Spain tomorrow, or was it always your intention to marry for a title and money and be damned how I would feel?'

Charlotte looked intently into Adam's eyes. 'I never asked you to buy the villa, it was always supposed to be a joke!' she said calmly.

'A joke! Yes, mother said you thought I was a joke. But then I heard her tell you that she'd decided to delay the payment because she overheard you telling your friend all our plans. She made up a story about the account needing two weeks' notice. She *lied* to me – because of you! And then I found out something else, that changing the villa's completion date brought me to the attention of the property developers, one of whom is a Mr Lord, an unpleasant character with whom I had dealing in London. He sent his thugs after me and I realised why they were at the Hall. I'll have to pay them back now, but if we had gone to Spain quietly, as I'd intended, then they wouldn't have known where I was.' Adam blurted out.

'Wait a minute, Adam, old man!' Hugo began. 'Are you saying that those two chaps who were arrested were sent by Lord and Baron?'

'Yes,' Adam told him. 'I didn't know of course that Mr Lord was the property developer – I bought the villa through you. But when Mother wanted to delay the payment of the balance and you sorted it all out, I'm guessing that our address was on some of the paperwork and that's how they found me.'

'How did they know you would be at the Hall though?' Charlotte chimed in.

'Because Mrs Buckley had a drink with them and succumbed to the charms of a conman,' Doreen said from behind the bar. All attention turned to her. 'I didn't like them when they checked in, so when I saw that Terry Sharp was flirting with Mrs Buckley, I kept my eyes and ears open, I don't hold with any shenanigans in my pub. Mrs Buckley mentioned the name Adam Lewis, the wedding fair at Ashdale Hall and she made arrangements to go with the Sharps.' Doreen folded her arms and looked directly at Vivienne.

'For Christ's sake, Vivienne!' retorted Vinnie, looking with disgust as his wife.

Adam howled like a caged animal. 'So, *you* blabbed to your friend about our affair which Mother overheard,' he yelled at Charlotte, 'and *you* blabbed to the Sharps,' he pointed at

Vivienne. 'Between you, you managed not only to destroy the future I had mapped out, but bring about the circumstances which resulted in my mother's death. All you had to do, was to keep your mouths and legs shut, but you're both too selfish to do that.'

Lydia glanced at Will again who nodded and pushed himself away from the wall. Greg opened the door and beckoned to someone outside. DS Helen Oakley appeared with two more officers. Adam was read his rights and handcuffed.

'I had no choice, I had to kill her...I was pushed into a corner...it's their fault ...' he yelled as he was led away.

There was a general hubbub of conversation in the ensuing moments and Greg came over to where Lydia stood. 'Gerald has been arrested—' Greg began, breaking off as Vinnie wandered over.

'I didn't know you were coming back up here?' Lydia said to her ex-husband, who looked forlorn.

'I was asked to come and oversee the PR, what with the magazine coverage of the wedding, but I guess that won't be necessary now. We'll go home tomorrow, we've some talking to do,' Vinnie said quietly. 'I had an inkling that she was getting money from somewhere as her treatments no longer appeared on the credit card statements. I had her followed – she picked up a man on Tuesday afternoon, I just got the pictures emailed to me.'

Greg glanced uncomfortably at Lydia and they both looked to where Vivienne stood near the bar, scrolling through her phone. Next to her was Charlotte, who had waited for the police to leave with Adam before fluffing her hair, lifting her chin, and, defiantly ignoring the nudges and glances, marching out of the pub in their wake.

'Wait here, I just need a word with Charlotte,' Lydia told Greg and she quickly followed her outside. Charlotte walked to where her car was parked on the Market Place and unlocked it,

'Charlotte!' called Lydia. Charlotte stood still without turning around.

'What!' she said ungraciously as she opened the car door.

'I need to speak to you,' replied Lydia as she hurried to reach the car.

'I have nothing to say.'

'There's something you need to know…about Gerald.'

Charlotte let out a breath. 'Really?' she said sarcastically.

'Really…he's been arrested.'

Charlotte spun round to face Lydia. '*What?*' she exclaimed.

Lydia glanced at people around and about on the Market Place. 'Can we get into your car and talk?' she asked.

Charlotte nodded and once they were settled inside, Lydia told Charlotte about Gerald's conversation she'd overheard earlier, outside the Hall.

'So, it wasn't Adam that told Gerald about the affair?' mused Charlotte, tapping her long nails on the steering wheel.

'No, Gerald was talking to the anonymous Mr Lord, but how *he* found out – I don't know,' replied Lydia.

'So, Gerald knew that this Mr Lord was looking for Adam and it was pure coincidence that Adam had bought his villa from Top Drawer Properties…and that I was involved with him?'

'I'm afraid so, but when Hugo brought the delay in payment to Mr Lord's attention and the name Adam Lewis came up, they knew where to find him.'

Charlotte thought about this for a few moments and then asked, 'And what if Beatrice had paid the balance on time? Would Adam have been safe from these thugs?'

'For a while, but I'm sure that eventually Mr Lord and Gerald would have noticed the name of one of their buyers.'

'Hmph! You're saying that the wedding would have been cancelled anyway because Gerald's been arrested, and not because of my affair. So, if I hadn't come to the pub for a showdown with Adam, no one would have known about the affair – is that right?' Charlotte clamped her lips together and Lydia thought once again that she was holding back tears.

'I think it would have come out anyway at some point, it was very unlikely that Adam would have been considerate enough to spare your blushes.' Lydia put her hand on Charlotte's arm.

'You should remember that in reality, you have had a very lucky escape, as becoming involved with a criminal linked to extortion, prostitution and money laundering may have had dire consequences for you.'

'It was that bad?' whispered Charlotte, a tear falling down her face.

Lydia nodded. 'That bad. We can only hope that now Gerald has been arrested, he will tell the police who Mr Lord is. Go home Charlotte and be with your family, they will protect you from the media. Lexie is very understanding and you have a loyal friend in Pen,' she advised.

Charlotte sniffed. 'Ok, Lydia, thank you for telling me what you know. I still can't believe Adam killed his mother – I certainly haven't made the wisest choices in men, have I?' she gave a watery smile.

'Not really,' Lydia replied kindly, with a wry smile.

She got out of the car and waited until Charlotte had driven away, then turning back towards the Coach, she saw Will beckoning her back.

As Lydia approached the pub, Tasheka squeezed herself past him. 'Hey girl, I gotta get back home. We're getting' a takeaway tonight an' I don't wanna be too late for Shanice,' she said.

'No problem, Tasheka, we sorted out what we needed to, I'll catch up with you next week.'

'I'm lookin' forward to workin' with you 'cos it sure ain't gonna be borin'!' And with that, Tasheka sashayed to her car.

'Lydia, I just need to clarify some things with you, please,' said Will kindly. 'Let me buy you a drink. I think you could do with one. Greg has kept your table.'

A few minutes later, when Will sat down with them both, he asked Lydia what had put her onto Adam in the first place.

'The photograph of the *The Sandringham Suite* with the sun shining through the windows. I realised that he must have come downstairs after he left Vinnie in the office, and yet he denied doing so. The assumption was always that he had been with

Vinnie until after two o'clock but there were a couple of things that showed otherwise; one was that he had seen the Sharps downstairs according to Charlotte, and the second thing was that Elsa went for her comfort break around two o'clock and that's why she didn't see the Sharps walk across the entrance hall, so that is when Adam must have quickly gone down the stairs and into *The Kensington Suite*.' Lydia told him.

'But how did you know he had gone to the pavilion?'

'I didn't, for sure, but Charlotte had no reason to go, other than to meet Adam.'

'They could have been in cahoots though and both been involved in Beatrice's murder. No one saw Charlotte return to the Hall and if Adam hadn't just told us what really happened, Charlotte may have been implicated.'

'I imagine the family have their own private entrance into the Hall which Charlotte used. I knew she wasn't involved because once we found out about her visit to the pavilion, she would have told us about Adam if she had known he was there. There was absolutely no way Charlotte would have taken the rap for him, she wanted him out of her life.'

Will nodded. 'I can agree with all of that. I can't thank you enough Lydia for helping out once again, especially now we have one of the Top Drawer directors, although Sir Gerald did deny his involvement with anything Spanish. Fortunately, you told me what Amy had told you and we've been able to confirm that it is indeed Sir Gerald aka Gerry who has a girlfriend that he takes to Spain. It also transpires that he rarely goes to London, his time has been spent in Mar Menor all along.'

'Presumably, you can now find Mr Lord as well?' asked Lydia.

Will shook his head. 'Unfortunately not. Like the Sharps, Sir Gerald had never met Mr Lord and the phone number and any other methods of contact he used have been discontinued.'

'Crikey! Did Adam owe Mr Lord a lot of money?'

'He certainly did,' said Greg. 'I've been going over the information gleaned by Rick and his colleagues and we now know that Adam led a pretty extravagant lifestyle – far more expensive than his salary could support.'

'So where does that leave the investigation into Mr Lord?' Lydia wondered.

'Still ongoing I'm afraid. There will be a full investigation into Top Drawer Properties so I don't think we shall be buying from them,' Will said ruefully. 'Although I do quite like the idea of a long weekend away before winter,' he added with a grin.

'Well, look on the bright side, now that the Beatrice Lewis case is closed, we can at least make plans to enjoy a bit of sunshine somewhere – cheers!' said Greg holding up his pint of lager. Will and Lydia clinked their glasses with his.

'Just one more thing,' Lydia said to Will, 'the Housemans are at an awards dinner this evening and I know that Sheila is worried because you told Derek that he was still a person of interest – can I just send a simple text to her and say that Beatrice's killer has been arrested and Derek is in the clear?'

Will sighed. 'Normally of course I would have to say 'no' but, seeing as how Adam confessed in front of a pub full of drinkers, it's hardly a secret. So go ahead and send the text, but just don't mention names right now.'

Lydia nodded and tapped away on her phone. She pressed Send and smiled at Will. 'Thank you, I'm crossing my fingers that they win an award and that my text will just put the icing on the cake so to speak,' she quipped.

Will and Greg both groaned at the pun.

Sheila Houseman

The British Bakery Awards were being held in the ballroom at the Majestic Hotel in Harrogate. There were over three hundred and fifty people attending from all around the UK, some were nominees for one of the several awards whilst others were simply member of the association who wished to attend the glamourous occasion. The evening was being filmed for the internet and members of the press were also in attendance, Cliff being one of them.

Sheila and Derek were with three other couples, all of whom were fellow bakers. From where she was sitting, Sheila could just see the Blenkhorns a few tables away and, from the disparaging looks she got from them, they clearly thought that they had the trophy in the bag.

It was a glittering, black-tie occasion, and everyone was dressed up to the nines – Sheila, at Derek's insistence, had bought a new dress especially for the event. The food was delicious and normally, Sheila would have been in her element chatting to like-minded bakers, but tonight she was also trying very hard to forget that Derek was still a person of interest to the police in a murder investigation. The worry had quite taken the edge off her evening and, although she smiled and talked – inside her heart was breaking, just in case…

'Sheila love, this waiter has agreed to take a photo of our table, can you give him your phone?' Derek's voice broke into her thoughts.

'Just a sec,' she replied dipping into her evening bag. The eight of them arranged themselves neatly in a group and the waiter obligingly took the photo, then the other couples wanted the same. When Sheila's phone had been returned to her, she noticed there was a text message from Lydia.

The lights dimmed and the chatter died down as the awards were about to be announced. As the compere introduced the celebrity baker, Christophe Armand, Sheila pulled out her glasses and read the text message. Sheila beamed and felt as though a great weight had lifted from her shoulders and she squeezed Derek's hand. He turned and looked questioningly at her, so she passed him the phone. She saw the smile grow on Derek's face as he read the short message, then he leaned towards her and whispered, 'I told you not to worry – now you can really enjoy the evening.'

Sheila nodded happily in response and sat back, applauding enthusiastically as each winner was given their trophy. As the award ceremony drew to a close and there were only two category winners to be announced. Sheila felt nervous – this was it, Best Independent Baker. Christophe Armand announced the nominees which included her Derek, the Blenkhorns and three other bakers. The gold envelope was opened and Sheila held her breath.

'…and the winner of the Best Independent Baker Award goes to – Housemans of Ashdale, here in Yorkshire!'

'Oh my God! Derek! That's us! We've won!' Sheila exclaimed.

Derek stood up amid a rapturous applause – he held out his hand for Sheila and together, they made their way onto the stage. Christophe Armand kissed both of Sheila's cheeks and handed Derek a silver trophy and a sought-after silver spoon. They were asked to stay on stage and the other trophy winners were invited back to join them. This was the big announcement – British Champion Baker.

Christophe Armand made a little speech about how much he had enjoyed the evening and how it now gave him great pleasure to announce that the winner of the most coveted award in the baking industry, British Champion Baker of the Year was…Derek Houseman!

18

Lydia Buckley

Greg left after breakfast to help Tom assemble some flat-pack wardrobes and, as it was a Saturday off, Lydia decided to have a lazy day. After doing the usual morning chores of clearing up and making the bed, Lydia decided to go and see the Housemans. She picked up her phone from beside the bed and realised there was a message – from Bella! *I welcomed my baby daughter at 1a.m. this morning.* Lydia immediately sent a text back sending much love and congratulations and she was surprised to receive a response straight away from Bella to say that she would be home later today and would Lydia be able to call in. Lydia texted back to say that she would love to meet the baby, and feeling a little bit emotional, she decided to go and buy some flowers to take with her. Picking up her handbag, she left the flat.

She noticed straight away that the poster and photographs of the Spanish Sun, Mar Menor properties had been removed from the estate agent's window, and, glancing inside, she could see Hugo in Tom's office looking a bit forlorn. Lydia suddenly decided to go and see him.

As she opened the door, Miss Reid, the efficient and loyal office manager, looked up and almost smiled. 'Good morning, Mrs Buckley,' she said politely. Lydia noted that she still wore her trademark cream blouse tied in a pussy bow at the neck and she privately wondered if her wardrobe had a whole rail of identical blouses. Miss Reid had worked for Hugo Marshall when he and his brother-in-law had owned the estate agency and she still reminded Lydia of her old school headmistress.

'Hello. Felicity. Please – call me Lydia, there is no need to be formal,' Lydia replied kindly. 'I wonder if Hugo might be able to spare me a few minutes.'

Felicity Reid didn't have time to reply as Hugo flung his office door open. 'Lydia! What a pleasant surprise, please come through – I wonder if I might have a little word.'

With a smile at Felicity, Lydia walked past her and into Hugo's, now Tom's, office.

'Sit down, sit down,' said Hugo warmly as he closed the door. 'I – I, well dammit – I just wanted to say something, but to be honest I'm not sure what. The last time you solved a murder which involved me, I thanked you, but somehow that doesn't seem appropriate now – with Adam being…arrested and charged, so—' Hugo broke off and Lydia was taken aback as she realised he was close to tears.

'Hugo,' she began kindly, 'you don't need to say anything and I'm so sorry that it was Adam. Ideally, his arrest wouldn't have happened quite so dramatically in the Coach, but one thing led to another. I didn't get a chance to speak to you after the police took Adam away, as I think you left pretty much at the same time, didn't you?'

Hugo had got himself under control and nodded his head. 'I had to get home and speak to Celia before anyone called her. She's in a bit of a state, as Beatrice and Adam were all the family she had. We're going to have to stay here for a bit, things to deal with and so forth.'

'Of course,' Lydia said sympathetically. 'Will everything be all right with your business, Spanish Sun?'

'I imagine so – of course you know that I don't actually own the business, it belongs to Bruce Harvey. The police will question him about how he came to be involved with Top Drawer Properties, but I believe it was in quite a proper way. The sales of the properties themselves were quite legitimate, but unfortunately there are questions about the original monies used to purchase the land and pay for the development – the police suspect that it was the proceeds of money laundering or funds ill-gotten in other ways, off-shore accounts – that sort of thing. Spanish Sun is involved with other developers though, and it's still a good little business.'

'Well, I'm pleased to hear that, Hugo, maybe we shall still come over and have a look.'

'Please do, I can arrange somewhere for you to stay, if that helps. I've arranged favourable rates at one or two very nice hotels or I can organise an apartment if you'd prefer.' Hugo smiled briefly. 'You know, if *I* had guaranteed his completion date extension and not involved Beatrice, she may still have been alive and—'

'And if Adam had not been involved with Mr Lord in London, if he had not had an affair with Charlotte, if Beatrice had not overheard Charlotte talking about it, if Sir Gerald had not been Mr Baron…ifs, buts and maybes. Hugo, there were many facets to this case, none of which were *your* fault, everything just came to a head, but whatever else happened, Adam did what he did – nobody forced him to do it.'

Hugo sighed. 'I know you're right, Lydia – it's just that…I *feel* responsible, guilty almost.'

'You're still in shock, Hugo and need some time to come to terms with what happened, there are people here to help you, you know.'

'Oh yes! Tom will sort out Beatrice's house – it will have to be sold, and Albert Wilks was Beatrice's accountant so he can deal with that, Adam used Freddie Flanigan…and, well I know him because… Anyway, I've to organise Beatrice's funeral, it will be a civic do because she was a serving councillor and eventually, Celia and I will go back to Spain. Celia has become the sole beneficiary of Beatrice's estate, because under the law, Adam cannot now benefit from his mother's death. I never really warmed to Beatrice, but I wouldn't have wished this on her.'

Lydia could see that Hugo was struggling with his emotions again, which was quite out of character for this normally ebullient man, and she decided that he needed some space, so she stood up and held out her hand,

'You have much to do so I'll say goodbye for now. I'm sure I'll see you around. Give my condolences to Celia and take care, Hugo.'

Hugo took her hand and shook it warmly. 'Thank you, Lydia, I can say that with conviction now and I do hope that you and Greg will come out to Spain.'

Lydia left Hugo and walked back into the office where Felicity hovered, a worried expression on her face. 'He's fine, albeit a bit shell-shocked, it's been a nasty business,' she told the office manager.

'Yes, and I'm here to support him, Mrs Buckley,' was the firm reply.

'Thank you, Felicity.'

Lydia stepped out of the estate agents. The weather had turned cool and there was a threat of rain – she wished that she had put a slighter warmer jacket on now. As she walked past the bakery, she glanced in and saw Sheila beckon her to come in. As Lydia came through the door, she was delighted to see that not one, but two trophies in pride of place on a shelf behind Sheila.

'Lydia!' Sheila came from behind her counter and gave Lydia a warm hug. 'Thank you so much for sending me that text – it made all the difference. Elsa has been in and told me everything that happened in the Coach, what a to-do!'

'I just thought it would lift your spirits as I knew how worried you were. But look at those trophies! Congratulations! You're both so deserving of them.'

Sheila blushed with pride. 'It's all Derek really, I'm so pleased for him.'

'Take some credit for yourself, Sheila. You both work so hard to make this a thriving business and you give so much back to the community,' Lydia interrupted.

Derek appeared in the kitchen doorway. 'I thought I heard your voice, Lydia. I want to thank you for even thinking about us last night and sending that text after all that went on, it really perked Sheila up. *I* knew that I hadn't killed Beatrice, but I could see that as loyal as my wife is, she was worried that the police might think that I had,' he said.

'Elsa said that Adam had taken the nut allergy sign himself hoping that Beatrice would die here and we would be blamed.'

Sheila shuddered, 'I can't bear to think of the consequences of that!'

'At least the truth is out and we can all get on with our lives. I've just spoken to Hugo; he and Celia are very shaken, so we might all need to be a bit understanding whilst they are here in Ashdale,' Lydia told them.

Derek nodded. 'Aye, I guess so, it was a nasty shock.'

'On a much happier note, tell me more about this award,' said Lydia. And she listened as Sheila explained that they would be on the local evening news on the television, having given an interview last night, that Cliff wanted an interview for the local paper, and that they would be featured in all the Bakers' Association marketing campaigns over the next twelve months. And that, maybe, there would be other offers in the pipeline.

'It all sounds very exciting and I'm so pleased for you both. Here are your next customers so I'll leave you in peace,' said Lydia as the shop door opened. She allowed two ladies to enter the shop and then slipped outside.

'Lydia!'

She turned at the sound of her name being called and saw Cliff hurrying across the Market Place towards her. She waited for him to approach her and smiled. Morning, Cliff!' she greeted him.

'Have you some time for a chat? Can I buy you a coffee?' he puffed.

'Hmmm, let me think what we could possibly have to talk about,' she teased him.

'I can't believe so much has happened in twenty-four hours,' he exclaimed.

'Come on then, let's make ourselves comfy in the café and have a proper chat,' said Lydia amicably.

Having got coffee and cake, they settled in a quiet corner.'Where shall we start?' asked Lydia.

'Do you mind telling me the whole story about why Adam murdered his mother, or at least what you know? I don't know about the Spanish property part.'

Lydia began with Adam's involvement with Mr Lord in London, his escape back to Ashdale, the affair with Charlotte and his villa purchase.

'So, it was just pure coincidence that Mr Lord was also a director of Top Drawer Properties?' he asked.

'It was, and of course nobody would have guessed that Sir Gerald was involved.'

'Will the police find this Mr Lord character now?'

'It'll take a lot more investigation as he has cut all the lines of communication that were used for both the Sharps and Sir Gerald and has gone to ground. It's a hug web of deceit that may take months to unravel.'

'And at the wedding fair, it was Derek who I glimpsed through the trees, not Lucy.'

'Yes, and he heard you on the phone and thought it was the murderer speaking.'

'Dear me! It's understandable though. Charlotte has had a lucky escape really, hasn't she?' Cliff pointed out.

'She has and she'll realise that, once she gets over the embarrassment of last night.'

'Tell me about that, I'm gutted that I missed it.'

'I'll tell you what happened, although might I suggest that Charlotte's affair is not included in your article. Why don't you speak to Lexie and see what they have told the guests, the minister and so on? I'm sure the fact that Sir Gerald Pemberton has been outed as a criminal and the big society wedding was therefore cancelled will be enough sensationalism for the press. I know that everyone in Ashdale will know about the affair, but I see no reason why the whole of the UK needs to know as well.'

'I understand, although I can't guarantee that it will remain a secret,' Cliff said candidly.

'I realise that, but it just may give Charlotte some breathing space and by the time it does get out, it won't really be so sensational,' pointed out Lydia.

Cliff nodded in agreement, then Lydia told him about the drama in the Coach which led to Adam's arrest and when she finished, he exhaled a long breath.

'Good grief! What a drama! It's such a shame as well because Lexie and Lady Victoria had done an incredible job with the décor. Let me show you some photos.'

'You got photos?' exclaimed Lydia.

'I did, I told Lexie that they could use them in any of their advertising, look ...' Cliff passed his phone to Lydia and she scrolled through the impressive pictures.

'They are fantastic, it all looks absolutely stunning. Thank goodness you took them.'

'I'll ask Lexie if she wants them when I speak to her later today,' he said as he put his phone back in his jacket pocket. 'I'm so looking forward to moving here,' he added, 'there's so much excitement.'

'Well, I'm not sure that murder is 'excitement',' Lydia replied warily. 'I'd much rather we didn't have any murders at all.'

'Oh no, I wouldn't wish harm on anyone, but heck! I've been stuck in a flat in Leeds city centre for the last few months, this has got to be better that that! But talking of murder, please tell me about the last one. I keep hearing bits of it, but I would really like to hear it from you. I'll buy you another coffee?' he said enthusiastically.

Lydia laughed. 'Thank you, but I don't need another coffee, I'll just tell you the story.'

Lydia told him about the murder that had taken place earlier in the year during the annual panto.

'Did Bella keep the baby in the end?'

'She did, as a matter of fact her little girl was born only this morning, I was on my way to buy flowers when you caught me.'

Cliff was quiet and took a drink from his cup, he seemed to be struggling with his emotions, so Lydia said nothing for a few moments.

'Now how about you? How are you feeling?' she asked eventually.

'It's going to take me a little while to come to terms with what Trissie did, but I've got Fran and Michelle as my family and I'm grateful for that.'

'And what about the MG? Are you still buying that?'

Cliff thought for a moment. 'The police took the photo of the MG and seemed to think that it was possible that the damage had been caused by hitting something rather than an object being dropped on it,' he explained.

'And could that something have been a pedestrian?'

Cliff nodded. 'It could, but they can't say for sure, although the date, time and location point to the possibility that Trissie…Beatrice *could* have killed Sam. The thing is, Lydia, that in my heart of hearts, I kind of know that she did it because, for one thing, she lied about the damage to the car, it would also explain her shock and, well…horror at seeing me and then Fran and Lucy at the wedding fair.'

'Oh Cliff! I'm so sorry, it's quite shattered your memories of her, hasn't it?'

'*She* did that last Sunday. Her reaction when we met shook me to the core. I really wanted that car,' replied Cliff playing with his teaspoon, 'but I can't drive around in it knowing that it may have killed Sam, especially when I move here. I couldn't hurt Lucy and Sarah like that. I don't *need* an MG, it's just a silly pipe dream, a mid-life crisis, clutching at youthful straws—'

'I get it, Cliff! Honestly, you're as bad as Greg with clichés,' Lydia told him.

'Mikey was very understanding when I explained about everything and said that he is sure that he'll find another buyer.'

'Mikey needs to be an understanding kinda guy, he's married to Tasheka,' Lydia said.

Cliff chuckled. 'She is certainly a character.

'She is. She has a heart of gold and I count her as one of my dearest friends,' said Lydia sincerely.

Cliff stretched. 'Well, I can't put the clock back, but I can move forward. I'm going to make my home here in Ashdale and become an active member of the community,' he said determinedly.

'Well, I'm pleased to hear it, we look forward to having you join us.'

They had both finished their coffee and Cliff took Lydia's hand. 'Thank you for listening to me, your advice and, well...just being a friend really,' he said sincerely.

'Cliff, we've been through a bit of a trauma during the last few days, but it's over now and I want to reassure you that I count you, Fran, Lucy and Sarah as my friends, too.'

'It's good to know that, Lydia. Now, I suppose I must get on, I've a column to write but I need to speak to Lexie first.' They both stood up and moved to the door.

'Thank you for the coffee, Cliff, it was lovely to chat to you. Take care.'

'You certainly will. TTFN,' he said as he held the door open for her.

It was now looking decidedly like rain, so Lydia hurried across the Market Place to the florists. Sarah looked up from the flowers she was arranging in a large urn and beamed when she saw that it was Lydia. 'Hi! I hear you cracked the case last night!' she exclaimed.

'Has Elsa been in here by any chance?' asked Lydia.

'She certainly has, I think she's been all around the Market Place – she was fit to bursting with excitement.'

'Well at least it's all over and you're no longer a person of interest to the police, Sarah.'

'I can't tell you how pleased I was when the police told me that Saffron's sister, Scarlett, had spoken to them and confirmed our conversation on the terrace. *I* knew that I hadn't done it, but I suppose I was rather vocal about Beatrice being the person who killed my dad,' Sarah admitted.

'You were a bit, but I've spoken to Cliff this morning and he thinks you may have been right. I hope that whatever *you* think happened, enables you find some solace at last.'

'Well, I still believe it *was* Beatrice and, although I don't condone what Adam Lewis did, I do feel a sense of closure now rather than the hatred that was inside me.'

'I am pleased, Sarah. Carrying hatred around inside for so long is not good. Anyway, on a brighter note, I would like some flowers for a new mother please. Bella Sturdy had her baby girl only this morning and I'm going to see her this afternoon.'

'Oh, some happy news! I'll make a pretty bouquet for you, and I also have some gossip,' she said mischievously.

'Really? Do tell!' encouraged Lydia.

Sarah selected flowers as she spoke,

'Well, Mum has gone into Harrogate to find something "nice to wear" – is how she put it.'

'Nice to wear? Is it a special occasion?'

'I didn't think so, but she's going to a lot of effort.'

'Ok, but what is the occasion?'

'Dinner with Cliff Walker tonight! I told her that she didn't need anything new, but I guess she opened her wardrobe door and nothing took her fancy.'

'How sweet! You know Cliff had a bit of a thing for your mother, he admitted to me that if she hadn't been seeing Sam, then he might have…well, stepped in.'

Sarah had an armful of flowers by now. 'Goodness, wouldn't things have turned out differently? Just give me a minute to put these together.' Sarah disappeared into the back room, reappearing a couple of minutes later with a beautiful bouquet wrapped in cellophane and tied with pink ribbon.

'Sarah! They're beautiful, thank you so much.' Lydia took out her purse and handed over her credit card. 'So where are Cliff and Lucy going for dinner?'

'Somewhere fancy in Harrogate, I believe. I'm really happy for Mum, it's been a long time since anyone took her out and she's really looking forward to it.'

'Well, you can tell her from me, that I hope they both enjoy their evening.'

After leaving Flower Power, Lydia remembered that she needed to call in at MegaMart and buy some bits and pieces, and on her way out of the supermarket, she bumped into Saffron.

'Oh! Hi Lee…Lie …' Saffron began awkwardly.

Lydia mentally eye-rolled. 'Lydia,' she said.

'Oh yes, I can never remember how to say your name, 'cos it's like, got a 'y' in it,' Saffron explained.

'Cos it's got a 'y' in it? Lydia repeated incredulously to herself.

Saffron smiled happily. 'Is it true what Elsie said about Adam Lewis? That he, like, killed Cllr Lewis last Sunday?'

'Yes, unfortunately she's right.'

'It's just as well that I, like, didn't want to go out with him then 'cos he might, like, have murdered me.'

'I think you would have been all right, Saffron—'

'Well, we don't know that for certain, do we? I mean my Connor might have, like, been in trouble before, but he, like, hasn't killed anyone.'

'Well, I'm pleased to hear that – that he hasn't killed anyone I mean, not that he has been in trouble.'

Saffron frowned as she digested Lydia's words, then she nodded as she grasped their meaning.

'Anyway, it means, like, I won't get any more flowers now 'cos, although they were really beautiful, it, like, freaked me out, you know?' she said.

Lydia nodded vaguely as Saffron continued. 'And that Lady Charlotte's wedding was cancelled, that was, like, a real shame 'cos I was looking forward to seeing her dress. I think me and Connor are gonna get married next year. Hey! I just thought, do you think she might like, sell her dress to me? 'Cos she won't want it now, will she?'

'I don't know, Saffron, she might consider it. Would you like me to ask her the next time I see her?'

Saffron's eyes lit up. 'Oh, would you? That would be, like, amazing,' she gushed, and then her face suddenly became serious. 'I'd better get on or Maggie will tell me off again, see you soon, Lisa.' Saffron waggled her fingers and hurried away into the supermarket.

Lydia sighed, as much as she liked Saffron, it was difficult to have a meaningful conversation with her – however, she made a mental note to ask Lexie if Charlotte would consider selling her dress. She wondered how Charlotte was feeling this morning – Upset? Sulky? Embarrassed? Angry? All of those, probably. She knew that Lexie would have been busy last night cancelling everything and informing the many guests that the wedding was off and that today they would be dismantling the marquee. Thank goodness Cliff had taken those photographs.

Lydia went straight back to her flat and made herself a sandwich before setting off to Harefield Park to see Bella. The drive to the Sturdy home was between dry stone walls and hedges until the road rose up and she could see the spectacular Yorkshire Dales, where the leaves were turning gold, amber and bronze, their colours standing out in front of the backdrop of green hills. Driving around a bend, she slowed as she came up behind a tractor and she had no choice but to follow it at a sedate twenty miles an hour. The tractor indicated and then turned right to a small hamlet named Bedlam. *Just what we should rename Ashdale*, thought Lydia, before she was able to accelerate and continue on her way. The terrain flattened out and Lydia passed the old entrance to Thornberry Farm, which was now part of Jonathan Sturdy's estate of Harefield Park.

When Jonathan Sturdy had originally inherited Harefield House Farm from his father, he had developed the two redundant barns resulting in rather nice four-bedroomed properties which he had then sold for a healthy profit. This had been ploughed back into the new business venture, Harefield Park, whereby the farmland was converted into a holiday park for campers and touring caravans. The park had high-quality facility blocks with bathrooms and laundry areas, picnic tables, country walks and trails and the holiday park offered discounts into local attractions. The business had flourished, and, following the purchase of his uncle's neighbouring Thornberry Farm, Jonathan had recently applied to the council to build a static caravan park and log cabin lodges along with a swimming pool and clubhouse.

Lydia pulled into the gateway of Harefield House and the front door opened immediately. Bella stood in the doorway, a huge grin on her face.

'Hi!' she called, 'I can't wait to show her to you, you're my first visitor. Mum said I should rest, but I'm absolutely fine!' her eyes sparkled and Lydia was amazed at how well she looked. She picked up the bouquet of flowers from the front seat of the car and held them out to Bella,

'For you, I'm just so happy for you,' she said.

Bella took the flowers and kissed Lydia on the cheek. 'Thank you so very much,' she said sincerely.

'Did everything go ok?'

'I went into labour around eight o'clock last night and she was born at eleven with no problems, so I was tucked up in bed by midnight. I came home this morning and, to be honest, I just feel a little shell-shocked that it has happened at all, but then I look at my beautiful baby.' As Bella talked, she led Lydia through into the sitting room where Claire Sturdy was gazing fondly into a Moses basket.

'Hello Claire, how are you?'

Claire looked more shaken and tired than Bella. 'I'm fine, thank you. You know Lydia, I cannot believe she's ours, she is simply beautiful,' she whispered.

'There is no need to whisper, Mum,' admonished Bella, then turning to Lydia she said, 'Lydia, please let me introduce you to Thea Elizabeth Sturdy.'

Lydia looked at the little bundle sleeping peacefully in her basket, she had soft blonde hair and long black eyelashes.

'She is truly gorgeous and what a lovely name,' she said.

'I'll go and put the kettle on. Lydia, will you have tea or coffee?' asked Claire.

'I would love a coffee please.'

'Bella, let me take those flowers and put them in water.'

Claire disappeared with the flowers and Bella turned to Lydia. 'Sit down and tell me everything about the Beatrice Lewis murder, I'm dying to know all the details,' she implored.

Lydia laughed. 'You've just had a baby and you want to hear about a murder?' she teased.

'I certainly do, Mum is completely gaga about Thea and, as much as I love my little daughter, that's all we've talked about today, so you're a refreshing change.'

Lydia began the story for the second time that day, and she had just reached the wedding fair part when Claire came in with a tray. As she put the tray down, Thea began snuffling and whimpering. 'It looks as though someone wants to join us for afternoon tea, I'll get her bottle ready,' said Claire and she disappeared once more.

Bella picked Thea up and gave her to Lydia. 'Have a quick cuddle before Nonna gets back.'

'Nonna?'

'That's the name Mum wishes to be known by, so…'

Lydia rocked the little baby who simply screwed up her face and waved her little fists around as she slowly woke herself up.

Claire returned with a bottle. 'Shall I go and feed her in the nursery and you can chat to Lydia?' she asked, her eyes on her granddaughter.

'That would be lovely, Mum, thank you,' replied Bella.

Lydia duly handed over the baby and Claire immediately talked baby talk as she soothed the little mewing noises.

'Mum is absolutely besotted with Thea, which is completely the opposite of what I thought she would be like,' Bella said.

'I think I would just be the same,' replied Lydia.

'Now, you were up to the bit where Tasheka and Vivienne went upstairs, so go on.'

Lydia continued her story. '…so, it's unlikely that the police will find Mr Lord for quite some time,' she finished.

'It's so weird though, how he found out about Adam and Charlotte's affair, isn't it?' mused Bella.

'That's what niggles me,' agreed Lydia.

'I've missed working in Ashdale, although I'm not sure I want to go back to work full-time.'

'Zoe might be able to accommodate that if she can find another receptionist willing to job share. I think Saffron would prefer full-time though as she said she was getting married next year.'

'I think I would want a job that was flexible and…well, please don't laugh, but there is something else I think I might like to do – eventually, of course.'

'Oh? What's that?'

Bella paused and looked at Lydia. 'I quite like the idea of being a lash technician,' she said hesitantly, 'because then I could work my own hours and actually be trained in something.'

'I think that's a great idea and, strangely enough, you're not the first person to want do that.'

'I'm not? Who else has spoken to you?'

'Tasheka,' replied Lydia, 'she had the details of the training course and I believe she'll sign up next week.'

'Oh!' said Bella, a little despondently.

'Why so sad about that?'

'Because I thought I might work with you, but if she's going to do that then…' Bella broke off and shrugged, '…it was just an idea.'

'It's a very good idea and, when you're ready in a few months, I would very much like to be your tutor.'

'You would?' exclaimed Bella.

Lydia nodded and explained about her idea of an academy and agency.

'But that's a brilliant idea, I would love to be a part of that.'

'I would be more than happy to have you on my books *if* you make the grade,' Lydia told her seriously.

'I'll work blooming hard to make sure I'm the best,' replied Bella fiercely.They chatted more about the Ashdale Players and the forthcoming production of Cinderella and eventually Lydia took her leave, promising to come again soon.

Once home, Lydia wondered about doing a bit of work on her novel, it was nearing the end and with a push, she could probably finish it by the end of next week. But just then, her phone rang, the ID told her that it was Vinnie and she frowned. 'Vinnie? Is everything ok?' she asked with concern when she answered it.

'Not really, I just need to talk to you,' he replied.

'Ok,' Lydia replied tentatively.

'You were right!'

'About what?'

'Vivienne!'

'I was?'

Vinnie sighed. 'I was fooled by her obvious charms and now I'm stuck with her. I think we both want a divorce, but I can't afford one...'

Lydia frowned, was he going to ask for money?

'Vinnie, I—' she began.

'... so I've decided that I'm not going to give her the benefit of any settlement nor pay for a divorce. Do you know, I actually think I was *tricked* into marrying her? I'm not sure she was ever pregnant. I think she just wanted a fancy lifestyle, but when I paid your settlement, we had to tighten our belts – she doesn't like that. To think that she's been sleeping with other men – *for money!* I'm so shocked, I can't talk to her.'

None of this was a surprise to Lydia, in fact Vinnie was merely echoing her own thoughts.

He continued talking. 'So, what I wanted to tell you, no...ask you was – would you mind terribly if I moved to Harrogate or Ashdale? You see, my clients are in the north now and it might give me and Vivienne a new start?'

Now, Lydia was shocked, *Vinnie and Vivienne on her doorstep?*

'I can't stop you moving house, Vinnie,' she replied non-committedly.

'No, I know, but I just wanted to run it past you first, to let you think about it rather than it be a fait-accompli, so to speak.'

'That's very considerate of you.'

'Well, I like to think that we can be civil about things.'

'We can certainly be civil, but are you sure it's what you want?'

'Oh yes! Matt will find it easier to see us both if we're in the same area, for one thing and for another, it will take Vivienne away from *those* people she knows.' Vinnie sounded as though his mind was made up.

'She might not be very happy about it,' Lydia said.

'I don't care, it's my house and I'm selling it. She can come with me or make alternative arrangements on her own, but I am *not* shelling out for another divorce settlement!' he said with conviction, 'And that is not a dig at you!' he added.

'O-kay, well it's up to you of course.'

'Well, that's that then! I just wanted to let you know how things were, in case you were wondering.'

If Lydia was honest, she hadn't given Vinnie and Vivienne any thought at all since the showdown last night – was it only last night? It seemed ages ago, already.

'You do whatever is best for you, Vinnie – I won't mind at all.'

After they had said goodbye, Lydia exhaled a long breath, she didn't feel at all like work now, she just wanted to relax, so she switched on the television and found some Sarah Millican videos on YouTube – her go-to for good humour.

A

Towards the end of the afternoon, in an office somewhere in England, a man took out his mobile and made a call to a florist. He asked for a luxurious bouquet of neutral hued flowers to be delivered to a Ms Saffron Lawson, c/o WOW! Market Place, Ashdale.

'Is there a card to go with that, sir?' asked the florist.

'Yes please,' was the reply, 'the wording is *I'm still thinking about you, 'A'*. Could you have them delivered next Wednesday please?'

'Certainly sir.'

After the phone call had ended, the man sat back in his chair and smiled. *Saffron, you have stolen my heart and one day you will be mine.*

Notes from the Author

I hope you enjoyed the second book in my Ashdale series and if so, the third book *Murder Covered By Snow,* will be published later in 2022 and will be available on Amazon.

Printed in Great Britain
by Amazon